"How do..."

What was the matter with her? She sounded like a fool, and she didn't seem to be able to stop it. "I mean to you. How can you tell?"

"Lack of eye contact." He moved closer. "A tense, closed expression, halting speech, hesitation."

He certainly didn't look tense. He looked powerful, in control and way too sexy.

"Take now," he said, leaning ever so slightly forward. "Your expression is open. You're not nervous. It's like you're inviting me in. Like you want me to see your innermost thoughts," he continued.

She definitely didn't want that.

"Like you're thinking of physical contact..." He brushed her fingers, gently holding the tips of hers with the tips of his. He drew in a deep breath. "Wouldn't be a bad thing."

She felt a warmth rise over her wrist, up the inside of her arm and through to her chest. She didn't want him to let go.

* * *

One Baby, Two Secrets
is part of Mills & Boon Desire's No. 1
bestselling series, Billionaires and Babies:
Powerful men… wrapped around
their babies' little fingers.

ONE BABY, TWO SECRETS

BY
BARBARA DUNLOP

First Published in Great Britain 2017
By Mills & Boon, an imprint of HarperCollins*Publishers*
1 London Bridge Street, London, SE1 9GF

© 2017 Barbara Dunlop

ISBN: 978-0-263-92802-0

51-0117

Our policy is to use papers that are natural, renewable and recyclable products and made from wood grown in sustainable forests. The logging and manufacturing processes conform to the legal environmental regulations of the country of origin.

Printed and bound in Spain
by CPI, Barcelona

To my husband.

One

Stale cigarette smoke warred with sharp memories as Kate Dunhern stood in the doorway of her mother's tattered third-floor walk-up in south central Los Angeles.

"Darling," her mother Chloe cried, pulling her into a bony embrace.

Chloe's hair was cut spiky short, her tank top crisp with colored sequins, and the scent of Vendi Dark Mist wafted in an invisible cloud around her. The floor seemed to shift momentarily, and Kate was transported back to her childhood.

"I didn't think you'd come," Chloe singsonged, rocking Kate back and forth in her arms.

"Of course I came," Kate said, firming her stance and waiting for the embrace to end.

"It's been terrible on us all," Chloe said with a sniff, finally pulling back and giving Kate space to breathe.

"I can't believe she's gone." An image of her sister, Francie, formed in Kate's mind.

She saw Francie as a teenager, grinning as they dug into a bowl of ice cream with colored sprinkles. The memory was good. But it was followed swiftly by the memory of Francie shouting that she hated Chloe before storming out of the apartment and slamming the door.

Not that Kate blamed Francie for bailing. Chloe had never been a candidate for mother of the year.

She had loved her daughters when the mood struck her and ignored them when it didn't. She'd criticized them when she was in a bad mood, which was most of the time. She claimed they had cramped her style, ruined her figure and kept her home with their snotty-nosed whining when she'd rather be out with an eligible man. In Chloe's mind, the only thing between her and happily ever after with some handsome, wealthy Prince Charming had been the anchor of Kate and Francie.

Kate had followed Francie's lead, leaving for Seattle with her best friend, Nadia Ivanova, as soon as they'd graduated high school. She and Nadia had supported each other through teachers' college, and she'd never looked back, at least not until now. Not until Francie had been killed in a car accident.

"She was drinking, you know," Chloe said, closing the apartment door and crossing the worn braided rug on high heels.

"I read the news article." Kate was the last person to defend Francie's actions, but she bristled at the critical tone in her mother's voice.

Chloe lifted a glass of orange juice from the small, chipped dining table. "She should have known better."

Even if ice cubes hadn't clinked against the glass as she drank, Kate would have guessed the juice was laced with vodka.

Because of the great example you set for us? The sarcastic question rang silent in Kate's mind.

"When is her service?" she asked instead.

Chloe waved a dismissive hand. "She didn't want a service."

"It doesn't have to be big or fancy," Kate said.

They were anything but a close-knit family, but they were Francie's only family. They needed to say goodbye.

"The body was already cremated."

"What? When?" Kate's knees went unexpectedly weak, the finality of her sister's death suddenly hitting home.

She was never going to see Francie again. Visions of her sister bloomed in earnest now, at eight years old, reading *The Jolly Green Frog* to Kate on their shared mattress in the back bedroom, the time she'd tried to bake peanut butter cookies and nearly lit the kitchen on fire, the two of them on the floor in front of the television, watching a thoroughly inappropriate late-night crime drama with Chloe passed out on the sofa.

Kate moved now to touch that sofa, that same old burgundy brocade sofa. She lowered herself to the saggy cushion.

"Why would you do that?" she asked her mother, her throat tight.

"It wasn't me," Chloe said.

"The hospital decided to cremate her?"

Had Chloe pleaded poverty? Was cremation the default decision for patients who died without the means to pay for a funeral? Chloe should have come to Kate. Kate didn't have a lot of money, but she could have buried her own sister.

"Quentin decided to cremate her. He said it was what she wanted. He can afford anything he wants without blinking an eye, so I expect he was telling the truth." Chloe took a large swallow of the orange juice drink.

"Quentin?" Kate prompted.

"Francie's boyfriend, Annabelle's father."

"Who is Annabelle?"

Chloe blinked at Kate for a moment. "Francie's baby."

Kate was glad to be sitting down. "Francie…" Her voice failed her before she could finish the sentence. She cleared her throat and tried again. "Francie has a baby?"

"You didn't know?"

"How would I know?" Kate hadn't spoken to either her mother or her sister in nearly seven years. "Is the baby all right? Where is she?" Kate found herself glancing around the apartment, wondering if her niece might be sleeping in the bedroom.

Chloe obviously guessed the direction of Kate's thoughts and drew back in what looked like alarm. "She's not here. She's where she belongs, with her father, Quentin Roo."

As he had for nearly a month now, Brody Calder pretended to be amused by Quentin Roo's crude, misogynistic remarks. The man's current target was swimsuit model Vera Redmond, who was clad in a clingy black sheath of a minidress, sipping a crimson martini across the crowded pool deck of Quentin's Hollywood Hills mansion.

"Could bounce a quarter off it," Quentin stated with a low, meaningful chuckle.

"I have," said Rex Markel, causing Quentin to laugh harder.

Brody smiled at the joke, wishing he was someplace else, quite frankly anywhere else on this Saturday night. But his family had put their faith in him, and that faith had put their fortune at risk. Brody had made a bad calculation, and now it was up to him to set things right.

He was standing, while Quentin and Rex lounged in padded rattan chairs on the second level of the multitiered pool deck. Light spilled from the great room, its sliding glass walls wide open in the still August night as guests moved inside and out. Quentin liked to party, and the massive profits from his gaming company, Beast Blue Designs, ensured he had the means.

"Did you catch her baby owl tattoo?" Brody asked Rex, putting on the cocky confidence of the rock concert promoter he was pretending to be.

Rex looked surprised, causing Brody to suspect he hadn't bounced a quarter off or anywhere near the former Miss Ventura County's rear end.

Brody had caught a glimpse of the tattoo last Wednesday morning. It seemed Vera liked string bikinis and sunrise swims, while Brody had been the only punctual arrival at breakfast that day. It was all quite innocent, but he wasn't about to mess with his street cred by explaining the circumstance.

Quentin raised his highball in a toast. "Rock on, Brody."

"I do my best," Brody drawled.

"Take a seat," Quentin invited.

While Rex frowned at him, Brody eased onto another of the rattan chairs. Music from the extensive sound system throbbed around them. A few guests splashed in the pool, while others clustered around the bar and the dessert buffet.

"Well, hello there, gorgeous," Rex drawled, sitting up straight, prompting Brody to follow the direction of his gaze.

A new woman had appeared on the pool deck, leggy and

tanned in sparkly four-inch heels. Her dress was a skintight wrap of hot, shimmering pink. Her short blond hair flowed sleekly around her face, purple highlights framing her thick-lashed, wide blue eyes. She wore sparkling earrings and chunky bangles. And when her bright red lips curved into a sultry smile, Brody felt the impact right down to his bones.

"Who is she?" he asked, before remembering to play it cool.

"Kate Dunhern," Quentin answered.

"Francie's sister?" Rex asked with clear surprise.

"It seems that's the little sister," said Quentin, a thought-ful thread running through his tone as he perused the woman with obvious curiosity.

"Who's Francie?" Brody asked, cataloging the women he'd met since striking up his acquaintance with Quentin. He didn't recall anyone named Francie.

"My baby-mama," said Quentin.

The revelation surprised Brody. "You have a child?"

"Annabelle."

Quentin had a daughter. Brody couldn't imagine how his research had overlooked that fact.

"How old is she?" he asked, looking to fill in the blanks while trying to imagine Quentin as a father.

Quentin glanced to Rex, as if he didn't know his own daughter's age.

"Around six months," Rex answered.

"I had no idea," Brody said.

"Why would you?" Rex asked, his smirk of superiority clearly intended to remind Brody he was a newcomer to this social circle, while Rex had known Quentin since junior high.

"She died last week," Quentin said in a matter-of-fact tone.

A sick feeling invaded Brody's stomach. "Your baby died?"

"Francie died," said Rex.

Brody was relieved, but then he was immediately sorry for Francie, and he was appalled by Quentin's apparently callous attitude toward the mother of his child. Not that he should have been surprised. Aside from the extravagant spending, what he knew so far was that Quentin Roo was cold, calculating and self-centered in just about every aspect of his life.

Brody's attention moved back to the jaw-dropping woman named Kate. He pondered her notice-me appearance. Her sister had died last week? And she was at a party, in a place like this, dressed like that?

Nice.

"I'm sorry for your loss," Brody offered to Quentin.

Quentin gave a shrug. "She was fun, I suppose. But if she hadn't got knocked up, it would have been over a long time ago."

Just when Brody thought his opinion of Quentin couldn't sink any further, it did.

"Did she live here?" It seemed a long shot that Francie was involved in the Beast Blue Designs' intellectual property theft. But information was information, and Brody was gathering all he could.

"I let her use the gatehouse. Made it easier. I could sometimes see the kid when I had time."

Between drunken bashes? Brody bit back the sarcastic retort. Quentin's personal life was none of his business.

"What's the sister's story?" asked Rex, ogling Kate from the tips of her purple highlighted hair to the heels of her glittering sandals.

Brody found himself doing the same. He wasn't proud of the behavior, but he was mesmerized. Even in that gaudy getup, she was a knockout.

"Don't know," said Quentin. "Don't really care."

"She showed up out of the blue?" asked Rex.

"Apparently she came down from Seattle."

"Had you met her before?" Although this Kate person had nothing to do with his investigation into Quentin's gaming technology company, Brody found himself curious.

"Never even knew she existed," said Quentin.

Suspicion grew thick in Rex's tone. "So today was the first time you met her?"

"You want me to check her ID?"

"Being Francie's sister doesn't entitle her to anything," Rex said. "You can't hand out your money to every person who crosses your path."

"It's a whole lot easier than fighting them."

"It's stupid."

"Path of least resistance. Besides, the money train's not about to derail."

Brody clenched his jaw then downed the remainder of his Shet Select single malt. The taste grounded him, reminding him of his home in the Scottish Highlands, of his parents, his brother and his purpose for being here. Quentin's money train might still be going, but only because he'd ripped off the Calder family's technology.

Brody was here to prove Quentin had stolen from his family. And he was determined to send that money train right off the nearest cliff.

"You have better things to spend it on than opportunistic gold diggers," said Rex.

"Really? Name one." Quentin then turned his attention back to Vera, Miss Ventura County. "Think I'll get me a look at that baby owl."

Brody reminded himself to stay in character. He gave a salacious grin of approval to Quentin. "Go get 'er."

Quentin smiled in anticipation, polished off his martini and rose to his feet.

Two steps later, Kate Dunhern moved into his path.

"Hello, Quentin," she said.

Her tone was smooth, cultured, far different than Brody had expected. He thought he detected an underlying trace of nervousness. He wondered why she was nervous. Was she going to make a pitch for a payout right here and now?

"Hello, Kate," Quentin responded in a level tone. "Good to see you."

"Thanks for inviting me."

He gestured expansively around the deck. "It's a party."

"I wondered if there was somewhere we could talk?"

Quentin's gaze flicked back to the sexy Vera. "Depends on…"

While Kate obviously waited for him to finish the sentence, Vera caught his attention and sent a friendly smile his way.

"Maybe tomorrow," he said to Kate.

Though she tried to hide it, her disappointment was obvious. "Uh, sure. Okay."

"Catch you later." He moved past her.

Rex made to rise, but Brody was quicker. He didn't know what he hoped to gain from talking to the sister of a woman who'd had nothing to do with Beast Blue Designs, but he didn't want Rex hitting on her. He didn't know why he felt that way. But it didn't really matter.

He stepped up in front of her.

"Brody Herrington," he said, using the last name he'd temporarily adopted from his grandmother.

She took a long moment to focus on him. Then she seemed to study him. While she did that, he detected an unexpected intelligence behind her eyes.

"Kate Dunhern," she finally responded.

"Can I get you a drink?"

She appeared to be gathering her bearings, even sizing him up. Then her mouth suddenly curved into a bright smile. In a flash, her assessing intellect was replaced by overexuberance and friendliness.

"Love one," she said. "Champagne?"

He couldn't help but puzzle at the cause of her transformation. Had she recognized his designer jeans? Had she noted his expensive watch and shoes and decided he was worth chatting up? Whatever it was, now she was behaving the way he'd expected when he first saw her purple-streaked hair and her crystal-studded sandals.

He offered his arm. "This way."

She took it, her bright pink manicured nails shimmering against his skin.

He did a double take at the distinctly sensual image and felt a spike of lust shoot through him. It was a normal reaction, he told himself. She was a gorgeous woman in an outfit designed to display it. She was likely disappointed at losing Quentin's attention, but she had the attention of every other red-blooded man here. If it was money she was after, there was plenty of it unattached and at the party.

"You're a friend of Quentin's?" she asked in a bright, friendly tone.

"An acquaintance," said Brody. He shouldn't, nor did he have any desire to lay claim to more.

"Are you in the video gaming business?"

"The entertainment industry. I'm a concert promoter from Europe."

"Scotland?" she guessed.

He'd wished he could keep it more generic, but his accent gave him away. He could only hope the fake profession and fake name would keep Quentin from making a connection to his father or, more significantly, to his family's ownership of Quentin's competitor Shetland Tech Corporation.

"You got me," he answered.

"I'm guessing it's not classical music you're promoting." Her gaze seemed to take in the party which was growing more raucous by the hour.

Brody knew it was only a matter of time until a fight broke out or someone got tossed into the pool. Breakage was a given. Quentin seemed to have a cleanup crew on perpetual standby to deal with whatever carnage was wrought at the late-night parties.

"Rock 'n roll," he answered.

"Anyone I might recognize?"

"Confidential, I'm afraid."

It was his pat answer whenever anyone pressed for details. Luckily, so far nobody had probed further. He had enough money to buy credibility, and he doubted anybody really cared beyond that. He suspected most of the people in Quentin's circle lied about their background or profession in some way or another.

"Are you in LA for a concert?" she asked.

"I'm on vacation."

"Amusement parks and surfing?"

"Something like that. What about you?"

A cloud crossed her eyes. "You may have heard my sister was killed."

"I did." He wondered if he might have misjudged her. In this moment, her remorse struck him as genuine. "I'm sorry."

But then she seemed to shake off the melancholy. "We were estranged. I hadn't seen her in seven years."

They made it to the bar, and he placed their order—champagne for her and another Shet Select for him.

"Bad blood?" he asked, finding himself curious.

"Different goals and objectives in life." She accepted the flute of champagne.

"How so?"

She seemed to hesitate. "Hard to put my finger on it now." Then she grinned, the happy-go-lucky expression coming back into her eyes. "Interesting that she was with Quentin." The new tone was searching.

"Interesting," Brody agreed, thinking Quentin was probably right. Kate was here to trade on her sister's relationship with an enormously wealthy man.

"Quentin said you were down from Seattle," he continued.

"I live there."

"That wouldn't have been my first guess."

Her eyebrow arched. "Why not?"

"It doesn't seem like a very exciting town." His rock 'n roll alter ego jumped in. "And you seem like an exciting girl."

"Seattle might surprise you." She flashed a secretive smile, clinked her glass to his and turned to walk from the bar.

He could have let the conversation end there. It would have been the smart move. Kate was a distraction, and he didn't need any distractions right now. He was here to schmooze Quentin and the Beast Blue Designs team, get inside information on who was who and then pump them for details so he could prove they'd stolen intellectual property from Shetland Tech.

So far, his conversations with Scotland Yard and the LAPD had gotten him nowhere. Both police forces were focused on murders, kidnappings and drug crimes and had little time for possible corporate espionage. Not that he blamed them. They had to prioritize.

His second plan had been to hire a private investigator. But the guy they'd put undercover at Beast Blue Designs had been caught snooping, and the company was a veritable fortress of security and secrecy. He hadn't found out a single thing.

Running out of time, Brody had taken matters into his own hands. He was trying to gain Quentin's trust on a personal level to find a route into the company.

He told his feet to walk away from Kate. But they didn't.

"What do you do in Seattle?" he asked instead.

"This and that," she answered vaguely.

The answer likely meant she was unemployed, or perhaps embarrassed by her profession. Maybe she was a criminal, or a con artist, or simply a shameless opportunist.

Whatever she was, she was sexy as hell. He should be sprinting away from her and focusing on business. Instead, he eased closer, gazing into her blue eyes, touching his glass to hers a second time.

"To this and that," he said.

Two

The party was confirming Kate's worst fears. It was a rambunctious crowd, fuelled by throbbing techno music and excessive drinking. She was no expert, but she thought she detected the scent of marijuana wafting up from the gardens. And she feared there could be other recreational drugs being passed around Quentin's mansion.

She couldn't imagine what her sister had been thinking to bring a baby into an environment like this. On second thought, she supposed she knew exactly what Francie had been thinking: nothing, at least nothing beyond enjoying the next ten minutes of her life. She'd inherited that trait from Chloe.

As recently as this morning, Kate had convinced herself Annabelle would be fine. Chloe had sworn that Annabelle was the luckiest little girl in the world. Chloe had read all about Quentin Roo and was more than impressed with his money and his success.

He was in mourning now, she had said, and not ready to introduce Annabelle to anyone from the family. Impatient to get away from her childhood memories and back home again, Kate had been willing to buy into Chloe's optimism.

She'd made it as far as the airport, her bags checked, and arrangements made with Nadia to pick her up in Seattle. But while she waited for her flight to board she'd done an internet search and found some news items featuring Quentin. One showed him outside a downtown nightclub a few weeks back. He was clearly intoxicated, a sexy woman on his arm, confronting a police officer over the right to drive his fancy sports car.

Disturbed by the images, Kate had searched further. His social media presence painted a picture of a party animal. She also found clips of his belligerent behavior and descriptions of wild times held at his mansion. He might be rich, but he definitely wasn't responsible.

Protective instincts had welled up inside her. She'd cancelled her flight and left the airport, determined to confront him, determined to demand access to Annabelle and the right to ensure the baby was safe. But halfway to his mansion, she'd stopped herself, realizing the confrontational approach was almost guaranteed to fail.

She knew she needed a better plan, something more subtle in order to get close to Annabelle without spooking Quentin. The best way she could think of to do that was appear amicable and nonthreatening, to fit seamlessly into his world. She'd decided the best option was to get to Quentin and pretend she was just like Francie.

One crazy makeover later, she did look like Francie. And now she was inside the party. And she'd met Quentin. Even if it was only momentarily, it was still a start.

The man named Brody kept pace with her along the pool deck. Whoops of delight echoed around them. Groups of people talked and laughed, drinks in hands, eyes alight with enthusiasm and exhilaration. The staccato of the bassline pummeled through to her bones.

She kept an eye on Quentin, waiting for the right moment to approach him again. He was engrossed in conversation with a tall blonde woman. She was model-thin, taller than Quentin, with impossibly long limbs and a gorgeous face that would do justice to any magazine cover.

"I've never been up north myself," Brody stated conversationally.

His deep, rolling accent purred over her. Ordinarily, she would have enjoyed that. But chatting up anyone but Quentin wasn't in her plans tonight, even if the man was distractingly attractive.

And Brody was definitely that. He had a strong chin with just enough beard stubble to be rakish. His eyes were slate gray, his brow quizzical, and he had a sexy dark shock of hair swooping across his forehead. His mouth was firm, slightly

stern, some might even say judgmental. Although exactly
what someone living in the thick of the rock-and-roll lifestyle would have to be judgmental about was a mystery to her.

"No rock concerts to promote in Washington State?" she
asked, telling herself to keep it light and stay in character. Everybody with anything to do with Quentin needed to believe
she was just like Francie, a girl looking to enjoy life without
worrying too much about the details.

"North America is a secondary market. Here we mostly
stick to New York City. I have been to Boston and Chicago,
and once to Florida, but that was a vacation."

"Miami's a fun town." She was guessing. She'd only ever
seen it on television, but it seemed like a good bet.

She kept watch on Quentin, poised to interrupt as soon
as she had a chance. She'd decided to downplay her interest
in Annabelle tonight. A party girl wouldn't be fixated on a
baby's welfare. But she was growing impatient. Quentin was
getting rapidly drunk, so who was with the baby?

"The Keys," Brody said beside her.

"What keys?" she asked.

"The Florida Keys."

"Oh." Kate told herself to focus and try to use the conversation productively. She'd track Annabelle down as soon as
she could. "How long have you known Quentin?"

"I've been in LA for a few weeks," Brody replied. "But
I've known of him for quite a bit longer."

She leaned casually against a rail that overlooked the
sweeping lights of the city, keeping Quentin in her peripheral vision while the breeze blew her newly short hair back
from her face. "And what do you think of him?"

Brody turned to face her. "In what sense?"

"I've seen the news reports, and I wonder how much of
it is true."

He took in her outfit, and she was reminded of her heavy
makeup, tight dress and the funky hair. She wasn't exactly
comfortable with the impression she must be making, but she
had to see this through.

"He knows how to have a good time," said Brody.

Kate gave her head a little toss and tried to look like a woman who was very much interested in having a good time. She glanced pointedly around the party, the pretty people, the exotic clothes, the expensive food and liquor. "This is definitely a good time."

There was an unfathomable expression in his eyes that could have been sarcasm or resignation. "Isn't it just."

The odd reaction made her curious. "You must be used to parties in your line of work."

"I've been to parties of all kinds."

"Wild ones?" she asked, striving to look intrigued and excited at the possibility.

"Some." He gave her a warm smile.

"Sounds terrific." She half expected him to toss out an invitation, at least a generic one: *maybe I'll take you sometime, baby...*

She'd refuse of course, politely. She wasn't here looking for dates. She was here for Annabelle and nothing else. But he didn't ask, and she found herself wondering if the purple highlights weren't working for her.

Just then Quentin left his conversation partner, and she spotted her opening. She made a quick move toward him, but her heel caught on a concrete seam, and she stumbled, sloshing her champagne.

Brody grasped her elbow, stabilizing her.

"Sorry." She quickly apologized for her clumsiness, hoping she hadn't splashed anything on his clothes.

"You all right?" he asked, still holding on to her.

"I tripped."

"You were in a pretty big hurry."

"I was—" She hesitated over her words. "I'm hoping to catch Quentin."

Brody glanced past her. "Someone beat you to him."

She turned to see two new women laughing with him. She cursed under her breath.

"He was just with your sister." There was censure in Brody's tone, and she looked up to see his gaze had hardened.

"It's not that." It was clear from his frown that he didn't believe her. "I'm not here to make a play for Quentin."

"You nearly injured yourself trying to get over there to chat him up."

"Not for that."

"Listen, it's not really any of my business."

"You're right. It's not. But I'm going to tell you anyway. I'm not romantically interested in Quentin."

She couldn't imagine any circumstance where she'd be romantically interested in a man like Quentin Roo.

Brody's gaze took a leisurely tour of her outfit. "Good news, Kate. Romance is not at all what you're projecting."

Despite the fact that she'd done so on purpose, she was offended by his implication that she'd dressed provocatively. "I'm not after Quentin in any way, shape or form."

"Of course you're not."

She didn't care what this Brody person thought. At least she shouldn't care about his opinion. But for some stupid reason, she did care.

It was on the tip of her tongue to explain that this was all about her niece. She was playacting here, making sure Annabelle was going to be okay. But she stopped herself just in time. Instead, she looked up at him and gave her highlighted hair another defiant toss. "I'm here for a good time."

His eyes reminded her of flints. "Aren't we all."

Brody watched the fleet of tiny electronic spaceships blast their way through an asteroid field on the wall-mounted wide screen. The ships changed colors, using different weapons, all jockeying for position while trying to avoid being annihilated by other players.

"See that? Right there," said Will Finlay, the head programmer from Shetland Tech. "The organics on the planet surface."

"All I see are a bunch of things exploding."

"It's the way they're exploding," said Will. "Or rather, the way they've changed the way they're exploding."

"If you say so." Brody wasn't a software engineer, and he wouldn't pretend to come close to Will's technical understanding.

"This is the best evidence yet. I've checked with a few contacts at MIT, and they agree Shetland Tech has been ripped off."

"Can we prove it with this?" Brody asked.

Will had managed to get his hands on a prototype of the Beast Blue Designs' new game, "Blue Strata Combat."

"Not without the source code," Will said. "We can prove they're using advanced algorithms that trigger object evolution within an AI environment, but we can't prove they stole it from Shetland."

"But they did," said Brody.

"They did."

"If we move now?"

"I'm told that if we make a move based on the evidence we have right now we'll be tied up in litigation for a few decades. And after that we'll probably lose."

Brody sat back in the burgundy leather armchair that was positioned in the living area of his hotel suite at the Diamond Pier Towers. He'd been away from home for over a month now, and he was growing impatient.

Back in Scotland, his brother Blane had too much to worry about already. Suffering from the neuromuscular disease Newis Bar Syndrome, Blane tired more easily than most people. But as eldest son, the Viscount and the future Earl of Calder, the responsibilities for the family seat fell to him. Brody had to at least take the money trouble out of the equation.

"We need to get inside their facility," Will said. "Proving our case still hinges on accessing their resident servers and finding our proprietary code."

"We already tried that."

The attempt had been a dismal failure. The technical security was impenetrable, and the server room was on lockdown twenty-four hours a day. The private detective they'd hired to go undercover as a technician was caught trying to gain unauthorized access and was summarily fired.

"Do you think Quentin might confess something?" Will asked.

"To me?"

"To anybody."

Brody found his thoughts moving to Kate. If he looked like Kate he might be able to get Quentin to spill his darkest secrets. But he didn't look like Kate, and so far Quentin didn't want to talk business with outsiders.

"I need to find an opportunity to search his house," Brody said. "If we can't get into their corporate headquarters, Quentin's house is the next best bet."

"You get caught snooping around? Well, I have to say, those security guys he's hired seem very serious."

"I'll be careful."

"They have Russian accents."

"I know."

Brody had heard rumors about Quentin's financial backers, that they had shady backgrounds and even shadier connections to overseas criminal organizations.

"I don't see we have any choice," he said.

"There's always a choice," Will said.

"You mean I can make the decision to bankrupt my family?"

"It's better than being shot."

"Marginally," Brody said.

Quite frankly, he'd rather take a bullet than be responsible for losing the Calder estate. The earldom had been in his family for twenty-two generations. They'd had ups and downs over the years. The land had been mortgaged before, but the family had always made it back to better times.

Five years ago, their financial position had become particularly precarious, and Brody knew they needed to modernize. His brother Blane, the viscount and eldest son of the earl, wanted to develop tourism infrastructure on the estate, starting with a hotel. But Brody worried about the high investment and slow rate of return that were part of Blane's plan. He knew they needed something faster, so he'd convinced his father to buy Will's start-up company and go into high-end gaming technology.

At first, it had worked brilliantly. They'd paid down their debt and were looking forward to moving into the tourism sector. But then Brody got overconfident. He'd borrowed again, borrowed more, and plowed the money into expanding Shetland Tech, creating a new game that he and Will were sure would revolutionize the industry.

Their logic was solid. So was their research. It should have been a success. It would have been a success. But then Beast Blue Designs had stolen their code and stood a frightening chance of beating them to market.

If Beast Blue succeeded, it would be impossible to recoup Shetland Tech's sunk costs, and the company would most certainly go bankrupt. The Calder estate and the castle on the banks of the River Tay would be lost to the family forever.

"I'm serious," Will said, setting down the controller. "You can't mess with those guys."

"They already messed with me."

Will uttered an exclamation of disgust. "You're going to get all macho about it?"

"I'm not getting macho. What I'm getting is smart. If we can't infiltrate the company, then we'll come at it from another angle, through Quentin. The man drinks and parties to excess. He's not as sharp as he should be, and I've succeeded in becoming his new pal."

"That's because you're pretending to be exciting and likable."

"I like to think I'm generally both," Brody said with a straight face.

Will flashed a grin. "Right. Sure. Let's call you that. But you can't expect to meet Quentin Roo's standards."

"I'm definitely not the life of some parties," Brody said. He had absolutely no desire to be the life of Quentin's parties.

His phone buzzed on the low table in front of him.

Will stayed silent while he picked it up.

"Blane," he answered warmly. He didn't have any good news for his brother, but he was still glad to hear from him.

Blane coughed into the phone. "Hi, Brody."

Brody was immediately concerned. "What's wrong? Are you ill?"

"I'm fine."

"You're sure?"

Blane coughed again. "It's nothing. Mother has me steaming in the bathroom."

Brody relaxed a little, since he knew that at the first sign of a problem their mother would hover over Blane. He glanced at his watch. "It's late there."

"Have you signed up to be my nanny?"

"If you're sick—"

"A tickle in my chest is not sick. I'm humoring her. I don't need to humor you."

"Okay."

"Oliver Masterson came by today."

The information gave Brody pause. Oliver Masterson was the head architect on the family's hotel development project. Oliver shouldn't have much to do at the moment, because it was a long-term plan, with nothing substantive happening for years down the road. Brody thought they were all clear on the timing.

He spoke to his brother in a cautious tone. "We're only looking for preliminary drawings right now."

"We were. We are," said Blane. "He only wanted to see the site. He likes the view of the lake."

"Who wouldn't?"

The east meadow was one of Brody's favorite spots on the entire three-hundred-acre estate. If he'd had his way, they'd have built a house there and turned the castle into a hotel.

But his mother wouldn't hear of moving from the family's traditional home.

"He wants the building to go higher," said Blane.

"Higher than three stories?"

"I know that puts us into a whole new category of construction. But we need to think of the long term, our children's children and beyond. The high-end market provides the best return on investment."

"You've been talking to the town council again." A large, five-star hotel on the Calder lands would have spin-off effects to any number of local businesses.

Blane coughed again. "You know they're right."

"I understand where you're coming from, Blane."

"And you agree with me."

Brody did agree. Like their ancestors before them, they had an obligation to support the surrounding community. He agreed there was growth potential in luxury tourism. The only problem he had was cash flow. They needed significant cash to flow in order to underwrite his brother's dream. Right now, they didn't have it.

"Don't sign anything today," he said.

"I won't. Are you close?" Blane knew only the broad strokes of the problem with Beast Blue Designs. He didn't know how precarious their financial situation had become.

"Getting closer," said Brody, knowing he was going to have to make something happen soon or confess to his family the full extent of their problems.

"Let me know how it goes." Blane's coughing started again.

"I will. Get better."

Blane wheezed out a laugh. "I'm in good hands."

Brody couldn't help but smile as he set down the phone. Their mother the countess was a force of nature.

"Problem?" asked Will.

"They want to make the hotel bigger."

"Let me guess. They accomplish that by spending more money."

"I knew you weren't just a pretty face." Brody suddenly felt tired and momentarily defeated. "It's always about more money. We need to win this thing, Will. And we need to do it soon."

"Okay," said Will, squaring his shoulders. "Let's hope Quentin is the kind of guy who brings his work home with him. If you can get in front of his home computer, I can tell you what to look for. But don't get caught, and whatever you do don't get shot by the Russian bodyguards."

Brody frowned. "I have no intention of getting shot."

"Nobody *plans* to get shot," said Will. "It happens all of a sudden and usually at the most inconvenient time."

Three

Kate had wrangled an invitation back to Quentin's Sunday night. She had been hoping to talk to him alone and maybe even meet Annabelle. But she'd been disappointed on both fronts.

Annabelle had been put to bed by the nanny before Kate arrived, and Quentin didn't even show his face. His friends didn't seem to care, though, guzzling liquor, dancing on the furniture and frolicking in the pool to music from a live band in the gazebo.

She'd had no desire to party, but she was more determined than ever to meet Annabelle. So when she saw a woman passed out on a sofa, she'd come up with an idea. As the party wore down, she found a quiet corner and pretended to do the same.

There was no way she was dozing off amidst intoxicated strangers. So she lay there awake until 4:00 a.m. when the last guests had stumbled away.

Chilled and exhausted, she'd finally closed her eyes.

At five, the cleaners showed up and began straightening the furniture and clearing up the debris—empty bottles, broken glass, garbage and cigarette butts discarded everywhere. At six, they turned on vacuum cleaners and began to filter the pool water.

Giving up on the idea of sleeping, Kate found a bathroom. She gazed at her smudged makeup, mussed hair and the dark circles under her eyes. Lack of sleep made her look exactly like a woman who'd partied too hard two nights in a row. It was depressing, but there was no denying it would help her disguise. She ran a comb through her hair and wiped away the worst of the mascara smudges, then her thoughts turned to coffee.

As she moved down the hallway, she heard a woman's voice chirping happily about it being a beautiful day and how she was warming a bottle that would be delicious. Kate guessed it had to be the nanny talking to Annabelle. Her chest swelled with anticipation, and she picked up her pace, following the voice.

"You look so pretty this morning," the nanny singsonged. "Such a smiley girl."

Kate moved through the archway into a bright, airy kitchen, to see a young woman in blue jeans and an orange T-shirt, holding a baby against one shoulder and a bottle in the opposite hand.

"Are you hungry?" the young woman asked Annabelle in a gentle voice, and then she spotted Kate.

"Oh," she said, her expression sobering. "Hello. I didn't realize anyone was here."

"Leftover from last night," Kate offered in an apologetic tone, smoothing a hand over her messy hair.

"Can I help you with something?" the woman asked, her voice and manner becoming reserved.

Kate couldn't keep her gaze from Annabelle. The baby girl had blond hair and big blue eyes in a sweet, delicate-looking face. Her pink mouth was perfect, and she was dressed in a white romper dotted with colored hearts.

"I'm…" Kate struggled for words. "I was hoping to meet Annabelle."

The woman's gaze narrowed, and she drew almost imperceptibly back.

Kate was reminded of how she looked and of the impression she must be giving.

"I'm Kate Dunhern," she quickly put in. "Francie's sister."

When the woman didn't immediately respond, it occurred to Kate that she might be new on the job.

"Did you know Francie?" Kate asked.

"I didn't know she had a sister." The woman was still obviously cautious.

"We weren't close."

"She never mentioned you."

Kate kept her voice calm and mild. She didn't mind that the nanny was protective. "I can answer some questions about Francie. Or I can show you some identification."

The offers seemed to dispel the woman's fears. "That won't be necessary. I'm Christina Alder, Annabelle's nanny."

"I guessed that," said Kate, taking a step forward. "She's adorable."

Christina smiled fondly at Annabelle. "Isn't she? She's a sweetheart, good as gold."

"Have you been taking care of her long?" Kate moved closer still, taking it slow, smiling at Annabelle, trying not to startle the baby.

"From the day she was born," said Christina.

Kate reached out and touched Annabelle's little hand with her finger.

"Baa," said Annabelle.

"Baa, yourself." Kate smiled. "I'm your auntie Kate."

Annabelle wiggled, and Christina shifted her hold.

"You're a friend of Quentin's?" asked Christina.

Kate shook her head. "I only just met him on Saturday. I came home for…" She paused. "Well, I was disappointed they didn't have a service for Francie. And then I learned about Annabelle."

Annabelle wrapped her fist around Kate's index finger, and a shaft of warmth shot straight to Kate's heart.

"She misses her mommy," said Christina. But there was something off in her tone, as if she was being polite rather than sincere.

"It's good that she has you."

"Yes," said Christina, sounding more sincere. "It helps."

"And there's Quentin," said Kate, opening the door for a comment about Quentin's abilities as a father.

"There are a lot of demands on his schedule." Christina's tone was neutral.

"He seems very busy."

"He is very busy." Christina paused. "He loves his daughter, though."

"I'm sure he does."

Annabelle started to squirm, and her face twisted into a frown.

"She's hungry," said Christina.

"I'm sorry I interrupted."

"Not at all. I just need to sit down to feed her."

Kate stepped back to give them some room. She wasn't sure if she should leave, but she desperately wanted to stay.

Christina climbed into a padded chair at the breakfast bar and adjusted Annabelle across one forearm, popping the bottle into the baby's mouth. Annabelle began to suck and her eyes fluttered closed.

"She's very patient," said Christina. "Most babies cry from the time you get them up to the time they get their bottles."

"Have you cared for a lot of babies?"

"I've had my diploma for four years. I did a lot of fill-in work for the first two, and my last posting was newborn twins." Christina smiled. "They were a handful." She smoothed a lock of hair across Annabelle's forehead.

"Boys or girls?" asked Kate, easing her way onto one of the other chairs.

"Boys. We got them into a routine at about four months. Mom took them on by herself when they hit six months. She still sends me email updates."

"They're doing well?" Kate continued to watch Annabelle.

"They just had their first birthday. They're finally both sleeping through the night." Christina sobered. "I'm very sorry about your sister."

"Me, too," said Kate. "I hadn't seen her in a long time. Well, I guess you would know that since I haven't been to see Annabelle. I didn't even know Francie was pregnant."

Christina didn't respond to that. Kate supposed there wasn't a whole lot more to say on the subject.

"I'm glad she had Annabelle and Quentin in her life," said Kate.

Christina's brow furrowed ever so slightly "You know we lived in the gatehouse, right?"

Kate wasn't sure what that meant. "The gatehouse?"

"Quentin and Francie, they weren't… They weren't together as a couple. He said he liked having Annabelle close by, but I understood his relationship with Francie was short-lived." Christina glanced away, as if she was aware that she'd shared too much.

"Thanks for telling me that. I didn't know."

Cristina didn't answer, instead adjusting the bottle at Annabelle's mouth.

"It was nice that Francie could live here," said Kate, glancing around at the huge, ultramodern kitchen.

From where she sat, she could see the estate grounds and the city beyond. The great room was behind her with its expensive furniture and art, the plush carpeting and a massive stone fireplace across one entire wall. If the gatehouse was any comparison to the main house, Francie had lived in the lap of luxury.

"She did enjoy the lifestyle," said Christina.

Kate could well imagine, at least from what she remembered of her sister. "Quentin seems to throw her kind of parties."

"He does," said Christina, removing the bottle from Annabelle's mouth and holding the baby against her chest to pat Annabelle's back. "She definitely liked the nightlife better than the mornings."

"I remember that about her."

"But she had me. So she didn't need to worry about the mornings."

A male voice interrupted their conversation. "Sorry to barge in."

Kate stood, turning to see the man she'd met Saturday night.

Brody Herrington looked a whole lot fresher than she felt in her crumpled cocktail dress. He'd topped a pair of well-worn jeans with a crisp charcoal dress shirt.

"I wouldn't have taken you for an early riser," he said to Kate.

She stuck to her story. "The vacuuming woke me up."

"I'll get out of your way," said Christina, her demeanor immediately changing to deference as she rose with Annabelle.

Kate wanted to tell her not to leave, to ask her to please stay and talk some more. She wanted to learn about her sister and Annabelle's life here with Quentin. But she couldn't risk tipping her hand. If Quentin knew she was here to judge his fitness as a parent, he would send her packing.

"It was nice to meet you," she said instead.

Christina gave her a brief nod and left the room.

"You crashed here last night?" Brody asked.

"One too many martinis," Kate lied, pushing past her embarrassment to stay in character.

What must he think of a woman who passed out at a party? Then she told herself he probably didn't think anything. He likely met that kind of woman all the time.

"I may have left my watch behind last night," he said, holding up his bare wrist as evidence. Then he seemed to spy a coffeepot. He smiled and crossed to it.

"Want some?" he asked.

"Kill for some."

He retrieved a pair of mugs from a glassed-in cupboard. "I was going to take a look around and see if I could find it."

"It must be expensive," she observed.

He looked puzzled. "Expensive?"

"You're here at six in the morning. I assume you were worried about it."

"Oh. Yes. Well, it is a nice watch. It was a gift. From my mother on my twenty-first birthday. It's engraved."

"So, sentimental value."

"Sentimental value," he agreed as he poured the coffee.

The revelation surprised Kate. Brody didn't seem like the sentimental type.

"You need anything in it?" he asked.

"Black is fine."

He held out one of the mugs, and she moved to take it. In addition to a movie-star-handsome face, he had the most extraordinary eyes. They were dark and deep, slate gray in some lights, shot with silver in others. Right now they seemed to shimmer with contemplation. For a second she worried he saw right through her disguise.

"Want some help?" she asked, more to break the silence than anything else.

"Help?"

"To find your watch."

"Oh. Sure. It has a black face and a platinum band."

She couldn't help but grin at that. "To help me distinguish it from all the other watches lying around the mansion?"

"It was a great party."

"Yes, it was," she lied.

She simply couldn't understand the appeal of such a rowdy event. It was impossible to carry on a conversation over the loud music, music that grated in her ears. The guests were all drunk or high and only interested in gossip and fashion and bragging about their money or their connections.

"You don't say that with a lot of conviction," Brody observed.

She covered her expression with a swallow of the coffee. It tasted fantastic. "I guess I'm still recovering from the fun."

"You do look a little rough around the edges."

"Aren't you suave."

"You want me to lie?"

"Sure. Why not?"

His dark eyes warmed with humor. "You look fantastic this morning."

"Lukewarm delivery. But I'll take it."

His gaze moved downward, noting her one-shouldered, jeweled, sea-foam cocktail dress. It was tight and stiff and terrible to sleep in.

"I like the dress," he said.

"It's too late for you to try to flirt with me."

"I disagree."

"Then it's too early for you to flirt with me." She took another satisfying swallow of the coffee. "Chat me up later, when my brain is fully functional."

"I'll hold you to that."

Kate knew flirting with Brody was a mistake. She needed to keep him and everyone else at arm's length.

"Where did you last see it?" she asked him.

"See what?"

"Your watch."

"Oh, right." He glanced around. "I don't know. I'm not sure. I was going to start with the great room."

She polished off her coffee. "Lead on."

Kate decided that looking for Brody's watch was a plausible reason to hang around the mansion a while longer. She might get another chance to see Annabelle or a chance to talk to Quentin. Thus far, she hadn't managed to get the man to stand still long enough to have more than a ten-second conversation.

Brody pulled up the sofa cushions, checking behind each one. Kate took the opposite end of the room, scanning the floor, the tabletops, the windowsills, eventually making her way into the dining room and hunting around its corners. The cleaners were still working and nodded politely to her as they passed. They seemed used to encountering leftover party guests.

It occurred to her they would assume she'd had a companion last night. After all, that was the most common reason for a woman to be dressed in a cocktail dress in the early hours of the morning. She told herself not to care. But then she found herself wondering if Brody thought the same thing.

Had he believed her when she said she'd fallen asleep? Did he think she'd had a one-night stand? He might even think she spent the night with Quentin.

She shuddered at the very idea.

She told herself again not to care what Brody thought. What Brody thought of her was completely irrelevant. Still she found herself retreating to the great room to set the record straight.

He wasn't there.

She listened, but she didn't hear anything. So she headed down the hall, toward the main staircase, glancing into the rooms with open doors. She found Brody in an office, standing behind a desk plunking the keys of a computer.

"Find anything?" she asked.

He looked guiltily up, and she couldn't help but wonder what he was doing.

"Nothing," he answered.

She waited to see if he'd elaborate.

"I was taking a quick check of my emails." He hit a couple more keys. "We've got a big tour in the works."

"Sounds exciting."

He shrugged. "Fairly routine. But you know rock stars."

"Big egos?" she guessed.

"Big everything. They need a lot of TLC." He moved from behind the desk.

She struggled for an opening to broach the subject, but there was no way to nonchalantly work it in. She decided to tackle it head-on. "I did fall asleep last night."

"Huh?"

"What I said earlier. That was how it happened. I had a few too many drinks and accidentally fell asleep on a sofa."

His gaze narrowed, and he looked intrigued.

"I was telling you the truth," she said.

"Okay."

"Was that sarcasm?" She couldn't tell if he believed her or not.

"That was. It's none of my business."

"I wasn't with Quentin."

Brody looked so genuinely surprised that she felt foolish.

She tried to backpedal. "I was remembering what you said Saturday night. You seemed to…well, allude to me possibly being after Quentin in an unsavory way."

"You said you weren't."

"I'm not."

"I believed you." He seemed sincere.

Now she really felt foolish. "Good. That's good." She told herself to stop talking, but for some reason she kept on. "Why?"

He flexed an amused grin, brushing his fingers along the top of the wooden desk as he moved toward her. "You didn't look like you were lying."

"How does lying look?" What was the matter with her? She sounded silly, and she didn't seem to be able to quit. "I mean to you. How can you tell?"

"I don't know. How does anyone tell?" He stopped in front of her.

It was too close for comfort, but she didn't move.

"Lack of eye contact," he continued. "A tense, closed expression, halting speech, hesitation."

He certainly didn't look tense. He looked relaxed. He looked powerful, in control, and too, too sexy. She should look away and break the spell. She didn't.

"Take now," he said, leaning ever so slightly forward. "Your expression is open. You're not nervous. You're looking straight at me. It's like you're inviting me in."

Uh-oh.

"Like you want me to see your innermost thoughts," he continued.

She definitely didn't want that. Her innermost thoughts were her business and hers alone.

"Like you're thinking physical contact…" He brushed her fingers, gently holding the tips of hers with the tips of his. He drew in a deep breath. "Wouldn't be a bad thing."

She felt a warmth rise over her wrist, up the inside of her arm and through to her chest. She didn't want him to let go.

He eased in, his intention clear. His hand wrapped itself fully around hers, intensifying the sensations. She lost track of time and place, forgot about everything but Brody as he drew her close.

His lips touched hers. The kiss was gentle. She hadn't expected that. His free hand came to rest at her waist, again the lightest of touches. If he'd kissed her hard or pulled her fast and tight, she might have had the presence of mind to break away. But he was stealthy in his approach, slipping past her defenses, his actions so soothing that she didn't realize her mistake.

The kiss deepened.

It felt good. It felt great.

She stepped forward, bringing her body against his, chest to chest, thigh to thigh. His hand moved along the small of her back, splaying warm and smooth against her spine.

Her lips parted, and he groaned, pulling back, breaking the kiss.

"I'm sorry," he said.

She felt her face heat in embarrassment. "No, I'm sorry. I shouldn't—"

Then she remembered the part she was supposed to be playing. Girls like Francie didn't get rattled by a kiss. So instead of apologizing, she gave him a sultry smile and walked her fingers down his chest before dropping her hand to her side. "No problem. Just so we're clear on Quentin."

Brody looked confused for a moment. Then he seemed to give himself a little shake. "Glad we got that out of the way."

She wanted to ask him if it was the question of Quentin that was now out of the way, or if their kiss was the thing that was out of the way. Had he been curious about kissing her? Had he been disappointed? Was he moving on?

A dozen questions bloomed in her mind, but she couldn't ask any of them. The kiss was definitely out of the way. It was done. She was moving past it, past Brody, and back on to Annabelle.

Four

Brody heard deep voices in the mansion hallway and kicked himself for getting distracted by Kate. She was gorgeous and sexy, and who could blame him for kissing her. But he'd let his guard down. Quentin's computer was still on, and somebody was approaching.

It sounded like two of them. Their voices were guttural, speaking in Russian, Quentin's security guards for sure.

He grasped Kate's arm and drew her out of sight.

"What?" she started to ask.

"Shhh," he cautioned.

She looked puzzled but stopped talking. For that, he was grateful.

The voices rose. The footsteps paused by the door. He pressed himself and Kate flat against the wall, ready to kiss her again if the men came into the room. He assumed a clandestine sexual encounter would be something they'd understand and accept.

Luckily, instead of looking in, they resumed walking and talking.

Kate whispered, "Are we doing something wrong?"

"No," he lied.

He was definitely doing something wrong. She thought she was searching for his lost watch.

"I didn't want to embarrass you," he lied again.

"Embarrass me how?"

He made a show of taking in her outfit from last night.

"Oh." She wrapped her arms around her front, covering her cleavage and bare shoulders. "They'd think I spent the night with you."

"They would."

"Thanks, then."

"No problem."

A split second later, she gave a little shrug, dropping her hands to her sides. "But what would I care?"

It was a good question. He wasn't sure why he thought she'd care about the opinions of strangers. He did know pretending to be chivalrous was a whole lot better than explaining to her that he'd been checking out Quentin's computer.

"Who are they?" she asked, still keeping her voice low.

"Security guards. Quentin has a lot of them. Every one brawny, ill-humored and uncommunicative."

"What did they mean that Quentin had better be persuaded?"

The question surprised Brody. No, not surprised. It shocked the heck out of him. "You speak Russian?"

"No. But they were speaking Ukrainian."

That was another surprise. All along, he'd thought the guys were Russian.

He gave her a beat to elaborate.

She didn't.

"Same question," he prompted.

"Only a little. I understand it better than I speak it." She moved away from the wall, peeping out the open door.

"And?" he asked, struggling to keep the impatience from his tone. "That's because?"

"Oh. My best friend Nadia is Ukrainian. She grew up with her grandmother who lived across the hall from our apartment. Mrs. Ivanova was a crotchety old thing, and she didn't speak much English. She wore baggy stockings and embroidered cloth shoes, but I liked her because she baked incredible honey cookies and Kiev cake."

"And she taught you Ukrainian?"

Kate seemed to have a peculiar way of getting around to a point.

"Nadia and I tried to teach her English," said Kate. "Turns out, we weren't very good teachers."

"But you were a good student?"

She made a tipping motion with her hand. "I was okay. Nadia's fluent. I dabble."

"You understood those two."

"Only part of it."

"What else?" Brody didn't want to drag an unsuspecting Kate into his web of intrigue. But what she'd overheard could be important.

There were rumors Quentin had originally been financed by an Eastern European criminal organization. Assuming the rumors were true, Brody had wondered if the bodyguards might be connected to the financier. If they were, maybe they were into other kinds of crime, like corporate espionage.

One thing was sure: given the snippet of conversation Kate had interpreted, there was a real chance those men were more than just bodyguards.

"I didn't understand most of it," she said. "And I might be getting it wrong."

He tried not to sound too earnest. "What exactly did you hear?"

"That Quentin could be or maybe had to be persuaded. Something about him accepting or maybe embracing Ceci."

"Ceci?"

"That's what I heard."

Who was Ceci? "Did they mention a last name?"

"No."

"Accepting her as what?"

"A girlfriend, maybe?"

"They said that?"

"I'm tossing out random guesses," she said.

"What about the context?"

"I'm not that good."

"But—"

"Brody, it was a tiny snippet of conversation in a foreign language from a distance. What do you want from me?"

He immediately regretted grilling her. "You're right. I'm sorry."

"Why do you care so much?"

"I don't." He ordered himself to take a beat and relax. "You had me curious is all. I've listened to those guys talk amongst themselves for weeks now and never knew what they were saying."

She peered at him for a moment, seeming to assess his expression. Once again, she appeared smarter than he would have guessed. But then she blinked, and the expression was gone.

"Maybe that's why he broke up with Francie," she speculated aloud. "To be with this Ceci person."

"I've never seen him with a steady girlfriend." Then again, Brody hadn't ever come across Francie, either. There could be any number of people in Quentin's life that Brody didn't know about.

"Do you suppose he has another child?" asked Kate. "Maybe those guys want him to marry Ceci because they have a baby."

That seemed like a long shot to Brody, and not at all helpful to his investigation. He wanted the bodyguards and the mysterious Ceci to be clues to Beast Blue Designs' theft from Shetland. Though he acknowledged that was a long shot, as well.

The thought did remind him of why he was here and what he was doing. He needed to get back at it.

"No sign of my watch in here," he said to Kate. "Did you happen to check the dining room?"

She nodded. "I did."

"What about the kitchen?" He wanted to get her out of the office so that he could turn off Quentin's computer.

"Would you like me to check there?"

"That would help. I was in there a few times last night."

"I'm surprised I didn't see you at the party."

"I spent most of the evening in the garden." Lying was becoming easier and easier for him. He wasn't sure how he should feel about that.

He hadn't even been at last night's party, never mind lost his watch. It was a ruse he'd concocted as an excuse to snoop around the mansion. It wasn't the most complicated plan in the world, but he'd decided simpler was better.

She seemed to expect him to elaborate on his statement.

"With a woman," he lied again. "Somebody I just met."

A bit of the friendliness vanished from her expression. "Right."

He wanted to tell her he was lying. He wasn't like Quentin and the rest of the partiers. He didn't have sex in the garden with random women. But telling her the truth was dangerous. Like everybody else in this world, she needed to believe he was Brody Herrington, a freewheeling concert promoter living the rock-and-roll lifestyle.

If one surprisingly interesting woman thought he was some kind of a player, then that was the price he'd pay.

"I'll check the kitchen," she said, turning away.

"Kate?"

She stopped without turning back. "Yes?"

He knew he was selfish to ask for her cooperation, but his family was at stake. "Don't let on."

She twisted her head to look at him.

"Don't let on that you understand Ukrainian."

Her brow furrowed in puzzlement.

"I don't trust those guys." That much was definitely true. "It's probably better if you just listen." He wished he could ask her to report back to him on what she heard, but he didn't dare go that far.

"I wasn't planning to let on," she said.

"Good."

"I'll go check for your watch."

"Thanks."

"Maybe if you kept your clothes on," she muttered under her breath. "You might not lose things."

He watched her walk away, her hair slightly mussed, her shoulders bare, her legs long and shapely beneath the tight, short dress. It struck him as odd that she'd criticize his behavior. But a split second later, she only struck him as gorgeous, and he forgot about anything else.

* * *

Kate took a quick look through the kitchen, and then decided Brody could find his own watch. It was probably in the garden, falling off when he'd stripped down for a quickie.

It had annoyed her to learn he'd spent the evening hooking up. She acknowledged the reaction was absurd, since it had absolutely nothing to do with her. With his job, he probably had one-night stands all over the world—him and all the other single, wealthy men hanging out with celebrities and groupies.

But for some reason she wanted him to be better than the rest. Maybe it was because she'd kissed him. Or more important because she'd enjoyed kissing him. She should have better taste than to enjoy kissing a man who was into one-night stands. What was the matter with her?

She made her way back into the main hallway, focusing on Annabelle again, and wondering how long she dared hang around. She didn't want anyone to get suspicious, but she also didn't want to squander this opportunity.

Time was ticking. Banking on Quentin being a late sleeper, she decided to have a look upstairs before she left.

She guessed Annabelle's nursery would be on the second floor and hoped Christina and Annabelle had gone back there when they left the kitchen. If anyone questioned her, she could always use the excuse of Brody's lost watch.

At the top of the stairs, she heard the gentle pings of a lullaby. She walked toward them, coming to an open bedroom door.

Annabelle was lying in a white crib, cooing softly, her hands and bare feet wiggling in the air as she watched colorful cloth jungle animals circle above her.

The rest of the big room was a jumble, containing a change table, two armchairs, a rocking chair. Through an open doorway to a connected room, she saw a single bed and a dresser. Everything was covered in cardboard boxes. Some were open, some taped shut. Plush toys were strewn around the nursery, and the walk-in closet was wide-open, revealing empty shelves and more packing boxes.

"Wow," said Kate. "You've got some work on your hands."

Christina looked surprised by the sound of Kate's voice.

Kate knew she was being unforgivably brazen barging in on them. She squelched her discomfort. "Do you want some help?"

"That's not necessary."

"I'm happy to do it." Kate forced herself to ignore Christina's obvious lack of welcome, moving to one of the open boxes of baby clothes to look inside. "Shall I put these in the closet?"

"No, really." Christina started toward her.

Annabelle let out a cry.

"I'll get her," Kate impulsively announced.

"No," Christina said sharply.

Their gazes met.

Kate realized she couldn't pull it off. Maybe in the midst of a party she could pretend to be self-centered and oblivious to the needs of others. But she couldn't do that to Christina.

"I'm sorry," she said. She took a step back. "I don't mean to put you in an awkward position." She took another step back, steadying herself on the doorjamb. "I wanted to see Annabelle is all. I'll leave the two of you in peace."

Disappointment running through her, Kate turned for the door.

"Wait," said Christina.

Kate paused and turned back.

Christina took a deep breath. "I'm not trying to be suspicious. It's just that most of Quentin's friends are…"

"Untrustworthy?" Kate guessed.

"I try to keep Annabelle out of their paths. They think she's a toy, and they're not always…"

"Sober?"

Christina looked stricken. "I shouldn't be saying these things."

"I'm not like them." Kate realized she was ready to come clean with Christina.

"Not like who?" Quentin appeared in Kate's peripheral vision.

For a second, her heart lodged in her throat. How much had he overheard? She scrambled for a plausible response.

"Not like those uptight people who hate mess and noise." She gave a brilliant smile.

Christina looked confused.

"You mean the Vernons?" asked Quentin.

"Who are the Vernons?"

"The people next door. Did they complain about the music again?"

"I loved the music," said Kate. "But, I fell asleep on the sofa. Too many martinis. My bad." She gave a giggle.

"There's no such thing as too many martinis," said Quentin.

Annabelle let out another cry, and Quentin winced at the sound.

"Now that kind of noise will make a man nuts."

Christina moved quickly to shush the baby.

Kate bit back a reproach. He shouldn't blame a baby for crying.

"Do you have parties every weekend?" she asked instead.

He gave a shrug. "People tend to drop by."

She wanted to ask how that was going to work with Annabelle living in the main house, but she held back.

One of the bodyguards appeared beside Quentin, holding out a cell phone. "Mr. Kozak for you."

Quentin clenched his jaw. Mr. Kozak was obviously not someone Quentin was pleased to hear from.

The bodyguard met Quentin's annoyed expression with a level stare.

"Not now," said Quentin.

The bodyguard stayed silent. He waited, obviously expecting Quentin to change his mind.

Kate could feel the tension in the air.

"Tell him I'll call him back," said Quentin.

After a long moment, the bodyguard turned abruptly, raising the phone to his ear. He spoke in Ukrainian as he walked away, but it was too fast. Kate couldn't make out any of the words.

Christina had moved to the far side of the room, jiggling Annabelle in her arms and cooing softly in her ear.

Annoyance was radiating from Quentin.

Kate's stomach clenched, and her instincts told her to leave, to get out of the room, even out of the house. She didn't know what was going on here, but Quentin clearly had a temper. She had no desire to be in his line of fire. But she didn't want to leave Annabelle and Christina alone with him.

"I, uh…" She scrambled to think what Francie would do.

After only a second, she came up with a plausible solution. Francie would have been completely oblivious to the undercurrents. She'd be thinking solely of herself. What was Francie feeling? What did Francie want?

Kate was exhausted, and she was hungry. She went with it.

"Any way to get some breakfast around here?" she asked him coyly.

Quentin looked taken aback. But his surprised expression didn't last long. He seemed willing to be distracted.

"You're hungry?" he asked.

"Famished. I usually have blueberry muffins for breakfast," she rattled off. "Except on Sundays. On Sundays I go to this little bistro on Backwater Street. It's about a block from the ocean, and they have the best eggs Benedict I have ever eaten." She grinned invitingly. "With a mimosa. To die for, really."

Quentin's expression had relaxed.

She couldn't help thinking it was easy being Francie. There was no need to worry about empathy or propriety or even good manners. You just led with your emotions and lived in the moment.

"Eggs Benedict it is," he said. He gestured to the nursery doorway.

Kate was disappointed to leave Annabelle. But in the short term, getting into Quentin's good graces was the most important thing. If she played her cards right, she'd have time to see Annabelle again later.

"You have a really gorgeous house," she told him as they walked down the hallway. She ran her fingertips along the white panel molding.

"I bought it from Deke Hamilton," he said.

"The movie star?" She put what she hoped was the right amount of awe and admiration into the question.

"He had it custom built," said Quentin. "Cost ten million, but I got it for nine."

"Nice."

"The divorce."

Kate wished she could remember something about Deke Hamilton's love life, but she couldn't.

"You always lose money on a divorce," she said.

"True that," said Quentin. "I'll sure never fall for it."

"Marriage?" she guessed.

"Marriage, common-law, palimony. Whatever."

It occurred to her that was probably why Francie and Annabelle had lived in the gatehouse. Quentin didn't want to risk a lawsuit. She couldn't help but think he had to have plenty of money to spare.

As they descended the stairs, she pointed to a huge, dramatic crystal chandelier. "Swarovski?" she asked, dredging up the only famous name she knew.

"Of course."

She tilted her head to admire it.

"Are you here for Francie's things?" he asked.

The question surprised Kate. She hadn't thought of that. But she realized it was a fair assumption. The woman Kate was pretending to be would probably covet anything Quentin might have bought for Francie.

Then again, if by "things" he meant Annabelle, the answer was rapidly turning into a yes.

She put a speculative gleam in her eyes, and a faux coy tone in her voice. "What things?"

Quentin laughed, clearly pleased with himself for having guessed her motive.

Kate was happy to let him think he had her figured out.

"You seem like a generous man," she said, playing it up even further.

"I just told you I'd never get married and risk alimony," he responded.

"True," she conceded. "But that doesn't mean you don't like to make women happy."

Brody's voice joined the conversation. "I assure you, he does."

Brody's gaze was judgmental as he peered at Kate, and her heart fluttered in a nervous reaction. He was going to think the worst of her all over again.

She didn't care, she told herself one more time. She couldn't and wouldn't care.

"Brody's got me pegged," said Quentin. "What about you?" he asked Brody. "You willing to risk it all for some woman?"

"Depends on the woman."

Quentin laughed. "I can't even picture who that would be."

Kate found herself waiting for Brody's answer.

"Tall," he said. "Large breasts and big hair."

She involuntarily glanced down at her chest. No, not so much. Plus, she was only five feet five, and her hair was sleek rather than puffy, shorter than it had been three days ago. And he hadn't mentioned liking a woman's hair to be purple, so she supposed she was nowhere near his demographic.

"You'll want to visit Texas," said Quentin, chuckling.

"I'll think about it," said Brody.

She supposed she could wear high shoes and a wig, but she drew the line at cosmetic surgery. Her breasts were staying the size they were.

Not that she wanted to attract Brody. He kissed very well, but she didn't want it to happen again. Okay, so she did want it to happen again. But that was an emotional reaction, nothing based on reason. It was definitely better all around if it didn't happen again, not ever. Logic told her that. And she was nothing if not logical.

"I'm saving the jewelry," Quentin said to Kate.

"Huh?" She wasn't following him.

"I'm saving Francie's jewelry for Annabelle."

Kate told herself to look disappointed. "Oh."

"That seems fair," said Brody.

Kate agreed, but she didn't chime in with her agreement. It was better if Quentin thought she was opportunistic and greedy instead of judging his fitness as a father. She switched to a safer topic, again trying to be Francie-like.

"We're having eggs Benedict," she said to Brody. "Because I'm famished."

He looked bemused by the observation.

Rex, who Kate had learned that first night was Quentin's right-hand man, made his way down the hallway, his deep frown obviously sending an unspoken message to Quentin.

Quentin took in the expression. "I've got a phone call," he announced to no one in particular. To Kate he said, "Just tell the cook what you want."

"Something up?" Brody asked Quentin, his tone unconcerned, his body language casual and relaxed.

"Just puttin' out a fire. Nothing new."

"Can I help?" Brody asked.

Quentin looked puzzled by the offer, while Rex looked annoyed.

"Most of what messes us up in my organization are international issues," Brody said.

Quentin looked at Rex. "He does have international connections."

"Is this a Europe thing?" Brody asked.

"Let's talk," Quentin said, giving a nod toward the office.

As the three men moved away, Quentin turned back.

"Check out the gatehouse," he told Kate.

She didn't understand and must have looked confused.

"Take a look at Francie's jewelry. You're welcome to pick something. There'll still be plenty left for Annabelle."

Kate started to shake her head in protest. But she quickly stopped herself.

"That's very generous," she called out instead.

Brody smirked.

She knew what he was thinking. She didn't blame him. And it was what she wanted him to think anyway. She shouldn't feel so bad that her plan was working.

Five

Quentin's problem turned out to be mundane, which was disappointing for Brody. He didn't learn anything new about Beast Blue. There were some content issues with one of his games in the China market, and approvals were bogged down in red tape with a government agency. Brody had dealt with similar problems in the past and was able to give some advice on making it through the bureaucratic maze.

Brody wasn't wild about helping Beast Blue Designs make more money, but he did recognize the value of increasing his stature with Quentin. Rex was obviously annoyed that Brody got to play the hero. But then Rex was always annoyed about something. With respect to Quentin, Rex acted like a jealous lover.

Though it was only midmorning, Brody had had enough for one day. There were too many people around to take another run at Quentin's computer, and he didn't want to annoy Rex any more than necessary. The man might be obnoxious, but he was firmly in the inner circle of Beast Blue Designs. He might be valuable at some point.

On the way back down the driveway, Brody's attention caught on the gatehouse. He saw Kate though the window. The glimpse was fleeting, but it was enough to take him back to their kiss. That kiss had been amazing. It had all but short-circuited his brain and that never happened to him.

He repeated to himself that it wasn't something he could pursue, not here, and definitely not with someone like Kate. Forget about his problems with Beast Blue, she was nowhere near his type, nowhere near the kind of woman who normally attracted him. He acknowledged all that. He all but mentally shouted all that to himself. For all the good it did him, because his hormones didn't seem to care.

He found himself swinging into the parking space between the fence and a small patio. What the heck he was doing, he didn't want to guess.

A French door with glass panels was standing open, so he cut around the garden and poked his head into the modest foyer. Kate was at a small desk in the living area. A drawer was open, and she was working her way through a stack of papers.

"Looking for appraisal certificates?" he asked, attempting to open with a joke.

She jumped and turned guiltily at the sound of his voice.

Her reaction aroused his curiosity, and he took a few steps forward.

"Good guess," she said, with a nervous-sounding laugh.

He wasn't buying it. He'd caught her at something. He moved closer to get a look.

She quickly stuffed the papers back in the drawer and pushed it shut, turning to block it.

"What were those?" He made a show of looking around her.

"Nothing." She gave an airy wave of her hand. "A bunch of bills and stuff."

"Francie paid her own bills?"

Kate seemed to become even more flustered. "Well, not bills exactly."

"Are you looking for a will?"

"What? No."

He reached for the drawer.

"Are you allowed to do that?" she asked.

"Are you?" he challenged.

"Quentin told me I could look around."

"At her jewelry." Brody closed his fingers over the drawer handle.

She grabbed his wrist.

The contact startled him, but it didn't stop him. Although her cool fingers were distracting, she was absolutely no match for his strength. He slid the drawer open.

Inside, there were takeout menus and a couple of celebrity magazines. Kate's guilty reaction made absolutely no sense.

"Are you embarrassed to be interested in Trey Chatham's latest girlfriends?" he joked.

He pulled out the magazine to take a closer look. And then he saw it, a shallow, clear-topped jar of marijuana. Next to it were rolling papers and a lighter.

"Seriously?" he asked her.

A blush moved up her cheeks, but then she gave her streaked purple hair a defiant toss. "I wasn't going to smoke it."

"Of course not," he drawled.

"I was looking…" She seemed to have stumped herself. "I was just looking, okay?"

"It's eleven o'clock in the morning," he said.

"Thank you for that update."

"I'm saying it's a little early to get high."

"I'm not getting high. I don't do drugs. Don't make assumptions about me just because your rock-star friends indulge before noon."

"That wasn't why I was making the assumption."

She put her nose in the air. "Not that it's any of your business."

"You're young," he said.

He knew he shouldn't care one way or the other about what she did with her life. But she was fresh and vibrant. Since arriving in California, he'd seen what a few years of the hard-partying lifestyle did to most people. Kate could still choose a different path.

"I'm twenty-three," she said.

"Do you want to make thirty?"

"I am definitely planning to make thirty."

"Then stay away from Quentin. Sure, today it's marijuana and champagne. But tomorrow it'll be cocaine. Add to that a few dozen sexual partners, and you'll—"

"Excuse me?" She came to her feet, glaring daggers at him.

He looked her up and down, taking in the provocative

dress, her rounded breasts and those long, lanky limbs. With that funky hair and heavy makeup, she all but screamed sex.

"You know nothing about my lifestyle." She seemed genuinely offended.

"*I* kissed you," he said, without knowing why he said it.

She was right. He knew nothing about her lifestyle. He was making assumptions. But they were reasonable assumptions considering the evidence he had in front of him.

"You consider that a promiscuous lifestyle?"

"It was a really great kiss."

His answer seemed to give her pause.

"You want to do it again?" he asked, shamelessly taking advantage of the conversation. Against his better judgment, against anything remotely resembling judgment, his desire to repeat the experience was growing by the second.

"No, I don't want to do it again." She tilted her chin in the air. "I'm going to check out my sister's jewelry."

"You haven't looked at it yet?"

"No." She began walking toward the bedrooms.

He followed. "You've been here for more than an hour."

"And aren't you an old busybody. Can't you leave anything alone?"

"I've never been called a busybody before." He couldn't help but be amused by the archaic term.

"That's what you are."

"I have a perfectly ordinary sense of curiosity."

"Why are you following me?"

He realized it was a reasonable question. "With all this talk, you've got me curious about Francie's jewelry collection."

"As we've established, it's really none of your business."

"At least I'm consistent."

They'd entered what had obviously been Francie's room.

Kate stilled in silence, her expression going neutral. He couldn't help but wonder at the impact on her, entering the last place her sister had lived.

He waited to see what she would do.

She just stood there, her eyes darting around, her nostrils slightly flared, while her fingers curled into her palms.

"Do you recognize anything?" he asked gently.

No matter what he might think of her, this had to be hard. She had his sympathy on a human level.

She shook her head. "I hadn't seen Francie in a very long time. Not since she stormed out on my mother seven years ago."

"It was bad?" he guessed.

"It was bad. She was eighteen. There was a lot of shouting. Not that the shouting was anything new. But that time she left and never came back."

"Did you try to find her?"

Kate shook her head. "I wouldn't have known the first place to look. We were very different people back then." Then she seemed to catch herself. "Two years later, I graduated high school and left LA."

"I'm sorry," he said, thinking about his own brother. He couldn't imagine his life without Blane.

Instead of responding, she crossed the room to a big maple dresser, opening what was obviously a jewelry box on the top.

She stared at the contents for a moment.

"Wow," she uttered, her tone reverent.

He moved up behind her to see what was there.

The box was six tiers of polished, patterned wood. Two earring trays opened up on each side, the walls of the compartments lined with white satin. Necklaces hung from two wings, and a ring compartment popped out on the front.

Crystal-clear and colored gems winked from gold and platinum settings. To his surprise, amidst the riches, Kate zeroed in on a delicate gold chain with a small, gold bird charm. She lifted it in her fingers.

"What's that?" he asked.

She dropped it, as if he'd startled her. "Nothing." She moved on to a pair of diamond earrings. "Do you suppose these are real?"

"They are if Quentin bought them." If Brody had learned

anything about Quentin these past weeks, it was that he tossed money around like parade candy.

She fingered a large emerald-and-diamond pendant. Then she lifted a bracelet of gold-linked, square rubies, draping it over her wrist. "Annabelle is going to have everything, isn't she?"

"Everything money can buy," Brody agreed.

Quentin lavished luxury on those around him. He might be a criminal, but he wasn't selfish with his stolen wealth.

"There's more to life than money," said Kate.

"You won't get me to disagree with that."

"I grew up poor."

He thought of his family's thirty-five-room castle, his mother's diamond tiaras and the art collection in the grand hallway. He wanted to be honest. He couldn't be detailed, but he didn't have to lie. "I didn't."

She gave a nod, putting the bracelet back. "I wouldn't wish poverty on Annabelle."

"I doubt Annabelle will ever have to worry about money."

Even if Beast Blue lost everything on their new game, and even if they paid massive fines, Quentin would still be many times a millionaire. He and Annabelle would scrape by.

"Is that why you're here?" he asked Kate.

She looked guilty again. "What do you mean?"

"For the money. So you'll never have to be poor again."

She seemed to ponder the statement for a moment. "That would make sense, wouldn't it?"

"It would make perfect sense."

"Then yes. Yes, that's exactly why I'm here." She turned her attention back to the jewelry box. "I bet some of this stuff is really valuable."

"Are you for real?" he asked.

"What?"

"One minute you seem…I don't know, principled. And the next you're the material girl."

"It must be the recreational drugs."

"You said you didn't do drugs."

"It's not like I'm going to admit to anything illegal."

"So, you do take drugs?" He was very sorry to hear that.

She turned, holding a sapphire-and-diamond choker to her neck. "What do you think?"

It looked fantastic. It would look even better without the dress, better still without anything at all. Except the shoes. She should definitely keep the shoes.

"Are you going to wear it or sell it?" he asked.

She gave a giggle. "I haven't decided yet."

"Material girl," he muttered.

"This?" she asked, switching to an elaborate diamond pendant.

"You'd need a security guard with you if you're actually going to wear it."

"I know a couple of guys from the Ukraine," she responded without missing a beat.

"See?" said Brody. "You're quick."

"Quick at what?" She selected a pair of ruby drop earrings.

He stared at her.

She looked guilelessly back.

"Those would suit you," he said, instead of trying to figure her out.

"You think?" She removed her own earrings and settled the rubies into her ears.

He stood back. "You'd have to lose the purple hair."

Her hand went to her head. "You don't like my hair?"

He took a look in the jewelry box, selecting a pair of sapphire studs and a matching pendant. "These will go with your hair."

He watched while she tried them on, helping her with the clasp on the necklace.

"What do you think?"

He stepped back again.

She was perfect. Even with the crazy hair, she was undeniably elegant. The sapphire gems brought out the blue in her eyes. The jewels were neither too large nor too small.

"You need a ballroom around you," he said. "Chandelier

light shining down, an orchestra playing, gold filigree, fine art and a gown of sky-blue silk swirling while you dance."

He was picturing the grand hall of Calder Castle. She would look good there.

"I've never danced in a ballroom."

"You should."

"Have you?"

"I have." He found himself holding out his arms. "It's really quite easy."

She didn't fight as he drew her into his embrace. He danced a few steps, and she easily followed.

"You've danced before," he noted.

"Everybody's danced before."

He twirled her in a spin then pulled her back into his embrace. She felt fantastic against him.

"Are you keeping them?" he asked, nodding to the earrings.

"Are they the most expensive?"

"I don't think so." He'd bet on the emeralds.

"Then no."

"So, you are going to sell them." He was disappointed.

"Sure I'm going to sell them. The odds of me having to pay rent are a whole lot higher than the odds of me dancing in a ballroom."

He lowered his voice, settling her closer. "And if I could come up with a ballroom?"

"You'd better come up with a wealthy prince to go along with it."

"Would a viscount do?"

"Sure," she answered brightly. "So long as he's rich."

Brody thought about his home again. "He is. Well, for the moment anyway."

They swayed in silence in the small room. He held her close, breathing her essence, feeling her lithe form shifting against him, musing that he had no desire to let her go.

"It's a nice fantasy," she said against his shoulder.

After a moment, he drew back to look into her pretty eyes.

"It is." He touched her earlobe, the contact with her tender skin feeling intimate in a way that was arousing. "You should keep these."

She gave a sigh. "A good sister would do that."

"You're not a good sister?" He desperately wanted to kiss her. He wanted to kiss her over and over again.

It was hard to figure out exactly what was going on between them. But it was surprising and compelling all at once.

"I'm not a good anything," she said in a small voice "I'm a survivor, that's it, Brody."

The sound of his name made his chest contract. "We're all survivors."

Then, unable to stop himself, he slid his hand to her neck, stroking the soft skin, drawing her gently toward his waiting mouth, every fiber of his being anticipating the kiss. But she suddenly clapped her hands on his shoulders, her body stiffening before she moved out of his arms.

She turned to the jewelry box. "What do you think?"

What had just happened? Why did she back off?

"About what?" he asked, struggling to get his emotional bearings.

"What's the most expensive thing in here? I don't want to be greedy, but I don't want to be stupid, either."

Her words were like a bucket of cold water. That's what had happened. He'd been a fool. He kept seeing things in her that weren't there. She was a party girl like all the rest, frivolous, superficial and self-gratifying.

"The emeralds," he said.

She took the earrings, along with a matching necklace and bracelet, wrapping them in her hand.

Disgusted, he turned and headed for the door.

She didn't immediately follow, and when he glanced over his shoulder, he saw her also pocket the little bird necklace before shutting the jewelry box.

Six

After Brody left the gatehouse, Kate had returned the emeralds to the jewelry box, keeping only the gold chickadee necklace. She'd given it to Francie fifteen years ago, back when they were a team, when they'd stood together in the chaos wrought by their mother. It had been around Francie's neck the day she'd walked out.

Kate then drove back to her room at the Vista Family Inn and indulged in a long nap. When she woke, she showered and changed into comfortable blue jeans and a cotton blouse, relieved to have all the makeup off her face for a while. Then she dialed Nadia.

"Tell me how it's going?" Nadia opened without preamble.

"I don't even know where to start," Kate said. So much had happened in the last couple of days. She decided to begin with the most important point. "I met Annabelle."

"That's fantastic."

"Quentin's totally bought my act. He thinks I'm after Francie's jewelry."

"That's brilliant."

"His idea, not mine. But I'll use it."

"Good for you. And well-acted."

"And there are a couple of bodyguards there who speak Ukrainian."

"Did you talk to them?" Nadia asked.

"They're not overly friendly," Kate said. "And I think it's better to keep a low profile. The fewer people I talk to, the less chance I have to screw up."

"If you did talk to them, I bet they'd be impressed."

"Right. You've been teasing me about my accent since I was eight. Besides, I'm giving them an especially wide berth."

"So, what did you find out about Quentin? Is he a decent

father? Can you come home now? I got a notice from the condo association that they're redoing the roof."

"Quentin is a self-indulgent child. Is it going to cost us any money?"

"They're doing an estimate. And I guess that's what you expected, wasn't it? He sure doesn't come across as a candidate for father of the year."

"I'm beginning to think…" Kate paused. She wasn't sure she was ready to complete the thought.

"What?"

"That I might have to try to get custody of Annabelle. Is that terrible? Do you think I'm jumping to conclusions?"

Concern came into Nadia's voice. "Is it that bad? You're not a conclusion jumper."

"The nanny seems great." Kate didn't know what would be going on if not for Christina. "But Quentin's lifestyle is positively frightening. And the people he has coming and going. They're drinking. They're smoking. I'm positive some of them do cocaine."

"So, he's a criminal? That might help in the custody battle."

"Maybe," Kate allowed. "I'm not sure how seriously they take rich people doing recreational drugs in LA."

"Yeah," Nadia said. "Nobody we know ever got arrested for it, and they weren't even rich."

"I don't know what to do."

"I guess that depends on how serious you are."

Kate wasn't following. "What do you mean serious?"

"I mean are you really ready to take on the responsibility for Annabelle's care twenty-four-seven? Because that's huge, and you have to be positive you're in a position to see it through."

Kate realized it was a fair question. "I think I'm positive."

"That's not positive."

"I am positive."

"You're not picking out wallpaper."

"I know that." Kate might not have started the week trying to get custody of a baby. But now that the problem had been laid bare in front of her, she knew she had no choice. "You know what happens if nobody steps up."

Both she and Nadia had had less than ideal upbringings. Annabelle was so sweet, so innocent. She had so much promise and potential. She deserved a good parent.

Nadia didn't answer right away. "I do," she said in a soft voice.

"It's not happening on my watch."

"You're right. You're completely right. And I'm in."

"You'd still be willing to live with me?" Kate's chest tightened with emotion.

Francie might have been her sister by blood, but Nadia was the sister of her heart. They'd been together through thick and thin since they were five years old. They now both taught grade school in Seattle, and they'd bought a cheery, two-bedroom-plus-den condo nearby. For all intents and purposes, they'd created a family.

"There's a little girl who needs someone," Nadia said. "Neither of us is walking away. So, first off you need to find out what the grounds are for declaring someone an unfit parent. You're her aunt. Hopefully, that puts you next in line."

Mind completely made up, Kate spent most of the next day in the library, reading law books and checking legal websites, researching. Then, in preparation to visit Annabelle again in her Francie persona, she went to a secondhand store, finding a pair of skintight, cartoon patterned slacks and a black net crop top.

She found herself impatient to get things rolling, but she didn't want to seem pushy and alienate Quentin. So she waited one more night before donning the new outfit and heading back over to the mansion.

Luckily, the housekeeper who answered the door recognized her and let her straight in. It was ten in the morning on a Wednesday. She hoped Quentin would be at work and that Annabelle would be awake.

She checked the kitchen first, peeked at the patio and pool, and then headed toward the staircase that led up to the nursery. Partway along the hall, she heard Quentin's voice coming from the office.

"Back off," he shouted at someone. He sounded very angry.

Kate halted, wondering what she should do. The open office door was directly opposite the staircase, and she couldn't slip past it without risking being caught.

"How many times do I have to say it," he continued. "Forget Ceci. I'm not going there."

There was a silent pause, so she assumed he was on a phone call.

"No," he said sharply. "Because I'm not cut out for prison, that's why."

A wave of anxiety washed through her. She took a couple of reflexive steps backward. If Quentin caught her eavesdropping, he'd never trust her again.

"It's different," he stated emphatically. "With Ceci, we're talking a whole other level."

Suddenly, he appeared in the doorway, phone to his ear. His vision instantly zeroed in on Kate.

She pretended to be walking forward, moving swiftly, making her tone cheerful and oblivious. "Morning, Quentin." She pointed to the staircase. "I was going to stop by and see Annabelle."

His gaze narrowed, as if he was deciding whether or not to believe her.

"She wasn't in the kitchen. Does she nap midmorning?" Kate stopped in front of him, a guileless smile pasted on her face.

"Call you back," he growled into the phone.

Kate neutralized her expression. "Is this a bad time? I didn't mean to disturb you."

"Work," said Quentin, ending the call. "What did you need?"

Kate smiled breezily again. "I wanted to say howdy to Annabelle, maybe get a picture of her for my mom. I promised I would."

It was a flat-out lie. Chloe hadn't shown the slightest interest in Annabelle, except as a way to get to Quentin and his wealth.

He still seemed tense, causing Kate to wonder again about the seriousness of the phone call. He'd talked about prison, and Ceci again. Was he planning on something more than party drugs? She told herself to stop speculating in front of him, afraid her suspicions would show on her face. There'd be plenty of time to think it through later.

But was somebody pressuring him to sell drugs? Maybe Ceci was a new designer drug. Even as she considered the possibility, it seemed ludicrous. Billionaires didn't need to sell illegal drugs.

"Quentin?" A male voice sounded behind her.

She turned to see Rex coming toward them.

Rex gave her a wide, overly friendly smile. He'd gotten more suggestive each time he'd seen her. He was way too touchy, too flirty, and he kept giving her lingering looks that seemed to say they shared a special secret.

He clearly considered himself a ladies' man, and he didn't catch on to any of the subtle hints she was sending that she wasn't interested. Either that or he was ignoring them.

"Morning, gorgeous." His gaze took a tour of her sexy top, tight pants and purple spike-heeled suede boots.

It occurred to her that she was partly to blame. Her looks and actions sure weren't warning him away. She wished she could have it both ways, keeping up the facade while keeping her distance, but she couldn't.

"Morning, Rex." She forced herself to smile back, masking her dislike.

He gave her a hug. It was too tight and too lengthy, but she gritted her teeth and played along.

Then he gave her a kiss on the cheek and drew back, squeezing her hands for good measure.

She resisted the urge to wipe the kiss away.

"I'm heading up to see Annabelle," she told him, making a move toward the stairs. "Nice to see you again." She looked at Quentin. "Thanks for this. I really appreciate your hospitality."

Quentin seemed to finally relax. "Brody said you took the emeralds."

Kate's hand went involuntarily to the chickadee necklace she'd put on that morning. Then she reminded herself to look thrilled about her new riches. "The emeralds are spectacular."

"You have good taste," said Quentin, considering her closely.

"And you are extraordinarily generous."

"So I've been told."

"Francie was lucky to have you."

Quentin greeted the observation with a knowing smirk. "Francie knew how to take care of herself."

Kate wasn't surprised to hear that, but she pretended to be oblivious to the undertone. "She was a good big sister."

Quentin's phone rang in his hand. He glanced at the number, and then looked past her to Rex, his expression irritated.

"I'll get out of your way," she said cheerfully, and quickly headed for the stairs.

More footsteps sounded in the hall, and a gruff, Ukrainian voice joined the conversation. The bodyguards were back.

"Take the call," one of them said in English.

Kate glanced fleetingly back to see that it was the tall bald one who had spoken. He met her gaze. She looked instantly away and quickly trotted up the stairs.

She was relieved to find Annabelle awake, sitting in a padded plastic chair on the carpet, grinning and kicking happily. Christina was folding a basket of baby clothes.

She greeted Kate with a friendly smile. "Good morning."

"Am I disturbing you?" asked Kate, her gaze drawn to the baby.

"Not at all. She's in a very good mood."

"I can see that." Kate crossed the floor to Annabelle.

"She slept right through the night," said Christina.

"Aren't you the clever girl," Kate cooed.

"She finished all her cereal at breakfast."

"Is that a good thing?" Kate couldn't keep the smile off her face as she crouched down. "Hello, sweetheart." She gave Annabelle her index finger to squeeze.

"Bah, bah, bah, bah," said Annabelle.

"I've just introduced solid foods," said Christina. "She seems to love eating. I was thinking maybe pureed carrots next. Either that or peas." Then she paused. "I'm sorry. This is probably boring for you."

"Not at all. I want to hear everything." Kate hesitated. "Would it be okay to hold her?"

"Go ahead," Christina said softly. "It's nice for Annabelle to have family."

Kate put one hand behind Annabelle's back, and cradled her head, lifting her gently to her shoulder. She was wearing a stretchy red one-piece outfit with a yellow giraffe embroidered on the front. She was soft and warm, and she smelled sweet.

Her hands immediately tangled in Kate's hair and pulled.

"You get in the habit of pulling it back." Christina laughed, pointing to her own sensible ponytail.

"It's fine." Kate could comb it out later.

Then Annabelle's legs went stiff, her face screwed up, and a distinctive rumble emitted from her bottom.

"Oh, dear," said Christina.

"Don't worry," said Kate. "It's what babies do."

Christina quickly came over. "I'll deal with that."

Kate didn't want her time with Annabelle to end. "I can help. Or I can change her. I don't mind."

"So, you're experienced at this?" Christina looked relieved.

"Not exactly," said Kate. "Maybe you could talk me through it?"

"Aren't you the brave auntie," Christina teased.

"I'm not overly squeamish."

"That's a switch." Christina pointed to a white, padded

change table with diapers, wipes and creams laid out on a shelf.

"Quentin doesn't do diapers?" Somehow, that didn't shock Kate.

"Neither did Francie."

"How is that possible?" Kate couldn't say she was surprised to hear Francie didn't like diapers. But how could a mother avoid changing her own baby?

"She thought that's what nannies were for." Christina's expression sobered. "She didn't seem prepared for the day-to-day job of being a parent."

"I'm sorry," said Kate as she laid Annabelle gently down on the change table.

"There's nothing for you to be sorry for." Christina took a step back to give Kate some elbow room. "I have to admit, I'm interested to see how you do at this."

"Given my dysfunctional parenting genes?"

Christina laughed at the joke.

"My mother wasn't much of a mother, either. So, Francie came by it honestly." Kate located a long zipper on Annabelle's outfit.

She might not have done this before, but obviously the outer layer had to come off before she could get down to business. An odor was now wafting through the air, and she could only imagine Annabelle wouldn't be comfortable for long. Though, for the moment, the baby seemed perfectly happy, still grinning and kicking her feet.

"You don't have to take her arms out of the sleeves," Christina instructed. "Just push the rest out of the way. Undo the tapes. Be careful she doesn't turn over."

"I've got her." Kate held on to Annabelle's legs, lifting just enough to slide out the soiled diaper.

Christina handed her a wet wipe.

It was decidedly awkward, but Kate managed to get the baby's bottom cleaned.

"Here's a fresh one." Christina handed over a folded diaper. "Spread out the tapes, then slide it under."

Annabelle was wriggling in earnest now.

"She's hard to hold." Kate laughed.

"She loves being naked."

"I don't blame her." The diapers might be functional, but they are also bulky and constraining.

"You should see her in the bath. She's in heaven."

"I'd like that," said Kate as she wrapped the diaper around Annabelle's tummy. "I'd like that a lot."

"I bathe her before bed," said Christina.

Kate couldn't resist. Without even doing up the onesie, she lifted Annabelle back into her arms, cradling her close. "She's an angel."

Christina stroked the baby's hair. "She is that."

"Am I interrupting?" Brody's voice was distinct in the nursery doorway.

Kate turned, and his attention seemed arrested by the sight of Annabelle in her arms.

It took him a minute to speak. "She looks like you."

Kate reflexively glanced at the baby. "She looks like a baby."

"It's the blue eyes." He moved closer, seeming to consider Annabelle.

"Francie had blue eyes."

"Let me," said Christina, taking Annabelle from her arms and making a discreet exit into her own connected bedroom. She shut the door behind her.

Kate didn't want to give up Annabelle, and she was annoyed with Brody for interrupting her visit.

After Christina left, Brody was still considering her.

"What are you doing?" he asked.

She went on alert. "About what?"

"I keep tripping up against it." His gaze was far too astute, too penetrating. "You're up to something here."

"Are you hungry?" she asked, hoping to change the subject. "I'm hungry. Maybe some eggs Benedict?"

"It's got nothing to do with the emeralds, does it?" he asked.

"Or waffles. I could definitely go for some waffles."

He moved, starting to circle her.

"Brody, what are you—"

"It's Annabelle. You're here for Annabelle."

Kate's mouth went dry, and she swallowed trying to relieve it. "Sure." She pretended to misunderstand his point. "That's right. I thought I'd get a picture of her today."

"No." He shook his head. "I saw your expression when I walked in."

"I don't know what you're talking about. I had no expression."

He took in her outlandish slacks and the sexy top. "What's your plan?"

"I don't have a plan."

"You're lying."

"Brody."

"I saw Bert and Ernie down there."

She assumed he meant the bodyguard team. She was only too happy to let the subject change, but she was frightened by how much he'd already guessed.

"I'll make you a deal," he said, his expression turning calculated. "You report to me on what they say, and I'll pretend you're here after money."

"I am here after money."

"No, you're not. But I'm willing to pretend you are. So long as you help me in return. You do that, and your secret will be safe with me."

"I have no secret."

"Stop," he told her with quiet finality.

She quickly weighed the pros and cons, and realized further denial would get her nowhere. "Okay," she said. "I admit nothing. But I'll do what you want."

"You know, you don't have to admit something out loud for us both to know it's true."

She didn't bother to acknowledge his words. "They did say one thing this morning. It was Bert. And it was in English."

"Which one is Bert?"

"The tall guy. Which one is Bert to you?"

"Same one," said Brody. "What did he say?"

"Take the call. He told Quentin to take the call."

Brody's brow furrowed. "What call?"

"I don't know, but Quentin got another call a couple of days ago. He refused that one. And Bert didn't seem happy at the time."

"Do you know who called?"

"Someone named Kozak. Maybe he called back today."

"Why didn't you tell me?"

"Because I didn't know I was on your payroll."

"You're on the payroll now."

"So it seems. Are we done?" She wanted the conversation to end, and for Brody to be on his way.

But he didn't leave. Instead, he took her fingertips gently in his, like he'd done before. And just like before, she felt a warmth travel all the way to her chest.

"You're not who you pretend to be," he said.

"Are you?" she asked in return.

She instantly knew she'd touched on something. There was a momentary flash in his eyes—shock, or maybe even fear.

But then his expression smoothed and he eased in close. "I'm a man who finds you attractive."

It was easy to see that this time it was Brody trying to throw her off the scent of something.

She wasn't falling for it. "What's going on, Brody?"

"I'm about to kiss you."

"You know that's not what I meant."

"Doesn't matter. I'm going to do it anyway."

"Brody—"

His kiss cut off her words.

His lips were warm and firm. Unlike the last kiss, there was nothing tentative about it. She didn't care. If it was possible, this kiss was even better. And in seconds she was kissing him back.

His free hand went to the small of her back, pulling her intimately against him as he tilted her head, deepening the kiss.

She knew she should push him away, and she promised she would in just a second, just a moment, just a few more minutes of paradise.

But when he was the one to draw back, it was all she could do to keep from whimpering at the loss.

"Admit you have a secret," he said.

She wanted to say no, but the word wouldn't form.

"Like I said, it's safe with me." He cupped her face with his palm. "I promise, it's safe with me."

He gave her a brief parting kiss, and then he was gone.

Seven

Brody told himself to stop obsessing about Kate. But it was harder to do now that he'd confirmed there was more to her than met the eye. Plus, she'd become part of his investigation, so he needed to think about her. It was only prudent for him to try to figure her out. It was a double-edged sword, because thinking about her forced him to admit just how attracted he was to her.

It was Friday, and everyone seemed to understand what that meant. There would definitely be another party. He knew she'd be there, trying to listen in on Bert and Ernie. She'd be wearing something sinful, sipping champagne, and men would flock to her by the dozens and make a play. It was all he could do not to toss them one by one into the pool.

It was still afternoon, and he'd ducked into Quentin's home office again to take another shot at his computer. Will thought there might be a secure link from the home computer to the Beast Blue servers. If there was, it could net them the evidence they needed.

He heard footfalls in the hallway and froze at the keyboard. Just then, his cell phone rang. He swore under his breath, quickly jumping up from the desk chair, cursing himself for forgetting to turn off the ringer.

He swiftly crossed the room, leaning nonchalantly against a wall and put his phone to his ear.

The office door banged open, revealing Bert and Ernie. Both had their sport jackets parted, hands on the firearms in their holsters.

"Hello?" Brody said into the phone, measuring his breathing and schooling his features.

"Brody?" It was his brother Blane.

"Hi." He was always careful not to use names. He didn't want to give out any hints to his true identity.

"What are you doing in here?" Bert demanded, accent thick, while Ernie did a sweep of the room.

Brody pointed to his phone, feigning impatience at the intrusion.

Ernie checked the windows and the closet.

"Brody?" Blane repeated.

"Yes," said Brody.

Blane coughed into the phone.

"Are you okay?"

"Getting better," said Blane. "Mother's got herself in a flap about the community ball."

Brody inwardly sighed. "Of course she has."

"I know you hate these things."

"Get out," Bert ordered Brody, pointing at the office door.

Ernie moved to the computer, and Brody forced himself not to watch him. He didn't want to telegraph his fear.

"Tell her I'll be there," he said to Blane.

"Will you?"

"I think so. I hope so." The ball was only two weeks away, so Brody really wasn't sure.

"Get out!" Bert repeated.

Brody levered himself slowly away from the wall.

Ernie was reaching for the mouse. If he brought the screen up, he'd see the computer had been turned on. It wouldn't take a genius to know it had been Brody.

Bert said something in Ukrainian, and Ernie looked swiftly up at him.

Ernie answered back.

"You know what'll happen if you don't show up," said Blane.

Brody knew his mother would be upset. But if things didn't go well here, missing a ball would be the least of Brody's worries.

"I'll try," he promised his brother.

Bert stormed forward, and his meaty hand clamped around Brody's upper arm.

Brody shook him off, giving the man a glare as he moved toward the door.

"Gotta go," he said to Blane.

"Is everything all right?"

"It's fine."

"You sound upset…"

"Someone here is annoying me." Brody glared at the two security guards. Then he moderated his tone as he passed through the doorway. "It's no big deal. Can I call you later?"

"No need."

Ernie shouted something in Ukrainian behind him, and a chill went through Brody's chest.

"What was that?" asked Blane.

"Call you later." Brody quickly ended the call.

He turned, expecting to see their guns drawn and trained on him. But they were shouting at each other.

A second later, he sensed another presence. He looked to see Kate standing in the hall beside him. Her blue eyes were wide. She was dressed in black leather leggings and a tight pink tank top. Her heels were spiked, the ankle boots shiny black.

His brain flatlined.

"What happened?" she asked in a nervous voice.

He stepped in front of her, moving them both out of Bert and Ernie's line of vision. "What are they saying?" he whispered to her.

Her expression said she was concentrating.

He tried to be patient. "Can you understand?"

"Ceci again," she whispered back.

"What about her?"

Kate listened. "She's important. She's here. Bert wants to… It's not making sense."

"Did you get a last name?"

"No, but they're fighting about Quentin. Ernie wants to hurt him, and Bert wants to wait. Maybe Ceci is their sister?"

"Did they say that?"

"No. I'm guessing."

The voices stopped and Brody heard the men's footsteps. He grasped her arm. "Let's go." He hustled her along the hallway, around the corner and into the kitchen.

She glanced back around the corner.

"Don't look," he hissed.

She suddenly shrank against his chest. "They're carrying guns."

"They're security guards."

"They have guns in this house with a baby."

"They'll protect her."

"I'm not so sure they're even protecting Quentin."

Brody was beginning to think the same thing, but he wasn't about to throw that possibility out on the table. "If they weren't doing their job, Quentin would fire them."

She didn't argue the point.

As the immediate danger passed, he became acutely aware of her body against his, his arm around the curve of her waist. Her tank top was slinky and clingy, the pants were smooth, so smooth against his thighs. Her hair smelled like rich vanilla. It would take nothing at all for him to slide his palms up to her breasts, turn her, kiss her, peel off any and all of those silly, sexy clothes.

He rasped a deep breath. He wanted very badly to sweep her into his arms and carry her off.

She pulled away, breaking the contact, peeping around the corner again.

He willed his heart to return to normal.

"I think they're leaving," she said.

He curled his hands into fists and ordered himself to get it under control. She was beyond complicated, and she was confusing on so many levels. His family's future hung in the balance, and he was letting lust rule his brain.

After the run-in with Quentin's bodyguards, Kate's instincts told her it was time to take action. She didn't trust

Quentin, and she sure didn't trust Bert and Ernie. Quentin might be irresponsible, but Bert and Ernie seemed downright dangerous. Brody was a puzzle, for sure. It was clear he wasn't with Bert and Ernie. But it wasn't clear he was with Quentin, either.

Whose side was he on? And how many sides were there?

Later that evening, from her hotel room, she dialed Nadia.

"Hey," Nadia answered. She was breathing hard.

Since it was seven in the evening, Kate assumed she was out for a bike ride.

"Where are you?" Kate asked, sitting down on the bed.

"Coming through the university. Where are you?"

"In my motel room."

"What's up?"

"Are you sure you can talk?"

"It's fine. It's good. Talk away."

"Well…" Kate struggled to frame an opening. "Things keep getting stranger. And I'm worried. I'm really worried about Annabelle."

"What's Quentin done now?"

"It's not just Quentin. It's beyond just Quentin. It's everything."

"Define everything."

"To start with, there's this guy named Brody. He's figured out I'm interested in Annabelle." Kate hadn't yet worked out if Brody represented a danger to her ruse or not.

"Will he tell Quentin?"

"He said he'd keep it a secret if I'd spy for him."

There was a pause before Nadia spoke. "You may have to elaborate on that."

"Brody wants to know what the Ukrainians are saying."

"Why?"

"Because they're up to something. And they have guns. And they don't get along very well with Quentin."

"Hang on. I'm stopping."

"Don't stop."

"I'm stopping and sitting down." The bike clattered in the background. "Okay. What on earth?"

"Something tells me I should trust him."

"Brody, right? Not Quentin."

"Yes, Brody."

"Why would you trust him?"

"Because he hasn't blown my cover so far. And he seems smart. And at least he's not armed, and he's not doing recreational drugs."

"Well, there's a resounding recommendation."

"I need to get Annabelle out of there. I'm starting to worry about waiting too long. It feels like things at the mansion are getting more tense by the day."

"Can you call the police?" Nadia asked.

"I don't have anything to report."

"The drugs?"

Kate pulled her legs up onto the bed. "I'm afraid it won't be enough. And it would tip my hand. And Quentin would probably refuse to let me see Annabelle again."

Nadia went silent.

"That's why I'm thinking about Brody," Kate said. "He wants my help, so he might help me in return."

"Who are Bert and Ernie?"

"The Ukrainians."

"They're named Bert and Ernie?"

"I don't know their real names. Those are nicknames. Do you think I should do it or not?"

"Trust Brody?"

"Yes." Kate's heart rate sped up as she gave the answer. She realized how badly she wanted to trust Brody. She felt completely alone in this. And she was growing frightened for Annabelle. She needed an ally, and she desperately hoped Brody was the guy.

"What do you want me to say?"

"I want you to tell me that my instincts are right."

"Well, to be honest—"

"Yes, please be honest. I need you to be honest," Kate said.

"Since it seems like he already knows a big part of it, you don't have a lot to lose, Kate."

"You're right. What he doesn't know, he'll probably figure out anyway."

The risk was low, or at least most of it was already in play. That was what Kate wanted to hear.

The Friday party was well underway, with a crowd of people out on the pool deck and others in the great room and the kitchen. She looked for Brody, but didn't find him. There was also no sign of Bert and Ernie.

She was about to do another loop when she caught sight of Christina heading for the front door. She moved for a better view, curious about where she might be going, and she saw Annabelle, wide awake, gazing over Christina's shoulder at the party all around them.

It was nearly ten o'clock. Surely Annabelle should be asleep by now.

Kate hurried to catch up. She made it onto the porch as Christina was opening the back door of a silver sedan.

"Christina?"

Christina turned at the sound of her name.

Kate started down the stairs. "What are you doing?"

"We're going for a drive." Christina bent down to lay Annabelle in her car seat.

"Where?" asked Kate in astonishment. "Why? Now?"

Christina clicked the harness into place and tucked a blanket snugly around Annabelle.

She straightened. "She does okay falling asleep during the week. But on weekends the music gets pretty loud in there."

Annabelle couldn't sleep in her own room? Kate couldn't believe it. Or rather she could believe it, but she found it appalling.

"Have you talked to Quentin about the problem?" she asked.

Christina coughed out what sounded like a laugh. "Uh, no."

"You don't think he'd tone things down for his own daughter?"

"I don't think he'd stay still long enough to listen to the request." Christina seemed to realize what she'd said, and she snapped her mouth shut, worry coming into her expression.

"It's all right," said Kate. "I'm not going to say anything to him. I wish I could." She wished if she did say something it would have a hope of making some kind of positive difference.

"You must have guessed by now that he won't change his lifestyle for anyone or anything."

Kate struggled to control her anger. "How does he expect this to work?"

"He doesn't care how things work. He pays other people to make things work for him."

Kate silently acknowledged the truth in the statement. Quentin's development seemed to have been arrested in college. And he saw Annabelle more as a novelty than as a living human being.

"Where are you taking her?" Kate asked.

"Just out for a random drive. She likes the windy roads. They put her right to sleep."

"Doesn't she wake up when you come back?"

"We come back after the music stops."

"You drive around all night?" Kate couldn't believe it. What about Christina? How did she get any sleep?

"We'll come back around three," said Christina.

"That's ridiculous."

Christina gave a shrug, shutting the car door. "That's reality."

Kate made a quick decision. "I'm coming with you."

She'd tried to find Brody, and she'd tried to find Bert and Ernie. Brody wasn't the only person who needed information. Kate needed it, too. And Christina might be able to give her something she could use against Quentin.

Christina took in Kate's formfitting black-and-silver cocktail dress. "I have to say, it looks like you had a whole lot more in mind than babysitting tonight."

Kate waved a dismissive hand. "I'm only trying to fit in."

"Fit in with the 'billionaires who want trophy wives' club?" Again, Christina looked regretful. "I'm sorry. I don't know why I keep speaking out of turn."

Kate laughed. "I'm not vying to be a trophy wife. But it's easy to see that's how it looks."

"You seem so down to earth. I keep forgetting you're one of them."

"I'm not one of them. I'm pretending to be one of them."

Christina looked doubtful, but didn't dispute Kate's assertion as she headed for the driver's seat.

Kate didn't bother waiting for permission. She hopped right in on the passenger side.

"You're serious about this?" Christina's hand hovered near the ignition.

"Completely serious."

"So, you're really not here trying to snag a rich guy?"

Kate was realizing that she had to start being honest with the people who could help her. It was the only way she'd succeed.

Christina seemed trustworthy. And she was in charge of Annabelle. Honesty seemed like the best path forward.

"I'm only here because of my niece," she said, just throwing it right out there before she could change her mind.

Christina glanced into the backseat, and all vestiges of friendliness vanished from her eyes. "What do you mean?"

"We might not have been close, but Francie was my sister. I owe it—"

"So, her inheritance," Christina said coldly.

"No." Kate quickly shook her head.

"I get it. You want to set yourself up to control Annabelle's money."

Annabelle began fussing.

"I don't know that Annabelle has any money." Would Annabelle inherit money? It seemed like Quentin had gone to some trouble to protect all of his assets from Francie.

Christina was still frowning.

"That's not what I mean at all," Kate said.

"I should have known."

Annabelle's cries grew louder.

"You've got it wrong," Kate said. "Please, just go ahead and drive. Let her sleep. I'll explain."

Christina didn't look happy. But she did pull away from the curb.

It took Kate about half an hour to walk Christina through the family history, her job in Seattle, her recent arrival in LA, and her plan to imitate Francie as a party girl in order to check on Annabelle's welfare. She hesitated, but left out her ultimate decision to try to prove Quentin was an unfit father.

After Kate stopped talking, there were a few minutes of silence.

"That's really nice," said Christina, a slight quaver in her voice. "I'm so glad Annabelle has someone who cares about her."

Kate immediately felt guilty. She hadn't meant to sound self-righteous. "You've done a whole lot more for her than I have."

"A nanny's not the same as family."

Kate gave in to an urge to reach over and cover Christina's hand. "You were here. I wasn't."

Christina glanced over at her, eyes shiny in the passing streetlights. "You're here now."

"I'm trying."

Christina gave a little laugh. "I never would have guessed, not in a million years. I thought you were just like her."

"Then I'm a better actress than I expected." Kate couldn't help thinking about some of the exchanges between her and Brody. She knew she'd been convincing, but she hadn't been able to fool him. At least not for very long.

"What are you going to do now?" Christina asked.

"I'm figuring that out," Kate said as they passed by hedges, porch lights and manicured lawns through the Hollywood Hills. "I don't suppose you know anything about Brody Herrington."

Christina gave her a curious look. "He hasn't been around long."

"He seems different."

"I try to stay away from all of them," Christina said.

"Not the worst choice in the world."

"Do you like him?"

"What? No. That's not why I'm asking."

"He's a great-looking guy."

"There are lots of great-looking guys in the world."

"I've seen the way he looks at you."

"How do you mean?" Kate knew she shouldn't be asking, but she couldn't help herself.

"Like he wants to eat you for lunch."

"He does not."

"I think he has a lot of money. He wears expensive clothes."

"You can tell?"

"Poor people don't hire nannies. So I've had some experience with how the rich dress."

"I'd never know a designer suit."

"That's because you're not a gold digger."

"Neither are you," Kate told her.

"Oh, I'd take the gold in a heartbeat if it came with the right man."

Kate smiled. "There's your key. The right man."

"I guess I'd take him if he was poor, too. But Brody's not poor, and he's got a thing for you."

And they were back to Kate and Brody again—not the place Kate wanted to go. Protesting hadn't gotten her anywhere, so she turned it into a joke.

"Well, I've got a thing for Annabelle, so Brody's going to have to get in line."

Eight

Brody couldn't understand what had happened to Kate. She'd said she'd be here tonight, and he'd counted on it. Just when his opinion was starting to change, she pulled something like this.

Bert and Ernie had been huddled in a corner talking half the night. If she'd been here, if she'd showed up, it would have been a prime opportunity to gather more intel. He was holding up his end of the bargain. He was going to make sure she held up hers.

He headed down the front stairs of the mansion, deciding on his next move. And there she was, coming out of the passenger side of a car, looking super-sexy in a tight, short black-and-silver dress and a pair of high heels.

She'd been on a date? Seriously? Her love life couldn't go on hold for one day?

He strode for the car, prepared to confront her. Whoever she was dating could stand aside. The driver's door opened, and Brody braced himself. But the guy who stepped out was no guy at all. It was the nanny.

He was more confused than ever.

Before the issue could sort itself out in his mind, the nanny retrieved Annabelle from the backseat. Brody couldn't imagine where they had been at this time of night.

"You promised you'd be here," he said to Kate.

"I was here," she retorted. "You weren't."

"I've been here for hours." He lowered his voice. "And so have Bert and Ernie."

"Annabelle couldn't sleep."

Brody had no idea how to respond to that. "And…" he all but sputtered.

Annabelle started to fuss in the nanny's arms.

"We took her for a drive," Kate said.

"I should get her inside," said Christina.

"You were touring the neighborhood instead of being here?" He was trying to wrap his head around her thought processes.

"Thanks for your help," Christina said to Kate.

A look passed between the two women before the nanny hustled up the stairs.

"You want to tell me what that was all about?"

"My niece. The *baby*," Kate said. "Crying. Lots. And motion puts her to sleep."

"I'm not buying it."

"You know you have a suspicious mind?"

"That doesn't mean I'm wrong."

She went silent, an intense expression coming over her face. Everything he'd ever suspected about her intellect was there in front of him to see.

"Tell me what you're thinking," he said.

She made him wait a moment longer. "Is there somewhere we can talk?"

"Absolutely." Whatever she was thinking or doing, he wanted to know about it.

"Somewhere that's not here."

"My car." He pointed to his black Audi rental.

They were both silent as they walked. Then they slid into the leather seats and buckled up.

He pushed the starter button and moved the shifter. "Start talking."

It took her a minute or so to answer. "Not yet. I want to be able to see your eyes while I talk."

"This is starting to feel like some kind of a game." He wasn't interested in being jerked around for whatever reason she might have.

"I'm trying to decide if I can trust you, Brody."

"You can."

"You're going to have to let me be the judge of that."

He gave up. He was curious enough that he'd do it her way. "My hotel has a nice lounge."

"That'll work." She slumped back as the car started to move. She seemed distracted, gazing out the window as the streetlights flashed past.

They cleared the driveway, and he pulled the car onto the winding mountain road.

He told himself to be patient, but his interest was piqued. "If the lounge isn't private enough, we can go up to my suite."

"Sure," she answered distractedly.

"Kate?"

"Hmm?"

"What's going on inside your head?"

"What?"

"You just agreed to go up to my hotel suite."

She blinked at him. "Did I?"

"Are you planning to seduce me?" He knew that wasn't the case, but a man could hope.

"No."

"I'm sorry to hear that."

Her tone turned tart. "You can't be surprised."

He grinned. "There we go. Now you're back."

He picked up speed, and the route took them down to the beach at Santa Monica. In front of the hotel, Brody handed the keys off to the valet and swiftly rounded the car to open Kate's door.

He couldn't help admiring her shapely legs as she stepped out of the car.

She caught him staring. "We're not on a date."

"It feels like a date. It could be a date."

"This is serious, Brody."

"Fine." As he righted his gaze, he couldn't help but notice the little bird necklace dangling against her chest. He touched a finger to it. "I thought you'd decided on the emeralds."

He hadn't intended to call her on stealing the pretty necklace. But the fact that she'd taken it, along with so many other things about her had him more than a little confused. He wanted to see how she'd explain it away.

She glanced down. "I put the emeralds back."

"You did not."

They were worth a fortune, and she'd had Quentin's permission to take them. Kate might not be a fortune hunter, but she wasn't a fool.

"He said I could take one thing, and I wanted this instead," she said.

"Why?"

"Because I gave it to Francie for her birthday." There was regret in Kate's eyes. "A long time ago. When things were better between us."

Now Brody felt like a prize jerk.

"Can we go inside?" she asked.

They crossed the lobby to the quiet lounge in the back and found an empty table with deep cushioned chairs and a candle flickering on the polished black surface.

"Drink?" he asked.

"I'll take a club soda."

Brody also ordered a beer for himself and debated whether he should apologize.

Before he could decide, she spoke. "I've come to the reluctant conclusion that I'm going to have to trust you."

"Reluctant?" It was hard to take that as a vote of confidence."

"Look at it from my side, Brody. I don't know anything about you, or your relationship to Quentin, or what's going on with Bert and Ernie."

"But you need something from me." That much was clear.

She toyed with one of her dangling earrings. "I need to tell you that I'm a fraud."

"You're a criminal?" He certainly didn't want that to be the case.

"No." She pointed to her hair and her dress and her fingernails. "I mean I'm not this."

He wasn't following. Was she saying she wasn't Francie's sister? He hadn't even considered that as a possibility.

"I'm not like Francie. I don't like parties and loud music, and I certainly don't do recreational drugs."

"But you are her sister?"

His question seemed to confuse her.

"Of course I'm her sister. Who else would I be?"

Brody didn't know. But he was through taking anything at face value.

"What about the marijuana in the gatehouse?" he asked.

"You walked in just as I found it. I was putting it back."

"Okay."

She squared her shoulders. "Do you believe me?"

"Yes." He did. He hadn't seen anything else that indicated she was into any kind of drugs. When he thought back about it, she barely ever drank the champagne she ordered.

"I'm a first-grade teacher," she said.

"Really?" That wouldn't have even been his hundredth guess.

"I'm giving you the truth here. And I can prove it all. I cut my hair. It's not usually purple. I don't wear this amount of makeup, and my closet is full of ordinary dresses and blazers."

He found himself smiling. "So, I'm assuming this was part of some master plan?"

"I wanted Quentin to like me. I wanted to blend in. I wanted a chance to make sure Annabelle was being properly cared for."

What she said seemed to pull a lot of the pieces together, and Brody couldn't help but admire her ingenuity. "Well, you pulled it off. And you managed to look good doing it."

"I look tacky doing it."

"But sexy. Tacky can be very sexy."

"Stop."

"It's hard to stop when you're sitting right here in front of me."

"Be serious, Brody."

The waiter arrived and set down their drinks.

Brody waited until he left. "I am serious. But this is hardly the most damning secret in the world. You did a good thing."

"That's not all of it." She twirled the plastic stick in her icy drink.

She had his attention.

"I need someone close to Quentin to help me."

Brody almost told her he wasn't close to Quentin. But he didn't want to stop the flow of information. And he didn't want to disappoint her before he had to.

"I know he does illegal drugs," she said. "And I can probably get proof of that."

"I don't think that's a good idea, Kate, it would be dangerous for you to try."

"Even if I was successful, I don't think that's going to be enough."

"Enough to what?"

"To prove he's an unfit parent. I've been reading up, and it's not going to be enough to show I'd be a better parent. There has to be something significant to get her away from him."

Brody couldn't help but see the irony in the situation. If his own plans came together, Quentin wouldn't be in a position to raise Annabelle or any other child for a very long time to come.

She continued in the face of his silence. "Francie and I didn't have it very good growing up. Our mother was a narcissist and an alcoholic who didn't particularly like children."

"That sounds bad."

"It was bad. Maybe worse for Francie than it was for me. She reacted one way to the disaster that was our childhood. I reacted in another. Thing is, I survived. I'm doing really well in Seattle. I've got a great job. Great friends. I own a condo—well, half a condo. I fought hard and I climbed out of a truly dismal start in life. I'm in a position to take care of Annabelle. She doesn't have to be stuck with Quentin. The cycle doesn't have to repeat with her, because I can stop it."

Brody couldn't help comparing Kate's upbringing with his own. And he couldn't help picturing Annabelle. She was a beautiful little baby, cherubic, happy, curious. And she had Kate's blue eyes.

He didn't care that they were also Francie's blue eyes. As far as he was concerned, they belonged to Kate. And for some reason that told him Annabelle should be with Kate. And he wanted to help.

He knew the safe thing to do was keep quiet about his family. But he found he didn't want to play it safe. He wanted to go out on a limb for her. And that meant sharing more than he should. But she'd trusted him and, like him, she was trying to do the right thing by her family.

"I don't mean this the way it sounds," he said. "But would you come up to my hotel room?"

"How do you think it sounds?"

"Like I'm making a pass at you."

"But you're not."

"No. There's something I want to talk to you about, and I can't do it here."

It looked like she was fighting a smile. "'Come up to my hotel room, baby, and I'll tell you a secret'."

"If I was making a pass at you, it would be a lot smoother than that."

"I'm not judging."

"You were mocking."

"I guess I'm just relieved that now you know the truth about me and why I'm here."

He reached forward and took her hands. "That wasn't such a terrible secret. What you're doing is admirable. And if you'll trust me a little further, I have an idea."

"I trust you." She paused. "I guess in part because I have to. You're the only one of Quentin's friends who doesn't make the hair stand up on the back of my neck."

"Your instincts are good. You should keep going with those."

Kate was drawn to the glass doors that led to the balcony of Brody's hotel suite. He had a sweeping view of the ocean and stars, and a quarter moon that hung low in the sky, and she gazed out at the panorama.

"Open?" he asked, coming up beside her.

"That would be nice."

It was coming up on three in the morning. Her energy was waning, but as he pulled aside the doors the ocean air blew in, reviving her.

"Thirsty?" he asked.

"I'm fine."

"Would you like to sit?" he asked, gesturing to the sofa.

"You're making me nervous," she said.

"Don't be."

If only it were that easy. She wasn't completely sure she was ready for whatever he had to say that was so private. She hoped it was something good about Annabelle.

He took the opposite end of the sofa, then he seemed to hesitate. "Right. Here it is."

She waited.

"Here's what?" she asked, her curiosity beginning to turn into anxiety. Was it something bad?

He gave a tight smile then pressed his lips together. "My name is not Brody Herrington."

A warning tingle flooded Kate's body.

"What?"

"I'm not—"

She came to her feet, the hair on the back of her neck standing on end. Why had it seemed safe to come up here with him? She didn't even know him. She didn't know him at all.

"Wait," he said.

She turned to leave, and he jumped up from the sofa.

"It's Brody Calder," he called after her. "Kate, stop. It's nothing sinister, I promise."

Her hand was gripping the door handle. She didn't let go, but she stared at him cautiously.

"I'm Brody Calder. My grandmother's name is Herrington. My family and I own Shetland Technology Corporation. It's a Scottish firm that's a direct competitor of Beast Blue Designs."

She tried to wrap her head around what he was saying. "You're not a concert promoter."

That much was clear.

"I'm not."

"So you're some corporate spy? You're a criminal? Are Bert and Ernie the good guys?"

"No! And I'm not a criminal. And Bert and Ernie are definitely not the good guys. My family and I are the victims. Quentin stole from us, and I'm here to prove it."

"What did he steal?" She couldn't imagine what Quentin would want that he couldn't buy for himself.

"Intellectual property. Computer code."

Her instincts were at war with themselves, some telling her to get away from Brody, the rest telling her to trust him. "Why should I believe you?"

"Because you've met Quentin, and you've met me. Which one of us do you think is a thief?"

"There's no way to know."

"There are dozens of ways to know."

"Name one." She kept a firm grip on the door handle.

If he made a single move toward her, she was running out into the hall and shouting for help.

"Do a search on me. Use my real name. You'll find my family, and you'll find my company. You'll know I'm telling the truth about that much."

"You'll stay where you are?" she asked.

"Absolutely." He sat back down and held up his palms in mock surrender. "Go ahead."

She took out her phone and pulled up the browser. "You said Calder."

"Yes. Try the Earl of Calder. My father."

She studied his expression. "Is this a joke? Some kind of con?"

"You're about to find out."

She typed.

The photo was small, but it was clearly Brody. He was the second son of the Earl of Calder. She let go of the door handle, somewhat relieved.

"You can use my computer to look further," he offered.

She glanced up. "You're a viscount?"

"My older brother, Blane, is a viscount. When my father dies, Blane will be Earl. That's how it works."

"But you're the son of an earl."

"Guilty."

She was thoroughly confused. "What are you doing? Why are you here? You're taking a huge risk. Why not just call the police?"

"That was the first thing I tried," he said, looking suddenly tired. "On both sides of the Atlantic."

She moved back toward the sofa, her fear dissipating. She found she believed him. "This is a lot to take in."

"I understand that."

She studied him, wondering if there was something she should have seen, something that should have stood out, setting him apart from the rest. Then she realized there was. She'd come to him for a reason. Of everyone near Quentin and Annabelle, Brody was the one she'd innately trusted.

When she looked at him now, his honesty, his intelligence and his integrity shone through.

She sat down. "Quentin is a thief."

"He is."

Her mind cataloged the implications and the possibilities. "And you're trying to prove it, to get him fairly and justly charged, convicted and maybe sent to jail."

"I am."

"Okay." She nodded. "Okay. I'm in. What do we do?"

Brody smiled. "Thank you."

"You don't have to thank me. This is for Annabelle. I should be thanking you." If Brody was right, and if they could prove it, she'd have more than a fighting chance with Annabelle.

"We think there might be proof on Quentin's home computer."

"Who is we?"

"My head programmer, Will Finlay, and me."

"So that's what you were doing the day you said we were looking for your watch." She saw all of his actions through a whole new lens.

"Again, guilty. There was never any watch."

"You kissed me to throw me off." Her mind went back to the moment.

"I kissed you because I wanted to kiss you. But I'd have done it again then to keep Bert and Ernie off the scent." He paused. "Heck, I'd have done it again then or any other time, and with any excuse, or with no excuse at all."

The atmosphere shifted, their kisses thrown out front and center. The air seemed to warm, and the room seemed to shrink around them.

"I knew you never quite fit," he said, and he shifted across the sofa towards her. "You were crazy and sane, smart and scattered. Your ridiculous clothes and outlandish hair never meshed with your core personality. The real you kept slipping through."

"I kept wanting to trust you," she said.

"I'm an honorable man."

"Is that a viscount thing?"

He reached up and slowly cradled her cheek. "That's my brother's title."

She liked the feel of his hand. She loved his closeness. She was so relieved that they were being honest with each other.

"You were conning me while I was conning you."

"I don't know who won that round." He touched his forehead to hers.

"Call it a draw."

"Sure. But in honor of our new spirit of honesty and full disclosure. Fair warning. In about three seconds I'm going to kiss you."

"I think…" She tipped her head for his kiss. "It's good to be on the same side."

"I think so, too."

His lips claimed hers, tender at first but then with a deepening passion and a hardening purpose. She wrapped her arms around his neck, molding her breasts to his body, giving in to the desire she'd been fighting for days.

He was sturdy and strong, an anchor point she desperately needed. She opened to him, and their kiss went on and on, sexy and impatient, probing and exhilarating.

His hand slid to the small of her back, splaying over her spine. He shifted her to his lap, his slacks arousing friction against the backs of her bare legs.

His lips moved to her neck, planting hot, moist kisses in the sensitive hollows. He pushed a strap of her dress from her shoulder, kissing his way to the tip. Her nipples hardened and tingled, aching for his touch.

He read her mind, and he cupped her breast.

She moaned his name, arching her back, sighing with pleasure as he pushed her dress down. It pooled at her waist.

"You are incredible," he whispered, then he kissed a path from her neck to her breasts.

She all but melted in his arms, letting the pleasure wash over her.

Her dress rode up, and his thumb brushed the lace of her panties.

"I want you," he said on a rasp. "All of you. Every inch…"

"I want you, too," she managed to say. "Now." She'd never been so brazen, but she had no intention of stopping him.

He stripped off her panties in one deft motion.

Her body contracted with intense sensations, the cool air, his hot touch, his kisses that went on and on, along her neck, up to her mouth.

Her lips were swollen and burning and eager for more. She turned in his lap, facing him, straddling him, gripping his shoulders tightly. She had no desire to control the wild passion building between them. For now, for a moment, in this tiny space and time, nothing existed but Brody.

She plucked at his shirt buttons, releasing them one by one. Then she pulled the sides open and pushed his sleeves down. His shoulders were magnificent, smooth, toned and tanned. She kissed one of them, tasting his skin, smelling his skin.

He stripped off his shirt, wrapping his strong arms around her, pressing them together. The heat of his chest fanned the pulse in her core. She reached for his pants, releasing the zipper. He helped, raising her up, freeing himself, then splaying her hips with his hands and bringing them together as one.

She gasped, staring into his eyes. "That is…"

"You're amazing," he whispered as he started to move.

"Oh, Brody."

"I know."

Pleasure and joy pulsated through her. She rocked her hips in time with his. She held on to his shoulders, tighter and tighter. She kissed him again, their tongues tangling, deeper and deeper still.

The world disappeared. Her whole body was alive, alight with the buzz of pleasure. She turned hot and then cold and then hot again.

He trailed his fingers on the curve of her breast, circling in, closer and closer until he reached the center.

She cried out, bucking against him, striving desperately to close any last space between them.

He wrapped her in his arms. Then he turned her, pressing her back onto the sofa, stretching them chest to chest, thigh to thigh, toe to toe. He linked their hands, raising them over her head.

Then he watched her. He held her gaze, and she felt like she was falling headlong into his polished-pewter eyes. His strokes were taking her to heaven, and she let it come. She lay still. She absorbed his pace. She let him into her body, her mind and her soul.

The pulses of pleasure came faster and harder, as she soared to an unbearable height.

"Kate!" he cried out.

His body shuddered around her, and she catapulted to the edge of oblivion.

She couldn't see. She couldn't hear. She couldn't move.

She was floating, blissfully.

"Kate?" His voice was a long way off.

"Hmmm?" She wasn't capable of forming actual words.

"You are the most incredible woman I've ever met."

She smiled. Then she opened her eyes. He was blurry in front of her.

"You're very good at this," she said.

"I'm not that good." He kissed her shoulder. "I'm not this good. I think it must be you."

"I'm not that good, either." She had never had sex that came close to this experience.

"Then it must be us."

"I bet it was the relief."

Now that it was over, she could take a step back and analyze her intense feelings for Brody.

"The relief?"

"You're going to help me with Quentin, with Annabelle. It's a huge relief to have someone on my side."

"And that translates into mind-blowing sex?"

"It seemed to."

"Because, Kate." He looked completely genuine. "I don't know what sex is like where you come from, but that was off the charts."

She knew what he meant, but she wanted to keep it light. "You don't have sex that good in Scotland?"

"Man, I'm going to have to visit Seattle."

Kate grinned.

He captured her hand and kissed her fingers. Then he smoothed back her hair, his voice going lower. "You have rocked my world."

She gave in to honesty. "You rocked mine, too."

He wrapped her in another tight hug.

The last thing she wanted to do was break the spell. But

they were running out of night, and their problems would still be there in the morning.

"But right now," she said. "We need to talk about Quentin."

He heaved an exaggerated sigh. "I know."

Brody rose, and she watched him stride naked to the bathroom. He emerged a few minutes later with two fluffy robes and dropped one beside her.

"You know this moment could be truly sublime," he said, shrugging into the other. "We could order some room service, feed each other truffles and champagne, talk about our hopes and dreams and plans for the future."

She sat up and put on the robe, grateful for the warmth. "Our plans for the future are to annihilate Quentin."

"And that hardly lends itself to afterglow, does it?" He sat next to her.

"Buck up, Brody." She gave him a playful elbow. "Tell me how I can help."

"Aren't you the no-nonsense schoolteacher."

"If I can keep twenty first graders in line, I can handle one almost-viscount. What should I do?"

He sat back, a serious expression coming over his face. "The best thing you can do is spy on Bert and Ernie."

"I really don't like those guys."

"Like I said, your instincts are good."

"Is there a reason you think they know something?"

"They're not your run-of-the-mill bodyguards. If I was running a criminal enterprise, those are the guys I'd want on my team."

"Do they seem like overkill to you?" she asked.

"That's a good question." Brody seemed to consider the point. "If all Quentin did was steal our computer code, why does he need those guys? He needs techies to incorporate the code into his game. And he needs a sales staff to get it to market. But why those two running around his house all the time?"

"Maybe he's stealing something else."

"It's possible." Brody looked unconvinced. "Even if he is, in Quentin's world, you need nerds for thieves, not thugs."

"I'll do my best to find out."

Kate might prefer to stay away from Bert and Ernie, but she agreed with Brody's assessment. And she was grateful for his help. Her chances of helping Annabelle had now drastically improved, and it was thanks to Brody.

Nine

Kate and Brody slept for a couple of hours, and then she returned to the mansion to execute their new plan.

It was quiet there, with no sign of Christina and Annabelle on the main floor. So Kate made her way up the staircase. Near the top, she heard Annabelle crying.

The crying grew louder. She found herself hurrying, pushing open the nursery door, wondering what could be wrong.

She was surprised to find Annabelle alone. As she rushed to pick her up, a figure on the floor caught the corner of her eye.

"Christina?" she said out loud as she scooped Annabelle from her crib.

The baby's eyes were swollen, her face red, her nose running. Kate cradled her against her shoulder as she rushed to Christina's side. She was unconscious, lying motionless, her face pale, her hair streaked with sweat. Her forehead was hot to the touch.

"Christina?" Kate tried again, juggling Annabelle and reaching into her pocket for her phone.

Christina's eyes blinked open. They were glassy and confused.

"Are you okay?" Kate asked, even though it was obvious she was not. "I'm calling for an ambulance."

"Annabelle," Christina croaked out.

"I've got her," said Kate. "She's upset, but she's fine."

Christina tried to sit up.

"Don't," ordered Kate.

"She's hungry."

"I'll get her a bottle." Kate pressed 911.

"Fire, police or ambulance?" came the immediate response on the line.

"Ambulance," said Kate, and she gave them the address.

"You need to feed her," Christina mumbled weakly.

"I will."

Footsteps sounded in the hallway.

"Help," Kate called out.

The footsteps stopped, and Rex was in the doorway. When he took in the scene, his jaunty, expectant smile was gone.

"I've called an ambulance," said Kate. "Christina's burning up, and Annabelle needs a bottle."

"I'll get someone to help," said Rex.

He disappeared, and almost immediately one of the housekeepers entered the nursery.

"I'll stay here, miss, and someone will meet the ambulance downstairs," the woman said.

"Thank you," Kate said to the housekeeper. "I'll get Annabelle a bottle." Kate gave Christina's hand a squeeze, but Christina seemed oblivious.

Kate juggled Annabelle as she walked, shushing her and promising food was on its way.

She'd watched Christina prepare bottles, so she knew where everything was kept, how to heat up the formula, and to test the temperature on her wrist. She also knew how to hold Annabelle. It was a bit awkward, but between the two of them, they got it sorted out, and Annabelle settled down.

She heard the ambulance arrive, and people going up and down the stairs. She was grateful that Christina was going to be in good hands. After a while, the noise subsided, and Rex came into the kitchen.

"How is she?" Kate asked him.

"They took her away."

It wasn't exactly an answer, but she supposed that was all she was going to get. She hoped it was nothing serious. She'd come to like Christina very much.

"How are you doing?" Rex asked, moving closer to her.

Kate felt her guard going up. His tone was solicitous, but there was something about him that always seemed calculating and cunning. He tried to flirt with her whenever he got the chance. So far, she hadn't responded with any encouragement. Yet he persisted.

"We're fine." She had to struggle not to feel intimidated. "I mean, Annabelle's fine. She's the only one we need to worry about."

His glance went fleetingly to Annabelle. "I assume that smell is her?"

"I decided hunger was more pressing than a fresh diaper."

Rex wrinkled his nose. "I'm not sure you made the right choice."

"That's only because she's quiet. If she was still crying, you'd agree with me."

"Maybe," he said.

His gaze on her was distracting, and it made her want to shift in her seat. She wished he would back up a bit. As it was, with her sitting, it felt like he was looming over her.

"Is Quentin up?" she asked, instinct telling her to remind him there were other people in the house.

"Not that I've seen."

"He must have heard the ambulance."

Rex gave a shrug. "He's a sound sleeper."

He awkwardly wriggled Annabelle's foot, and it was all Kate could do not to slap his hand away. She didn't want him touching the baby.

"So, tell me, Kate," he said. "How are you enjoying LA?"

"I grew up in LA."

"Not in a place like this."

She found herself glancing at the surroundings. "No, not in a place like this."

"You like it?"

"What's not to like?" She tried to figure out where he was going with this conversation. Surely, after all the worry and concern only minutes ago, it wasn't the time now for chitchat.

He sat down in the chair next to her at the table.

She resisted an urge to scoot back.

"How long are you planning to stay?" He rested his hand on the tabletop.

"I don't know. I haven't given it much thought."

Rex was plummeting along with Bert and Ernie on her trust meter. She didn't know how he might factor in to Quentin's crimes, but she definitely didn't like being alone with him.

"Oh, I suspect you've given it some thought." He moved his hand closer to her.

Her grip tightened on Annabelle, and the baby squirmed. Kate forced herself to relax.

She pretended to misinterpret his question. "I can take care of Annabelle as long as Christina's sick."

"Is that what this is about?" He brushed the back of his knuckles against her forearm. "Annabelle."

Kate didn't like him getting anywhere close to the truth. She subtly pulled away from his touch. "She is my niece."

"You don't strike me as the maternal type."

"I'm not." She told herself to think like Francie again. Her sister wouldn't have been intimidated by Rex. "I'm the cool-auntie type. I plan to take her shopping and stuff."

"With Quentin's money?"

"He is her father."

Brody barged full force into the kitchen, his gaze immediately locking on Kate. "What was with the ambulance?"

She was incredibly grateful to see him.

Rex gave him a glare. "Look who's still hanging around."

"Christina is sick," she said, adjusting Annabelle in her arms. "Everything else is fine."

"What kind of sick?" Brody asked.

"A fever, maybe only a flu or something. But she had passed out when I found her."

"Are you all right?"

Rex came to his feet. "Does she look like she's not all right?"

"I'm fine," Kate said.

Annabelle's suckling was slowing down, so Kate removed the bottle and raised her to her shoulder to burp her.

"She needs a change." Kate was glad for the excuse to get out of the conversation.

"What are you doing here?" Rex asked Brody.

"I came to see Quentin."

"Quentin won't be up for hours."

"I'm up now," came Quentin's voice as he sauntered into the room. "What's going on?"

Kate jumped in before anyone else had the chance. "Christina's sick. So I'm taking care of Annabelle."

Quentin seemed to digest that for a moment.

She held her breath and waited. She wanted all the time she could get with Annabelle, and the more she hung around, the more opportunities she'd have to eavesdrop on Bert and Ernie. Not to mention Rex. She was starting to get suspicious of Rex.

"Oh," was all Quentin said.

She let go an inward sigh of relief, taking his lack of interest as permission to stay.

Brody gave her a subtle look of approval.

"Welcome aboard," said Rex, a mocking edge to his tone and a predatory glint in his eyes.

She was definitely going to have to be careful around him.

"Annabelle needs a change," she announced.

Quentin inhaled and scowled. "You're telling me."

Kate hopped to her feet and headed for the hallway.

Brody stopped her with a gentle hand on her arm. His touch had a ripple effect across her body.

"You sure you're okay?" he asked in an undertone.

"It's all good," she said.

Rex broke in. "What's with the whispering?" he asked them.

She pulled her arm free. "Brody's offering to change the baby."

Brody made a show of surrender. "I'll pick up formula, shake a rattle or move the car seat. But you're on your own for the sticky stuff."

"I guess I misunderstood," she quickly told Quentin, adding a giggle for good measure.

Rex seemed to be getting far too suspicious. She and Brody were going to have to be careful to keep up their charades.

She gave Quentin a smile and thought airy Francie thoughts.

She held Annabelle up like an accessory. "I thought we'd go to the mall. I could pick us out matching outfits and get our picture taken. Or maybe I should get her ears pierced. She'd look darling, don't you think?"

Before anyone could react to the outrageous statement, she breezed from the room.

The next day Brody watched Rex head up the main staircase. He knew where the man was going and he didn't like it. Kate had moved into the mansion yesterday, taking Christina's room, since it was connected to the nursery. Moving in was a good move from the perspective of spying, but now Rex was stalking her.

Brody took the stairs two at a time.

"Soundproof?" Rex was asking as Brody rounded the corner into the nursery.

"Sound dampening, anyway," said Kate.

She was on the floor, a cutting tool in her hand, colorful rolls of material and cardboard cartons strewn around the room. Annabelle was cooing in the crib which had been pulled away from the wall. All of the furniture was moved toward the center of the room.

"What are you doing?" Brody couldn't help but ask.

Redecorating seemed like an odd choice given their current plan of trying to have Quentin arrested. Then again, he supposed Quentin wouldn't suspect she wanted to take Annabelle away if she was nesting in the nursery. If that was the plan, it was pretty good.

Rex gave Brody an annoyed frown. It was clear he wanted Kate all to himself. Too bad, because Brody wasn't going anywhere.

"Quentin told me I could make a few changes."

She was dressed in worn jeans, a plain red T-shirt and

a pair of runners. Brody was sure this was the first time he'd seen her without makeup. Except for the purple hair, she looked like the perfect girl next door.

He found the look very sexy. Truth was, he found all of her looks sexy. This was just another in a long list.

"Wallpaper?" he asked.

There had to be easier means to accomplish the same objective.

"It has a sound barrier on the inside." She pointed to the quarter-inch material. "And on the outside, well, you can see the pretty trees and birds."

Brody wasn't sure he followed her complete logic. But he was willing to go along with it.

"You're going to need help with that," he said.

If Rex stayed, Brody stayed.

"That would be great." She gave him a grateful smile as she came to her feet, retrieving a measuring tape.

He had to admire her acting. Rex thought she was planning to freeload. Quentin likely did, as well. It was good to feed into their mistakes. It would keep them from thinking about other possibilities.

"I'll give you a hand, too," said Rex, rolling up his shirt-sleeves.

No surprise there.

"Thanks," Kate said.

Brody knew she was no fan of Rex, so he applauded her acting once again. Then he rolled up his sleeves, as well. He was far from a home decorating expert. But if she was determined to do this, he could provide brute strength.

Annabelle's vocalizations grew louder, as if she wanted to participate in the conversation. She rolled from her back to her stomach, blinking at them.

As always, he was struck by her eyes—Kate's blue eyes. Her cheeks were plump and rosy pink, and she had a soft halo of light hair. For a moment, Brody thought of his mother and her intense desire for grandchildren. She was anxious for an heir, and his parents were pushing his brother, Blane, to get married.

He suspected it was more than just the need for an heir to the earldom. His mother had a soft spot for both babies and children. Her charitable work focused on children, and there was nobody more enthusiastic about the annual summer children's festival that took place on the grounds of the Calder estate.

"The directions say to start with plumb lines," said Kate.

Annabelle picked that moment to cry out. Her little face screwed up, she quickly began to wail.

Kate glanced at her with worry, her hands already full. "Oh, baby. Does it have to be right now?"

Brody impulsively stepped forward. "I'll get her."

Kate looked surprised by the offer. "Are you sure?"

"I'm sure."

"Do you know what you're doing?"

He frowned at her. But it was true that her instincts were bang on. He'd never held a baby before. Not that he was about to admit it. It couldn't be too complicated. Annabelle was soft, warm and fragrant.

His confidence faltered. She was a little too fragrant, and not in a good way.

She gulped down a sob, eyeing him with surprise and trepidation.

"Hey there, Annabelle," he said softly, giving her what he hoped was a reassuring smile. "Something bothering you?"

She sniffed a couple of times, clearly deciding whether or not to keep crying.

"Your auntie's busy right now," he crooned.

He could hear Rex guffaw in the background, but he ignored him. Rex might be too macho to take care of a baby, but it was clear to Brody that holding Annabelle was the most practical thing to do to help Kate. And he was on Kate's team now. He wanted Kate to know they were a team.

"You do know what's bothering her, right?" There was amusement in Kate's tone, laced with an obvious challenge.

"I can guess," said Brody.

"You're not scared?"

"I'm made of pretty stern stuff."

"Okay, tough guy. Change table's over there if you're up for it."

Rex laughed more clearly this time.

Brody had no intention of backing down. It would take more than a teeny, tiny little girl to do him in.

"I've got this," he told Kate and received a twinkling grin in return. He realized he'd change a dozen diapers in order to put that expression on her face.

Then she turned her attention to Rex. But at least she wasn't smiling at him. Brody was grateful for that. And a little smug, too.

"We're working with nine-foot ceilings," she said.

Brody muttered softly to Annabelle. "I'd say we're working with a twenty-six-inch baby."

"I heard that," said Kate, laughter in her voice.

"Your auntie is a meddler," he said to Annabelle, moving to the change table.

He knew they'd need a new diaper. He understood the concept of wet wipes. On the shelf below the table was an assortment of items, including a jar of diaper cream. And there was a covered trash can beside the table. He was sure he could work this all out.

He laid Annabelle down on the vinyl changing pad.

"Careful she doesn't roll off," Kate called.

"Careful you make your lines straight," he called back. "Meddler," he whispered to Annabelle.

Surprisingly, the baby smiled up at him.

"That's the spirit," he told her. Then he located a row of snaps down the inside leg of her stretchy sleeper.

He unfastened the garment and peeled it out of the way. She kicked her legs as soon as they were free, and she did try to roll. But he placed his palm on her tummy and gently held her in place.

He released the tapes on the diaper, memorizing their position for use with the fresh one. The smell immediately became stronger. He swallowed against a gag reflex, but he refused to give in.

Rex wasn't so lucky. He made a choking sound in the back of his throat and bolted for the exit.

Brody smiled between shallow breaths. But he also discovered an error in judgment. He should have retrieved the wet wipes before releasing the fasteners on the diaper.

"Got a problem?" asked Kate.

"We're fine."

But then she was beside him, the blue box of wipes open in her hand, offering them to him.

"Thanks," he said, taking one, shaking it out, and using it to make a pass over Annabelle's bottom.

"I'm impressed," said Kate.

"That I can clean a baby or keep my breakfast down?" He glanced meaningfully at the doorway where Rex had disappeared.

"Both," she said.

"At least we know how to get rid of Rex now."

"I expect he'll be back."

Brody helped himself to another wipe. "Oh, he'll be back. Don't encourage him."

"Encouraging him is the very last thing on my mind."

"Good." Brody had suspected as much, but he was glad to hear her say it.

"Do you think he's involved?"

"I'm not sure. He probably knows something. But I don't get the sense he's the key to anything. Don't try to spy on him."

The last thing Brody wanted was Kate trying to get close to Rex.

"But if an opportunity presents itself…" she said.

"No." He realized his tone was sharper than he'd intended. Annabelle's face screwed up.

"It's okay, little girl," Brody crooned.

"I'm not saying I'll do anything risky," Kate said.

"Don't do anything at all. He's determined to make a move on you." And Brody was equally determined to keep that from happening.

"If he does, I might be able to use that."

"You're not your sister."

"Excuse me?" There was a challenge in her tone.

"I mean that in a good way."

"Are you saying I'm naive and unsophisticated?"

"I'm saying you're honest and…" He hesitated. "Okay, yeah, I'm saying you're maybe a little more innocent than Francie."

"I can take care of myself." She snapped the lid on the wipes container and put it back on the shelf. "I was doing great the past few days."

He dropped the soiled diaper into the trash. "But I'm here to help now, and we're a team."

"And you're the captain?"

"I'm…" He wasn't sure how to frame it. "I'm less vulnerable than you. I can't stay here twenty-four hours a day. So you'll be alone and unprotected."

"Quentin's here. And I don't get the sense that Rex will try anything in front of Quentin. All I'm going to do is keep my ear to the ground."

Rex took a diaper from the small pile. "I don't trust Quentin to protect you. Keep your ear to the ground, by all means. But make sure that ground is nowhere near Rex."

"Yes, sir. Would a snappy salute be in order?"

"Don't be melodramatic." He spread the clean diaper out beneath Annabelle.

"You've got it backwards," said Kate.

"How do I have it backwards?" Brody wanted to end this conversation. It was getting them nowhere. "I'm a man. If push comes to shove I have a good chance of taking Rex. Add to that, he doesn't have any sexual designs on me."

"I meant the diaper," she said. "You've got the diaper backwards."

He took in the orientation of the snowy white diaper. "Oh."

She reached out and turned it a hundred and eighty degrees. "There."

"Right. So, all that other stuff…"

"I get it. I'll be very careful. And I'll try to keep my distance from Rex."

"Try hard."

"Yes, sir." She gave him a mocking salute.

He shook his head as he folded the diaper around Annabelle and fastened the tapes. Then as he put her little feet back into the sleeper, he realized an oversight. "I forgot the cream."

Kate lifted Annabelle into her arms. "Don't worry. We'll get it next time."

His worry magnified as he gazed at Kate's small frame, her fresh face, the cherubic Annabelle cuddled in her arms. His thoughts went to his mother again, and how incredibly delighted she would be to have a daughter-in-law and a grandchild that looked just like that. He paused and couldn't help but smile—perhaps not so much the purple hair.

Kate gave Annabelle a kiss on the top of her head. "I just want this to be over."

"So do I."

He fought an urge to draw them both into his arms. He needed all this to be over so that his family would be financially secure. But he also wanted it to be over for Kate's sake, as well.

He stopped abruptly on that thought. When this was over, the two of them would be on opposite sides of the world. He was finding it hard to get excited by that prospect.

Ten

The soundproofing wallpaper, along with some quilted wall hangings, a couple of enormous stuffed animals and a white-noise machine seemed to do the trick for Annabelle. Kate had also discovered the room was equipped with a high-end baby monitor that came with an earpiece. So, once Annabelle was in bed that night, she was free to join everyone downstairs.

She'd looked through Francie's closet for something appropriate and had chosen a pair of purposely tattered denim shorts and a white lace top. Her midriff was bare. She'd spiked her short hair with gel. And her feet were clad in high-heeled white, chunky sandals.

She was ready to blend in and more than ready to hunt down Bert and Ernie.

"Hello, gorgeous," said Rex as he approached her.

He handed her a glass of champagne, the drink she'd decided early on to identify as her favorite. She'd chosen it because it was weaker than a martini, and because it had the air of extravagance. Also, she didn't mind the taste.

"Hi, Rex." She mustered up a smile.

He edged up close and wrapped an arm around her waist. "You look like someone ready to have fun."

"That's me," she singsonged. She desperately wanted to pull away, but she forced herself to endure the embrace.

"That's what I like about you," Rex whispered against her neck.

She caught Brody's glare. She assumed he was angry with her for not staying away from Rex. But the glare was aimed squarely at Rex, and it was intent. For a horrible second she thought Brody was going to stomp over and tear Rex limb from limb.

She quickly put some space between herself and Rex, past-ing a carefree expression on her face. "I'm going to look for Quentin. We can catch up later?"

Rex reached out and grasped her hand. "Not so fast."

She forced herself to giggle in an effort to defuse the situation. "In these shoes? I guarantee you, I'll be going really, really slow."

Rex glanced down at her shoes, and she took the opportunity to pull away. She kept her momentum going, sauntering toward the pool, making sure she mixed with the crowd.

Brody came up beside her. "What happened to the plan to stay away from him?"

"He approached me."

"No kidding." He glanced at her outfit. "And there's a lineup forming after him."

"I'm wearing Francie's clothes. I can't change back to me."

"That was the best she had?"

"It was one of the things she had. There were worse things in that closet."

"You're all but wearing a neon sign that says 'make a pass at me, because I'll probably say yes.'"

"Now who's being melodramatic?"

"You can't be that oblivious to how men react to you."

"And you can't be that paranoid. This party's full of people. I look flirty. I'm trying to look flirty. It's part of the plan."

She'd been wearing funky clothes for days now—she couldn't understand why Brody was suddenly so worried about it.

"Look further into her closet. There has to be something better than this."

"Focus, Brody. Have you seen Bert and Ernie?"

Brody let out an exaggerated sigh. "They're beside the gazebo, checking out the woman in the pink net cover-up."

Kate casually glanced in their direction. "And you say *I'm* dressed provocatively."

"She's trying harder, but it takes you less effort to have the same effect."

"Is that a compliment?" She truly wasn't sure.

"It's a compliment. And it's a warning. You have a lot of power. Use it wisely."

She coughed out a laugh. "You're losing it, Brody."

The bar was next to Bert and Ernie, so she quickly downed her champagne and handed the glass to Brody.

"You sure that was a good idea?"

"I'm going to the bar for a fresh drink."

"You could have dumped it in a plant."

"Didn't think of that." She had to admit, it would probably have been a better idea.

Just then, the wind shifted. She caught a whiff of smoke and wondered if they were doing burgers and brats again tonight. It reminded her that she was hungry. She hadn't wanted to eat much before prancing around in such a revealing outfit, but maybe she could snag one a little later on. In fact, she'd have two because—

Someone screamed.

"Not again," Kate muttered. She truly wished they'd stop tossing people into the pool.

But then someone shouted the word "fire!"

Her heart all but stopped.

Before she could turn to look, Brody was running. While others fled the flames that were curling up the side of the house to the second floor, he was running toward them.

Annabelle. Fear overtook Kate.

She started to run, almost instantly tripping up due to the shoes and falling to the grass. She kicked them off and jumped to her feet, running barefoot into the house.

She sprinted through the kitchen, down the hall and up the stairs. The smoke was coming in through the open windows, stinging her eyes. Though she was moving as fast as she could, she felt like she was running through wet concrete.

She finally made it to the nursery and wrenched open the door. Annabelle was still asleep. Faint bands of smoke hovered in the light from the window. She looked to be perfectly fine.

Kate scooped her up in her blanket, covering her head and

face, then rushed out the door. The return trip seemed to go faster. And by the time she was outside, the flames were out.

Brody was standing over a charred lounger with a fire extinguisher in his hand. A burned wicker basket stood nearby. The wall was scorched at least twelve feet in the air.

Quentin clapped Brody on the back. "That was awesome." His voice was slurred, and he stumbled a little, steadying himself on Brody's shoulder.

Somebody let out a whoop.

"It's all clear, folks," Quentin yelled, turning to the crowd. The music started up again, and everybody cheered.

Kate stared at Brody's rigid posture as Annabelle squirmed in her arms. She told herself, if she hadn't been there, Quentin would have remembered he had a baby. If the fire had gotten worse, surely he would have rescued Annabelle.

But then a shudder went through Kate's body, because she wasn't certain at all.

Even with the distraction of the fire, it was 3:00 a.m. before the party broke up. Brody was appalled by the behavior of the party guests. Even Quentin seemed to think it was funny that his house had nearly burned down.

Speculation was that someone had disposed of a cigarette butt in a towel hamper. The hamper had ignited, the fire spreading to the teak lounger beside it and up the wall of the house.

Once it was out, Kate had taken Annabelle back to the nursery. She hadn't returned to the party. Brody didn't blame her. Bert and Ernie would have to wait until tomorrow.

Brody was horrified to think about how badly it could have gone. He was sick of hanging out with Quentin and his friends. He didn't want Kate near any of them, and Annabelle seemed to be in genuine danger.

He needed to get the evidence he required and turn this whole thing over to the police. It was late, and the mansion was finally quiet, though adrenaline was still pumping through his system.

He marched into Quentin's office and sat down at his computer. He turned it on and dialed Will.

"Hello?" Will's voice was groggy.

"I'm at his computer," Brody said without preamble. "Tell me what I'm looking for."

Will became alert. "You're looking for a network connection."

Brody went to the control panel. "I see three."

"Read them to me."

Raised voices sounded down the hallway.

"Hang on," said Brody.

"What?"

Brody came to his feet, moving toward the door.

"We've already had this conversation," Quentin shouted.

"Gotta go," Brody said to Will, ending the call.

Brody pocketed his phone and carefully cracked the office door, peering out. The hallway was dim, but he could make out three figures.

"I'm going to bed," Quentin stated with determination.

He marched up the staircase and disappeared.

Bert said something to Ernie, and then Ernie answered back. The exchange became heated, and they moved down the hall, entering another room and shutting the door.

Brody knew he needed Kate right now. He hated to drag her out of bed after the evening she'd had, but he needed to know what those two were saying.

He left the office and took the stairs two at a time, letting himself into her bedroom. In the dim light, he quietly closed the connecting door to the nursery.

"Kate?" he whispered. He flicked on the bedside lamp.

"Kate?" he repeated. "It's Brody."

She blinked her eyes. For some reason, she didn't seem surprised to see him. "What's going on?"

"Can you come downstairs?"

She glanced at the clock on her bedside table. "It's after four."

"Bert and Ernie are having a fight. I need to know what they're arguing about."

She gave herself a little shake. "Sure. Yeah. Okay."

"You awake?" he asked.

She nodded. She flipped back the covers and rose from the bed. She was dressed in a pair of shorts and an old T-shirt. The outfit suited her, and her tousled hair and sleepy eyes were incredibly sexy.

He told himself to get a grip. "They're downstairs."

"Okay." She padded silently beside him.

"If they come out," Brody whispered to her as they descended the stairs. "If anyone sees us."

"You can pretend it's a tryst."

"I think that's best."

"They'll buy it. I have it on good authority that I looked provocative earlier tonight."

He couldn't believe she was making jokes. "We should be quiet."

She stopped talking.

They came to the closed door at the end of the hallway. The men's voices were muffled but audible.

"Something about a Mr. Kozak," she whispered.

It was the same name that came up before. Will had looked into the name but found far too many Kozaks to know who they might be talking about.

"Whoever he is," Kate said. "He's coming to California tomorrow, and they need to pick him up at the airport."

She listened a few minutes longer. "They're back to Ceci again. If Quentin doesn't agree to Ceci, they're going to…" Kate went pale.

"What is it?" Brody asked.

Kate's voice dropped to a whisper. "They're going to threaten Annabelle. They want to use her to control Quentin."

Kate swayed, and Brody grasped her shoulders to support her.

"Brody, what do we do?"

He'd heard enough. "Let's go."

She stumbled as she followed him. "What are we going to do?"

Turning into Quentin's office, he pressed his speed dial for Will. "Whatever it is we need to find, we're doing it now."

He closed the door, locking them inside the office.

He sat down behind the computer.

"They're threatening Annabelle," he told Will. "And we're running out of time."

Will's tone turned all business. "You're at the computer?"

"Yes."

"Read me the name of each of the network connections."

Brody read, and Will asked more questions, becoming more technical the deeper they went.

Kate paced the floor.

"Okay," Will finally said. "That's it. That's the proof."

Brody could hardly believe it. "We found it?"

Kate looked sharply up.

"It's time to call the police. I know exactly where to point them."

"Good. That's good." Brody was afraid to hope it would all come together. "Tell them the guy named Kozak is coming into the country tomorrow. Whoever he is, he's got to be connected somehow. Can you take another look for him?"

"Will do," said Will.

"And something about someone named Ceci. They keep saying they want Quentin to do something with Ceci. He's resisting, and that's why they're threatening Annabelle."

Will was silent.

"You there?" Brody asked.

"You know for sure that Ceci's a person?" asked Will.

Brody looked to Kate. "Ceci's a person?"

"I believe so. It's the only thing that makes sense."

"That's Kate's best guess."

"Did they ever actually say it wasn't something else?" Will asked.

Brody relayed the question.

She shook her head. "Not explicitly."

Brody went back to Will. "We thought maybe Kozak wanted Quentin to date or marry someone named Ceci. Maybe he has another illegitimate child out there?"

Will took another pause before responding. "Why would Bert and Ernie care about Quentin's love life?"

"It was only a theory."

"Got any other theories?"

"None. Do you?"

"Tell me exactly what they said about Ceci."

"I'll give you Kate." Brody handed Kate the phone. "He wants to know exactly what they said about Ceci."

She took the phone. "Hi, Will. This is Kate." She paused, obviously listening. "At first I thought they said Quentin would have to embrace Ceci, but then I thought maybe it was more closely translated to accept Ceci."

She paused. "Is this important? Because I'm not very good at translation. I don't want to mislead you."

Kate paused again. "No, they didn't. Okay."

She handed the phone back to Brody.

"Did that help?" he asked Will.

"Oh, man," Will said.

"In a good way or a bad way?"

"Ceci."

"You do realize that wasn't an answer."

"It's not Ceci, it's C E S I." There was stark astonishment in Will's voice.

"That made even less sense." Brody wished he could reach through the phone line and shake Will's brain back to life.

"CESI isn't a woman, it's an acronym. It stands for Cryptography Enabled Steganography Instances."

"Was that English?"

"Steganography hides messages inside other objects. Cryptography encrypts those messages."

"What kind of messages?"

"Any kind of message." Will's level of excitement was clearly growing. "Any kind of data."

A lightbulb went off inside Brody's brain. "Kozak wants to use 'Blue Strata Combat' to move secret data, hidden data."

"That would be my guess," Will said.

"To millions of computers worldwide?"

"Yes. Do you have any idea what this could be?"

An unnerving picture was forming in Brody's mind. "Through millions of servers, into countless countries."

"This is way above my pay grade."

"Could it be financial data?" Brody's astonishment and worry were both growing as the moments passed. This had to go far beyond stealing computer gaming code.

"It could be financial," said Will. "Or something even more sinister. It could be trade secrets, or even military secrets."

"Are we talking national security?" Brody asked.

"You need to get back here," Will said. "We have to call FBI Cyber Crimes."

"I'm not leaving Kate."

Brody's words caught her attention. Worry was etched in her face.

"You should get Kate and Annabelle out of the house as soon as you can."

"Agreed," Brody said. He wasn't leaving them in danger any longer.

Kate tried to quell her nerves as she packed a diaper bag for Annabelle. It was barely five in the morning, so they'd be gone long before Quentin woke up. But she couldn't quell her nervousness.

She wasn't taking much. If they got caught leaving, she wanted her story of taking Annabelle for a drive to put her back to sleep to sound plausible. And she could buy anything they needed in the short term.

As soon as Quentin was arrested, she'd try for temporary custody of Annabelle. Once she had that, she was taking the baby to Seattle. Annabelle would be safe there. She'd be safe and she would be happy.

Kate zipped up the bag, afraid to believe it might be almost over.

She slung it over her shoulder and took Annabelle in her arms, stopping at the kitchen for a bottle. Brody was moving the car seat to his car and would meet them out front.

Annabelle whimpered as they made their way down the stairs.

"Shhh," Kate whispered. "We'll get you a bottle, honey. It's coming right up."

Kate removed a bottle from the fridge and warmed it in the microwave. While she waited, every sound seemed magnified. She imagined she could hear Brody's car out front, and Annabelle's soft cries seemed to echo in the room. The microwave's beeps sounded piercing sharp.

"You're not nearly so sexy with a baby weighing you down."

Kate cringed at the tone of Rex's voice.

"I'm not trying to look sexy," she said, trying to sound casual.

"Going somewhere?"

"For a drive. Annabelle's fussy, and it quiets her down."

Rex moved closer. "Doesn't a bottle usually work?"

"Sometimes. But a drive works better."

Kate tested the formula temperature on her wrist. Thankfully, it was just right. While she'd prayed Annabelle would stay quiet, she now wished the baby would make some noise. It would add credibility to her story about going for a drive.

"Thing is," Rex said. "You don't have a car."

His words flustered her, and she hesitated. It was just for a moment, but she could tell it was enough to raise his suspicions.

"Brody offered to drive," she said, collecting the baby, her supplies and moving for the door.

"What's Brody doing here?"

"I…I…"

Rex's eyes narrowed.

"I slept with him," she blurted out. "I slept with Brody. That's why he's here in the morning."

"Why don't I believe you?"

She tried a pout. "Why would I lie about that?"

Rex gave his head a slow shake. "I don't know."

She tried to intimidate him. "Who I sleep with is no concern of yours."

"Maybe not," he said, stepping fully into the center of the door, blocking her path. "But what goes on in this house is my business."

"Sex doesn't normally go on in this house?" She tried to be sarcastic.

"People don't normally leave with Quentin's daughter."

Kate's stomach lurched. What did Rex know? What did he suspect?

"I say we go talk to Quentin," he said.

"Quentin's asleep." She could feel her courage deserting her. Her heart rate was spiking and her mouth had turned dry.

"We'll wake him up," suggested Rex.

"We shouldn't do that."

"Oh, I think we should." Rex's hand clamped onto her arm.

There was no way to fight him off, not with her holding Annabelle. She scrambled for the right action. Should she try to make a run for it, should she yell, or should she brazen it out and hope Quentin fell for the story?

He normally didn't care what went on with Annabelle as long as it didn't cause him any trouble. If she held off on the bottle a few more minutes, Annabelle would start crying. Quentin hated it when Annabelle cried. He'd agree to anything so long as Kate was taking her out of earshot.

"Fine," she said, giving him a defiant look. "Let's wake Quentin up. But you better be ready to tell him it was your great idea."

Rex tugged on her arm, urging her down the hall.

"You can let me go," she said.

"I don't think so."

He marched her up the stairs and down the hall to the master bedroom.

He banged on the door. "Quentin?"

Annabelle started to cry.

"Shhh," Kate said automatically. But she was secretly cheering for the baby's lungs.

The door flung open, and Quentin appeared. "What the hell is going on out here?"

"Kate is taking Annabelle," Rex said.

"For a drive," Kate quickly put in.

"With Brody." Rex frowned.

"What the hell time is it?" Quentin bellowed.

Annabelle cried louder.

There was a sudden commotion on the first floor. There were loud shouts and running feet. It took Kate a second for the words to make sense.

"FBI! FBI! Everybody out where we can see you!"

Before she could react, Rex shoved her through the bedroom door and locked it behind them.

"What are you doing?" she demanded. She looked to Quentin, hoping against hope he would intervene. Surely he cared about the safety of his own daughter.

Then Rex pulled a gun from beneath his shirt and trained it on her. She automatically turned to protect Annabelle.

"What on earth is going on?" Her voice quavered with fear.

"You tell me," Quentin shouted.

"I don't know." Kate was becoming terrified.

Where was Brody? Was he going to be able to help her?

"Start talking," Rex growled.

"I don't know what's going on," Kate cried. "Put down the gun. You might hurt Annabelle."

"Annabelle is the least of your worries," Rex said.

Kate held the baby closer to her chest.

Annabelle kept crying.

"She knows," Rex said to Quentin.

"I don't know anything," Kate said.

Somebody banged loudly on the bedroom door. "FBI. Everybody out. Hands in the air."

"We have a baby in here," Rex shouted back.

The door burst open, and two armed men entered the room.

Rex grabbed Kate and pushed the gun to her chest.

"Let Annabelle go," Kate pleaded. "Just let me put her down on the bed."

"No," Rex growled.

"Quentin," Kate pleaded. "She's your daughter. Please don't let her get hurt."

Quentin looked like he was making up his mind.

"Quentin!" She couldn't believe he was hesitating.

"Quiet, ma'am," one of the officers ordered sharply.

Kate's panic was rising. She couldn't think straight. She didn't know what to do. She couldn't just stand here with Annabelle's life in danger.

"Take me," she told Rex. "You don't need Annabelle."

"Shut her up," Quentin demanded.

"I can give her the bottle," Kate said. "Let me put her on the bed. She can have the bottle. Then she'll keep quiet."

"Quiet, ma'am," the officer ordered again.

Kate wasn't inclined to listen to him. He wasn't likely to shoot her. Rex just might.

"We're walking out of here," Rex spat.

"We can't let you do that," the officer said.

"You can't stop me. Come on, Quentin."

"We have a search warrant for the premises," the officer said. "Are you Quentin Roo?"

"And we have hostages." Rex sneered at the man.

"Let them go," the other officer said.

Kate knew she was probably losing it, but she couldn't help but think it was about time they made that suggestion. Shouldn't that have been the first thing they said? Please let go of the nice hostages?

Rex started to push her toward the door.

"No closer," the officer ordered.

Rex ignored him.

Quentin moved in. He reached for Annabelle.

"No," Kate moaned, clasping the baby tighter.

"Give her to me," Quentin said.

"No. You can't."

"She's my daughter." He pulled hard, and Kate was terrified.

A split second later, Annabelle was in Quentin's arms. Rex had Kate held tight, and they were moving toward the door.

She stared at the officers. Surely, they wouldn't let them past. They'd do something, disarm Rex or shoot him or something.

"Out of the way," Rex shouted. "Get back!"

Annabelle's cries reached a new decibel.

"Shut up," Quentin muttered to the baby.

When the FBI agents stepped aside, Kate's terror rose to a whole new level.

Rex forced her down the stairs. The four made their way through the entry hall and out the front door.

There, they were surrounded by a dozen armed officers.

"Give yourselves up," someone shouted over a megaphone. "There's nowhere to go."

"What do we do?" Quentin asked Rex.

"Let us go," Kate said.

"Shut up," Rex demanded. "We'll take your car," he said to Quentin.

"There's no way out," the megaphone man said.

"They've blocked the driveway," Quentin said.

"We've got hostages," Rex called out and kept walking.

Suddenly, Brody was standing in front of them. "Release them."

"I should have known," Rex said. "There was always something off about you. Didn't I tell you that?" he asked Quentin. "FBI?" he asked Brody.

"No," Brody said. "But give me Annabelle and let Kate go."

"Not a chance."

"The only way out of here is through me."

"My pleasure."

"That's murder," Brody said calmly. "You want to be arrested for corporate espionage or murder. You want a white-collar prison or the death penalty?" He looked to Quentin. "You'll be charged, too."

"Big talk," Rex sputtered.

Brody didn't move a muscle. "I'm not bluffing. Let her go, or shoot me. It's one or the other."

Rex aimed his gun at Brody.

"Brody, no." Kate was overcome with sheer, blind panic.

She saw Rex's face, and she knew in her soul that he was going to shoot Brody. Brody was going to die right here on the front steps.

Before she could even think about it, she was pushing Rex with all her might. A shot rang out. Brody lunged forward. He grabbed Annabelle from Quentin's arms.

"Down," he screamed at Kate.

The world went into slow motion. She looked straight in his eyes, and did exactly as he asked. She dropped down, lying flat on her stomach while Brody covered Annabelle with his body.

More shots echoed.

She covered her ears, and squeezed her eyes shut.

"Kate." It was Brody's voice. His hand touched hers. "Kate."

She blinked to find him lying beside her, Annabelle still crying in his arms.

"I have her bottle," she said.

"Are you all right?" he asked.

She nodded. She was sore, but she didn't think she was injured. "Is it over?"

"It's over."

"Are they…" She swallowed, looking around at the chaos. She couldn't finish the sentence.

"Don't worry about it right now. Don't look back. Don't look at anything." He led her up the front steps. "Just focus on the house, Kate. And hand me the bottle."

Eleven

The hotel had brought a crib up to Brody's suite, and Annabelle was now sound asleep. It had been a long day. He and Kate had given statements to the FBI, who had picked Kozak up at the airport. There they'd also arrested Bert and Ernie who'd come to meet him.

Will was now working with the FBI IT experts, determining the extent of the theft from Shetland Technologies and whether or not they'd managed to use the cryptography enabled steganography to commit any other crimes.

Brody wanted nothing more than to be here with Kate and Annabelle. He carried two snifters of cognac to the sofa where she was curled up.

"Kate, you holding up okay?" he asked, handing one to her.

She didn't answer, and she didn't take the drink, so he set it down on the coffee table in front of her.

"It may take a while," he said, sitting down beside her.

She was silent for a moment more. "I can't believe it's over."

"It's over."

"He was going to shoot you."

"I don't think so."

Her voice rose. "Did you see his expression, his eyes? I saw it in his eyes, Brody. Rex was going to shoot you point-blank."

Brody leaned across her knee to pick up the glass. This time when he handed it to her, she took it.

"It's over," he repeated with finality, and he clinked his snifter to hers.

She stared into space.

"You should drink now," he told her.

She took a sip. "You just stood there, a great big target only five feet away. You wouldn't move."

"I wasn't about to let him take you and Annabelle."

"But he had a gun." She waved the glass. "The cops. They were smart. They let him by. But you... You..."

"The cops don't know you the way I do."

She gave him a quizzical look, but he wasn't ready to elaborate on that statement.

He swallowed some of his cognac. It tasted good going down. "You were smart to push him off balance."

"I had to do something. He was going to kill you, Brody. I'm positive of that, and there's nothing you can say to change my mind."

"Okay. He was going to kill me."

For some reason, that seemed to satisfy her. She turned on the sofa, coming up on her knees. "You saved my life. You saved Annabelle's life."

"Listen, we can talk about this as long as you like, or as long as you need to in order to feel better. But I did what I had to do, and so did you, and everybody is okay. Well, everybody that counts, anyway."

She paused. But then her shoulders dropped, and the intensity went out of her expression.

"We can stop talking about it now," she said.

He was dying to touch her, so he smoothed back her hair. "We've got the emergency custody hearing tomorrow afternoon."

She trapped his hand and kissed his palm. "Thanks to you."

He set down his glass. "It was nothing. You deserve Annabelle, and Annabelle deserves you. Quentin is gone from her life."

Kate's hand started to shake, and Brody took her glass, setting it next to his on the table.

"I can't believe he's dead," she said in a quiet voice.

"It's sad. It didn't have to happen like that."

She nodded. "I hope Annabelle won't have any memories of what had happened."

"She won't. She's so young."

"I shouldn't repeat it now that Rex is dead, but I really didn't like that man."

Brody leaned in, pulled her forward and kissed the top of her head. "You must be tired."

"I'm numb."

"Let's go to bed." He realized he was sounding and acting presumptuous. "I mean, I can convert the sofa and sleep out here, if you'd rather."

She tipped her head to look up at him, giving a ghost of a smile. "We can share the bed. I'd like to share the bed."

"Good." He wasn't near ready to let her go.

He rose and held out his hand to her, walking her into the bedroom where he pulled back the quilt. They both took off their clothes and climbed in.

He drew her into his arms, and she was asleep in moments.

He gazed at her pink cheeks, her cute little nose and the dark eyelashes resting against her skin. He touched her crazy purple hair and smiled. She'd done that for Annabelle, for a niece she'd never even met. She'd chopped off her hair and walked boldly into Quentin Roo's stronghold and took him on.

With all the dysfunctionality in her upbringing, with her estrangement from her sister, she'd still stepped up.

He couldn't help comparing Kate's family to his own. The Calders weren't as close as some, and they'd had their share of scandal and betrayal in past generations, but he liked to think he'd do anything for his brother, Blane.

The family was small right now. His father had only one sibling. A sister, and she'd died in a horseback riding accident in her twenties. She hadn't married and had no children.

Brody's father was late to marry, and his grandparents had passed away a few years back. Brody and his brother, Blane, were now the future of the Calder dynasty. They were expected to marry and produce heirs, and that was fine with Brody.

He'd always looked forward to children. He'd decided a long time ago to have as many as he could. But having children meant finding a woman willing to take him on.

Up to now, he hadn't found the time to focus on that facet of his life. He'd dated, and there was no shortage of women with a romantic notion of what it meant to marry into the Calder family. Some of them seemed like wonderful people. But it wasn't just a matter of compatibility. It was no small thing for anyone to take on the demands of joining the nobility.

As the second son, his social obligations were far less intense than his brother's. But given Blane's health problems, Brody expected to spend a considerable amount of time supporting Blane. His future wife would have to be prepared for the reality of that life.

Aside from the complications of his family, the past few years had been focused on business. If he couldn't save the family fortune, there'd be nothing to pass on to any children of his or of Blane's.

He realized he ought to share the good news. He calculated the time zone difference, and guessed Blane would be up and around.

He dialed the number and let it ring.

He was about to give up when the line connected.

"Brody?" To his surprise, it was his mother's crisp voice.

"Hello, Mother." He kept his voice low so he wouldn't disturb Kate. He couldn't help but feel disappointed. He'd wanted Blane to be the first to hear the news.

"Blane can't talk right now, Brody." She seemed annoyed about something.

"Are you sure?" Brody was certain Blane would want to interrupt anything he might be doing for this. But he didn't want to tell his mother it was important, because she'd ask to hear the news herself.

"Give me the phone." Blane's voice was faint in the background.

"Is he with you?" Brody was surprised his mother would scoop Blane's phone right from under his nose. That was high-handed even for her.

"He can't talk," his mother said in her most officious countess voice.

"Why not?"

"He's with the doctor."

Brody went on alert, sitting up straight, remembering his last conversation with Blane. "What doctor? Where are you?"

"We're at the hospital."

"Is it the cough?"

Kate blinked her eyes open.

"Sorry," he mouthed to her, regretting waking her.

"It's his lungs," said his mother. "They're doing tests."

There was coughing in the background.

"What kind of tests?" asked Brody, his attention turning fully to the phone call.

"We'll know more when they're done. It might be congestion, or there might be deterioration."

"Deterioration of his lungs?" Brody's worry was now in full force.

"Give me the—" Blane's voice turned to coughing again.

Brody met Kate's eyes.

"I'll call you back," his mother said.

"But—"

"They say we'll know more later tonight," she said.

"Call me as soon as you know anything at all."

"I will. But since you're not here…"

Guilt spiked in Brody. "What I'm doing here is important, Mother."

"Maybe so."

Blane spoke in the background again. "Mother, don't."

"As you say," she said to Brody.

"Call me," he reminded her.

"Fine."

The conversation ended.

Kate moved into a sitting position "Who was that?"

"My mother."

"Something's wrong." It wasn't a question.

"My brother, Blane," said Brody, staring at his phone.

"Is he ill?"

"Yes. He has a condition called Newis Bar Syndrome. It's a rare neuromuscular disease."

She dipped her head to his shoulder and gave him a gentle kiss. "I'm so sorry to hear that."

"He may have developed a complication."

"Oh, Brody."

"Deterioration of his lungs." Brody could barely say it out loud. It sounded very serious, even critical.

His brother couldn't be critically ill. Blane had an important future. He had to inherit the earldom. He had to get married, have children, produce the new viscount and other heirs.

Kate shifted next to Brody, wrapping her hand around his arm and leaning in close. "Is there anything I can do?"

"No. Not tonight. I know he's getting the very best care. I wanted to tell him about Shetland Tech." Brody had looked forward to telling Blane directly. "Maybe I should have told my mother. The good news might give him a lift."

Kate tucked her arms around his neck and just stayed there, silently holding him close. After her traumatic day, he found it nothing short of amazing that she had it in her to comfort him.

He hugged her back, burying his face against her fragrant hair and closing his mind to everything but the peace she seemed to bring to his world.

Her small body curled against him, soft and yielding. He held her close, feeling her heartbeat, his chest hollowing out with emotion. He touched her face. Then he gave in and kissed her neck.

She smoothed her palm over his cheek, then she cradled his face, drawing back, gazing deeply into his eyes. He willed her lips to his, and she moved toward him, her kiss a gentle whisper of empathy.

He kissed her back, then again, and again. Desire flowed through him like honey.

"Is this okay?" he whispered.

"Yes," she returned, her kisses growing deeper. "It's…" She arched against him. "Good."

He splayed a hand across her back, turning her into the soft bed. Her crazy hair stood out against the white pillow, her breasts rose and fell with her breaths, her pink nipples beautiful in the dim light. He loved her breasts. They were soft, smooth coral-tipped wonders. He loved her neck, her stomach, her face. He could have gazed at her for eternity.

Desire, tenderness and hope all rose within him, neutralizing the exhaustion of the day.

He kissed her, then he kissed her again, then he deepened the kiss and let her essence fill him.

"You aren't too tired, are you?" He didn't want to be selfish. She'd been through enough.

"Don't stop," she whispered.

He moved on top of her, skin to skin. He ran his hand from her shoulders down her back, to her hips and bottom, pulling her intimately against him.

"Oh, Brody."

"You bring out the best in me, Kate." His kisses roamed her neck and her bare shoulder, moving to the softness of her breasts.

"I need you," he rasped.

"You've got me. Please make love to me."

He'd never heard sweeter words. He eased her thighs apart, pressing slowly inside, drinking in every inch, every second as her heat surrounded him. And then he was inside her, rocking against her, kissing her tenderly, and feeling her heartbeat sync with his.

He closed his eyes and gave himself over to sensation. He could hear her breaths and her small moans. He could smell her scents, fresh and floral, deep and earthy. She was soft to his hard, gentle to his harsh.

He rode the sweet rhythm, until the waves grew larger, their crests going higher. He tried to hang on, never wanting the feeling to end.

But sweat broke out on his body. His muscle fibers tightened their way to the breaking point. He couldn't slow down. He had to speed up.

"Yes," she cried against his mouth. "Just...like..." Her body contracted around him, and he roared his way to paradise.

It was early.

Kate was sated and content in Brody's arms. The sun was barely filtering through the sheers on the hotel window. They had minutes, maybe seconds until Annabelle woke up.

Annabelle was an early riser, but a happy one.

"Did you know this could happen to your brother?" she asked Brody.

His brother's health scare was their one immediate worry.

"I didn't expect it." Brody was behind her, his body spooning hers, his arms wrapped around her. "There are dozens of potential complications. This is the first time it's hit his lungs."

"It must have been hard." She toyed with his fingers where they lay against her stomach. "To leave when Blane was sick."

"It was. But I had no choice. And he was doing quite well last time I saw him." Brody paused. "But I was the one who put my family's fortune at risk. And it was up to me to fix it."

"How did you do it? How did you put it at risk?"

"You going to make me show you my weakness, aren't you?"

"I'm going to make you be honest."

"And if I'd rather not tell you? If I'd rather you thought of me as the brave and dashing hero who saved your life yesterday?"

"You're going to use that one for a long time to come, aren't you?"

He turned silent, and she regretted her words. They were too lighthearted for this conversation. And they were presumptuous. She was implying they'd be together for a while. He'd never suggested any such thing.

"I got into trouble because I got cocky," he said. "Blane and my father wanted to go into the hotel business. It's much safer, but the financial returns are low and a lot slower coming. We needed money right away, so I took a risk."

"And you lost the money?"

"Not at first. At first, I had some real success with software development. But I got carried away. I wanted to be the savior. I wanted Blane to be able to build his dream hotel and run it for years to come. I thought…"

Kate waited. "Thought what?"

"I thought if he could live his dream, his health might improve. I thought taking money worries off the table would allow him to get out and meet a great woman. But it had the opposite effect. When I lost the money, he worried even more."

"Did he meet a woman?" Kate hoped he had. If he was anything like Brody, he deserved to be happy.

"No. And now it may be too late."

She turned in Brody's arms. "Don't talk like that. They haven't found anything wrong with him yet."

"Except for Newis Bar Syndrome."

"Which he's had all along, and has nothing to do with anything you did or didn't do."

"It could be bad," he said.

She looked into his eyes. "And it could be nothing." She leaned across his chest and reached for his phone. "Call him again."

He accepted the phone but stared at it without dialing.

"Not knowing won't change anything," she said.

After a long moment, he pressed a number. Then he raised it to his ear.

It occurred to her that he might want privacy, so Kate started to rise. But he held her back.

"Stay right there," he said.

"Are you sure?"

"Yes." He slipped an arm around her shoulders and drew her close.

She settled in against him, trying not to feel too desperate about this stolen time together. Annabelle would wake soon, and they'd attend the custody hearing later today. Then Brody would return to Scotland. And Kate would go back to Seattle.

In the blink of an eye, this unexpected feeling of closeness would be nothing but a memory.

"Hey, Blane," Brody said.

Kate closed her eyes in relief. Then she let the timbre of his voice vibrate against her skin. She loved his voice.

"You feeling any better?" Brody asked.

Kate listened to his heartbeat, felt his chest rise and fall, smelled the tang of his sweat, and tasted the salt of his skin.

"They did?" Brody asked. He sounded relieved. "That's fantastic news. But don't go home too soon."

She couldn't help but smile.

Brody laughed. "You'll be dancing again in no time. But don't let Mother pick your suit." He paused. "I don't care if it's tradition. There'll be women there, eligible women. You need to look like you live in this century, not the last."

Brody absently stroked Kate's hair.

"You're a viscount, heir to an earldom. You're eligible already." He chuckled again. "You use what you've got, man."

Kate felt a sudden desire to meet Blane. It was clear the two brothers had a close relationship. Was he as smart and interesting as Brody? It was hard to imagine there were two such men in the world.

Then just as quickly as the idea had formed, it disappeared. She knew it would never happen.

"I have more good news," Brody said, pure joy evident in his tone. "Our cash flow problem is solved. It's a bit of a long story, one you don't have to worry about right now. But nobody will be illegally using our intellectual property."

Kate gave him a hug, remembering yesterday all over again, gratitude blooming inside her.

"I can, and I will," he said. "Soon. You rest and get better."

Brody signed off and set down his phone.

"That sounded good," she said.

"It was only congestion. His lungs are fine, and he's on the road to recovery."

"I'm so glad to hear that."

Brody slid down in the bed and cuddled her closer. "It's a huge relief."

They both lay quiet for a few minutes.

"They didn't know the details, did they?" she asked him. "Your family didn't know what you were doing over here."

If they'd known about Quentin, Brody's brother would surely have asked some far more specific questions.

"I didn't want to worry them all. There was nothing they could do, and I was hoping I could solve it before we went bankrupt."

"Bankrupt?"

"It was a possibility. If Beast Blue had made it to market first with their game, Shetland would have folded. And with the loan guarantees we signed, we'd have lost the castle."

She turned her head to look up at him. "I can't believe you have a castle."

"It's on the River Tay."

"It's a *castle*." Its location wasn't the most pertinent information as far as Kate was concerned. She was trying to come to grips with Brody's expansive lifestyle, his family, Brody himself.

"It's not as exciting as it sounds. It's old and pretty drafty. It's been in my family for twenty-two generations."

"I'm sorry, Brody. One more time. You have a castle?"

"We're the Scottish nobility, Kate. Everyone has a castle."

"I have a thousand-square-foot condo," she said, mustering up a faux note of superiority.

"You told me that." There was answering humor in his tone.

"It's been in my family for nearly a year."

"That's impressive."

"Well, half of it, anyway. My friend Nadia owns the other half."

"I bet it's not drafty."

"Tight as a drum."

"I'd like to see it sometime."

"Well, you coming to Seattle seems a lot more likely than me going to Scotland."

"I'm serious." He sat up. "It makes sense. I'll go with you and Annabelle to Seattle."

She couldn't tell if they were still joking. He seemed serious, but he wasn't making sense. "We don't need an escort. The danger is past."

As if hearing her name, Annabelle vocalized from her crib in the living room.

"I've become invested in the little tyke," he said. "I want to make sure she's in a good place. I'm definitely coming to the hearing."

"My condo is a good place. It might not be a castle, but it has everything she needs."

"I didn't mean it that way."

"What way did you mean it?"

"I want to make sure she stays with you."

Kate rose from the bed and retrieved one of the hotel robes, tightening it around her waist. "Is this because you changed her diaper?"

"I like to think we bonded over that."

She couldn't help injecting a note of teasing sarcasm. "You were definitely her knight in shining armor."

He got up and shrugged into the other robe. "A few generations ago. Yeah, I could have done that."

"Can you ride a horse?" she asked, moving into the living room to get Annabelle.

"I play polo," he called from behind her.

"Oooh, la di da. Hello, sweetheart," she crooned to a smiling Annabelle. "Uncle Brody is here to change your diaper."

"Walked right into that one, didn't I?"

"Yes, you did." Kate lifted Annabelle and handed her off to Brody.

Twelve

The more Brody thought about it, the better he liked the idea of going to Seattle. It would take Will a few more days to tie up loose ends in LA. They'd already put a team of lawyers on the case to make sure *i*'s were dotted and *t*'s crossed. It would take months for the techs to go through Beast Blue's code.

Brody could stay in LA until Will was done, or he could take a quick trip to Seattle, get Annabelle settled. Then he could come back to close things off before he returned to Scotland.

For today, he'd borrowed one of the lawyers at their newly engaged firm to help with Annabelle's case. Brody was encouraged by Kalvin Moran's youth. He knew the firm was anxious to please Shetland Tech, so if they'd put a junior associate onto Annabelle, that meant they expected it to be straightforward.

It was a small hearing room, with a single row of chairs behind the lawyer's tables.

"Ms. Dunhern is the child's aunt?" the judge asked Kalvin. "Yes."

"Is she the only known relative?"

"Mr. Roo's parents are deceased. He has a half brother who is currently incarcerated in Illinois."

The judge read a paper on her desk. "The child's grand-mother, Chloe Dunhern is—"

"Right here," came a smoke-husky voice from the back of the courtroom.

Brody turned along with everyone else to see a sixtysome-thing woman with spiky, dyed-blond hair walk shakily into the hearing room. She wore a pair of skintight black-and-white diamond-patterned slacks and a royal blue sleeveless sweater.

"Oh, no," Kate groaned beside him.

"I'm Annabelle's grandmother," she announced with a little wave.

"Mom, please," Kate said.

"Are you petitioning the court for custody?" the judge asked.

"Yes," Chloe Dunhern said. "Yes, that's right."

"You can't have custody, Mom."

"Hello, Kate. I don't see why not." Chloe pointed her finger. "You're just after the money."

"Please address me," the judge said.

"Yes, Your Honor," Chloe said. "Where do I sit?"

Kate leaned over to Kalvin. "Ask her if she's been drinking."

"She's not a witness," Kalvin said.

"Can you ask?"

Kalvin stood up. "Your Honor, can you ask Ms. Dunhern, Ms. Chloe Dunhern if she's been drinking?"

The judge's brows went up. "Ms. Dunhern, have you had anything to drink today?"

"Orange juice."

"Vodka," Kate whispered to Kalvin.

"Your honor, Ms. Dunhern has been known to drink vodka in her orange juice. Could we clarify if that's the case today?"

"Ms. Dunhern?" the judge asked.

"Yes?"

"Did you have vodka or any other alcohol in your orange juice."

"No."

"Breathalyzer," Kate whispered.

"Would Ms. Dunhern be willing to submit to a breathalyzer test?" Kalvin asked.

"Ms. Dunhern?" the judge asked.

"What about her?" Chloe asked, pointing at Kate while holding the back of a chair for support. "Nobody's asking Kate to take a breathalyzer."

Kalvin looked to Kate.

Kate nodded. "You bet."

"I'm ordering a breathalyzer test for both petitioners," the judge said.

"Well," Chloe said. "Well, in that case…" She seemed uncertain about what to do.

"Mom, we've talked about this," Kate said, sounding carefully patient.

"We didn't agree on anything," Chloe said.

"We did agree, Mom. You're busy. You're tired. Annabelle will be a lot of work."

"I…" Chloe didn't seem to have an answer for that.

"Can we talk later?" Kate asked.

Chloe looked around at the participants, seeming to be making up her mind. "I don't need a breathalyzer." She stated emphatically. Then she turned and walked from the room.

"That's my mother," Kate said helplessly.

There was a moment of dazed silence.

"Your Honor," Kalvin continued, regrouping. "Other than, uh, Chloe Dunhern, Kate Dunhern is the child's only known relative. She's a teacher in the Seattle public school system. She owns residential real estate in Seattle. We've submitted work and personal references, along with her credit report. She has no criminal record, and is willing and able to care for Annabelle on an immediate and emergency basis."

The judge looked at Kate. "Have you had anything to drink today?"

"No, Your Honor."

"What is your average weekly consumption of alcohol?"

"Two to three drinks."

"Ever in the morning?"

"Only on Christmas Day. A mimosa with brunch."

"Very well." The judge brought down her gavel. "I've reviewed all the submitted documentation, including the police reports, and grant temporary custody of Annabelle Dunhern to Kate Dunhern."

Brody gave Kate's hand a quick squeeze.

"Thank you," she said to Kalvin.

"Happy to help out."

Brody shook Kalvin's hand. "Thanks."

"My pleasure, sir." Kalvin shut his briefcase and took his leave.

Brody pulled Kate into a hug. "Well done."

"You mean my not drinking in the mornings?"

"That little fact didn't hurt your case."

"That was so embarrassing."

"It was interesting to meet your mother. Whatever else she did, she raised a wonderful daughter."

"That's a very nice thing to say."

"I mean it." Brody put a hand on the small of her back as they walked from the hearing room. "Now, what should we do first? Plane tickets, baby gear, lawyer's office?"

Kate had already said she didn't want to go back to the mansion to pick up any of Anabelle's things. She had Anabelle and the chickadee necklace, and that was all she wanted. She was after a fresh start, and Brody didn't blame her.

"You don't need to babysit me, Brody."

"That's not what I'm doing."

"You must have things to do."

"I have a lot of things to do. But what I want to do is help you. Let's start with a lawyer."

"We just finished with a lawyer."

"That was step one. Next you need to hire someone to represent Annabelle's interests."

"They told me she'd have a court-appointed advocate."

"You still need a lawyer. It's going to be a complicated estate."

"What about Kalvin?"

"He's a junior associate, and Beast Blue is worth millions."

Brody couldn't help but wonder if Annabelle might be better served by someone more experienced. But it wasn't his decision. Kate's comfort level was what counted.

"I liked him."

"He is backed by a solid firm. So he would have the more senior partners to support him."

"We could ask him if he's interested."

Brody couldn't imagine any circumstance under which Kalvin wouldn't be interested. "Okay. Let's see if we can catch him in the lobby."

Kate was relieved to finally be home.

Nadia greeted them at the door, oohing and aahing over Annabelle, giving Kate a warm hug, and politely greeting Brody who carried in armloads of baby paraphernalia.

"Will you come to Auntie Nadia?" she cooed to Annabelle.

Annabelle looked perplexed for a moment, but then smiled. Kate handed her over.

"We're going to get along just fine," Nadia singsonged as she wandered away. "Do you want to see the kitchen?"

"Anywhere in particular I should put all this?" Brody asked.

"In the living room, I guess." Kate's condo suddenly felt small. "The bedrooms are upstairs, and there's room in the basement for storage. But I can see this is going to take some organizing."

"You're here," he said. "That's what counts."

Kate blew out a big breath of relief. "I'm here. And Annabelle's here. And everything else will work itself out."

Nadia reappeared. "Are you staying in Seattle?" she asked Brody.

There was something funny in her tone, but Kate couldn't put her finger on it.

"For a few days," Brody said.

"Downtown?"

Brody hesitated.

Kate realized they hadn't talked about where he'd stay. They'd spent the last three nights in his hotel suite. They'd slept together there—partly because there'd only been one bed, but mostly because their physical attraction had shown no signs of fading.

She wondered if she should ask him to stay at the condo. Should they continue to sleep together?

"I was going to check for a hotel nearby," he put in

smoothly. Unless a person had been looking for it, the pause in the conversation was barely noticeable.

"The Seabreeze is about ten minutes away," Nadia said.

"I'll check them out." He set the packages down on the sofa.

"Good idea."

His expression was puzzled for a few seconds while he looked at Nadia. But then it softened, and he turned his attention to Kate. "Do you want to shop later on? You'll need a crib right away."

"Yes," Kate said, enthusiastically. "Are you going to be around this afternoon?" she asked Nadia.

"I can be here for this one." She gave Annabelle some mini kisses on her fingers, and Annabelle laughed.

"If I get Annabelle down for her nap before we go, do you mind watching her?"

"Not at all."

"It'll be a big help to pick up a few things right away."

"In the meantime," Brody said. "I'll go check out the hotel."

"Are you sure?" Kate asked. She felt like she was rushing him out the door. "Are you hungry? I can make us something for lunch."

"Don't worry about me." He gave her a squeeze on the shoulder. "I'll call you in a while."

"Okay."

It felt strange to have him leave. They'd been together pretty much constantly since the FBI raid. She realized she was coming to depend on him.

When the door closed behind him, she felt strangely alone.

"Tell me everything." Nadia pushed aside the bags, packages and boxes, and sat down on the sofa, settling Annabelle on her lap.

Kate perched on an armchair. "I don't even know where to start."

"Start with Brody. Who is he, and what's his angle?"

"What kind of a question is that? He doesn't have an

angle." Kate found herself looking to the front door where Brody had left.

"I don't trust him."

"Why on earth not?"

"He came out of nowhere."

"He came from Scotland."

"And now he's here?"

"He's helping. He's been terrific, Nad. He changes diapers and everything."

"And you don't find that odd?"

"It's not odd. What are you getting at?"

Nadia lifted Annabelle so that she was standing on her lap. Annabelle reached out to grab Nadia's nose.

"You said Quentin stole from him," Nadia said.

"He did. And—I hate to say it, because it sounds terrible—I'm glad he did. If it hadn't been for that, we'd still be in LA in that horrible mansion with those awful people, and I might be fighting a losing battle to get Annabelle."

"You don't think he's ticked about that?" Nadia asked, her focus still on the baby.

"You mean ticked at Quentin?" Kate wasn't following.

"At anybody who has anything to do with Quentin."

"You mean me?" The question didn't make sense.

Brody wasn't angry with Kate. Quite the opposite. He seemed to like her a lot, quite a lot, and he'd been nothing but helpful and supportive.

"From what you've said, he's stuck to you like glue since he found out you were going for custody."

"We've been in danger. It was real."

Sympathy and concern immediately flooded Nadia's expression, and she finally looked at Kate. "I know. I'm so glad everything turned out okay."

"Thanks to Brody." Kate couldn't believe she was having to defend him.

"I'm not saying he wasn't brave."

"He stood in front of a bullet for me."

"Earning your undying trust."

Kate came to her feet. "I don't understand what you're saying. It wasn't a ploy." The idea that Brody had risked his life to get her to trust him was preposterous.

"Tell me about the lawyer," Nadia said a little more softly.

"Kalvin? I like him a lot. He's young, but he's eager. And he's got a lot of support from the senior partners. They all came to the meeting, as well."

"And Brody introduced you to him?"

Kate did a double take of her friend. "I picked him. Brody would have supported anyone I chose."

"So he made you think."

"Good grief, Nad. You've been reading way too many conspiracy theories."

"Your lawyer is from a firm that represents Shetland Tech."

"They're a very highly respected firm. They represent a lot of clients."

"But Shetland Tech and Beast Blue Designs are competitors."

"Quentin was the crook," Kate said.

"He did crooked things. Absolutely. And I'm perfectly glad he's gone. But things linger, Kate."

"Whatever you're getting at, just spit it out."

"What I'm getting at is Brody and his company, Shetland Tech, have an innate conflict of interest in helping Annabelle because she will inherit Beast Blue Designs. That conflict extends to you as her legal guardian."

Kate stilled, parsing through the statement. "He's not thinking that way."

"I can guarantee he is. Consider it, Kate. A rich Scottish royal suddenly romancing you."

"Who said he was romancing me?"

Nadia coughed out a laugh of disbelief. "The expressions on both of your faces. It's plain as day that you're sleeping with him."

Kate considered denying it, but realized it was pointless to lie. "What if I am?"

"Oh, Kate."

"Don't 'oh, Kate' me. It's a fling. He's hot. I've had flings before."

"He's staying close to you and gaining your trust to benefit his corporation."

"I don't buy that." Kate refused to believe Brody would be so callous. She moved directly to the kitchen. She was thirsty, so she opened the fridge to look for a pitcher of iced tea.

Nadia followed, carrying Annabelle. "Please, just listen, Kate. You tell him you're going for custody. He knows about Quentin's crimes, so he knows you're going to win custody of Annabelle. And suddenly, of all the women in the world that Scotland's most eligible bachelor can be with, he chooses you?"

"Thanks a lot. Want some? And what makes you say he's Scotland's most eligible bachelor?"

"You're welcome. Yes. And I did a thorough search on him, and there's a reputable magazine that officially named him Scotland's most eligible bachelor."

Kate set two tall glasses on the counter. She didn't know why she was surprised. Brody would be a great catch. He was hot, wealthy and titled to boot. He was funny and smart, and he was amazing in bed. Word might have gotten around about that.

She poured the iced tea.

"I don't like the look on your face," Nadia said.

"I don't have a look on my face."

"Where do you think this is going?"

"Nowhere. It's nothing. He's here for a few days, and then he's got some wrap-up in LA, and then he's going back to Scotland. Where he has a brother. Who is going to be the earl. And who, by the way, is probably a more eligible bachelor than Brody."

"What's he wrapping up in LA?"

"The Beast Blue thing. They need to pull all the code from 'Blue Strata Combat'."

Nadia took one of the glasses. Her tone went softer. "Which will do what?"

"Give Brody's family back their rightful property." Kate took a drink, soothing her parched throat.

"What will it do to Beast Blue Designs?"

Kate hadn't thought about that. "It'll hurt the company for sure."

"It'll destroy the company. He may bankrupt Annabelle's company."

"It's not—"

"But it is. And he doesn't know what you'll do. You might fight for Annabelle's interests. You *should* fight for Annabelle's interests. And that would be counter to Brody's interests."

Kate pulled up a stool at their small breakfast bar. "It's not like that."

But she was trying to figure out what it was like. What was Brody planning? Was he worried she'd make some kind of a move to protect Beast Blue? He didn't need to worry. She didn't have the first idea of what that move might be.

Nadia took the stool beside her. "Shetland Tech could easily bankrupt Beast Blue. They probably will, and then Annabelle will have nothing."

"Annabelle doesn't need anything." Kate reached out and took Annabelle's little hand. "She has me. She doesn't need anything else."

"But Brody doesn't know that."

"He trusts me."

"He could be hedging his bets."

Kate refused to believe Brody was being manipulative. "He stood in front of a bullet for me. You didn't see it. Rex was absolutely going to shoot him."

"Maybe," Nadia said. "If you're right, then that's terrific, and he's an exceptional man. I'm just saying be careful. There's a lot at stake, and you're a babe in the woods."

"Your confidence in me is inspiring."

"I love you, Kate. But I've got to be honest. You need to go into this with your eyes wide-open."

"I will," Kate said.

She believed in Brody. Everything he'd done so far seemed to be for her well-being and Annabelle's. But she couldn't deny that Nadia had made some good points. Brody was a highly successful and eligible man who could have any woman in the world. Did it make any sense at all that he'd fall for Kate?

"Love the hair, by the way," Nadia said.

Kate's hand went to her short locks. Would the son of an earl honestly opt for a woman with purple hair?

Thirteen

Brody picked Kate up in his rental car, taking her to a nearby shopping mall while Annabelle napped and Nadia babysat. Kate had talked a lot about Nadia their past few days in LA. She made her friend sound intelligent, open and friendly.

That sure wasn't the vibe Brody was picking up. She seemed impatient and resentful. It was clear she loved babies, so it wasn't the introduction of Annabelle into their lives. It was equally clear she was suspicious of Brody.

She and Kate were obviously close. Maybe it was as simple as wanting to reconnect with Kate and settle into their new life without Brody around to get in the way. He had to admit, it was a reasonable thing to want.

He and Kate were strolling through the baby section of a department store. They'd picked a crib with a top safety rating, and they were now looking at blankets and something called bumper pads which apparently protected babies from the dangers of top safety rated cribs.

"I was thinking," he opened.

Kate stopped to look at a puffy blanket with an elephant pattern. "About?"

"About how long I should stay."

She turned to look at him. "Do you need to go back to Scotland? Because I wouldn't want to keep you from your family."

He wasn't wild about her enthusiasm to get rid of him. He'd hoped she'd seem at least a little bit disappointed.

"It's not about getting back to Scotland," he said.

"Oh." She didn't ask him to elaborate.

He elaborated anyway. "I don't want to overstay my welcome."

"In America? Is there a visa thing?"

"In Seattle."

She looked puzzled. "I don't think anyone cares how long you stay in Seattle."

"What about Nadia?"

Kate's expression faltered and she went back to checking out the elephant quilt. "What does Nadia have to do with anything?"

"I bet this is a lot for her, with Annabelle coming home. I don't want to get in the way."

"What do you want?" Kate asked.

He could be honest about that. "What I want is to spend more time with you. But your feelings are more important than mine. You've been through a lot. Your life has drastically changed, and I don't want to make your life any more difficult."

At the same time, he couldn't deny he was worried about her. She'd been catapulted into a world of big money and big stakes, about to be put in de facto charge of a company that had committed a major crime.

Beast Blue had hundreds of employees. Who knew how many of them were involved, and how would she ever sort through the mess? Lawyers, accountants and technical specialists could only help so much. Ultimately, she was going to have to look after Annabelle's financial future.

"I want to help you," he said, reaching out to draw her into a loose embrace. "If you'll let me."

At first she was stiff in his arms. He chalked it up to them being in a public place. But then she relaxed and leaned into him.

"I don't want you to go yet," she said.

"Good. That's settled." He gave her a light kiss on the temple. "I'm going to miss you tonight."

She smiled. "Absence makes the heart grow fonder."

Then she seemed to realize what she'd said. Her smile disappeared, and her cheeks flushed. "I didn't mean. That is…"

"You didn't mean to make it sound romantic."

"Yes."

He knew what had her uncomfortable. It was preying on

his mind, as well. They didn't know what this was, or if it was anything. And he knew they weren't in a position to figure it out.

He tried to put her at ease by lightening the mood. "I supposed it can only be so romantic here in the linens section."

She didn't smile at his joke.

"I don't know what this is either, Kate."

He truly didn't. And he was starting to wonder. His feelings for her were beyond friendship and support. But they'd been thrown together under such bizarre circumstances, and their lives couldn't be further apart. Still, he seemed to be falling fast and hard. And he couldn't begin to guess how far it would go.

"It's a fling," she said. "It's a wonderful fling, and in some respects, it's so much more. You saving my life for instance, and you proving Quentin committed a crime so that I got custody of Annabelle. That's beyond your average fling."

"No kidding."

"But the you and me part, we're just two people sleeping together for a while."

He wasn't ready to accept that. But he wasn't ready to argue it, either.

"I wish we could do that tonight," he said instead.

"I have a baby to take care of."

"You do," he agreed, knowing they weren't going to solve this here and now. "And that baby needs blankets."

Kate laughed then, and he loved the sound of it.

His phone rang in his pocket, and he checked the screen.

"Will," he told her. "Hey," he answered.

"It's a mess," said Will.

"Is that a surprise?"

"It's worse than we expected."

"In what sense?"

"They can take care of the steganography. That never made it into the mainstream programming, and we don't have a national security issue. But the Shetland Tech code is everywhere. They've used it in a dozen programs. It'll take years to pull it all apart."

Kate had moved farther down the aisle, and Brody put some additional distance between them.

"We don't have years," he said to Will.

"I've made that abundantly clear."

"Good."

"But we're going to have to bring them down, Brody. Beast Blue will cease to exist."

"So I kill Annabelle's company."

"To save your family."

"That's a terrible choice," Brody said.

"It's no choice at all."

"I suppose not."

Brody's loyalty had to be to his family. And they weren't the ones who'd committed a crime. It might not be Annabelle's fault, but it was her father's doing, and her legacy turned out to be based on theft.

"What about the mansion? Has there been any talk of Quentin's personal assets?"

"He signed personal guarantees. It'll all get eaten up in the bankruptcy proceedings."

"Everything?" Brody hated that this was how it would go.

"You might be able to make a case for Francie's personal possessions."

"The jewelry?"

"They weren't married. They didn't live together. And she didn't sign any of the personal guarantees."

"Isn't that ironic."

Quentin had tried to protect his assets from Francie, and he ended up protecting Francie's assets instead.

"You want me to pick them up from the gatehouse?"

"Can you legally do that?"

"With Kate's permission, I can. But, one more thing."

Brody braced himself.

"Kate's mother will get half. Francie had some kind of old will that was written before Annabelle was born."

Brody almost laughed. "There's really no justice, is there?"

"You got justice for Shetland Tech."

"I suppose I did. I'll ask Kate."

"Let me know."

"Will do." Brody signed off and caught up to Kate.

"Everything okay?" she asked.

"It's progressing. It's going to be a long haul." He saw no reason to give her the bad news before it was concrete. "Will did have one question for you."

She gave Brody her attention. "What is it?"

"It'll make things easier if Francie's personal possessions are separated from the mansion's assets. He can pick up her jewelry if you'd like."

"You mean I'm getting the emeralds after all?"

"You are."

"Is it just me, or is that kind of funny?"

"I almost laughed. One glitch though. Your mother will get half."

Kate rolled her eyes. "Oh, good grief. They shouldn't go to either of us. They should go to Annabelle."

"I don't suppose suggesting that to your mother would help?" Brody was sure he knew the answer. The woman he'd seen in the courtroom wasn't about to give up a windfall.

"There's no point in even asking," Kate said. "She will be firmly convinced she's entitled."

"Maybe it'll keep her away." As soon as the words were out of his mouth, he rethought them. "I'm sorry. She's your mother."

"I'm not going to pretend to admire her now. Her staying away from Annabelle is the best outcome of this. If it costs us a few emeralds, so be it."

"That's the spirit."

"Now, help me with this. Elephants or bunnies?"

"The bunnies are adorable."

"I thought so, too."

He leaned down to whisper, letting his lips brush the shell of her ear. "And you're adorable."

"No," she said in a firm voice.

"No?"

"I'm not going to your hotel before we relieve Nadia. You can make it through one night on your own."

He wasn't so sure about that.

Then again, he had a lot to think about and a bunch of phone calls to make. Will was right. Brody had to protect his family's legacy.

Kate and Brody walked along the path on Sunday morning, pushing Annabelle in her new stroller. Families were picnicking, children were riding bikes, and dads and sons were playing catch. She'd never paid much attention to the activities in the park near her condo, but she realized now it was a hub of activity.

"I'm having a hard time picturing it," Kate said as she watched a little girl climb up the slide. "I mean, I can wrap my head around a baby, but I can't imagine Annabelle as a child. She'll go to school, maybe take dance lessons, or soccer or fencing. She might like fencing."

"Fencing?" Brody asked, pointing to a vacant bench.

Annabelle had fallen asleep, and now he parked the stroller, and they sat down to take in the sights.

"You never know what she might like. Whatever it is, I'll support it. I'm going to be a regular mom. I'm going to bake cookies for the bake sale, register her in swimming lessons, buy her ice cream at the zoo."

"All the things your own mother never did," Brody guessed.

"She's going to be happy," Kate said with conviction.

"You want some ice cream?" He pointed to a concession stand. "You've given me a craving."

"Sure." Kate leaned back and tipped her face up to the sunshine. She couldn't remember being this happy. "Make mine chocolate."

"You got it." Brody rose from the bench and walked across the path, weaving his way through the picnic tables.

She watched him, admiring his great looks, his height and confident stride.

He placed his order and then turned back to her. He smiled and waved, and her heart took a flip. If family life in suburbia was like this, she was going to love it. Annabelle at three, at six, and nine. Brody—

Her fantasy screeched to a halt.

Brody wasn't going to be there. Brody was only hers for a short while. Soon he'd get on a plane. He'd fly off to Scotland. He'd play polo, attend fancy balls, meet glamorous women and eventually produce the next generation of little earls to live in his big, drafty castle.

But that was his life, and it made sense for him. She and Annabelle were much better here, she told herself.

And, who knew, over time maybe Kate would meet a nice man, an accountant or an architect. She could get married and have some brothers and sisters for Annabelle.

She tried to picture her future husband, but Brody kept getting in the way. That was understandable, she told herself. Because he was walking this way, a smile on his face, two chocolate ice-cream cones in his hands.

It was impossible to plan beyond Brody. And why should she try? There was nothing wrong with enjoying this moment. She was under no illusions. She wouldn't get hurt when he left. Her heart wouldn't be broken, because she'd been prepared for the end before it had even happened.

"Chocolate all around," he said, handing her one of the cones before sitting back down beside her.

They both licked the melting edge of their ice cream.

"This is nice," Brody said, gazing around at the trees and flowers. "It's a lot like Scotland—like the cities, anyway. The countryside is wilder, more rugged."

"I've always lived in cities," she said.

"I went to university in Edinburgh, but I mostly grew up in the country."

"In a castle. I heard. You don't have to brag."

He chuckled. "Believe me, it's nothing to brag about."

"Sure, it is. What kid doesn't dream of being a prince or princess, of growing up surrounded by finery in a castle with a beautiful, kindly queen as a mother?"

"Was that your dream?" he asked.

"For a while. When I was nine." She wasn't going to lie. "I just knew I'd have a beautiful golden dress, and a little gold crown, and jeweled shoes."

"Jeweled shoes?"

"What? You don't have any jeweled shoes?"

"Since I'm not an entertainer in Vegas, no."

"Well, I would have had jeweled shoes. Like I said. When I was nine." She licked her ice cream.

"And afterwards? Or before? You obviously had other dreams."

"This," she said, scanning the scene in front of her. "This was my dream."

He smiled at that. "You're living your dream, Kate."

"At least for a little while."

He adjusted the hood on the stroller to block the sun from Annabelle. "For a long while, I think."

Kate didn't want to disagree. But her dream had included a husband. And she couldn't imagine where that might be in her future.

"What did I say?" he asked.

"Nothing." She shook off her mood.

He slid closer. "Seriously, Kate. What happened just then?"

She opened her mouth to lie. But then she caught his gaze with her own.

"I'm going to miss you." The truth came out before she could stop it.

His expression softened, his eyes going opaque. He touched his index finger to her chin. "I'm going to miss you, too."

Neither of them moved.

"How did this happen?" she asked.

"I have no idea," he said. "There I was, busy minding my own business."

"You were undercover investigating a crime."

"You were undercover saving a baby."

"One minute we were arguing," she said.

"And the next we discovered we had something in common."

"I don't want to sleep alone tonight," she said.

Brody looked concerned. "What would Nadia think?"

"It doesn't matter what Nadia thinks. I know what I think."

He gave a wry smile. "She might throw me out of the condo."

"Not if we go to your hotel."

Annabelle stirred in the stroller.

Brody's hand smoothed Kate's shoulder. "You are welcome in my hotel room anytime you want."

Fourteen

Brody awoke to Annabelle's coos. She was in a portable crib in the corner of the hotel room playing with her toes in the morning light.

He looked down at Kate sleeping beside him, and his chest contracted with emotion. She was right where she belonged. And so was he.

His phone rang, and he quickly scooped it up, hoping it wouldn't wake her.

He slipped from the bed and padded into the small living room, keeping his voice down.

"Hello?"

"It's Will."

"Morning." Brody checked out the coffeemaker to see if he could figure out how to make a pot.

"I've been up all night."

"Anything wrong?"

"No. I had an idea. Well, it was Kalvin's idea, but I agree with him."

"Okay." Brody managed to free the small coffeepot from the holder. He turned to the sink and filled it.

"Hear me out?"

"Sure."

"It's going to sound crazy."

"I'm half asleep, trying to work a hotel coffeemaker. Talk slow and use small words, and you'll probably be fine."

"Why don't you call room service?"

"Because I'm talking to you." Brody located a packet of Colombian coffee and tore it open.

"Okay, I'm going to plunge right in," Will said.

"You're not plunging very fast."

"Shetland Tech buys Beast Blue."

"What?" Brody spilled the coffee grounds. He cursed.

"You said you'd hear me out."

"I'm listening." There was another package in the service basket and he took it.

"You could get it for pennies on the dollar. It's all but worthless as it stands. If Shetland buys it, then it doesn't matter who stole what. We get our game 'Mercury Mayhem' to market first as planned. But then we follow it up with some of Beast Blue's games, then more of ours, and we own the space."

"We compete with ourselves."

"Yes."

Brody immediately thought of one complication. "Beast Blue employees are going to be hostile. And some of them had to know about the theft. I don't want a bunch of dishonest people working for me."

He pressed the switch on the coffeemaker and stood back.

"That would have to be part of the process, yes," Will said. "We'd identify those who were involved and fire them."

"Before they could do any damage?"

"Oh, yeah. There are ways to keep people contained in a technical environment. We lock it down, and keep people out until we've vetted them."

"These are very talented programmers. You don't think they might break in and cause trouble?"

"Are you questioning my technological savvy?"

"No. I'm just a cautious man."

"Who stands in front of bad guys pointing guns," Will said.

"We're going to stop talking about that now."

"Okay, boss. But what do you think of my idea?"

The aroma of coffee filled the air. Brody inhaled and turned over a cup.

"Is it even possible to do right now?" he asked. "They're not going to let Kate make such a far-reaching decision while she's only Annabelle's temporary guardian."

"She'd have to do it in conjunction with the executor and the advocate appointed by the court."

"The court-appointed advocate has that kind of power?"

"They have a vote. Kalvin says they can do this kind of thing in cases involving minors and money."

Brody took a mental step back. "So Annabelle would get something out of this. She might do okay?"

"That all depends on you. But for her any kind of a sale is better than bankruptcy."

Brody began to get excited. He poured himself a cup of coffee, taking a first sip as he walked away from the mess. He wanted his brain to be fully functional. If this worked, it could be a win-win.

"I'll talk to Kate and call you back," he said to Will.

"If she has any questions, loop me in."

"Thanks." Brody ended the call.

He could hear Kate moving in the bedroom, her soft voice as she talked to Annabelle. Taking another sip of coffee, he moved to the doorway. He leaned his shoulder on the doorjamb, watching her.

In a fluffy hotel robe, hair mussed, feet bare, she leaned into the crib and lifted Annabelle.

"Did you have a good sleep, darling?" she asked, rubbing her nose to Annabelle's.

"Bah," Annabelle said. "Bah, bah."

"You always make your point so eloquently. Are you hungry, or would you like a change first."

"Bah, bah." Annabelle batted at her cheek.

"Change it is. Between you and me, I think that's a good decision."

Kate caught sight of Brody, and she smiled. "Morning."

"Good morning to you, pretty ladies." He moved into the room and gave Kate a kiss. Then he rubbed Annabelle's hair and stroked his thumb across her soft cheek.

He felt like a very lucky man. He wished he could stop time and stay in this moment forever.

But he knew he couldn't. Since he couldn't keep them, the best he could do was protect them. And he would. He wouldn't let his own family down, but he wouldn't throw Kate and Annabelle to the wolves, either.

"I have an idea," he said to Kate.

"For breakfast?" she asked.

"For life."

She looked startled.

"It wasn't exactly my idea. It was Will's. Well, really it was Kalvin's."

"You've been talking to my lawyer?" There was something odd in her voice when she asked the question.

"I've been talking to Will, why?"

She shrugged and her expression smoothed out. "No reason. What did Will say?"

"He said…" Brody hesitated. He didn't know why he was hesitating. This was good news.

Kate bent to the diaper bag and retrieved a diaper, the change pad and some wet wipes.

"He suggested Shetland Tech should buy Beast Blue Designs."

She looked puzzled. "You should buy it? Why would you want to buy it?"

"Two reasons, really."

Instead of looking at him, she spread the change pad out on the bed and laid Annabelle on top.

"First is, well I didn't say anything to you before now," Brody continued speaking. "Because I didn't want you to worry. But Beast Blue is in serious trouble. To stop using the Shetland code, they're going to have to dismantle most of their new games. They're going to have to pay hefty fines. And it's going to cost the company a fortune."

"You expected that, though." Kate was bent over the baby, and Brody couldn't see her face.

"I did. But it's worse than we anticipated. It'll bankrupt the company."

She looked up at that. "Would that be a good thing? For you, I mean."

"For Shetland Tech. Sure. Theoretically, losing a major competitor in the marketplace is good for Shetland."

"So, are you happy?"

He sat down on the bed to be level with her profile. "I'm not happy at the prospect of Annabelle losing all her money."

"It was Quentin's money."

"You can't be happy at the thought of losing it all."

She frowned. "I'm not my mother, Brody."

"What the heck is that supposed to mean?"

"I mean, I'm not looking for a big score. Getting Annabelle was never about the money." With one hand on Annabelle's stomach so the baby couldn't roll over, Kate shook out the new diaper.

"Nobody said it was."

"You just did."

"No, I didn't."

"You just tippy-toed up to telling me there wouldn't be any money. Clearly, you thought I'd care."

"Most people would care." He was trying to be patient here.

"Well, I don't." She deftly swooped the diaper beneath Annabelle's bottom.

"Okay. That's good. You're a better person than most."

"Thank you."

"You're welcome. And, well, this is going to seem rather anticlimactic then."

She waited.

"It's the second reason. Will and Kalvin—and I agree with them—figured out that if Shetland Tech buys Beast Blue, then we don't need to untangle their entire year's R&D. As a wholly owned company they—well, we—can use the stolen code and sell the products as they were designed."

She lifted Annabelle from the bed and straightened up. Her gaze narrowed on him. "And what does that mean?"

"It means what it sounds like. Shetland Tech pays for Beast Blue—in other words Annabelle—instead of causing the company to go completely bankrupt. Quentin signed personal guarantees. If Beast Blue goes down, the mansion and everything else is gone."

"But what does it mean for Shetland Tech?"

"That's the beauty of it. It's a win-win."

"But more a win for Shetland Tech."

"It was always going to be more of a win for Shetland Tech. We have the advantage of having not broken the law."

Annabelle started to fuss, and Kate patted her back. "And you came up with the plan with my lawyer."

"It was Kalvin's idea, yes."

"The lawyer you introduced me to." She reached into the diaper bag and produced a bottle.

"Kate, what is wrong?"

"A lawyer from a firm that just happens to represent Shetland Tech?"

"Are you accusing me of something?"

Annabelle reached for the bottle and cried out.

"What are we doing here, Brody?"

He came to his feet. "I honestly haven't the vaguest notion."

She popped the bottle into Annabelle's mouth. "If it's all the same to you, Brody, I think I'll hire my own lawyer from here on in."

"What?"

"I want a lawyer that I know is taking care of Annabelle."

"Are you saying Kalvin has a conflict of interest?"

Her gaze had gone hard. "I guess I am. This is all just a little too convenient. You and Annabelle's lawyer suddenly discover it's in her best interest to sell to you, ensuring Shetland Tech will have the market all to themselves and be wildly successful."

"You don't trust me." That surprised him. In fact it hurt him more than it surprised him. He didn't like the feeling.

"I did trust you. But Nadia had you pegged. I stood up for you. I figured any guy who'd stand in front of a bullet for me had to be honest."

"I have been nothing but honest." Even as he said the words, he knew they sounded ridiculous.

He'd lied to her from the moment he met her. But she'd lied to him, as well. And he thought they'd worked that out. He sure hadn't lied to her since.

"Right." She put Annabelle down in the crib, making sure

she had a grip on the bottle. "And a rich royal from Scotland is falling for a public-school teacher who owns half a condo with a sky-high mortgage."

"You think I'm a snob?" Hell, yes he was falling for her.

She started to get dressed. "Nadia said you were playing me, that you were sticking to me to get to Annabelle. I pretended it wasn't true. I pretended that you hadn't turned on a dime when you found out I wanted guardianship."

"I turned on a dime because you needed my help."

"And because you liked me so much." Her voice dripped with sarcasm. "And you wanted to be with me. I hope the sex wasn't too much trouble for you."

"Kate, you're losing your mind."

"No, I'm opening my eyes." She was fully dressed now, and she shoved her feet into her shoes.

"Are you leaving?" he asked. "Is that what you're doing? You're leaving?"

Brody's phone rang.

"I'm going to find Annabelle a new lawyer," she said.

"Find whatever lawyer you want." He immediately realized that would be a good thing. It would prove he was being honest with her. "That's the best thing you can do, Kate. They'll tell you I'm offering you a lifeline. I'm doing it for Annabelle."

He'd been doing it for Kate as well, but in this moment he really didn't feel like helping her.

His phone rang again.

He reached for it and saw it was Blane.

Kate lifted Annabelle from the crib.

"I have to take this," Brody said.

She paused in the doorway. "Don't let us stop you."

"Don't go."

"This was a mistake."

"I'm on your side."

"I don't believe you."

His phone rang a third time.

"Then go." He tried not to feel bitter, but he failed. "Talk to a lawyer who's never even heard my name before and see what he says. But when you come back, you better hope I'm still willing to buy the company."

She turned and walked out.

Brody answered the call. "Yeah?"

"Brody?" Blane's voice was rough.

Fear shot through Brody. "What's wrong?"

Blane had a fit of ragged coughing. "You'd better come home. Hurry."

Brody immediately headed for his suitcase. "Are you with a doctor?"

"They want to do surgery. Mother and Father are pretty upset."

"What kind of surgery? Never mind. I'll get the doctor's number from Mother. I'm on my way. You do what they tell you. Save your strength."

Brody threw his clothes into the suitcase. He shouldn't have stayed here with Kate. It was selfish. He should have gone home. Even if Blane seemed temporarily better, he should have gone home to support his brother.

Kate had spent two hours in a lawyer's office in Seattle that first day, tossing out all kinds of accusations about Brody, Shetland Technology and Kalvin. The lawyer had then spent at least that on the phone with Kalvin. They'd called in technical experts and financial experts, and Kate had paid him nearly a month's salary.

Now, close to a week later, she'd been told, in essence, that she was a fool. Everything Brody had said to her was accurate and correct. Shetland Tech would be throwing Annabelle a lifeline by purchasing Beast Blue. Sure, it would work out okay for Brody and his family, but Shetland Tech was going to do well in any event.

For Annabelle, Beast Blue, and all of their employees, most of whom were completely innocent, Brody's offer was the only way out.

Armed with enough information to make her feel wretched, she arrived home where Nadia was babysitting Annabelle.

"Well?" Nadia asked as soon as she walked in. "What did he say?"

Kate closed the door and leaned against it. "He said Annabelle should have accepted Brody's offer. And I shouldn't have doubted him."

Nadia's expression fell. "What do you mean?"

"Brody wasn't trying to take advantage of the situation. He wasn't after anything he couldn't have gotten without ever saying a word to me, never mind saving my life and helping me with Annabelle."

Nadia dropped into the nearest chair. "Oh, Kate."

Kate dumped her purse on the floor and walked into the living room. Her legs were feeling wobbly.

"Is it my fault?" Nadia asked. "I feel like it's my fault."

"It's not your fault. You didn't know him. I did. I knew him. I slept with him. He told me about his family, his brother." She groaned and sat down on the sofa. "I should have trusted him."

"He is royalty." Nadia paused. "I'm just sayin', the mathematical odds…"

"It wasn't like he fell madly in love with me." Kate only wished that could have happened. "He was attracted to me, and he was honest with me. And anything he said or did, when he held me and kissed me, it was because he wanted to, not because he was attempting to get at Annabelle."

"Was it good?" Nadia asked. "The sex, the romance?"

"It was amazing." Kate closed her eyes and remembered. "He was so, I don't know, so everything. Sweet and funny, and wicked smart. He got my jokes. He made them better. He understood that I had to take care of Annabelle. He never questioned that. And he was good with her. He was honestly good with her."

"Uh-oh," Nadia said.

"What?" Could things get even worse?

"You fell in love with him."

"No, I didn't."

That would be bad. That would be terrible. If Kate had fallen in love with Brody, she was going to have her heart broken. She refused to have her heart broken. Not on top of everything else. Not on top of losing Brody.

Losing Brody was the worst thing that had ever happened to her.

"Oh, no," she moaned. Her hands started to tremble. "How could I have let this happen?"

"What are you going to do?"

"Do? There's nothing I can do. Don't you think I've done enough?"

"You could apologize." Nadia's suggestion was tentative.

"I should." Kate didn't disagree with that. "I owe it to him."

"But?"

"I don't think I can. I don't think I can bring myself to talk to him."

"An email?" Nadia suggested.

"That would be lame. Not to mention insulting. He was really angry that last day, Nad. And he had a right to be angry."

Kate's mind went back. "That last morning. He looked so good. He was so happy. We slept together. We woke up with Annabelle. We'd gone to the park the day before. And then we ordered room service for dinner. That way, Annabelle could play in her crib while we ate. It was like we were this happy little family." She groaned and dropped her head into her hands.

"Uh, Kate?"

"What?"

"He would have gone back to Scotland."

Kate spread her fingers and peeked out.

"Fight or no fight, he wasn't staying in Seattle."

Kate straightened. "I know that."

"Do you? Because for a minute there it sounded like you were thinking happily ever after."

Kate tried to make herself laugh. "I didn't go that far over the edge."

"Uh-oh," Nadia said again.

"No," Kate insisted. "I had my head on straight the whole time. I know his life is over there." She stopped herself. What was she saying? Brody's life in Scotland was far from the only thing keeping them from happily ever after.

"I'm a rational person," Kate continued. "Even if his life wasn't over there, I get that I'm indulging in this fantasy all by myself. It was never his fantasy. He liked me, sure. I get that. And he wasn't conning me, which is noble. But he wasn't falling in love with me. I know that for a fact."

"Do you?" Nadia asked.

Fifteen

"Her lawyer called," Kalvin told Brody over the phone from across the Atlantic.

"We knew he would," Brody said.

It had taken a little longer than he'd hoped, but the lawyer had seen the value in Shetland Tech's offer.

"What do you want to do about the deal?" Kalvin asked.

"Let it go through."

"So, you're going to forgive her?" Blane asked from where he reclined in a lounger in the Calder Castle garden. The day was warm, and Blane was recovering quickly from the surgery on his airway.

"You're being way too generous," Kalvin said. "As your legal counsel, I have to advise you—"

"Advise away," Brody said. "But the deal stands."

It wasn't Annabelle's fault that Kate had trust issues. And it wasn't Annabelle's fault that Brody let common sense rush out the door the minute he'd laid eyes on Kate.

Annabelle hadn't chosen her parents. For that matter, she hadn't chosen her headstrong auntie, either. She was stuck with what life had dealt her. And Brody wasn't going to be the guy to take away her inheritance. He'd make sure both Annabelle and Kate could live comfortably for the rest of their lives.

"Are you making a bad deal?" Blane asked.

"I can email a scan of the paperwork," Kalvin said. "You'll need to get it notarized at your end."

"As long as she'll sign, too."

"Oh, she'll sign. I set that lawyer of hers straight on a few things."

Brody chuckled. "You shouldn't have such a thin skin."

"He initially threatened to bring me up on charges with the bar."

"You didn't do anything wrong."

"I know. And now he knows it, too."

"And Kate knows it?"

"She sure does."

Brody had half hoped for an apology from her. She'd made some wild accusations, and she'd been dead wrong about his motives. Now that she knew it for sure, you'd think the woman could pick up the phone and admit it.

She hadn't.

And his only conclusion was that she didn't want to speak to him. She was taking the money and putting the rest behind her. He didn't know what all that intimacy and sex was about, but clearly it didn't mean nearly as much to her as it had meant to him.

"It won't bring her back to you," Blane said.

Brody shot him a glare.

"Fax the paperwork," he said to Kalvin.

"It'll be there in the morning. Goodbye, sir."

"Goodbye, Kalvin."

"That's what you really want," Blane said.

"That's not why I did it." Brody didn't bother denying that he'd wish Kate would call.

"By 'did it' you mean overpay for a company we don't really need in the first place?"

"It's going to make us a lot of money." Brody wasn't going to accept the premise that he'd overpaid. He'd paid well, but he hadn't paid more than he expected to make on the deal.

"Since you saved us from ruin, I'm going to give you this one."

"Thank you so much. Since I'm the guy running the business end of this family, I'll do whatever I bloody well please."

Blane chuckled. But then his chuckle turned into a cough.

Brody sat up straighter, regretting his outburst.

"I'm fine," Blane wheezed.

"You sure?" Brody was poised to run for Blane's nurse. The coughing subsided. "I hate this."

"I know." Brody felt enormous sympathy for his brother.

The surgery had been a success, and a new medication had stabilized Blane's lungs.

"You know, at this rate you're going to be Earl," Blane said, recovering his breath and sitting back.

"I have no intention of ever being Earl."

"I may or may not outlive Father, but eventually, I'm going to die."

"Eventually is a long, long time," Brody said.

"I'm not getting married."

"You can't possibly know that." Brody refused to let Blane give up on having a family.

He knew his brother wanted children. And Brody wanted that for him. He also wanted it to be Blane's son to take over as Earl after Blane died as a very old man. And in the meantime, Brody wanted to live his own life.

"I'll probably live for a while," Blane said.

"You'll live for a very long time. You have to, if only because I couldn't stand all those ceremonial events. I've got businesses to run."

"And women to chase."

"I'm done with that for a while." Brody couldn't imagine who might follow Kate. He had no interest in anyone else, and he couldn't see that changing in the short term.

"You need to get married," Blane said. "This family needs a backup plan."

"Stop that. I'm serious. I'll get married. Eventually. But you need to go first."

"Maybe." Blane smiled smugly to himself. "Now tell me again about her purple hair."

"How did Kate get back into this conversation?"

"We're talking about you getting married."

"We're talking about *you* getting married. Where have you been the past week? Or did the anesthetic permanently addle your brain?"

"My brain's not addled. You're the one who's addled."

"I'm not marrying Kate."

Even if their relationship hadn't completely broken down,

she'd made it clear: her perfect life was in suburbia. Her perfect life was being a soccer and bake-sale mom for Annabelle. It was an admirable goal, but it didn't include Brody.

"You'd better marry her," Blane said.

"Why had I better?"

"Because you're in love with her."

Brody wasn't rising to the bait. "I was infatuated with her. I'm over it."

"You're the worst liar in the world."

"You didn't see me in California. I rocked at lying."

Brody had surprised himself with his acting ability.

"Maybe," Blane said. "But you suck at lying to yourself."

"I'm not lying. I'm accepting reality."

Kate was in Brody's past. There was nothing he could do to change that. He might miss her, and he might desperately wish he could be with her again. But reality was reality.

Blane wouldn't be deterred. "Give me one good reason you can't have her."

"I'll give you three. She doesn't trust me. She won't leave Seattle. And she has purple hair."

"Give me one that matters."

"Those all matter."

"No, they don't," said Blane. He counted off on his fingers. "She now knows she can trust you."

"On this, maybe. But what about the next thing?"

"Her hair will grow out. And Seattle's just geography."

"What does that even mean?"

"It means there are other places in the world to be a responsible, caring parent and raise a wonderful child. Right here, for example."

"You want me to bring Kate here?"

"That would be traditional."

"Well…I…" Brody abandoned his answer. There was no point in trying to talk sense to Blane right now. "You want something that matters?" he asked instead.

"I do."

"Okay."

Brody's brain conjured up a kaleidoscope of Kate, laughing beside the pool, dancing in his arms, pushing the stroller through the park and holding Annabelle on that last morning before he'd blown it with her.

"Brody?" Blane interrupted. "You're not saying anything."

"Here's the reason." Brody forced himself to be brutally honest. "I should never have fallen in love with her in the first place."

"I think you just made my point for me," Blane said softly.

"Yeah." Brody felt a giant weight had just settled onto his chest.

He loved Kate. He loved her more than life. Sitting here pretending he didn't was hopeless. It wasn't going to work, and his feelings weren't going to go away.

That left him with a stark choice. Live the rest of his life missing her and wondering what they might have had together. Or put his heart on his sleeve and go back to her. Maybe he was the one who should apologize.

He had to do something. He didn't want to keep living like this.

"I have to go get her," he said mostly to himself.

"You have to go get her."

"What if she says no? What if she won't consider Scotland?"

"Maybe you stay with her."

"In Seattle?"

"I don't know. All I know is that you don't give it up. If she's everything you say she is, you don't give it up."

Brody looked over his shoulder at the family castle. Could he give this up?

"It's just geography," said Blane.

Brody pictured Kate and Annabelle, and the little condo in Seattle. He pictured himself there, and it looked good.

In an instant, he knew he could give up the drafty castle. He could give up anything for Kate.

"You promise you'll get married and have a few sons?"

he asked Blane. "Because if I do this, we're going to need a few more Calders."

"Deal. But I might need your help finding a willing woman."

"Oh, get over yourself. As soon as you're up and around, there'll be a lineup halfway to the village."

Kate didn't think it was possible for her to feel worse. But she was wrong. She did feel worse.

Her lawyer put the contracts in front of her, all approved and signed by the executor of Quentin's estate and the court-appointed advocate for Annabelle. As soon as Kate signed, it would be a done deal.

Brody would own Beast Blue, and Annabelle would have a portfolio of investments that would give her the means to do anything she wanted in life. Kate could do anything she wanted as well, because the allowance for raising Annabelle was ridiculously generous.

Trouble was the only thing she truly wanted was the thing she couldn't have.

"Something wrong?" the lawyer asked.

"Nothing." Kate put the pen to the line on the last page and signed.

Wild thoughts rolled through her mind on the drive home, memories and regrets. Where had she gone wrong? What should she have done differently? Would it have changed anything if she had?

She had no way of knowing what Brody thought of her now. He might well be completely over their fling. He might not have given her another thought. He might have made the deal for Beast Blue solely because it suited him. It didn't mean he cared about her at all.

By the time she got home, she was no closer to an answer than she'd been when she started. She pulled into the short driveway and gripped the steering wheel. She had limited choices here, but she did have a couple of them. She could leave things as they were and move on with life. Or she could try to do the right thing. She could at least take a stab at doing the right thing, and maybe clear her conscience.

She stepped out of the car and slammed the door behind her. Her principles told her she needed to apologize. It was the same set of principles that had made her go after Annabelle in the first place, the same ones that had ended up putting their lives in jeopardy and lost her Brody.

"Sometimes you win. Sometimes you lose." But she knew deep down she had to stick with her beliefs.

She swung her purse over her shoulder and marched up the walkway. One thing was sure, without principles, she had nothing.

She opened the front door to find Nadia on the floor with Annabelle, a stack of blocks between them.

"I'm doing it," she said.

"Then I'm with you," Nadia said looking up. "What exactly are we talking about?"

"I'm apologizing to Brody. I signed the contracts. Annabelle's future is secure. But I was wrong. And I'm sorry. And I'm going to tell him so."

"You're calling him?"

Annabelle knocked the colorful block tower over with a clatter. She grinned up at Kate.

"Well done, sweetheart," Kate said. "I'm not calling him."

"Emailing? That's probably better. You might get tripped up trying to talk. If you write it, you can take your time, compose it just right. And you won't have to—"

"I'm going to Scotland."

It took Nadia a moment to speak. "Say again?"

"I'm going to Scotland. I'm not wimping out on this. I'm going to face him, look him in the eye and tell him I was wrong and I'm sorry."

Nadia came to her feet. "That's a bad idea."

"It's the right thing to do."

"No, honey. It's a bad thing to do. You're sorry. I know you are. But that's not why you're going to Scotland."

"Yes, it is." Kate had just gone over this in her mind in minute detail. She knew what was right and what was wrong.

"You're going to Scotland to see if he's in love with you."

"I'm not. He's not. I'm over that fantasy."

"I know you so well, Kate. I can tell you're not over that fantasy. And I'm worried about you. If you go to him, and it's not what you hope, you're going to get your heart stomped on. And it's going to happen in person, overseas, and you'll be all by yourself when it does."

"That's not why I'm going." Was it? "I have no expectations."

Nadia put an arm around her shoulders. "Your expectations are written all over your face."

"But—"

"But, nothing. You're going to lay your heart on the line, and there's a better than even chance it's going to go completely wrong."

Kate didn't want to hear this. She did not want to hear that her last hope was gone.

"But, what do I do?"

"I tell you what you do." Nadia paused for a long time.

"What?" Kate all but shouted.

"You take me with you."

Kate swallowed against a sob, but then Nadia's words registered. "What?"

"I'm your best friend. No way I'm letting you go through this alone."

Kate couldn't help a watery smile.

"Remember when I had to stand up to that awful principal and you stuck with me till the end?"

Kate remembered.

"You should do this, Kate. If you love him that much, and it's obvious to me that you do, then it's worth the risk. For you and for Annabelle. Whatever happens, I'll be there to cheer you on and have your back."

"You'd come to Scotland?"

"I'll buy the tickets."

* * *

The Calder butler Jeremy Clive entered the library where Brody and Blane were drinking brandy. Blane was getting better in leaps and bounds. His color was back. His energy was increasing. And he claimed he felt better than he had in years.

"Sir?" Jeremy said.

"Yes?" Brody and Blane answered simultaneously.

"Sorry to disturb you, but there's a young lady in the main foyer. She declined to give her name."

Brody reached out and rapped Blane heartily on the shoulder. "You see that? Word's gotten around already."

"She's here to see you, Mr. Brody."

"Me?"

"Yes."

"How young?"

The stately Jeremy looked confused. "I would guess in her twenties. She's not a child."

"Pretty?" asked Blane.

"I would say so."

"If you don't want her, I'll take her," Blane said.

They were on their second brandy, and Blane's tolerance for alcohol seemed to have diminished while he was sick.

Brody rose to his feet. "I'll get back to you on that."

As he exited the library, he tried to figure out who might be stopping by. Jeremy knew most of his friends, and he certainly knew the people in the village, better than Brody did in fact.

He'd met a woman in the airport a couple of weeks ago. So, she was a possibility. What was her name? Mandy or Sandy or maybe Katrina? If he couldn't remember by the time he got to the entrance foyer, this was going to be a bit embarrassing.

He came around the corner of the hall and halted.

Her back was to him, and her hair wasn't purple, but he could swear it was Kate.

He blinked his eyes and gave his head a shake.

Then Annabelle's little head popped up over her shoulder, and joy surged through him. He quickly set down his drink and strode forward.

"Kate?"

She turned, and he drank in her beautiful face. Her makeup was subtle, her hair had grown longer. She'd either cut off or colored the purple bits. She was wearing a fitted, smoke-blue dress with a navy cardigan.

She looked classic and beautiful beneath the portraits and shields that decorated the hall. She looked as if she'd been born to the castle.

"You're in Scotland," he said.

"Hello, Brody."

She looked and sounded so formal, he was afraid to hug her. He stopped a foot away.

He smiled. "Hi there, Annabelle. She's grown since I saw her."

"Every day," Kate said.

"Come in." He motioned. "I'm surprised to see you."

"I hope it's okay."

"It's more than okay."

"And who do we have here?" asked Blane, making an appearance in the hall.

"This is my brother, Blane," Brody said to Kate.

She gave Blane a broad smile. It was the smile Brody wanted for himself. He felt a shaft of jealousy and an urge to shove Blane back into the library.

"Hi, Blane," she said.

"This is Kate Dunhern."

Blane's eyes went wide. "This is Kate?"

"Yes." Brody instantly worried about the brandy consumption and what it might do to Blane's judgment.

Blane strode right over to her and took her hand. "And this must be Annabelle."

"Brody mentioned us?" Kate asked.

The question set Brody back. Did she think he wouldn't? Did she think he'd tell his family the story of Quentin and LA and leave her and Annabelle out?

"He more than mentioned you," Blane said.

"That's enough," Brody interjected, fearing what might come next.

"He's in love with you."

Both Kate and Brody went completely still.

Then Brody found his voice. "Are you kidding me?" he said to Blane. He could have socked his brother.

Instead, he took Kate's hand. "Ignore him. Let's go inside." He led her away from Blane, back down the hall where he shut them into the library.

"I'm so sorry about that. He's been sick."

"I know."

"He's a little drunk right now." Brody was mortified and scrambling for the right words. "And, well, he made some funny assumptions about things I said when I first got back."

"You don't have to explain."

"He was way out of line."

She moved closer. "You don't have to explain. I came to say I'm sorry, Brody."

"For what?"

She gave him a look of disbelief. "For not trusting you. For that last morning in Seattle when I accused you of plotting against me. For throwing out everything we had together because I couldn't bring myself to—"

"Stop." He put his fingertips across her lips.

"You won't accept my apology?" She looked positively demoralized.

He stepped closer.

"Gah," Annabelle told him softly. She reached out and patted his lips.

"Gah," he said in return. "Kate, you don't owe me an apology," he said.

"Yes, I do." He shook his head. "I behaved terribly, and you made the deal anyway. You took care of Annabelle, and of me."

"I love you." He couldn't hold it in any longer. "My brother is right. I love you, Kate."

She blinked at him, seeming completely flustered. "I don't even know what that means."

"It means I love you." It felt good to say it over and over.

"But… What…"

"I think the 'what' depends on you."

She still looked confused.

"Do you love me back?"

"Yes," she answered quickly. "Oh, yes." Then she gave a nervous laugh. "I guess I should have said that right away, shouldn't have I?"

"It's traditional."

"I meant, what does that mean for us? You live here and I live there, and…"

He smiled. He almost laughed. "What do you want it to mean?"

"You keep answering my questions with questions."

"That's because I don't care about anything but loving you. We can do anything. We can live anywhere. It'll have to be together. But beyond that, I'm open."

She looked around the room. "Hmmm. Well. This is a big castle."

"It is that."

"My condo's pretty small."

"No argument from me. But Seattle has other houses, bigger houses. And I understand you've recently come into some money."

"You'd do that for us? You'd move?"

"I'd do that."

This time when she smiled, her eyes shimmered with tears.

"I'm going to kiss you now," he said. "We can finish this conversation later. But right now I'm going to kiss you."

"Oh, please do." She raised her lips to his.

Epilogue

In the anteroom of the cathedral, Brody double-checked his tie. His gray vest was smooth under the crisp tuxedo jacket, and his cuff links bore the Calder family crest. He wanted to look perfect, not that anyone would be looking at him. All attention would be focused squarely on Kate.

The heavy oak door to the chapel hallway swung open, and he turned, expecting to see Blane checking on his parents.

Instead, it was Kate rushing into the room in a cloud of tulle and lace.

"You can't be here," he told her, quickly averting his eyes. It took about three seconds for curiosity to get the best of him, and he glanced up.

She looked wonderful, classy and elegant in a satin and jeweled snow-white gown. Lace decorated her smooth shoulders, the bodice was fitted to her slim waist, while the filmy, full skirt cascaded out from a satin belt.

"I'm not supposed to see you in that." Even as he said the words, he continued to stare at her.

Her hair was a soft cloud around her beautiful face, dark lashes emphasizing her brilliant blue eyes. And her lips looked dark and luscious. He couldn't wait for the part where he got to kiss her.

"I have an idea," she said, her voice bright and excited.

"Now? You're risking bad luck on our wedding day to bring me an idea?"

She swept closer. "With all we've been through, we're stronger than bad luck."

Coming closer still, she held out her hand to reveal a coin in her palm.

"Is the limo parked at a meter?" he joked.

"I've been thinking," she said. "We shouldn't get married without knowing where we're going to live."

The pressure was obviously getting to her. "You want to talk about which country to live in ten minutes before the ceremony?"

"Heads," she said, "we live in Scotland. Tails we live in Seattle."

"I can't keep up with you. What're you saying?"

"Or…" A mischievous twinkle came into her eyes. "We could buy a vacation home in the San Juan Islands."

"Is that in the Caribbean?"

"They're off the coast of Washington State, close to Seattle."

"A vacation home in Washington State? Is this some kind of a wedding present?"

Her grin went wide.

"Kate, sweetheart, are you saying what I think you're saying?" He felt like he'd won the lottery for a second time this year.

"We should stay in Scotland, Brody. I want to raise our family right here."

He wanted to pull her into his arms and hold her tight. But he didn't dare. She looked so perfect, he couldn't let himself muss her up.

"Okay with you?" she asked, looking suddenly uncertain.

"It's more than okay with me. You know my parents will be completely thrilled."

"I know." She took his hands. "Your mother and I talked last night. I know this is really important to your family."

He gave her hands a squeeze. "What's important here is us, you and me. You don't have to commit right now."

"I want to commit right now."

"Are you completely sure about this?"

"I'm completely sure, Brody. I thought about it all night."

"When my mother starts being 'the Countess' she can be formidable."

"I know she can. But she didn't intimidate me. It's what I want."

"In that case I couldn't be happier. Thank you, Kate." He hesitated for a split second, but then decided to share his own secret. "And… Well… Speaking of mothers…"

Kate sobered. It only took her a second to glean his meaning. "Brody, I told you, you can't call her."

"I know you told me that. But, well, you weren't going to call her." He sure hoped he hadn't made a mistake here.

"We were leaving well enough alone. She was happy about getting half of Francie's jewelry. Do you know how hard it is to make her happy? You don't mess with it once it happens. You don't need to put a target on your back."

"I didn't call her."

Kate looked relieved.

"I flew her here."

Kate's jaw dropped. "Here, as in Scotland?"

"Here, as in the cathedral."

Kate's hand went to her forehead. "Why would you do that?"

Brody held her other hand fast. "You can't get married without your mother. It's not right. She's your only family."

He reached out to touch the chickadee charm on her necklace. In Annabelle, Francie was still there with them, too. He was grateful to Francie. He always would be.

"I'm not worried about me," Kate said. "I can handle my mother. It's you. You're rich. You're royalty. She's going to latch onto you like—"

"I've taken care of that."

"Oh, really. You've taken care of my mother, have you?

Brody checked his watch. They only had about two minutes left to talk.

"I bought her a little condo in Santa Monica."

Kate's jaw dropped open.

"It's in a seniors complex. And they have people there to help her, keep an eye on her really."

"You didn't."

"I did."

Kate started to speak, but then her expression turned relieved and joyous.

She gave her head a bemused shake. "Okay. But you're a wonderful man. I think she's going to like it very much."

"I don't want you to have to worry about her."

"I won't worry. With you around, I've stopped having anything to worry about."

"Good."

"But I better go be a bride now."

"You better go be a bride. But one more thing." Brody wanted her to go into the ceremony on a purely happy note.

"Is it bad?"

"No, it's good. Christina is here, too."

Kate's face broke into a wide smile over that one. "You brought Christina all the way to Scotland for our wedding?"

"I did, but not just for the wedding."

"She's on vacation?"

"I hired her. She's staying to help with Annabelle."

"Do we need a nanny?"

"Well, you've got one whether you want one or not."

He could tell from her expression that she was warming to the idea.

"I don't know what you want to do," he told her. "Work or help my mother with charities, or be a full-time mom to Annabelle and all the other babies that come along. But you can have help to do it. I want you to have help to do it."

"Annabelle loves Christina."

"I know. And Christina is excited to be here."

"Brody?"

"Yes?"

"You can kiss the bride."

"I'm not going to wreck your pretty makeup." But he wanted to kiss her. He desperately wanted to kiss her.

He settled for a quick peck on her cheek.

Just then Blane arrived in the doorway.

He instantly zeroed in on Kate.

He gave her a mock scowl. "How did you get in here?"

"Through the door," she answered jauntily.

From minute one, she hadn't been the least bit intimidated by his brother the viscount. Brody couldn't help musing that Blane needed to find a woman like Kate. Not Kate, of course, never Kate.

"Out you go," he ordered, pointing to the door. "You have to know better than to let him see you before the ceremony."

"We're immune to bad luck," Kate said.

"Well, nobody's immune to Father Callum. Get back where you belong."

Kate grinned unrepentantly. "See you in five minutes," she said to Brody. "And your kissing better have improved by then."

Blane snickered as Kate left.

"Inside joke," Brody said.

"Uh-huh."

"I kiss just fine."

"I hope so. You're not going to hold on to a woman like that with lame kisses."

"She's not going anywhere."

"You sure?" There was a familiar teasing twinkle in Blane's eyes. Brody felt like they were kids again.

"In four minutes, she'll be mine for life. I'm grateful. I never thought I'd find someone so special." Brody meant every word.

"Let's go, brother." Blane clapped him on the back. "You've got a bride to marry."

Brody and Blane entered the chapel from a side door and made their way in front of the altar.

The church was completely filled with friends, relatives, a few London royals and people from the town. Blake met his mother's gaze in the front row. She was beaming. Sitting next to her, even his father looked proud. The earl was an aloof and exacting man. It wasn't often that Blane or Brody pleased him.

Then the piper's music rose, and Nadia appeared at the end of the aisle. She was carrying Annabelle, who was dressed in an opulent mauve gown. It set off Nadia's sophisticated royal purple.

"You've inspired me, brother," Blane muttered.

Brody rose a curious brow in Blane's direction.

"If you can find someone as wonderful as Kate, then it's time I went for it, too."

Brody found himself grinning with approval. "Good for you."

"I hear couples first meet at wedding receptions all the time."

"They do?"

"See that woman in row five? In the bright green dress?"

"She's pretty."

"I'm dancing with her first. If it doesn't work out, I'll try the redhead in row eight, left side, on the aisle."

Brody had to stifle a laugh.

Then the processional music came up, and Kate appeared. Brody had already seen her, but he was taken all over again by the beautiful dress, a heather bouquet from his highlands, the classic Calder diamond tiara and her serene smile that was all for him. The congregation gasped with her beauty.

She was stunning.

With every step that brought Kate closer to him, his heart filled with love and joy.

When she finally arrived, she handed Nadia her bouquet and gave Annabelle a kiss. Then she looked into Brody's eyes, hers filled with unconditional love. They joined hands, and he didn't look away until the vows were finished.

Then he kissed her properly. The congregation grew restless at the length, but he didn't care. When he drew away, she was well and truly his wife.

He took Annabelle from Nadia, and held her in his arms. Then he took Kate's hand to walk back down the aisle.

"Nice kiss," she whispered breathlessly, hanging on to his arm.

"I do aim to please."

"Your mother," she said.

"You want to talk about my mother right now?"

"I thought you should know. When we talked, she also said she expects us to get pregnant tonight."

Brody nudged Kate gently as they smiled to the people they passed. "Did you tell her we'd already taken care of that little thing?"

"I did not. I think we can save that announcement for another day."

"Good." He wasn't yet ready to share their secret.

Then the double doors opened in front of them. The bells pealed. A crowd on the grounds outside cheered loudly. And Brody introduced his family to his world.

* * * * *

*If you liked this story of a billionaire tamed
by the love of the right woman—and her baby—
pick up these other novels from
acclaimed author Barbara Dunlop.*

**THE BABY CONTRACT
THE MISSING HEIR
BILLIONAIRE BABY DILEMMA
AN AFTER-HOURS AFFAIR**

Available now from Mills & Boon Desire!

* * *

And don't miss the next
BILLIONAIRES AND BABIES *story,*
THE HEIR'S UNEXPECTED BABY
by Jules Bennett.
Available February 2017!

* * *

"I'm as qualified as you are to give marital advice."

"No, you're not," Erin teased. "You've never been engaged, so I've come closer to actually getting married."

Cade got up and crossed the room to her. "That gives you a little experience, but I've got a lot because I spent fifteen years growing up as the child of a bad marriage," Cade said. "That makes my advice more valid."

"You were going to stay on your side of the room tonight."

"See—this is why I shouldn't get married. I didn't do what I said I would. Scared of me?"

"Not in the least. I have no intention of marrying you. Now you go back to your side of the room and think about my brother."

"I want to know something else. Give me a straight answer. Did you miss any sleep after our first kiss?"

"Cade, we aren't going to do this."

"I think you just answered my question," he said in a husky voice as his gaze lowered to her mouth.

She couldn't catch her breath.

* * *

The Rancher's Nanny Bargain
is part of the Callahan's Clan series—A wealthy
Texas family finds love under the Western skies!

THE RANCHER'S
NANNY BARGAIN

BY
SARA ORWIG

MILLS
BOON

First Published in Great Britain 2017
By Mills & Boon, an imprint of HarperCollins*Publishers*
1 London Bridge Street, London, SE1 9GF

© 2017 Sara Orwig

ISBN: 978-0-263-92802-0

51-0117

Our policy is to use papers that are natural, renewable and recyclable products and made from wood grown in sustainable forests. The logging and manufacturing processes conform to the legal environmental regulations of the country of origin.

Printed and bound in Spain
by CPI, Barcelona

Sara Orwig is an Oklahoman whose life revolves around family, flowers, dogs and books. Books are like her children: she usually knows where they are, they delight her and she doesn't want to be without them. With a masters degree in English, Sara has written mainstream fiction, historical and contemporary romance. She has one hundred published novels translated in over twenty-six languages. You can visit her website at www.saraorwig.com.

To Stacy Boyd with so many thanks
for being my editor. To Maureen Walters
with special thanks for all the years together.
With love to David and to our family.

One

In his office at his ranch house, Cade Callahan sorted mail that had come while he was in Dallas at his commercial real estate office the past two days. But the letters blurred before his eyes.

All he could think about was the loss of his younger brother and his sister-in-law in the last week of June. How many times would he replay in his mind the moment he imagined their car had been struck by a drunk driver? Nate had been killed instantly, and Lydia had died on the way to the hospital. The drunk driver who hit them had died at the scene.

And Cade had been left as the sole guardian of his six-month-old niece, Amelia.

A shiver went down his spine as it always did when he thought about the tremendous responsibility he'd inherited. He knew nothing about caring for a baby. Which was why he needed Erin Dorsey.

He glanced at his watch. Within minutes she would arrive for an interview for the nanny job. He had high hopes for her.

At lunch, more than a week ago, with his closest friend, Luke Dorsey, Cade had complained about being unable to find a suitable nanny despite all the interviews he'd had. Luke had a surprising recommendation—his sister.

Recalling Luke's younger sister Erin, Cade had remembered a timid, freckle-faced, scrawny little redhead, hovering in the background and keeping away from Luke and his friends. Cade hadn't ever said more than hello to her and barely had received more than that in return before she'd disappeared from sight. She was years younger, probably twenty or twenty-one now.

When he'd mentioned to Luke that she was very quiet and very young, Luke's blue eyes had twinkled.

"Not as quiet as when she was a kid," he'd said. "And young is good. She's energetic, upbeat, loves kids and they love her. Trust me, she's great taking care of kids."

"Is she an environmental engineer like you?"

"Not at all." He'd gone on to list her credentials: an undergraduate degree in Human Development and Family Services, director of her church nursery, member of the Big Sister program while in college. "The only drawbacks for her would be a time limit and living on your ranch."

"What's the time limit?" Cade had asked, even though he'd had no intention of hiring Luke's little sister.

"Erin just finished her bachelor's degree. She'll be starting back at the University of Texas for her master's in January. She's staying out a semester to earn money. I've offered to pay for school but she won't accept my offer." He'd grinned. "My sister is independent and wants to do it her way. Frankly, I can understand. We're a big family and it will help Mom and Dad. I put myself through, something you know nothing about as Dirkson Callahan's son who set all of you up in business."

"Not Blake. Don't get me started on my dad, or my mom. Mom won't keep Amelia at all and made that plain from the first and flew to Europe with friends. Why the hell my dad had so many kids… Anyway, this is August, so it won't help me to hire a nanny for a few months and then start over," Cade had said before biting into a thick, juicy rib covered in dark red barbecue sauce.

"Think about it before you say no," Luke had replied. "Hiring Erin now would give you time to get a really good nanny, and before she has to leave she could help you select the perfect replacement and train her. It would remove the pressure that you're under now to choose a nanny quickly no matter how little you like any of them."

He'd felt a slight bit defensive. "They all come highly recommended. I hate turning a baby over to a stranger, but I have to do something quickly. Grandmother and my cook have been taking care of Amelia and Grandmother doesn't know much more about babies than I do. Maisie cooks, so she can't care for Amelia all of the time. Sierra, Blake's wife, has helped, too."

"Hire Erin and you won't be turning your niece over to a stranger."

Maybe not a complete stranger, but he barely knew Erin and he hadn't even seen her since he'd graduated from high school. He knew Luke's argument to that— Cade had known his family since they were both kids. He knew he could trust her and believe what Luke told him about her.

"I wouldn't recommend my sister to some of my friends," Luke had said, "but I know I can leave the country and be certain you won't hit on her."

Amen to that one, Cade had thought, but he hadn't say it aloud. "Well, hell—"

"You won't hit on her because she's not your type. She takes life seriously, while I know you're a carefree, love-'em-and-leave-'em guy. Last year when the guy she was engaged to broke their engagement to marry someone else, she was crushed and she hasn't gotten back into dating since then."

Cade had been surprised to hear she had been engaged, but he'd said nothing. He still could only think of her as a waif who drifted in the background of Luke's life. In addition to Erin, there were four younger kids in Luke's family and they, too, had usually avoided Luke's crowd.

"She has told a few people, but should you call her, I think you ought to know… While she was engaged, she was pregnant with his baby. She miscarried and that's why the guy broke off the engagement. The doctors said she might be able to have a baby, but there was a higher than normal chance she might miscarry again. Her ex-fiancé said he wanted to know for certain that he had married a wife who could give him kids."

"Well, damn, he must not have been deeply in love."

"That's what I thought, but what do I know—or you for that matter—about love and marriage? The breakup left her shaken and brokenhearted. We have a big family and she loves babies, so that loss tore her up because she wants marriage and kids. Plus she was in love with her fiancé. Now she doesn't trust her own judgment in men. In short, she's vulnerable. I know I can trust you not to cause her more grief."

"If she works for me, some of the guys who work for me might ask her out, but she should be able to deal with them."

"She'll handle them, I'm sure. And I won't have to

worry about you, especially since you know this about her."

"You act as if I've agreed to call her."

"Go interview some more nannies and then you'll call Erin."

"It's a shame you don't have any confidence in yourself," Cade had remarked.

Luke had laughed, then quickly sobered. "Look, Cade, she's had a rough year and I'd like to see her where she can focus on a baby and get back to normal living. Take my advice. Stop worrying and get someone you know who can do the job."

"I'll think about it. Tell me again, what is it you're doing?"

Luke smiled. "I'm an environmental engineer and I'll be working for the government in Antarctica on wastewater management, permitting, removal of solid and hazardous waste—mainly effective wastewater treatment in the Antarctic which is not the same as in Texas—"

"I've got it. At least I've got as much as I want to hear about what you do. I'll think about your sister," he repeated.

Two days of interviews later, Cade contacted her.

Unable to get the image of a solemn, skinny kid out of his thoughts, he expected the same whispered, minimal conversation he'd got from her when they were kids, but was surprised to find the grown-up Erin friendly and confident. She'd turned him down politely, thanking him for the offer, preferring to keep her high-paying secretarial job until she went back to school.

But Cade had taken Luke's advice to heart. He knew exactly what he needed: someone he knew, someone he could trust to watch baby Amelia. Using all his powers of persuasion, he'd convinced Erin to come interview before she made a hasty decision.

Now in his office at the ranch he glanced at the clock and saw she was due in four minutes.

As he shifted his attention to the papers in front of him, there was a light rap on the door. His tall, blond butler stood waiting. "Miss Dorsey has arrived."

He smiled to himself. Erin Dorsey was as punctual as Mary Poppins. "Thanks, Harold. Tell her to come in."

Harold stepped out of sight and in seconds she walked into the room.

For an instant Cade forgot his nanny interview. He could only stare at the tall, leggy redhead who entered the room. Blond streaks highlighted her long red hair that fell in curls around her face, framing her long-lashed green eyes. She wore what should have been a tailored, ordinary businesslike navy suit with a V-neck white blouse. On her, though, it was anything but ordinary or businesslike. The short skirt revealed long, shapely legs while a narrow belt circled a tiny waist. In a million years he would never have recognized her as Luke's younger sister.

Dazed, he stared at her until he realized what he was doing. Then he stood and closed the distance between them as she offered her hand. When his fingers wrapped around her soft hand, the contact startled him again.

"You've grown up since I last saw you," he said, causing her to smile, revealing a dimple in her right cheek. He didn't remember any dimple, but he also didn't remember seeing her smile as a little kid. But then again, he hadn't ever paid attention to her. Now, her dazzling, dimpled smile sent the temperature in the room climbing. For an instant he thought he couldn't hire her as a nanny because he wouldn't be able to resist flirting with her or wanting to kiss that delicious mouth. Somehow he managed to shake that thought and pull himself back to business in time to hear her speak.

"I believe you have, too. I'm not still Luke's ten-year-old kid sister which was probably the last time we saw each other."

He bit back the reply that she sure as hell wasn't. He waved his hand slightly toward two brown leather chairs that faced his wide cherrywood desk. "Please, have a seat," he said. When she sat, he turned the other chair to face her.

He had already decided before she arrived that he wanted her for the job because he knew her and could trust her. More importantly, he knew her family values and they were what he viewed as ideal, what he wanted for his baby niece. Luke's family was the family he always wished he'd had—caring and supportive of each other. His parents were invested in their kids and Luke had had his dad's guidance and friendship—things that Cade had never known from his dad beyond financial support. Yes, Erin would be the perfect nanny in so many important ways. He would just have to resist her stunning looks and assume his normal professional manner.

"It's been a long time since I last saw you," he said, smiling at her.

She flashed a warm smile in return. "I'm surprised you remember me at all. I tried to stay out of Luke's way when he had high school friends over. In those days tall, noisy boys intimidated me."

Looking at her now, he doubted if any male intimidated her, because Luke's sister had become a gorgeous, poised woman. Just the kind of woman that he hoped Amelia would one day grow up to be. As he thought about his little niece, he felt the too familiar dull ache that came each time he thought about her parents. He missed his brother and he always would. Little Amelia should have Nate and Lydia instead of an uncle and a nanny.

As if Erin guessed his thoughts, her smile vanished. "I'm so sorry about your brother and sister-in-law."

"It was a tragedy. The drunk driver who hit them died in the crash, too. Three lives lost," he replied, still thinking about his brother.

"At least their baby wasn't with them, and how wonderful for you to be her guardian."

"It's an awesome responsibility and one that I never expected to have," he replied, his thoughts shifting from Nate to Amelia. "You know, when Nate was working on their wills and he asked me if I would be Amelia's guardian, I thought the likelihood of this ever happening was zero." He remembered how shocked and dazed he had been over Nate's and Lydia's deaths back in June and how downright awestruck he'd been when he'd realized he had full responsibility for Amelia and would be his little niece's guardian. "I don't know one thing about babies."

"Luke said your niece is six months old now."

"That's right." He nodded. "Luke said you have experience taking care of babies and little kids. I—"

"Cade, I have to be honest with you." She didn't hesitate after her interruption. "As tempting as this job is, I have to decline. Out of courtesy to my brother, I'm here to talk to you, but I don't see changing from the secretarial job I have till school starts." Smiling, she shook her head. "I'm sorry, but this won't work out. We can both tell Luke we tried."

"Don't be too hasty. Let's talk about it," Cade said, unable to resist a glance as she crossed her long legs. How did that wisp of a shy, plain kid grow into this gorgeous, leggy redhead?

Once again he had to shift his thoughts to the reason for the interview.

"Before you turn down this job, listen to what I have to offer. My grandmother is currently minding Amelia, here on the ranch. Grandmother can't deal with the care of a baby on a permanent basis. In fact, she can't deal with it for many more days. Anyway, at least meet Amelia and then let's talk."

"That seems unnecessary because I can't take the nanny job."

"The nanny job will fit in a lot more with the degrees you're getting to work with children," he reminded her. "Also, your brother is going to ask us both about our interview and it'll make him a lot happier if you at least listened to my offer. Besides," Cade added, smiling at her, "how much time does it take to meet a baby?"

There was a flicker in the depths of her green eyes and for another electric moment, he was tempted to forget about Luke and the nanny job and just enjoy the beautiful woman who sat in front of him.

Then she blinked, glanced away and the moment vanished, but it resonated long after. It was another warning that hiring her might not be as problem-free as he had hoped. But as long as she could take good care of Amelia, he could resist the volatile chemistry that had to be off-limits.

"I suppose you're right," she said, nodding. "All right, I'll meet Amelia and we'll talk."

Stifling a triumphant smile, he rose. "If you'll come with me, we'll go see my grandmother. She's in Amelia's suite. Technically it's not a nursery, but it's what we could do on short notice."

When Erin walked beside him to the open door, he realized in heels she was taller than most women he knew.

He caught a faint scent of an exotic perfume that was enticing. Keenly aware of her, he motioned her ahead and she walked past him with a polite, "Thank you."

When she passed him, he couldn't keep from letting his gaze drift down her back and linger on her hips. There was a slight, appealing sway with each step she took, and he thoroughly enjoyed the walk to the baby's suite.

His grandmother, a tall, slender woman, stood in the center of the room holding Amelia. Strands of her gray-streaked brown hair had escaped the clip behind her head and a frown furrowed her brow. Her lavender blouse had come out of her slacks, adding to her disheveled appearance. Yet another reason to hire Erin instantly, Cade thought. His grandmother needed her rest.

Margo Wakely held her crying great-grandchild as she crossed the room. "Amelia is up from her nap and occasionally she doesn't wake easily."

"I'll take her," Cade said and instantly she handed Amelia to him. He spoke softly to his little niece while smoothing her pink jumper. Black curls framed her face and tears spilled from her big blue eyes. He kissed her lightly on the forehead while patting her back and talking softly to her for a minute before looking up.

"Grandmother, meet Luke's younger sister, Erin Dorsey. Erin, this is my grandmother Margo Wakely," he said, continuing to pat Amelia's back.

"I'm sorry for your loss, Mrs. Wakely," Erin said.

"Thank you. It's still difficult and so sad for Amelia."

"Here's our baby," Cade said, looking at Amelia who continued to cry. "Usually she's a sweetie who's happy." He shrugged. "This isn't good timing."

"I've had lots of experience with babies. Let me take her." She took Amelia from Cade and walked with her.

In seconds Amelia quieted while Erin lightly patted her and walked back to Cade and his grandmother.

"Luke was right," Cade said, looking at her handling Amelia with more ease than his grandmother had and far more ease than he felt. "You're good with babies."

"With my younger siblings I've been around babies since I was two. But don't let a few minutes fool you. Sometimes they cry with me, too, although usually they don't cry a long time. Probably because I'm relaxed around them. Besides helping with my younger siblings, I did a lot of babysitting, helped with the nursery at church, that sort of thing." She looked down at Amelia, talking to her softly. "You're right—she's a sweetie."

Amelia babbled, reaching out a small fist to grab Erin's suit lapel and tug on it.

Erin picked up a pink rattle from toys spread on a nearby table and in seconds Amelia focused on the rattle. She took it in her chubby hand, making it spin and shake.

"She likes you," Margo said. "I haven't seen you in years, Erin. I remember one time when Cade left his books at your house and your brother drove over. I answered the door and you handed me his books while your brother waited in the car. You seemed a lot younger than Cade or Luke."

"I am younger. Eight years, to be exact," she replied and Cade was surprised because she was older than he had guessed.

"Now you're all grown up and a beautiful woman," Margo said, causing Erin to smile another dimpled smile that carried an impact Cade tried to resist.

"Thanks, Mrs. Wakely." She gazed down at Amelia who was happily playing with the rattle. "Look at those big, dark blue eyes. Such a beautiful little girl."

"I have to agree," Margo replied, smiling at Erin, then

casting a nod to Cade, as if giving him her seal of approval.

Cade wholeheartedly agreed. Erin was perfect for the job.

As she looked at Amelia, Cade's gaze raked over Erin. There was only one drawback. His attraction. There could be no flirting with her—something he never thought would be a problem where Luke's younger sister was concerned. And no kissing, he thought as he watched her full red lips graze Amelia's soft cheek. Talking to Luke last week, Cade had dismissed anything sexual between them. Now he realized he had probably never in his life been as wrong about something.

He just had to remember Luke was her brother. Other than his brothers, Luke was his best friend, and Cade was not about to jeopardize their long-standing relationship for a brief flirtation that would be forgotten when Erin left for grad school.

Not one bit. Telling himself he could do this, he cleared his throat and got the attention of the two women.

"Grandmother, we'll give Amelia back to you because Erin has limited time."

"Thanks for quieting her down," Margo said as she took the baby. "You have a nice touch and she likes you."

Erin smiled again. "She's a sweet and beautiful baby."

"She looks a lot like her father and she has a resemblance to her uncle," Margo said, smiling at Cade.

"Grandmother, I'll be back soon. Call Maisie if you need some help," Cade said, referring to his cook. He had already made arrangements for her to help his grandmother with Amelia when she needed it.

"I always call Maisie when I need her," Margo said.

As he walked with Erin into the hall he said, "Amelia sleeps through the night, but it's still a lot for Grandmother to take care of her. I try to be here as much as possible so I can take care of her in the evenings, but because of business, there are times I can't be at the ranch. I need a nanny as soon as possible. You saw both of us with her. I'm a novice and Grandmother has forgotten what she knew about childcare," he admitted.

"You'll learn what to do."

"It's scary. When Amelia cries, I feel like I'm failing her and Nate and Lydia."

"Relax a little, Cade. You take care of a lot of things on this ranch that are far more difficult and complicated. She's just a little girl."

"I meant it when I said that I don't know anything about babies or kids. And I especially don't know any-thing about little girls," he confessed. Then he rolled his eyes and let out a groan. "I can't bear to think of trying to deal with a teenage girl."

Erin laughed softly. "She won't be a teen for a few years so stop worrying about that. You'll get accustomed to Amelia in no time." Erin paused in the hallway to face him and her expression sobered. "I'm sorry I can't do this. While I'd love to take care of Amelia and it would fit with my future career, living on your ranch or driving back and forth to my home in Dallas every day would be too much of a hardship. And I make a very good salary where I am. I wish you luck."

He looked into those deep green eyes that he knew he wouldn't forget for a long time and he knew what he had to do. "At least hear my offer before you turn me down."

He needed Erin. Amelia needed Erin. At the same time, he had known since she walked through his office door and he got his first sight of her, that resisting the urge to have her wouldn't be easy. But he hoped it would be possible. Besides, it was only a few months, not long enough to be much of a temptation.

"Come on," he said, turning toward his office and feeling her follow behind him. "Is there anyone you're seeing who'll be upset about you accepting a job on a ranch or being away from Dallas all week?" he asked as they walked.

"No, there isn't," she replied. "Luke leaves this week for the Antarctic and isn't scheduled to be back for the rest of the year. Mom is visiting her sister who lives in Arkansas—" She stopped, as if she suddenly thought of something. "I guess you weren't talking about my brother and family." She shook her head. "There's no man in my life."

"At the moment that works out better."

They entered Cade's office and sat in the leather chairs again. She crossed her legs and looked at him expectantly.

He placed his elbows on his knees and leaned closer. "I know you're capable and reliable. I know you and your family. I trust your credentials and I can trust you to care for Amelia like she was your own. You're perfect for this job."

"Thank you for such faith in me but—"

"I know. You don't think you'll make enough money for this nanny job to be worth your time. So, let's make it worth your time. It's five months counting December and then you'll leave for graduate school, right?"

"I'm quitting my job mid-December because I want to get ready to go to the university and I want a little time at home during Christmas."

"Okay. Only four months, plus two weeks, then. That makes a bigger salary even easier." When he paused to think, she waited quietly.

"Whatever your salary is for secretarial work, I'll quadruple it if you'll work for me," he offered.

Her eyes widened as she stared at him, saying nothing.

"You can have the use of one of my cars while you live here. That way you won't have wear and tear on your car or gas to buy when you come and go out here. You can have Saturdays and Sundays off after the first month and a ten-thousand-dollar signing bonus upon acceptance. The reason for asking you to stay on the weekends the first month is because everyone else is gone on the weekend. I'll get my cook to stay Saturday and take off one day during the week, but I'm not ready to be alone with Amelia and have full charge of her care."

"Mercy…" As her lips parted, his attention was drawn to them and his curiosity rose over what it would be like to kiss her. It still shocked him that the same person he could so easily ignore as a kid now took his breath away, made his pulse race and inspired fantasies about hot kisses. He had to force his mind back onto his offer when she finally spoke.

"What you're offering is ridiculous," she whispered, still staring at him as if he had offered her all the gold in Fort Knox. "It's definitely something I have to consider, now that I'm going to grad school." Her gaze flickered as she said, "You know, if I hadn't known you all my life and if you weren't really close friends with my brother, I would suspect some ulterior motive for that kind of money. As it is, I know you well enough to know you're offering me the job for the right reasons."

"Yes, I am. Because I trust Luke's recommendation. And because Amelia is the highest priority in my life and I want the best nanny I can possibly get." He had to, for her and for his brother. When he was away from Amelia, he didn't want to worry about her. Or even when he was with her. Funny, he thought, how he could handle all kinds of things on his ranch, but taking care of a little baby scared the daylights out of him.

He looked at Erin and held his breath, hoping she wouldn't take a lot of time to make a decision.

She shook her head slowly and he wondered if she intended to say no. He needed her desperately. If she turned him down, how much more should he offer to get her to accept the job?

"I don't need time. I can't possibly turn down your offer. When do you want me to start?"

Two

"As soon as you possibly can."

He felt relief surging in him and he could hardly stifle the smile that split his lips. Although temporary, he felt positive that he just hired an excellent nanny, and someone who could teach him how to be a parent so that later, he could select the best long-term nanny for his niece.

"I feel desperate and so does my grandmother, not to mention my cook who is doing some double shifts. Although sometimes I relieve her and cook for us so that she can help my grandmother," he explained. "Actually, tomorrow would be the best possible time for you to start, but I know you can't change your life that fast."

"No, I can't, but I can move to your ranch Monday and get to know Amelia. If you or your grandmother can be here the first day or two, it would be nice, so I can see Amelia's routine and learn what I need to know about her."

"I'll work that out. Move in Monday and if I can help

you, let me know. There are a lot of guys on this ranch willing to pitch in and help you move," he said. Every guy on the ranch would help once they got a glimpse of her. "I have a small plane and I also have a private jet I keep in Dallas. If you want, I can either have my pilot fly you here, because from the ranch it's a little over 160 miles to Dallas, or have someone pick you up in Dallas in a limo and move your things. From the ranch to Downly is twenty miles."

"My head is swimming. Let me think and I'll send you a text or call you later today. How's that?"

"That's excellent," he said, sitting back and smiling at her. She did look a bit overwhelmed.

"I'm stunned by your offer and am trying to adjust to the change in my life and what this job will mean to me," she said, her gaze shifting to his as she looked intently at him.

He became aware of how close they sat, her knees almost touching his, her exotic perfume filling the air. Her green eyes had darkened slightly and her rosy lips were turned up in a slight grin. He also became aware of how much he wanted to lean closer and taste them.

Would she always be such a temptation? he wondered. Or was it just the shock of seeing her looking so different, so mature, so feminine? He told himself he'd get used to the new Erin, with some time. Meanwhile, he had nothing to worry about where she was concerned. He had no qualms that she would be circumspect, professional, focused on Amelia.

He would, too, if he always kept in mind how vulnerable Erin was and how much she was into marriage, family and permanent commitment. Also, how much he valued her brother's friendship.

And she would never flirt with him or come on to him. He remembered how solemn she used to be. The reminder should be a reassurance to him, but for some reason it wasn't.

"When you're here, if you ever have any problems, don't hesitate to tell me," he said, his voice a deeper rasp.

"Thank you," she replied. "You know, I wouldn't do this if it weren't for your friendship with Luke and all the years we've known you."

"I wouldn't do this if it weren't for Luke, either," he said.

"And I doubt if I'll need any help, but I will let you know if I do. I don't even know what I need to bring."

"Let's go look at where you'll stay." He stood but paused as he exited his office. "One more thing," he said, "I'd like you to be on duty Friday nights. If you have some place you want to go on a Friday, let me know and I'll work around it, but on Fridays, I'd like to go out."

"That's fine. I think that would work out really well," she added and he smiled.

"Don't sound so happy to be rid of me," he said and she looked startled.

"I'm joking," he added swiftly, wanting to get back to being impersonal. "If you don't want to stay by yourself with Amelia, there are a couple of wives of the cowboys who work for me who live on the ranch. I can get them to stay on Friday night so you'll have someone else here with you."

"I'll be fine. They're all here on the ranch, so someone I can call won't be far away if necessary. Right?"

"Right. Come meet Maisie, my cook. She's still in the kitchen. She has a house here and her husband works for me, too. Harold, my butler, has a house on the ranch and his wife cooks for the people who work here." Cade took Erin's arm lightly to lead her out, and was surprised when the faint contact sent tingles up his arm. Yes, he thought, the woman was certainly tempting. Thank goodness once he had her situated and familiar with her charge and his staff, he could throw himself into work and see her less.

But how could he do that?

He needed to learn how to cope with Amelia. He needed to follow Erin around and see how to care for his charge. He also needed to bond with Amelia and when he did, Erin would be present, too. They were going to be thrown together, living together in his ranch house, spending a lot of time together with Amelia. And he had to remain cool and professional, the boss and his nanny.

He clung to the knowledge that even though Erin was gorgeous, there were other beautiful women who were far more lighthearted, ready to party, wanting the same freedom he did and who hadn't lost a baby or been hurt badly in a recent broken engagement. There were so many reasons to remain professional and distant with her, so why did they seemed to evaporate when he looked into her big, green eyes?

They entered the kitchen where a slender woman with braided blond hair wiped the countertops. "Ahh, hello, there," she said. "You must be Luke's younger sister. I can see a family resemblance."

Erin laughed. "I've heard that before, but not often."

"Erin, meet Maisie Elsworth, my cook and the person who keeps this place going. If you have questions about Amelia, the job or the ranch, or need help, Maisie is the person to ask."

"Absolutely," Maisie replied, smiling. "You'll love little Amelia and maybe you can teach this Wild West cowboy how to calm her. She's adorable." Maisie looked away and wiped her eyes, turning her back. "You'll have to give me a moment. I feel as if I lost one of my own boys when we lost Amelia's dad. The same for the little one's mother. So sad, and sometimes it hits me out of the blue," she said, still wiping her eyes.

Cade stepped up to put his arm around her and give her a squeeze. He stood quietly while she became composed again and turned to Erin.

"Sorry," Maisie said. "Moments come without warning when I realize they're gone forever and I think of little Amelia."

"Don't ever apologize because you love someone," Erin said. Cade thought about her miscarriage and how much she must have hurt over losing her baby, and how much she was still hurting.

"Ahh, you'll be a good nanny for our little baby," Maisie told her. "I hope your brother is fine. I miss seeing him. They were fun boys, but now they're grown men and busy and I don't see them."

"You see me plenty, Maisie," Cade said with a grin. "You'll see more of me today, but right now, I want to show Erin where she'll be staying when she moves in."

"It'll be good to have you with us," she said to Erin and Cade wondered whether he had just complicated his future while making Amelia's more secure.

Next, Cade took Erin to a suite that held four rooms. She walked into the center of the living area, turning to look at the room that had oak floors, a thick area rug in two tones of blue, watercolor paintings of horses on the walls, and glass and teak furniture.

Cade watched her turn to look around, his gaze running over her. He was still amazed by the changes in her appearance, even though common sense told him she wouldn't look the way she had at ten.

"Go ahead and look at the bedroom, the closet and the adjoining bathroom," Cade urged, wanting her to be happy with the job and where she would live. "There's also a small office with computer equipment."

He watched her thick red hair swing slightly across her shoulders as she walked out of sight into the bedroom. When she returned, she smiled—another friendly, dimpled smile that under other circumstances he would have accepted as an invitation to flirt.

"This is marvelous," she said. "I'll go back to the office and give notice today. They won't mind letting me go because I'm temporary anyway. I'll just leave sooner than I had planned."

He suspected they were going to mind letting her go, but he merely nodded. "Good. We'll stop by my office and I'll write a check to you for your signing bonus." They fell into step and he was aware of her close beside him. When they entered his office he hastily wrote the check, his fingers brushing hers when he handed it to her.

Every physical contact, no matter how slight or how much he tried to ignore it, was noticeable—all red flag warnings that he would have to deal carefully with her.

What made the feathery brushes of their hands noticeable besides his reaction was awareness that she responded, too. Her reaction showed in tiny ways: a surprised look, a flicker in her eyes, a deep breath. Some kind of chemistry existed between them, an attraction that he could not pursue and she didn't want.

When they walked to his front porch, she turned to face him, offering her hand.

"Thank you for this fantastic offer. I'm going to love taking care of Amelia and now I won't have to worry about finances so much," she said, withdrawing her hand that was soft and slender.

"Even though you're on a full scholarship, I know

your brother has offered to pay your college expenses and you've always turned him down."

"He put himself through school and I want to do this on my own, too, the way he did. I have my undergraduate degree now, so I'm making progress and I see the proverbial light at the end of the tunnel."

"Congratulations. That's commendable," Cade said, realizing she had a streak of independence that was so like her brother. "For the present, you have my phone number in case you need anything. And the offer of help to move still stands. I'll see you Monday."

"Thanks. I never dreamed I'd be in a business arrangement with you someday. And I'm sure you wouldn't have thought it possible to be in one with me," she said, her eyes twinkling. "I might as well have been wallpaper for all the attention you ever gave me back then."

He smiled and held back a reply that came to mind instantly, that he definitely noticed her now and she wasn't anything like wallpaper. He glanced at her full lips and wondered again about kissing her. More forbidden thoughts plagued him, thoughts that he would have to squelch. How many times would he have to remind himself?

"Cade, thank you again so very much for this job. I'm thrilled and looking forward to getting started," she said.

With an effort, he stepped back. "See you Monday," he said, taking a deep breath.

"Sure," she said, giving him one more long look before she hurried to her small black car. She waved as she drove away.

He had an excellent, trustworthy nanny—and a nagging worry that he might be bringing trouble home in a big way. Was he going to be able to ignore the chemistry that smoldered between them today? Was he going to be careful to avoid trying to seduce his nanny? He had to or he'd lose his best friend forever. Besides, he wasn't interested in commitment and Erin was the marrying kind. She had already been hurt badly and was vulnerable. He couldn't hurt her more.

Cade watched her car go down the ranch drive, but all he really saw were big green eyes and a rosy mouth that looked ripe for kissing.

When Erin glanced at her rearview mirror, Cade still stood on the porch of his sprawling ranch house. A tall Texas rancher, a man worth millions, yet he looked like other cowboys from ranches all over Texas. Except he was more handsome than most.

Smiling, she thought about how he had been shocked that she had grown up. He had never paid attention to her the years he was in high school. All her brother's friends had seemed big and intimidating and they had seldom taken notice of her, which was a relief to her. She just tried to avoid them and go ahead with what she wanted to do.

By the time Cade graduated from college, she was in her early teens and was attracted to him, thinking he was to-die-for handsome. She had a silly, schoolgirl crush that she told no one about. She knew the times he was at their house he didn't notice her any more than he had when she was nine years old and he had been in high school.

She hadn't seen Cade in years and it was a surprise to see an appealing, good-looking rancher. A grown man now—handsome, filled out and older, with that air of confidence that was as evident as it was with her brother.

Even though Cade was still her brother's closest friend, there was only a little she knew about him.

When she rounded a bend in the road and his house disappeared from the view behind her, she let out her breath. With the check he had just given her, there was no way she could turn down his job offer, but it was going to hurt badly at times.

She still wasn't over her losses completely, though the pain had eased somewhat. Losing her baby had been devastating and when Cade handed Amelia to her, she'd had a terrible clutch to her heart and felt tears sting her eyes. As she drove down the graveled, dusty ranch road, a pang still tore at her. She didn't think she would ever stop hurting over losing her baby, even though it had been early in her pregnancy, and she knew that Amelia was going to be a constant reminder of what she had lost.

Now she had taken a job that was going to dredge up that pain again every day until she got accustomed to dealing with Amelia and could focus on her charge without thinking about her miscarriage. Amelia looked so adorable, she should bring cheer just by being a sweet baby.

Cade, however, might not be so easily handled. He loomed, another giant difficulty because of his incredible appeal. What might make working for him difficult was the chemistry between them. Where had that come from? She felt it and she knew he had. Or maybe he stirred that reaction in all the women he met.

Several times today, he had looked at her intently, giving her the look a man gives a woman when he actually sees her as an attractive woman. She wasn't so out of practice that she didn't recognize it.

It wouldn't have mattered if he had spent the whole interview flirting with her. She didn't want to date, didn't want to fall in love, didn't want any kind of relationship. The pain of her broken engagement was still too real, too intense. The consequences of any relationship would bring back too many hurtful memories.

She didn't want to get involved emotionally with any man at this point in her life and definitely not Cade. She knew his views on relationships and his cynical view of marriage. She might not ever be able to have a baby, but she still wanted marriage and children in her future and that was not what Cade had ever wanted. If she could resist Cade's appeal and deal with the hurt and reminders of her loss that Amelia would unknowingly cause, this job would be great. A huge windfall for her, and good experience for her future career. Cade's offer had been irresistible. No way could she have turned it down.

Even though Erin tried to avoid thinking too much about her doctor's warning that she might not ever be able to carry a baby full-term, it was impossible to forget. If she couldn't bear a child, she would adopt. She would have a family, one way or another, but that would come in her future. Now she intended to concentrate on grad school and her career.

For a few months she would take care of a precious little girl. Amelia Callahan was a beautiful baby with lots of thick black curls and big dark blue eyes like her uncle. Erin remembered the few minutes when she held her and Amelia had stopped crying, looking into Erin's eyes as if they were bonding.

And you bonded with her uncle, too.

She ignored the insinuating voice inside her head. She hadn't bonded with Cade; she'd simply looked at him while he spoke to her. Yeah, and drowned in his eyes. And nearly ignited when he touched her.

Who was she kidding? Working for Cade was going to take difficult to new levels.

Living on the ranch, she could only hope Cade would be gone most of the day. It would make her job easier if he wasn't around. She was going to love precious little

Amelia and when December came, it would be dreadful to say goodbye.

In the meantime she'd simply avoid caring too much about Amelia's appealing guardian.

On Monday Erin changed clothes several times, finally deciding on practical navy slacks, a short-sleeve matching cotton blouse with a round neckline and navy pumps. She brushed her hair and stood looking at herself until she realized she was thinking about how Cade would view her. She had to stop that. And she had to put a halt to the heart-pounding, prickly awareness of him that had plagued her all weekend.

Her apartment bell buzzed and she went to the intercom to hear her brother's voice. "Am I too early?"

"No. I'm ready to go. Come up."

She opened her apartment door and in minutes Luke swept into the room. "Hey, you look nice," he said, studying her and then turning his eyes on her bags, laptop, carry-on and purse stacked near the door.

"Thanks, Luke, for helping me load my car."

"Sure. I'm glad you're doing this and I'm glad he's paying you well. I figured he would."

"The pay is fantastic. Now I don't have to worry about school."

"I still say, anytime you need anything or if you run short of money, let me know. I'm single, earning a good living and I'll be happy to help you. You don't have to pay me back, either—that's the best part."

She smiled at him. "The best part is that you made the offer. That gives me a secure feeling that I can always turn to you if something disastrous happens."

"Damn straight. Speaking of something disastrous… Let me remind you again—"

"Luke," she cautioned and laughed. "Don't tell me to avoid going out with Cade. He never even noticed me until he wanted to hire me. He knows I'm your little sister and he won't jeopardize his friendship with you. Now stop worrying about me."

"I'm worrying about what Cade will do, although I don't think he'll hit on you for the reasons you just gave. I can promise that he notices you now. He didn't when you were eight or nine years old, but...well, you look a lot different now. Let me remind you that while Cade loves the ladies, he is dead set against marriage. When it comes to long-term relationships, there's not a serious bone in his body. He doesn't know what a real family is—I know he always enjoyed being at our house partly because of our parents. He's close with his brothers and his mother had good intentions, but she was more interested in a social life. What I'm saying is Cade is not your type and you don't need another hurt."

"Luke—"

"Be advised. I will come back from Antarctica and punch him out if he tries to date you," he said, grinning at her.

She laughed, shaking her head and not taking him seriously. "No, you won't. He's your lifelong best friend. I think that covers it all. He knows how you feel and he knows I'm your little sister. I'm going to be the nanny. I'll be with his grandmother and his little ward, but I won't be with him. Frankly, I think he's scared to take care of Amelia by himself and he doesn't know how."

"You've got that right. For once in his life he is terrified. He told me as much when I spoke to him. He doesn't know anything about babies, even though he had younger brothers. They're too close in age for him to have learned anything about babies. Oh, and speaking of his brothers...

Little brother Gabe Callahan is single, closer to your age, likes to party and I imagine he'll ask you out. And Gabe doesn't take anything seriously—definitely not a relationship."

"Duly noted," she said, laughing at her brother. "If I get asked out, I can deal with that, and since I'll be the nanny and Cade is desperate and doesn't know how to care for Amelia, I'll have the best possible excuse to turn down any invitations by any guys I meet. Cade's already asked me if I would stay on Friday nights so he can go out. Stop worrying."

"Okay," he said, though she got the impression he really wanted to continue his dire warnings.

"Let's get the car loaded before I'm late arriving at his ranch. I'll text you and keep you posted on how I'm getting along. Everyone you work with there will wonder why you keep getting reports from me on my well-being."

"They'll know it's because I can't be there myself and I'm a class-A worrier when it comes to my baby sister. Cade is a great guy and my best friend, but I don't want you hurt by him."

"Luke, for the last time, you've got to stop. I believe you're the one who wanted me to interview with him and go to work for him," she said sweetly and Luke clamped his mouth shut. "Let's go," she said, picking up a bag which he took from her hands.

After her car was packed and her apartment locked, she hugged Luke. "I hope you love your work. You know, environmental engineers can find jobs in Texas."

He grinned. "This is a change and I'll learn new things. The South Pole needs protection. They have wastewater problems just like Dallas does."

"Don't give me one of your lectures about protecting our earth. I'm recycling."

"Keep at it. Every little bit helps. For my part, I'm excited about working there."

"Good. I'm excited about my new job, too. Amelia is a precious little girl."

Her brother studied her. "You'll work there a little over four months—you shouldn't get too attached in that time."

She brushed off his concern. "That little girl needs someone to care for her and I'm happy to get the job—and very happy to get the money," she added lightly. But inside, she was afraid she was already attached to Amelia, yet willing to care for her because her guardian was clueless about baby care. "It's too short a time for any attachment I form to get too strong," she lied. "Now you stop worrying and take care of yourself." She hugged him again.

"Don't I always?" Luke grinned as he held open the car door for her to get behind the wheel. He closed her door and stepped back, and she saw him watching her as she drove away. She turned the corner and he was lost to sight, but his warnings about Cade echoed in her mind.

Would this job be the blessing for all as she hoped? Or was she driving straight into trouble and more heartache?

When Erin arrived at the ranch, Cade came out in long strides to greet her. Her heartbeat jumped. This wasn't going to be the easiest job, she realized right away. The instant she saw him all her intentions to resist Cade's appeal vanished like smoke in the wind.

August sunshine spilled over him, and locks of his raven hair blew slightly in the breeze. Emitting a contagious vitality, he looked tan, strong and fit in his tight jeans, boots, and a red plaid shirt with the sleeves rolled up.

"Welcome to the ranch," he said, smiling at her. "My

grandmother is thrilled about your arrival today. Frankly, she's not accustomed to caring for a baby and she's worn threadbare."

Erin smiled at him, aware of his dark blue eyes as his gaze swept over her. If he had stayed in Dallas where he worked with his younger brother Gabe, in commercial real estate, and left her with his grandmother, Maisie, Harold and the rest of his staff, her life would be peaceful. As it was, while she looked up at such blue eyes and thick, black hair, she wondered if she would have another peaceful moment until this job ended in December.

"I'm eager to get started and to get to know Amelia," she said, trying to focus on her job.

Cade shouldered a carry-on and took her laptop from her hands. Their hands brushed in a casual touch that stirred more sparks.

"We'll get all your things," he said as Harold came out of the house and hurried to carry her luggage.

Holding Amelia in her arms, his grandmother stepped out and stood watching on the porch while Erin made her way up the walk, Cade beside her. At the top of the steps, she paused to greet Margo and Amelia.

"I'm so happy you're here," Margo said.

She returned the pleasantry. "Let me take Amelia," she said once she entered the house and set down her purse. Dressed in a blue-and-yellow jumper and yellow blouse, Amelia smelled sweet. When she studied Erin with her thickly lashed big blue eyes, Erin smiled at her.

"I'm glad you're here so you can tell me about her routine," Erin said quietly to Margo.

"We haven't exactly established a routine. It's been a long, long time since I've had the care of a baby. I had two girls and Crystal was my youngest. She's Cade's mother. By the time the boys were born, Crystal had a nanny

and help, so there was little for me to do about their care.
They're close together in age and I didn't raise boys, so I
didn't really have them with me often."

Erin nodded, thinking how different that was from her
mother's life and her own, caring for her little nephews
who stayed with her parents for a lot of nights. Her parents had raised a big family with boys and girls and they
loved having their grandchildren around.

"We'll go to what is the nursery for now," Cade said.
"Amelia's suite is between my suite and yours. The sitting room is now a playroom. Like I said earlier, we really didn't have time to change things when I got Amelia.
I wanted to get her settled and familiar with where she is.
I think she needs stability after the upheaval in her life."
He clamped his mouth closed and a muscle flexed in his
jaw. She guessed he was having a bad moment about losing his brother and sister-in-law, or possibly a bad moment thinking about Amelia losing a mommy and daddy.
She could understand because of her own heartaches and
she looked at Amelia, smoothing the baby's unruly curls
from her forehead.

Big blue eyes studied her solemnly and Erin smiled
at Amelia, knowing the baby would grow accustomed to
her as time passed.

She glanced at Cade to find him watching her and she
wondered what he was thinking. But she didn't ask.

Cade paused in front of Amelia's suite and motioned
her in, though he moved down toward another open door.

"I'll put these in your room and be right in."

Erin entered the baby's suite and turned to see Margo
settle on a sofa. She glanced around at a room she had
barely looked at the day of her interview. Stuffed toys
were scattered on a blanket on the floor. There were more

on a chair, plus rattles and blocks. A toy box overflowed with baby toys on one side of the sofa. There was a baby swing at one side of the room and a baby chair in the middle of the room.

Erin sat in a rocker and rocked while still holding Amelia. "She doesn't seem interested in getting down or in her toys."

"She woke early this morning, so she might be getting sleepy again," Margo said. "Cade is here with you and if you don't have any questions, I think I'll go answer my emails. Call me if you need me," she added and Erin nodded, wondering if she was going to be alone with Cade often or if he would disappear to work. Whatever happened, she realized her job as nanny had started instantly and she wasn't going to get any schedule from Margo regarding Amelia.

Getting down on the floor with Amelia, Erin rolled a clear plastic ball filled with sparkling objects and little silver bells. As she looked at the pretty little girl, she knew she was in for another heartache because she was going to love this baby so much by the time she finished her temporary job. Amelia was easy to love. Maybe she found reassurance from those who were taking care of her. Whatever made Amelia happy, Erin was drawn to her. In almost four months, she was certain she would love the girl as her own, but she would let her go because that would be best for Amelia.

If only she could guard her heart from falling in love with the handsome rancher who was Amelia's guardian. How was she going to resist him when they had to be together for Amelia's sake? How was she going to resist him, too, when he already made her heart pound and she wanted to be in his arms?

* * *

Cade entered the nursery and saw Erin on a blanket on the floor rolling a ball around in front of Amelia, while Amelia laughed and grabbed for it.

When Erin looked up at him, her red hair swung across her shoulders and he drew a deep breath. Why hadn't Luke told him his sister had grown into such a beauty?

He knew exactly why and he needed to remember that he had promised Luke he would not do anything to hurt Erin. As he gazed into her green eyes, he tried to remember what he had intended to tell her.

"Ah, Erin, I see Grandmother has already fled the scene and left it all to you," he said, looking down at her and looking at Amelia. "Amelia seems happy."

"For having such upheaval in her life, she's a happy baby. I think they sense what's happening around them."

He sat on the end of the sofa, so close he could easily reach out and touch her and Amelia. "She's doing better," he said as he shifted his attention to the baby. "At first she cried a lot. Thank goodness she doesn't cry as much now because that tears me up. When she's been fed and isn't sleepy and everything should be all right, but she still cries, I feel as if she wants Lydia or Nate."

"Cade, I'm sorry," Erin said softly, touching his hand lightly. She removed her hand instantly and drew a deep breath as he turned to look at her.

The moment had changed again as soon as she'd touched him. He was instantly hot, wanting to reach for her, wanting to flirt with her, to kiss her. That slight touch that was simply meant to console him stirred a potent desire within him.

Wide-eyed, Erin looked at him, then shifted away. When her cheeks turned pink, he decided she felt the same rush of desire as he had—and the knowledge only deepened his response to her.

"Amelia's happy now," she said, casting her gaze on the baby rolling the ball around. Erin laughed as she caught the ball and placed it back in front of Amelia.

"Now that you're here, my grandmother will be going home to Dallas."

"That's fine. You've hired me and I can manage. That's my job."

"I know you can take care of her easily, but I really expected Grandmother to at least give you a day. But I should have known because I know my grandmother. She's not into childcare."

"Your grandmother has been here since the accident?"

He shook his head. "No. Last May my older brother—actually my half brother—Blake Callahan married. His wife, Sierra, is expecting. She's been so good—she took Amelia for a week when I couldn't right after the accident in June. I didn't want to impose on her, but she insisted."

"That was nice of her," she said, smiling at him and turning back to Amelia. His gaze ran over Erin's profile and he noticed her dark lashes were long and thick. Her skin was flawless, soft looking. He realized the drift of his thoughts and tried to refocus. He told her more about his new sister-in-law.

"Sierra is like you are with Amelia, totally relaxed and competent with a baby. She has a big family with lots of kids. Her grandfather was involved in an agency in Kansas City that had a shelter for the homeless. They've branched out and have a home for kids who need a place, and this past year they opened a small animal rescue."

"I hope I get to meet her."

"You probably will because I'm close with Blake. Sierra's family is the opposite of ours. My dad, Dirkson

Callahan, is not into family and kids. He attended the funeral, left when it was over and we haven't seen him since. He's too busy making money."

"I've known you a long time, but I don't know your family."

"My dad is Dirkson Callahan and his first marriage was only eight months long, no children. He married Veronica next and had Blake, but divorced when Blake was a baby. He never acknowledged Blake, not until recently when Blake contacted him. Then my dad married my mom, Crystal, and I'm the oldest, then Nate and then Gabe. After Mom and Dad divorced he hasn't married again, but there were plenty of mistresses."

"You make me more grateful than ever for my parents."

"You're lucky. Anyway, when Nate's will was read, I was named guardian, but I already knew that because Nate asked me before they did their wills and set up a trust. Nate and I were always close. Anyway, Grandmother took pity on me and came to help me until I could get a nanny. And Maisie was around to help out, of course."

"It sounds to me as if you've had everything covered."

"I want everything perfect for Amelia. I owe it to Nate and Lydia." He reached out and cradled the baby's cheek before she grabbed her ball again. "Amelia seems fragile. I don't know whether she likes me, I don't know what to feed her. I'm at a loss," he admitted. "I've never felt so helpless."

"Now I'm here for her, and before I leave you can hire another nanny and you'll be fine. So will Amelia because you love her. Don't worry, Cade, I'll teach you how to care for her."

He bit back a reply that she could teach him a lot of things, but he wouldn't have been referring to Amelia.

"There's one rule of thumb when it comes to babies,"

she said. "Use common sense." Her eyes seemed to twinkle when she added, "You run this ranch and it's loaded with babies, just the four-footed kind."

"They're easy and that's different. I think you're on the verge of laughing at me," he said, looking into those green eyes that captivated him.

"Not really. You're worrying too much. She's going to love you. I've already seen her reach for you, so she likes you and trusts you or she wouldn't do that."

"I hope so," he said. "Look, I know Grandmother abandoned you but I have to make a long-distance call. Then I'll come back."

"You don't need to come back—not that I don't want to see you, but we'll get along fine."

"Can I get anything for you right now?"

"No. We're fine. We'll get to know each other. She'll probably take a nap later."

"I do know she had lunch before you came because I fed her. Don't hesitate to go get my grandmother if you need to. She shouldn't have left you the first hour you're here. Or go ask Maisie. She's polite and honest. And you can always call me on my cell if you need me."

"This isn't a difficult job," she said, smiling at him. "Go do what you have to do," she said, rolling the ball back and forth in front of Amelia who patted it and tried unsuccessfully to grab it. Erin glanced up to meet Cade's solemn gaze and the moment she looked into his eyes, he felt fiery sparks between them.

Unfortunately—or maybe fortunately—he needed to get some business taken care of, so he had to leave her. He suspected the better he got to know Erin, the more difficult it was going to be to keep a professional attitude with her. And he had to.

No matter if it killed him.

* * *

Only when Cade left the room did Erin let out the breath she'd been holding. How on earth was she going to get through the next few months when desire arced between them like that? Though the two times she'd been with him had been relatively brief, this heart-pounding, breathtaking fiery attraction had flared to life each time. It was as unnerving as it was unwanted. She was certain it would disappear and nothing would come of it, but until that happened, his appeal shocked her.

Amelia gave the big ball a push and it rolled away. She held out her tiny arms and waved them, wanting the ball back. Laughing, Erin got it and rolled it to Amelia. "Here's your pretty ball, sweet baby," she said softly, wanting Amelia to get accustomed to being with her.

This job wasn't really that different from the many she'd had as a babysitter except she would live on the ranch for the next few months. Living on his ranch with Cade—that was the difference. She had felt sorry for his hurt and wasn't thinking beyond sympathy for him and for little Amelia when she had placed her hand on Cade's as a reassurance.

The instant she'd touched him, everything had changed. Her sympathy vanished, replaced by a fiery awareness of Cade as an appealing, sexy man. The contact made her tingle; even more, the slight touch of her hand on his had made her want to be in his arms.

She hadn't felt a shred of desire for any man since she'd had the miscarriage last year. After Adam broke their engagement and called off the wedding, even the tiniest flicker of desire was gone. She hadn't wanted to date. No man had appealed to her. She had thrown herself into school and been numb otherwise.

That had ended the minute she walked into Cade Callahan's office and looked into his dark blue eyes. That strong physical awareness didn't diminish, even though she knew all about Cade's attitude toward commitment and his decision never to marry. She knew he liked to party and liked women who wanted to party. He was definitely not the type of man she would ever want to get involved with. Intimacy with Cade, however spectacular physically, would be meaningless emotionally.

So why did she have this volatile reaction to a mere look from him, or these tingles from an accidental contact of their hands or arms? He hadn't flirted or tried to kiss her, yet the slightest brush of their hands made her heart thud and made her want to be in his arms, to have his mouth on hers.

How could she have this reaction to a man her brother had repeatedly warned her didn't have it in him to be serious or to place any value on marriage and family?

How could she be drawn to a man like that?

She had to get more resistance to Cade and keep up her guard because she was going to be in close contact with him. They would have physical contact. They were sharing a baby and they would be sharing a house. Both their rooms opened into Amelia's room.

Luke had warned her and he was right. She did not want to go home with a broken heart when this job ended no more than her brother wanted her to. But she had a problem. A big problem. How was she going to resist Cade, a man she had been attracted to since she was thirteen, a man who could make her tremble by a look and make her want him by the mere brush of his fingers? How could she stay under the same roof, day and night, and say no to him?

Three

After playing for almost an hour with Amelia, Erin realized Amelia was tired and picked her up to change her
and rock her to sleep. Leaving the door open between
rooms, she unpacked her things.

That night for dinner they ate in the casual dining
area adjoining the kitchen on one side. There was a large
casual living area on the other side. Both areas were separated from the kitchen by islands, and there was a lot of
space in all three rooms.

During dinner with Margo and Cade, Erin's attention
was on Amelia, although she was well aware of Cade.
After dinner they moved to a sunny living area that overlooked part of the patio and flower beds of multicolored
blooms surrounded by a green lawn. The house and lawn
were an oasis in miles of mesquite and cacti.

Later when Erin left to put Amelia down for the night,
Margo went with her. Leaving the task to Erin, Margo
hovered in the background, sitting in one of the large

recliners in the baby's room until Erin stopped rocking Amelia. Erin put her down and stood beside her to make sure she stayed asleep. Finally, as they tiptoed out of the baby's suite, Margo turned to Erin.

"Thank you for taking her today. I knew you would do fine and it's an immense relief."

"I enjoyed taking care of her. She's a sweet, happy little girl."

"Well, I'm not as young as I was and I'm really worn-out from childcare. I'm going to turn in early so I'll say good-night now. But you go join Cade. There's a baby monitor in Amelia's room and you can hear it anywhere in the house so you'll know if she stirs. You can see her, too, with this iPad that Cade bought for this purpose. You've been a great help today, Erin. I'm thankful you took this job and Cade is relieved, too, that you're here. It's wonderful to turn Amelia's care over to someone who likes her and knows how to take care of babies."

"Thank you," Erin said, hating to tell Margo goodnight and go back to Cade when it was only the two of them. Reminding herself of his polite attitude earlier in the day, she parted with Margo, took a deep breath and left to join him.

As she entered the room, he stood, his gaze sweeping over her and, again, her fragile peace of mind shattered. When he had come in from work, he had showered and changed to fresh jeans and a blue knit shirt. Locks of his unruly wavy hair fell slightly on his forehead. Standing quietly, he dominated the room and made her pulse quicken, a reaction she wished she didn't have. Cade was too handsome, too appealing and she was thankful he had been professional and polite so far, because she wasn't ready to deal with him otherwise.

As she glanced around the room that had comfortable furniture, soft lighting and an inviting casualness, she noticed Amelia's toys had vanished, probably to her toy box.

"Thank you. You picked up her toys and put them away. Very nice, Cade, but I'll always be happy to do that. It goes with my job."

"Not necessarily," he said easily. "I'm able-bodied and can pick up toys. Also, congratulations. You made it through your first day. Want a glass of wine to celebrate?"

Smiling, she shook her head. "Instead, I think a glass of iced tea will do nicely." She followed him to the bar. "It was a good day," she said as he poured her drink and held it out to her. When she took it from him, their fingers brushed, another casual bit of contact that should have gone unnoticed, but instead only heightened her smoldering awareness of him. She intended to drink some of her tea, stay about half an hour and then go to her suite.

"Let's sit where it's comfortable," he said, grabbing himself a beer and moving to a brown leather chair, while she sat in a tan wing chair. "Anything new from your brother except warnings about me?"

"Not really. Since we graduated from high school each one of us goes on with life. Chunks of time pass between communications with him and once he leaves, I don't expect to hear much from him."

"That may be a good thing." Cade smiled and she laughed, her dimple showing.

"You know my brother well. Luke's the oldest, so he's accustomed to telling the others what to do. I'm the next, and even though I'm twenty-two and there are several years between our ages, we're close. It's a little amazing you're such good friends because you're both alpha males—very much alike probably."

"We don't see each other as much now and we never

did run each other's lives." He hesitated, then added, "Well, we both make suggestions, like him telling me to hire you."

"I imagine a better description would be *hounding* you to hire me until you were desperate enough to listen to him."

He smiled and her heart did another skip because it softened his features and it heightened his appeal.

"No," he replied. "I had mixed feelings about it until I saw you with Amelia. She took to you instantly and you were relaxed with her. Actually, anyone watching you who didn't know, would think you had been taking care of Amelia for a long time."

"I've spent a lot of time with babies."

"Well, Grandmother and I are grateful you've adjusted so quickly. She's worn-out. I don't know whether she told you or not, she's going home tomorrow."

Erin drew a sharp breath. "I thought she planned to stay awhile after I arrived," she said, instantly thinking of the moments she would be alone with Cade.

"Not anymore. She said you don't seem to need anyone, that you took charge from the first moment and she's just watched." His eyes narrowed. "Is there some reason you feel she needs to stay longer?"

His blue eyes were intent and she didn't want him to realize how on edge she felt with him. He might guess why she didn't want his grandmother to go.

"No, of course not." She hoped she sounded positive and casual. "I'll be fine. I just didn't want her to feel unwanted."

He stared at her a moment in silence and then shook his head. "Believe me, she doesn't feel unwanted. She couldn't wait to turn Amelia's care over to you."

Erin smiled at him. "I'm happy to have full charge of Amelia. She's easy."

"You'll be great with Amelia." He looked away with a muscle working in his jaw and she guessed that he was thinking about his deceased brother.

He sipped his beer and turned to look at her again. "When I'm out on the ranch, you can always get me on my phone and don't hesitate if you need me. I'll introduce you to my foreman and you can call him, too. Maisie is here during the day and you can get her if you need help. There will always be someone close."

"That's good to know."

"I promised you a complete tour of the house—want to look now?"

"Yes. This is a good time," she said, standing. She had the feeling that he was carefully trying to be friendly and yet keep a distance, which was a relief.

He showed her the formal, grand living area with elegant furniture and a massive stone fireplace with a large watercolor landscape above the marble mantel. She was relieved to see the fireplace had padding to protect Amelia if she fell against the stone hearth.

The open area had thick, handcrafted area rugs and columns that separated it from the dining room which was dominated by a polished cherrywood table that would seat twenty-four.

"Do you actually have this many people here for dinner?" she said, looking at the elegant table and then turning to catch him gazing at her with an intense look as personal as the touch of his hand, and made her forget his dining room.

"Occasionally," he answered. His voice held a husky note and she walked into the hall.

"Where do we go from here?"

He followed in silence, a brooding look on his face. Was he regretting hiring her? She didn't think the look he gave her was one of regret. Far from it.

They toured his house while conversation remained polite, impersonal, and she kept a discreet distance between them. In the entertainment room, she turned to him. "Amelia is a sound sleeper. I think I'll look in on her and turn in myself."

"Sure," he said, walking beside her. "I told you earlier that my suite is on the other side of hers. Come look. I'll show you," he said and in a few minutes ushered her through a wide-open door into a big sitting room with floor-to-ceiling windows along one side of the room that led to a patio and yard. The sitting room had a large Navajo rug, a polished hardwood floor, a beamed twelve-foot ceiling and a giant television screen on one wall. Bookcases lined another wall and a stone fireplace was on the fourth wall. He'd decorated with oil paintings of landscapes and Western scenes.

"Come on and see my bedroom," he said, taking her arm lightly and going through another open door into a spacious bedroom with another fireplace, more bookshelves, more glass. His oversize king bed with navy and light blue as a color theme, as well as his large leather sofa added to a room that appeared comfortable and a reflection of the man who lived in it. Through open doors, she could see a bathroom and to another side she saw a door open to an office with three computer screens on a wide glass desk. She was aware it was his room, more aware of him standing close beside her.

"I have baby monitors in here, plus my iPad so I can see and hear her if she stirs."

"So if she cries both of us are going to see about her?" she asked, wanting to avoid any such thing.

"No, I'm leaving that for you. It's in an emergency that I'll be around."

Relieved, she nodded. "You have a beautiful house. Lots of room for little Amelia."

When they stepped into the hall, she smiled at him. "I have some of my things to put away. I didn't finish today and I want to check on Amelia, so I'll say good-night now."

"Good night, Erin. I can't tell you how glad we are to have you here," he said.

She nodded and turned, going into her suite when she really wanted to stay and talk, but knowing which was the wiser course to follow.

Before she went to bed, she had on her blue cotton robe over matching pajamas. She opened the connecting door to Amelia's big room and looked around. Seeing no other occupant, Erin crossed the room to Amelia's crib. Amelia lay curled on her side, her black ringlets tangled and her dark lashes casting shadows on her rosy cheeks. Erin paused beside her bed and a tight pain squeezed her heart.

What would her baby have been like? How many times would she wonder about that? How long would this big empty void be in her life? How long would the hurt of losing her little baby continue?

There were times she couldn't stop the tears and her loss overwhelmed her. As time passed, her tears came less often, but she didn't think they would ever stop. The loss was too big and too important.

She heard a faint scrape and looked around. The door to Cade's room was closed and he was probably moving around in his suite. She needed to get back to her own suite.

Smoothing ringlets off the baby's forehead, Erin thought about Amelia's loss she would cry over when she was old enough to understand, but right now she slept in blissful peace, too young to know she had lost both mother and father, secure in the love of Cade and Margo and the people around her.

Erin wiped away her tears again and inhaled deeply. She had a wonderful temporary job that would pay her a small fortune. She worked with a sweet baby and very nice people. If she could keep from falling in love with Cade and giving her heart to Amelia as well, she would have a wonderful experience.

How simple it sounded—resist falling in love with Cade, and avoid loving Amelia, too. Would it really be that easy when they would be together daily?

It was midafternoon by the time Erin saw Cade the next day. He was standing beside his grandmother on the front porch, a limo waiting to take her to his private jet in Dallas.

Erin watched while Margo hugged and kissed Amelia, who in turn smiled at her great-grandmother. Once again she was struck by the resemblance to Cade. They looked so much alike, Amelia could have been his baby. Obviously Cade and his brother resembled each other. She had never met any of his brothers, at least that she could recall, although they might have been at her house at one time or another.

Margo was dressed in yellow linen slacks and a matching blouse and pumps. Coincidentally, Erin had dressed Amelia in a yellow jumper and white blouse. To say goodbye Erin had fastened a little yellow hair bow in Amelia's black curls. Erin didn't expect the ribbon to last long, but at least long enough for her to take several pictures of Margo holding Amelia.

When she handed Amelia to Erin, she smiled. "I'm

glad you're taking pictures. Cade never thinks about it and neither do I, so we don't have recent pictures of her. Please send some to me."

"I'll send you copies of all I take," Erin replied.

"Amelia is going to love you like one of the family," Margo said as she patted her arm. "You can do much better than I can for this delightful girl."

"I don't know about that," Erin said politely, smiling at Margo. "But I agree she's a joy."

"She is, but at my age she's also a handful. I'm glad you're here. Now I won't worry about Cade or Amelia. You take care."

"I will," Erin answered, aware of Cade patiently waiting and watching them. When Margo turned away, he held her arm lightly to walk down the steps with her, to kiss her cheek and help her into the limo. He stood watching it drive away and then came back to the porch.

"They'll get her on the plane and she has a friend picking her up when she lands. She is so happy you're here and you're so competent."

Erin smiled. "This is a great job," she said, looking at Amelia who was jabbering and pointing skyward. "She's a happy little girl."

"Nate was crazy about her and I can see why." He made a funny face at the baby and she giggled at him. "Much as I hate to leave, I've got to get back to work. Unless you need something," he said to Erin. "I'll see you both at dinner. Maisie will be in the house all afternoon and you can easily get in touch with me."

"We'll be fine. You go."

"Don't sound so eager," he said, smiling as he crossed the porch and held the door. "Are you two coming inside now?"

"Just long enough to get her stroller. I'll take her into the backyard. She seems to love being outside."

"Yes, she does. I know Nate would hold her in front of him on his horse."

"She's too little for that."

He held up his hands. "I'm not doing that yet. Right now I'm scared I'll drop her when I get her out of her bed."

Erin laughed. "Cade, you need to relax with her. You're not going to drop her when you pick her up."

"Everything I do with her I'm scared."

"That's too silly. Stop being so uptight."

"Stop laughing at me. I'm just an amateur dad," he said with a grin. "If you hadn't known me all your life, you wouldn't be laughing out loud at me and telling me I'm silly."

She had to admit he had a point there. She wiped away her grin and nodded at him. "You're doing great with her, Cade. We'll see you tonight."

When Cade went to his office, she looked down at Amelia as she strapped her in her stroller. "Your uncle Cade is scared to carry you, but he'll get over it soon," she cooed to the baby. "He's going to be a wonderful daddy for you, and he'll try to do everything your daddy would have done for you. And you'll love him because of it. In the meantime, I have to try to avoid falling in love with him." She pushed the stroller outside, all the time watching Cade walking toward the barns and garages.

Amelia began to babble and Erin nodded. "That's right." She laughed softly, thinking about Cade. She saw him already as a good dad and when he got more accustomed to Amelia, she knew he'd be a wonderful dad. She had a wistful pang and realized that his devotion to Amelia added to her attraction to him. It was one more strong pull on her heart, reinforcing an attraction that she was already fighting. An attraction that seemed to grow stronger every hour she was with him.

After Amelia's nap, Erin took her outside again. She was sitting in the shade on a lawn chair, Amelia in her stroller and gazing around, happy to be outside, when a bright red pickup pulled up by the back gate. The pickup had mud spattered on the tires and front bumper.

The door opened and a man—tall, broad-shouldered, wearing jeans, a Western shirt and wide-brimmed hat— jumped down. He opened the gate and stepped through, closing it and turning to come toward her.

"Hi. You must be Erin Dorsey. I'm Gabe Callahan, Cade's youngest brother," he said.

"I'm glad to meet you, Gabe."

"We may have met sometime way back in the past when your brother was over or I was with Blake to pick up Cade, but I'm sure you don't remember it and I don't, either. Now though, I couldn't possibly forget meeting you." He smiled at her, his grin lighting up his handsome face. "I had no idea Luke had a gorgeous younger sister. Neither Luke nor Cade told me."

She laughed. "I doubt that is how your older brother would have described me. As a matter of fact, I seriously doubt if he ever described me at all." She shrugged. "When I was a kid, I don't think he even saw me. He never acknowledged me when we were in the same room together."

"Like I said, I'm sure that's changed now." Gabe grinned, another irresistible smile, revealing white, even teeth. Then he hunkered down in front of Amelia.

"Hi, baby," he said. "How's my favorite niece?" She blew bubbles in his direction and he chuckled. "You're a cutie."

He stood and turned back to Erin. She motioned to another lawn chair. "Pull a chair over and join us."

He sat in the grass, instead, facing both of them. "This will do. I won't be here long. I really won't if Cade catches me."

"Now, why is that? Why wouldn't your brother want you here?"

"Because he won't want me to come over and flirt with his nanny or ask his nanny to go dancing."

She had to smile as she shook her head. "I'd say you don't waste time, do you?"

He grinned, another infectious grin that made Amelia laugh.

"She likes your smile."

"The ladies often do," he said, leaning forward to look at Amelia. "You have excellent taste and a beautiful nanny, so I'll come see you often."

Amelia patted his cheek and he leaned out of her reach.

"Smart move," Erin remarked. "That little hand might be sticky."

"Do you like your job?" Gabe asked.

"I love taking care of her," she answered.

"Good. I know Cade is relieved. Actually all of us are because he needs a good nanny. He knows nothing about taking care of a baby. Same with me and the same with Blake, although Blake is going to become a dad in January and then he'll know a lot. Until then, we're three guys who haven't been around babies. Now, we can help with other things."

She smiled. "Right now, we're getting along pretty well."

"I asked and was told that you're a city woman, so I figure you like to get out and about. Cade said you have weekends free. Let me take you to eat scrumptious fried catfish and do some fun boot-scootin' this Saturday night."

She smiled at him again as she shook her head. "Thank you very much, but I can't do that. I told your brother that I'll work the next couple of weekends because he's unsure about taking care of Amelia all by himself."

"Okay, we'll make it the first weekend you're off work, then. You surely didn't agree to do that all the time?"

"No, I didn't. I'll have weekends free, but I'm not dating right now."

His gaze raked her from head to toe. "A pretty young thing like yourself?"

Erin suddenly remembered her brother's warning about Gabe Callahan. A ladies' man, a flirt. Well, once again her big brother was right.

Still, the man was trying to be nice, so she'd give him the courtesy of a reason. "I had a broken engagement recently."

He got up, picked up a lawn chair and placed it very close beside hers, turned slightly so he could face her.

"To my way of thinking, that breakup is the best reason to go out. It's a fun evening, no strings, just dancing and eating and meeting fun people and forgetting everything else. If you give me a chance, I'll bet I can make you forget all about that breakup for a little while on a Saturday night."

She had to smile. "I think the Callahans are born filled with confidence. You're very convincing, Gabe, but my answer is still the same. I'm not ready for an evening out with an energetic, enthusiastic, good-looking rancher."

Gabe was a fun, sexy cowboy who wanted to take her out. He seemed sweet and genuine and kind, and probably every female in the county would jump at the chance to go out with him. But not her. She felt not one arc of sizzling attraction to him. The kind of attraction that blazed between her and his brother.

Why did Cade have that effect on her?

Before she could dwell on that thought, Gabe let out a laugh. Then he leaned in closer, assessing her with his eyes. "I think you may be a challenge, Erin. I hate to see you stuck out here with my brother, who will be wringing his hands over what he needs to do for the little one and he won't even think of asking you to go dancing. Don't you know physical activity is one of the best ways to deal with stress?"

"Yes, I do and your brother has a gym in his house and a pool and I can use them daily."

"I might have to ask him if I can swim over here."

She smiled at him. "I'll tell you what you should do," she said, leaning forward slightly herself. "You find one of those pretty Texas women who love to party and dance and ask her out for Saturday night and go have a blast because she'll love it and you'll have fun."

"That's exactly what I'm trying to do, because I can't imagine that back before your breakup you weren't one of those pretty Texas women who liked to get out and enjoy life."

"It's not going to happen, cowboy. I'm not dating right now, but I do appreciate your invitation and your enthusiasm. Now, if you'd like to visit one night with your brother and Amelia and me, I think you'll find that she is adorable company."

"I'll take you up on that one on some weeknight because she is a cutie, and I've been over and played with her." He leaned back in his chair and crossed one booted foot over his knee. "You know, I told my brother that I was coming over to meet you and I was going to ask you out and he told me to go right ahead. He said you weren't dating and I would get turned down because you turn everyone down, so I know it wasn't just me, which is a good thing to learn."

"No, it's definitely not just you. Far from it. It's more just me right now."

"Well, I'll try again sometime, so you'll have another chance for a night out with me," he said, laughter dancing in his vivid blue eyes, and she had to smile again.

He stood and walked around to Amelia. "She's happy sitting there, so would you rather I didn't pick her up?"

"No, go ahead. She'll like the change and I'm surprised she's been content where she is this long."

He leaned down to get Amelia, unbuckled her and picked her up. "Hello, Amelia," he said while she tried to grab his hat.

Talking quietly to her, he walked away with her. "Want to look at the yard and the fence and my pretty red truck?"

Erin watched him walk around and show things to Amelia, who seemed happy with him, and she wondered again at the lack of physical response she had to an outright flirting and very good-looking young cowboy. Especially when a single glance from his brother would set her heart racing. What was it about Cade and the chemistry between them?

Gabe spent a long time walking and entertaining Amelia before he finally returned to strap her into her stroller again.

"There she is." He sat back down in the lawn chair and for the next twenty minutes they talked about grad school and life in general. Finally Amelia began to fuss and Erin stood up to take the stroller.

"I think it's nap time so unfortunately, Gabe, we'll have to tell you goodbye."

He stood. "It's been fun to meet you, Erin. I'll be back another time."

"It was interesting to meet you. Thanks again," she said. "You're good with Amelia."

"She's a little doll." He waved to Amelia. "Bye-bye, Amelia," he said as he turned to walk back to his truck. As Erin reached the door to go in, she saw his red truck disappear down the road.

While Amelia napped, Erin got some more of her things put away and when the baby stirred an hour later, Erin got a bath ready. She bathed Amelia, washing her thin, soft curls and later dressing her in a pale blue jumper and matching short-sleeved knit shirt.

They stayed in the playroom, Erin entertaining the baby by holding a big furry bear in front of her face and popping out to say "Peekaboo."

The first time she did it Amelia laughed. Delighted by the new sound of her laughter, Erin giggled in turn and repeated it, saying "Peekaboo" in a funny voice and getting more laughter.

She couldn't resist the third and fourth times. Amelia looked so adorable. When she heard a noise behind her, she turned to see Cade standing in the doorway. He was dusty and had a smudge of dirt on his jaw. His hair was tangled as he stood there watching her. And once again she felt that electric charge zing through her.

"I've never heard Amelia laugh like that," he said.

"Neither had I. Listen." She repeated the game, popping out from behind the bear, and Amelia gave another hearty laugh that made both Erin and Cade laugh in turn.

"I'll be damned," Cade said, entering the room. "I'm too dusty to pick her up," he said, waving his hand at himself while still watching his little niece.

Erin repeated her game and got another laugh. As she

laughed she looked at Cade. "Adults will do anything to get a laugh from a little one. It's the most delightful sight and sound ever."

He studied Erin and she realized the cool remoteness he usually exhibited was gone. "You're great with her."

"I'm just playing with her," she said, but she was lost in his blue-eyed gaze that at the same time immobilized her and rocked her, no doubt from the sparks that flew between them. She knew he felt them, too.

Her pulse raced and then she realized how they were looking at each other, as if neither of them had seen the other before. As much as she wished she could sit there and feel his eyes on her all day, Amelia stirred and she turned to hand the child a rag doll. Then she picked Amelia up and placed her in her lap as she sat cross-legged on the blanket. All the time she felt as if Cade's gaze was still locked on her. When she finally glanced at him, she saw that she had been correct. He stood there watching her, his eyes like lasers trained on her and her alone.

She felt slightly uncomfortable, and searched for conversation. "Your brother came by today." It was the first thing that came to her.

"Gabe? He told me he would. Let me guess—he asked you out and you turned him down."

"You're right. He was fun and cheerful and very nice. I hope I didn't hurt his feelings."

"I don't think you did. Although he never gets turned down, so it's a new experience for him. He's even less serious with his women friends than I am."

The words came out before she could stop them. "Are these negative feelings about commitment all because of your dad? Your brother Nate married and so has your half brother, Blake."

"That they did. Nate never had negative feelings about

marriage, though. I'm a year older and I hated the fights our parents had. Dad cut Blake out of his life and Dad went from wife to wife with mistresses in between—he spread a lot of misery. You have a wonderful family, so be thankful. I don't want to marry and risk that kind of upheaval ever. As far as my brother—I don't think Gabe is avoiding any serious relationship because of our dad. I just don't think Gabe's ready to settle down. He came close once when he was in college and none of us know much about her, but they dated a whole year, which is amazing for Gabe. Then she moved on and that was that. I've never heard of her since." He shrugged. "As far as asking you out, he'll be back."

"That's what he said."

As much as she wouldn't mind another invitation, it wasn't Gabe she pictured asking her out for a Saturday night on the town. It was this cowboy right in front of her.

Startled by the mental picture her errant thoughts conjured up, she turned her attention back to Amelia, and shifted her in her arms.

Cade must have sensed an end to the conversation, because he backed up. "I'll go get cleaned up so I can come back and hold her for a while," he said quietly, and then he turned and was gone.

When she heard his boots scrape the floor in the hall she finally let out her breath she didn't realize she was holding. So much for hoping this job would be easy and Cade would continue to be cool, remote and professional. He might remain professional, but it was already too late for cool and remote. That wall he'd had up the first day had vanished and she didn't think it would return.

Maybe he would surprise her and come back his quiet self—her employer who was polite, nice and remote. Not the tall handsome rancher who could make her heart pound with a glance and cause the temperature in the room to climb when he spoke to her. How was she going to resist that man through the coming months?

Far more immediate, how was she going to resist him tonight when, after putting Amelia to bed, it was just the two of them in the house?

Cade spent the next two days getting up before sunrise and leaving, going out to work. On a ranch there was always work to do, and he was never so grateful for it. He intended to avoid the house—actually, he wanted to avoid Erin—as much as he could until evening when he wanted to spend time with Amelia.

He needed to get to know his niece and learn how to take care of her. From what he could see Erin was a marvelous nanny, as Luke had promised. Amelia liked her and every time he saw them together Amelia was happy. In the evening when Erin would play with her, he joined them. That was the most difficult part of his day. That was the time he couldn't avoid her anymore.

Flirting with Erin was a huge temptation. The more he tried to avoid her, the deeper his reaction was to her when they were together. She was a wonderful nanny and there was no way he could regret hiring her, but this was turning out to be a situation that left him sleepless at night.

Friday morning he changed his routine and lingered in the kitchen eating breakfast, thankful for Maisie's presence which helped him keep focused. Erin came through the door with Amelia in her arms. Erin's jeans were snug and a red knit shirt clung to a figure that made his pulse beat faster. Maisie was off on weekends, so they'd be alone after today. How was he going to ignore Erin all weekend, yet try to be with Amelia? Just the thought made his throat dry up.

"Good morning," Erin said, looking wide-eyed at him. "I'm surprised to see you here."

Amelia held out her arms to Cade. Startled, he stood to take her. "Good morning and hello to you, Amelia," he said. He looked back at Erin. "That's the first time she's made it obvious she wanted to come to me."

Erin smiled at him. "That's good. She'll do it more. You'll see. Can you stay and hold her for a few minutes? It'll be good for both of you to be together."

"Sure," he said, looking at Amelia as she ran her small hand over his jaw.

"There's our pretty girl," Maisie said, bringing a bowl of fluffy yellow scrambled eggs to the table. "Aren't you the cute one," she cooed softly to Amelia. The baby smiled and reached out for Maisie, making all the adults laugh.

"So much for her wanting to be with me," Cade remarked.

Maisie reached for her. "I'll take her. I'm through cooking now anyway." She took Amelia, who nestled against her as she walked away to the window. The cook talked softly to Amelia, trying to get her to look outside. "I'll take her out for a few minutes so you two can have breakfast in peace," Maisie said. "She likes to look around and then she can eat."

"Sure," Cade answered at the same time Erin said to go ahead. They looked at each other and laughed. "I'll try to let you field the questions about Amelia," he said as Maisie stepped outside with the baby and closed the door behind her, leaving them alone in the kitchen.

He held a chair at the table for Erin near Amelia's high chair. "Ready for breakfast?"

"Yes, thanks," she answered politely, taking a seat. As she did, he caught the faintest sweet scent, which could have been from baby powder, from perfume or from an early-morning shower. Instead of lingering on the scent, he tried to focus on breakfast, sitting down and passing the bowl of scrambled eggs to Erin.

"Thank you," she said without looking at him, keeping her attention on the bowl of eggs as she took it from him. Her fingers brushed his and she drew a deep breath.

"Maisie better get the hell back in here before I say something I shouldn't," Cade said, and Erin glanced up with a wide-eyed, startled look.

"I think you're right," she whispered, confirming his assumption that she had as much a reaction to him as he had to her.

"I hate to step out there and get her to come in because she'll think we don't want her to carry Amelia around, which is not the case. I'll be right back," he said, leaving the room. He forced himself to think about Luke and remember his best friend telling him that he felt certain he could count on Cade to be professional around his sister, telling him how vulnerable she was. It was a litany he chanted more and more often. Not that it seemed to be doing much good. He walked down the hall with clenched fists. He wanted her in his arms and he wanted to kiss her. To be truthful, he wanted to seduce her, make love to her. But he wouldn't—couldn't—cross that line. He couldn't allow himself to be the cause of any more hurt. And if he knew one thing about Erin, he knew she was way too earnest to take seduction lightly.

"Damn," he said quietly, feeling caught in a dilemma. It was August—how was he going to cope with being with her every day until mid-December?

He would be gone some because of business and during the day he was out working, but he wanted to bond with Amelia and the only way to do that was to spend time with her—time he'd also be spending with Erin. What was he to do?

He had reached the front door and stood looking through the sidelights flanking the wide, oversize door. He stared at his front porch and yard without seeing, either. In his mind's eye all he saw were Erin's big green eyes, her long legs, her tempting curves and ready smile.

"Where the hell is your willpower, Callahan?" he asked himself softly. But he couldn't answer his own question. He thought maybe the best thing would be to hear Luke's voice. More than anything he wanted to call his friend, but he was probably already out of touch. No, Cade was on his own here.

Taking a deep breath and determined to resist Erin and remain professional, he headed back to the kitchen. To his relief Maisie had returned, Amelia was buckled into her chair and Erin was giving her tiny bites of cut-up banana that she could pick up and feed herself. Erin talked softly to her as she placed a little cup with a lid in front of Amelia.

He figured he'd give it a shot. "Erin, do you know if I can get through to your brother?" When she looked at him questioningly, he bluffed. "I thought you might like to talk to him."

Her taut look eased. "He sends me texts. A phone call will be expensive. Right now he's in São Paulo, Brazil, for a few more days and then he continues on south." She glanced at the kitchen clock. "If you want to get in touch with him, the time is fine now. It's around noontime there."

"Great. Let's call him after breakfast." Cade resumed his seat and tried to keep his attention on his plate, Amelia, Maisie—everything around him except Erin—but he failed. His gaze swept over her, taking in each and every curve that her knit shirt revealed. Was he the only one who felt as if the temperature in the kitchen had climbed to uncomfortable heights? Finally, he stood, cutting short his breakfast, knowing he had to get out of the house before he did something foolish. Like flirt or ask her out.

He stepped into the hall, walked to his office, allowing himself to cool down. When nothing worked he called Luke and blew out a breath when he finally heard him answer. "Good morning. Or afternoon. It's Cade... No, everything's fine," he reassured his friend when he expressed concern. "I just thought we'd call you. Here's Erin." He walked back into the kitchen and handed her the phone, turning his attention to helping Amelia who was doing quite well on her own and sipping from her small sippy cup.

The reception had been fair when he'd told Luke hello and since Erin was speaking more loudly than normal, he assumed the reception was poor, but then her voice dropped back to the usual conversational level as she talked about Amelia and being on the ranch and the weather. He listened as she asked Luke what he was doing and finally, she looked at Cade.

"I'll let Cade say hello. This call was his idea and we're talking on his phone," she said, listened a moment and laughed as she handed the phone to Cade.

"Hi, buddy," Cade said. "I thought we'd see if you're frozen yet, but instead you're partying it up in Brazil."

"Long, tedious meetings that end tomorrow, thank goodness. Food is great here and the nights are fun, as a matter of fact." He paused a second, then said, "I know I don't have to ask you to know Erin is doing a good job."

"Absolutely. She's a marvelous nanny," he said, meeting Erin's green-eyed gaze and seeing her mouth form a "thank you."

"She has bonded with Amelia and I'm slowly, very slowly, learning how to deal with Amelia."

"Yeah." Luke's voice came clearly enough that Cade recognized the sarcasm in his tone. "I know why you called. You're having a difficult time trying to keep from flirting with her. Remember, she's vulnerable," he said slowly and clearly. "She's been hurt badly."

"I'm very aware of that," Cade said cheerfully, hoping Erin didn't guess the drift of the call.

"I know she can take care of herself, but you have a way with the ladies, so keep in mind that she's my sister, that she is hurting and she doesn't need to hurt even more."

"Sure thing. You keep from freezing if you ever leave São Paulo."

"I will and you remember what I've told you. I don't know if I can get through from where I'll be, so I'm glad you called and let me talk to her. She sounds happy, which means she likes being with Amelia and I think it's good for her to have to take care of your little girl."

"I hope so. Amelia's certainly happy over it. I'll give the phone back to Erin. Good talking to you." He wanted to add, "I think," but he didn't. He handed the phone to Erin carefully, making sure their hands didn't touch.

He stood and walked away from her, thinking about her brother, trying to focus on Luke, to think about Erin's broken engagement, her canceled wedding, her miscarriage. He vowed to himself that he would exercise self-control, willpower, and resist the attraction that seemed to increase by the hour.

It had helped to talk with Luke. He should be able to keep his promises to Luke, control his feelings and longings and remain professional. Erin obviously was fighting the same battle to some extent, but he didn't think she felt the attraction to the depth and intensity that he did. If she did…

Realizing where his thoughts were leading, he tried to focus on the ranch and the roof that needed to be checked after the last hailstorm.

He wanted to go to Fort Worth to a cattle sale and pick up a new bull.

"If you need me, call," he said, leaning down to brush a quick kiss on Amelia's cheek and getting a sticky hand on his cheek that made him laugh.

"Thanks, Amelia," he said, going to the sink to wash his cheek, then grabbing a paper towel to dry it, while Erin told her brother goodbye and ended the call.

"Do you see any food on my face?" He had intended to ask Maisie, but she had moved away and Erin stood nearby, so she stepped close to look at his face.

He inhaled and caught the faint sweet scent again. Her skin was smooth, flawless and her cheeks rosy. Her lips were full, heart-shaped, tempting. He was caught and held as he looked into her green eyes. "Anything on my face?" he repeated in a husky voice.

Her gaze moved slowly over him and his pulse raced so fast he could barely get his breath. He should turn and get out of the kitchen, but for some reason he couldn't seem to move.

She focused on his cheek and took the paper towel from him to dab at his face. "There. Now there's not," she said softly and met his gaze.

"Thanks," he whispered. He finally got his legs to obey his silent command and left the kitchen as if he was being chased. Outside in the cool morning air, he wiped his suddenly sweaty brow and let out his breath.

He had one humdinger of a dilemma on his hands.

He didn't want to stay away from Amelia. This was a critical time when she was adjusting to him, to new people and a new home. He needed to be there for her, but Erin was one of the most appealing women he had ever met. And he needed to steer clear of her. So what could he do? He stood outside, staring across the yard, lost in thought and not even knowing where he was.

Why did Luke's sister have to be this red-hot alluring woman who took his breath away, made his heart pound and muddled his thinking? Of all the women he had ever known, Erin Dorsey was the one woman he should not have any interest in other than as a nanny. She was far too vulnerable. She wasn't his type. And she was his employee. Most of all, she was his lifelong best friend's sister and if he hurt her, he would lose the best friend he had ever had.

As he headed to the garage to get his pickup, he realized Erin had probably gotten the same warnings from Luke to resist her boss and clear reminders how Cade would never be serious about a woman or have a real relationship with any meaning.

He hoped Luke had warned her. He had been on the verge of it himself.

He realized he was standing by his pickup, lost in thought about Erin. She was distracting. Maybe if he kissed her once, he would be satisfied and then leave her alone.

"Yeah, right," he said as he climbed into his truck and pulled out.

Erin had changed for dinner while Amelia napped, into a dark green, sleeveless, cotton sundress with a full skirt that was not too short, not too revealing. Just right for dinner with Amelia and Cade.

After Amelia's nap Erin changed her into a pretty new jumper and took her outside in the shady yard to take some pictures. Over the last few days she'd noticed that Cade had no photos of the baby anywhere in the house.

"You don't want to grow up without pictures, do you?" she asked Amelia. Despite knowing she wouldn't get an answer, she talked constantly to Amelia anyway, because that was how babies came to learn.

She took a couple of shots with her phone, then sent several to her parents and two to Luke. Since he was a bachelor, she didn't know how much he would be interested in Amelia's pictures, but she thought Amelia looked so cute, she didn't know how anyone could keep from enjoying seeing her pictures. Then she sent several to Cade so he'd have some on his phone as well as in his house.

Just thinking about him made her pulse quicken. In a few hours, when he returned and Maisie left for the evening, they'd be alone. With Amelia, of course. Until she went to bed. And then…? Every inch of her tingled as she let herself fantasize about what kind of night they'd have. Alone with a sexy man who had such a sensual effect on her—

No! She pushed those thoughts out of her mind, refusing to indulge those enticing images. What was she thinking? Cade Callahan may be a handsome rancher but he was her boss. And tonight was nothing more than work. Caring for her charge and sharing a meal with her employer.

That was all it could be.

She heard the gate open behind her and turned toward it. When she took in the sight, her breath caught in her throat. In a wide-brimmed black hat, tight jeans, boots and a fitted, blue cotton shirt that reflected his eyes, Cade strode toward her, his gaze never leaving hers.

And right then and there she knew she was in big trouble.

Four

Cade crossed the yard to them, his long legs eating up the distance. "Hi. What's happening?" he asked, his gaze going over her, making her aware of her sundress and the breeze tugging at her hair. She held down her skirt.

"We're out for a stroll," she replied, not liking the deep tone to her voice. She wanted to clear her throat but didn't want to be too obvious. "Amelia likes to be outside."

"It's cooling off some now and I suppose it's comfy in the shade, especially if you're not tossing trimmed brush into a truck bed." He dusted off his jeans and hunkered down in front of Amelia in her stroller.

"Hi, little doll," he said, smiling at Amelia who babbled and grabbed the brim of his hat, tugging lightly, but not able to pull it off. He pushed it back on his head. "Thanks for her pictures," he said without turning to look at Erin.

"You're welcome. You should have pictures of her on your phone to show people. And we should print some out and frame them for the house. I'll do that. Also, Cade, I think she'd like a swing out here. You have some big tree limbs that are low enough. She loves being outside and she likes her inside swing so…"

He stood to face Erin and her heartbeat quickened as she looked up at him. She rolled the stroller slightly back and forth to entertain Amelia. As Cade glanced around, her gaze ran over his jaw that now had a faint shadow from the stubble of his beard. His clothes and boots were dusty and he had a smudge on his cheek. Just the sight of him made her tingle from head to toe. Her body nearly cried out with longing, making it hard to hear the echo of her brother's reminders and warnings on the phone earlier. Luke had told her again that Cade would never be serious about a relationship. He'd repeated that Cade was a die-hard bachelor and intended to stay that way all his life. He was deeply opposed to marriage.

The words reverberated in her head till he smiled, and then she didn't hear a one of them.

"You're right," Cade said. "I don't know why I didn't think of a swing for her." He looked up at the tree they stood under, searching for the perfect limb. "I guess I was so busy trying to figure out what I needed to do to care for her each day, a swing never entered—"

He broke off as he turned to look at her and his eyes narrowed. He drew a deep breath and she felt her cheeks flush with heat. Suddenly self-conscious, she bent down to smooth Amelia's collar that didn't need smoothing. She didn't know what Cade had seen in her expression, but he must have guessed her thoughts were personal and on him.

"You look pretty," he said in a husky voice.

She was grateful she wasn't looking at him or he would have seen the desire that flared to life in her eyes. She busied herself with fidgeting with Amelia's jumper, which probably lasted only a couple of seconds but felt like an eternity. By the time she straightened, he was backing up, his hat in his hand.

"I'll go clean up and see you at dinner," he said abruptly and turned to stride toward the house, his long legs covering the ground swiftly.

She felt bereft at his departure. But she knew why he'd left so suddenly. His tone of voice had been thick and deep. There was no denying the fiery attraction he'd felt. She had felt it, too. And there was no way she'd be able to resist him if he ever broke down that wall of self-control he'd erected around himself.

If that happened, she'd be tumbling headfirst into heartbreak.

Taking a deep breath, she pushed the stroller back to the house and stepped into the much-needed air-conditioning just as Maisie was leaving.

"Dinner is ready. I told Cade and he left to clean up. Can I do anything else before I go?"

"No, thank you, Maisie. Thanks so much for all you did today."

"I'll see you Monday morning unless you need me before then."

"Thanks. Have a nice weekend," Erin said. But what she really wanted to say was that they needed her to stay for the weekend and be a third person with them. But that was wishful thinking.

She remembered from her interview that Cade had asked for her to stay with Amelia on Friday evenings so he could go out and she wished he was starting tonight, but he hadn't said a word about going anywhere away from the ranch. She'd better get a grip because it was going to be a long night.

She got Amelia out of her stroller and took her to the

sitting room where she spread out a blanket and sat down to play with her. She was playing patty-cake as Cade came into the room and for an instant she forgot what she was doing when she glanced at him. He had showered and changed. He still had a faint stubble of beard, but his hair was combed with waves already curling on his forehead, the ends still damp from his shower. He wore a blue dress shirt open at the throat and tucked into fresh jeans with a different pair of clean, black hand-tooled boots and a leather belt around his narrow waist.

"Come join us."

"How about a glass of wine? Or a beer?"

"I'll take white wine, thank you. Would you please bring her sippy cup with some water in case she gets thirsty?"

He nodded and returned with the white wine, a bottle of cold beer and a cup that he handed to Amelia. He joined them on the floor.

She latched on to a safe topic. "You asked me to stay these few weekends, so if it's all right with you, tomorrow you can help with Amelia and learn how to take care of her all on your own."

"That still scares the hell out of me. I don't know what to do, but I'm watching to see what you and Maisie do. My grandmother was almost as much at a loss as I am."

"She was sweet to stay until you got a nanny."

"You're a great nanny and I'm so thankful you took the job."

"Which brings up something I want to talk to you about."

His blue eyes focused on her and he arched a dark eyebrow in question.

"Amelia is babbling and imitating sounds. I'd like to start using words around her so she can begin to learn them. Is she going to call you daddy or Uncle Cade?" As he started to answer, she held her hand up. "Think a minute. You will raise her and you will be a dad to her."

"I'm never taking Nate's place," Cade said, frowning. "Nate was her dad and is forever her dad."

"Of course. I know that and she will, too, when she is slightly older and can understand, but in practical everyday living, you're going to be Dad to her. If this were reversed would you want your child calling your brother Uncle or Dad? She'll know Nate was her daddy because you'll see to that and have his pictures around, but in a lot of ways, you're going to have to be her dad and you need to decide what she'll call you."

Cade looked away and a muscle worked in his jaw. "Sometimes that wreck hits me. I miss Nate. I miss Nate and Lydia having their baby."

"I know you do," Erin said quietly, giving him a moment to deal with his emotions.

Finally he took a deep breath and faced her again. "Amelia isn't talking yet and I haven't given that a thought. Let me sleep on it."

"You do that, but let me know because before long, this little girl is going to be saying simple words and I can teach her something to call you before I go." She smiled. "Uncle Cade is a mouthful, I have to say, and will probably come out like *Unca Kay*. Or maybe she'll just call you *Okay*. That's an incentive to make a decision." He grinned and she smiled deeper, unable to resist his grin. When she put Amelia to bed tonight, she had to go to her room and get away from him, no matter how tempting it was to come back to talk to him.

"Will you entertain her while I put our dinner on the table and we can eat?" Erin said. "It smells wonderful, some kind of enchilada casserole."

"Sounds good to me," he said. "What's our baby having? More mashed stuff that bears little resemblance to real food?"

"Something healthy, pureed for babies."

"Good thing you didn't leave me to feed her tonight," he said, making a silly noise and causing Amelia to laugh.

As Erin got dinner on the table, she watched Cade playing with Amelia. For a man who didn't want to ever marry, he was such a good daddy. He seemed to be having as much fun playing as Amelia was having. Impulsively, Erin took their picture, both of them laughing while Cade held Amelia in the crook of his arm and made silly noises and faces. Erin couldn't keep from laughing at them— until she was struck by the power of the moment. It was one of those times when she was knocked over by the realization of her own loss and she felt a sharp stab of pain right to her heart.

Turning away from them, she hurried to get dinner on the table.

Later, after they'd finished, when she finally stood and told Cade she was taking Amelia to bed, she stopped in the doorway. "I won't come back tonight. I'll see you in the morning."

"I know you're not going to sleep this early. Come back and talk for a while. I'll stay clear over here on my side of the room and you can stay way over there and we won't cross the middle of the room. How safe is that?"

She stared at him in surprise that he had openly acknowledged they were trying to avoid each other. He hadn't admitted why, but they both knew why. "It might be safe, might not, but it's not very smart," she answered with a breathlessness that she couldn't avoid.

"Live dangerously, Erin. Your brother has warned you so much about me that I'm sure you'll do what he told you. He's threatened to punch me out if I do anything I shouldn't and I don't particularly want that, nor do I want to lose his friendship which goes way back in our young lives. So come back and let's sit and talk and keep our distance and all will be well. Otherwise, I might have to come get you and try to talk you into coming back here with me. That would throw us much closer together."

"You're a bit devious, aren't you?" she said, smiling and knowing she couldn't say no. "I'll be back."

"That's good," he said as she walked away.

At the door she turned. "It'll be a while. I rock her and read at least one or two stories to her. Don't look for me soon and don't come to get me because I'm not leaving her until she's down for the night."

"I wouldn't think of taking you away from rocking her or reading to her. I think that's wonderful. I'd love it if you—"

"Shh," she said, stopping him from voicing what she thought was coming. "Whatever you're about to say, don't say it. We're doing pretty well keeping things impersonal. Pretty well. I'd say maybe good enough to rate a C+. Don't pull down that grade."

"C+? I think I deserve an A."

"Don't push your luck," she said, turning to leave because they were verging on losing that professionalism they each had been struggling to demonstrate. She didn't look back as she left, carrying Amelia to get her ready for bed. Erin no longer wondered how she would get through the weekend with him. Instead, she fretted over how she would get through the next few hours.

She needed to continue the remote, polite, professional relationship of a rancher and his nanny.

Would that even be possible? Why was she so drawn to him? She had been hurt, and numb around all other men since her broken engagement. What was it about Cade that had been instant, intense and an irresistible attraction even when she knew she should never become emotionally involved with him?

Could she spend the next few hours with him without ending up in his arms and without kissing him?

Cade went outside and stood on the back porch, looking at the yard. He had yard lights and lights in the trees so it was easy to see close to the porch, and he looked again at tree limbs where he could hang a swing. He was losing his fear of carrying Amelia, of holding her too tightly, of scaring her with his deep voice. He no longer had to worry about what to feed her because Erin and Maisie both knew. Erin would be present when Maisie went home.

Now his worries shifted to Erin. His call to Luke brought back all the warnings, the emphasis on the heartaches she had just been through, the threats by Luke to end their friendship if Cade hurt her.

Cade knew exactly what he should do, but he was more drawn to her by the hour and he couldn't explain why, except she was sexy, gorgeous, fun and intelligent. That was a deadly combination when he was living under the same roof with her. It made him want to get to know the appealing woman she was. Get to know her and get her into his bed. But he could not do any such thing because too much was at stake—his lifelong friendship with his best friend and her fragile peace of mind after going through two heartbreaks.

No, he needed to fortify that wall around himself so he could stay on the ranch with Erin and learn how to take care of Amelia. But how in sweet hell would he survive night after night of putting Amelia to bed early and then staying alone with her nanny? Amelia's gorgeous, sexy nanny that he wanted to seduce?

"Dammit."

He went upstairs quietly because he had learned one thing—don't wake a baby that is dozing off. He had learned long ago how to move without making noise, so he tiptoed to open his connecting door.

As he looked into Amelia's room, he stood riveted. Erin held her close in her arms, rocking her. A small lamp burned with only low light in the room, but Cade could see the tears running down Erin's cheeks.

The lamp caught highlights in her red-gold hair that spilled over her shoulders. Taken aback because she was hurting, he closed the door quietly and walked away.

He wanted to cross the room and hold her and comfort her, but he didn't dare. Sympathy would turn to desire as quickly as a lightning bolt streaking across the sky.

He stood thinking about her and wondered whether she was crying over the baby she lost or the guy she lost or both. Was she still in love with him? The guy couldn't have really been in love and dumped her the way he did.

Cade thought of his dad and the three women he had married and the mistresses and the misery he had caused. Once again he promised himself that he would never get married. Returning to the sitting area, he picked up toys and put away the blanket. Then he cleaned the kitchen and was finishing when he turned to find Erin standing in the doorway.

"I was gone the right amount of time," she said, joking with him when she entered the room, and if he hadn't seen the tears on her cheeks, he wouldn't have guessed she had had a bad minute since she'd left him to put Amelia down.

"Ready for some relaxation—more wine, play a game, watch something or just sit?" he asked.

"I vote for just sit. For a little person who doesn't talk yet, I seem to have a lot of conversation with her."

"I'm getting a beer. I didn't drink that first one, but it's no longer cold." He grabbed a bottle from the fridge. "Now let's go sit and you can take one side of the room and I'll take the other and if we're tempted to meet in the center, we can imagine your brother sitting in the middle of the room."

She laughed. "Luke values your friendship. You know he does."

"Not as much as he wants his baby sister to avoid getting hurt. I don't blame him. I wasn't happy about my half brother getting hurt."

"How was that?"

"I figured you'd heard Luke say something because he knew. C'mon, let's sit and I'll tell you," Cade said, walking into the adjoining sitting area.

"Oh, my, you picked up all Amelia's toys and put them away. You're catching on to being a dad. Very good."

"I am very good," he said, flirting and not thinking about toys.

She blinked and her eyes sparkled. "Modest, too," she teased back at him. "Cleaned the kitchen, put away the toys. Very talented man," she said, turning swiftly to sit in a wing chair. The full skirt of her sundress swirled around her legs and flew up over her knees. She flipped her skirt down and crossed her long legs, looking up to see him looking at her legs. His gaze met hers.

"I'm talented in other areas, too," he drawled. "You'd be surprised."

She smiled at him. "I don't think I'll pursue what you're so talented at tonight. You were going to talk about your half brother. That should be a safe topic."

Cade crossed the room, sat in the big leather chair

he liked, propped his feet on the matching ottoman and settled back, thinking he could look at her all night. The soft light picked up the blond highlights in her red hair that spilled over her shoulders. The top of her sundress revealed the beginnings of the lush curves of her creamy breasts. Her skin was perfect, smooth, ivory and so soft-looking.

He wanted to cross the room, pick her up and place her on his lap and kiss her. He thought about her upstairs, crying over her losses, rocking and holding Amelia, who had also had big losses.

He didn't want to add any more hurt to what Erin had already gone through, so he settled back in the chair and looked out the window at the lighted yard while he went back to a safer topic.

"My family history is not the best ever. When Dad divorced Veronica, Blake was too little to understand what was happening. Dad cut Veronica and Blake out of his life completely. I don't think Blake was a year old. As a child, Blake had no memory of his dad ever speaking to him."

"He was a tiny baby. How could a dad not speak to his own child?"

"Blake said his mother told him that it was because his dad was angry with her. Whatever the reason, he ignored Blake. Blake wasn't any part of our lives, either—we didn't know who he was when we were little, and then had nothing to do with him because that's what we were taught. Our mothers didn't get along."

"That might have been because of your dad, too."

"I don't know. Actually, we never saw a lot of our dad, but our relationships with him weren't as bad as the way he snubbed Blake. He didn't pay much attention to the three of us and we all went to military schools."

"Was he a solitary person?"

Cade smiled. "He was a wealthy person. He spent his energies making money and that's what he loved. Money and power. He's a multibillionaire. There were mistresses and Mom divorced him. When Mom and Dad divorced, we hardly saw him, but he would show up at a graduation or something big."

"I can't imagine a father being that way," she said, shaking her head. "I have such a good dad."

"Yes, you do. I know him and he's a good father. He's friendly and great with kids. Anyway, Blake and I are the same age and in high school we realized there wasn't any reason to dislike each other. We became close friends and I brought him into the family. He never came to anything if our dad was there until the past year. We can thank Sierra for causing Blake to lose a lot of his bitterness and to actually contact our dad and want to meet him. They have a truce of sorts now."

"Sierra must have been a good influence."

"She was, but it's too late. Our dad means nothing to Blake. Our Mom, Crystal, was around, but her big interest was her social life, so we had nannies. Just like you and Luke, we grew up in Downly. Your family stayed in Downly, mine acquired a Dallas home, too, which is where Mom still lives if she ever comes home. Our grandfather had a ranch—that's where we spent a lot of time. Some of that you should know from Luke."

"I didn't ask Luke about his friends' backgrounds."

"Well, now you have a chunk of my sordid family history."

"It's awful he cut his son out of his life. Blake was only a little baby," she said again.

"Relationships are important. I don't want to lose your brother's friendship. He's meant too much to me for too long. Besides, I wouldn't want to do one thing to hurt his little sister."

He received one of her high-voltage dimpled smiles and felt his insides clutch. "Now why would you possibly hurt me?" she asked.

"Never deliberately."

"There must be a 'bad-boy' side to you that worries Luke," she said in a throaty voice.

The room suddenly became too hot and she was sitting too far away. He wanted to reach for her and toss an answer back at her. Before he could, she suddenly looked startled as if she just realized the direction of their conversation and her smile vanished.

"Whoops. I forgot the situation for a moment there." She fanned herself. "You made me forget all about my brother, his warnings and all I've heard about you. I remembered in the nick of time. I think we'll go on to a new topic." She paused a moment, then settled on a safe question. "Is this a cattle ranch, horse ranch? I don't really know much about you even though you and Luke have known each other for a long time."

For a minute he didn't answer her. His head spun with her changes, but he had discovered that she could be sexy, could be fun, could flirt and she might like to kiss— knowledge that aroused him, made him hot, made him want her more. He struggled to follow her to the safe conversation, fighting his way back to the guardian/nanny roles.

"It's a cattle ranch," he finally replied, "but I have other interests. I work with Gabe in commercial real estate, but I'm easing away from that because of Amelia. I prefer the life of a rancher and since I can afford to do what I want, I can live here and work at what I like best."

"I suspect being a rancher involves some rough, hard

and dangerous work—more than being in an office, although driving through traffic to get to work can be dangerous, very hazardous."

"There are challenges here, along with rewards, satisfaction for getting out and doing things that are physical. You want to work with children, which is good—you're great at it."

"I like child psychology. I like human services and counseling children. Actually, there are a lot of possibilities. I think I may be able to choose where I want to work. My brother, on the other hand, wants to be in the exotic spots, although an environmental engineer can work all over the world."

"He won't find any frozen tundra in Texas," he said, and she smiled.

As the evening passed, he found her easy to talk to which was no surprise because in some ways she was a little like her brother, plus they had grown up in the same general area and gone to the same schools, even though she was several years younger. He kept on track, constantly thinking about Luke, but it took an effort, especially when they laughed together over a humorous episode in their pasts.

Her laughter was infectious and enticing and always stirred the desire to kiss her. Kissing her was never far from his thoughts. Each time, he had to think about Luke, remember seeing her rocking and crying. He suspected from here on, he should find something else to do with his evenings after one or the other of them put Amelia to bed.

"You asked me about going out on Friday nights," she said at one point. "Please feel free to do so, Friday or Saturday night. I don't mind staying and I won't be going back to Dallas a lot of weekends, so I can take care of Amelia."

"You're trying to get rid of me," he said, amused that she was urging him to go somewhere.

"I might be," she said with that mischievous look she'd had a couple of times when she relaxed about being with him.

"Right now, there isn't anyone in particular I'm seeing and nothing much going on, so it's okay to stay home. I can say the same thing to you—the weekends are yours, after this first month. This one I'd like to stay at your side and see what you do to take care of Amelia and what I should feed her."

"I'd be glad to," she agreed. "You've got nothing to worry about. Amelia's a good baby. She's been sleeping so well, which is great because some little kids don't. She likes her food and she's happy most of the time. She's a happy, easy baby so you're in luck there." Erin stood and he came to his feet. "Sounds like we've got a busy day tomorrow, so I think I'll go to my room now. I'll see you in the morning. And remember, if you want to go out tomorrow night, go right ahead. I'll be here anyway."

Amused, he smiled because he was certain she was trying to get him out of the house. "I'll think about it. It would probably be better for both of us if I did something, even if it's just driving to Downly or points north, south, east or west and getting away from temptation."

As she nodded, her cheeks flushed. "I think that's an excellent idea. If you don't want to do that, maybe I will. It'll be a nice summer evening. "Good night, Cade," she said, and turned for the door.

Remaining where he was, he watched her leave without answering her. What he wanted to do was walk down the hall with her or try to talk her into staying longer because it wasn't late, but he knew better. As she left the room, he let out his breath.

He had to get out of the house tomorrow night because she had flat out asked him to do so or told him if he didn't, she would. He thought about women he usually liked to take out and quickly rejected each one. He'd go to dinner in Downly and find somewhere to go for a beer, spend some time and come home late.

He had a lot of nights and a lot of weekends ahead of him, so he better find something to do or someone else who interested him.

He stood with his hands on his hips. He was on edge. Maybe he should work out, he thought. But he didn't feel like going into his home gym. All he wanted was her back in the room so they could at least talk.

Finally he went to his room to change. He'd just pulled off his boots when he heard Amelia crying. He glanced at the closed door to her room and waited a moment, but as she continued crying, he crossed the room.

Her crying stopped and he wondered if she had gone back to sleep or if Erin was with her. He waited a moment and then knocked lightly on the door.

"Come in," Erin called, so he opened the door and entered to find Erin holding Amelia. The baby clung to Erin's shoulder, but turned when he entered to look at him.

"I heard her crying."

"Maybe she heard me say what a wonderful sleeper she is and decided she would prove me wrong," Erin said, smiling at Amelia. Amelia stared at Cade and held her tiny arms out, reaching for him.

"Hey, she wants to go to you. See, she likes for you to hold her," Erin said, crossing the room to hand Amelia to him.

He wanted to wrap his arms around both of them. Instead, he took Amelia who was warm, soft and smelled faintly of baby powder. "What's disturbing our baby?" he asked her softly, turning to walk with her. She wrapped her arm around his neck and clung to him, seeming to be happy as far as he could tell.

He should tell Erin to go on to bed, that he would rock Amelia back to sleep and put her in her crib, but he didn't want Erin to go. Still in her green sundress, she stood looking at him. In the soft light of one small lamp she looked more enticing than ever.

"I'd feel better if you'd stay," he said to Erin. "Do you mind?"

"Of course not," she answered, holding back a smile. "I wasn't going far away," she added, glancing at the open door to her suite.

"I know. I'll walk her a little and then rock her a little if she likes to rock."

"Fine, but give her to me whenever you want, although she looks very happy now with your arms around her. I don't know why she's awake."

"She'll go back to sleep," he said quietly walking around the room with her and then sitting in the rocker to rock her while Erin had already settled in a large, over-stuffed chair.

After a few minutes Amelia placed her head on his shoulder.

"When her eyes close, tell me," he whispered.

"Her eyes are already closed. I think she'll go to sleep," Erin said softly.

Cade continued rocking for another twenty minutes while he talked quietly to Erin.

"She is definitely asleep," Erin told him.

"I'll put her in her bed now," he said, handling her with great care as he stood and placed her in her crib. Erin came to stand beside him.

"See, she's sound asleep."

"It's early, Erin. I'm not going to bite. Come back and let's have cookies and milk or something and talk awhile longer."

Her green eyes widened as she gazed at him with a slight frown and didn't answer.

"I've kept my distance and haven't flirted. C'mon. It'll be more fun than sitting alone and I'm hours from sleep."

"Against all good judgment, I'll go with you for a while," she said. "It's early and Amelia seems sound asleep."

Satisfaction made him smile when she nodded and walked beside him. They paused at the door to both look back at Amelia, who was asleep curled on her side.

After he got some crackers, cheese, ice water for her and a cold beer for himself, they sat in the screened part of his porch on the darker east side of his house.

"I have fewer trees on this side of the house—the three oaks are it for now and they each have a couple of lights, but nothing like the other sides. I enjoy sitting out here in the dark sometimes. I can switch those lights off so it's dark enough to see some stars."

Their voices were soft in the quiet night. She had her iPad open, the brightness dimmed, but he could see Amelia hadn't moved since they left her.

He put his feet on another chair and talked quietly to Erin. "This is the most peaceful place on earth."

"You love it here, don't you?"

"Yes. I love everything about it except the paperwork. I can't totally escape that, what with keeping records, making sure taxes are right."

"Why don't you just do this all the time?"

"I wanted a business, to make money and not live on what Dad has given us. Just another little way to try to break away from him now that I'm grown."

"Cade, you're already becoming a good daddy for Amelia. You're not the same man as your dad, you know."

"Damn, I hope not. Are you going to give me a pitch on how great it would be to get married?"

She laughed softly, a tempting sound that made him want to draw her close. "It's just ridiculous for you to decide you'll never marry because your dad couldn't stay happily married. You're a different person."

"Amen. His blood is in my veins, though. I don't want any part of settling down."

"That's a shame," she said. "You're good with Amelia."

"I still feel nervous, but not as much as I did. Each day I feel closer to her. I hope she likes the ranch."

"She'll love it because it's her home."

"I suppose you're right there. Think you'll look for work in this area after you get your degree?"

"I'll look, but I'll go where the job is."

"That's good. If you end up somewhere else, will you come back and see us?"

"I can't answer that one now. Amelia may not even remember me because she's so young."

"I'll remember you," he said and she laughed.

"I'd hope. You've known me forever."

The later they talked, the longer they were together, the more he wanted to hold her and kiss her.

She finally stood and the last time he had looked at his watch, it had been after one in the morning. He guessed it might be after two. When she reached to pick up her glass and plate, he stood, his fingers closing around her wrist lightly.

"You don't—" Cade had started to tell her she didn't need to carry her dishes to the kitchen. The minute he took her slender wrist, the words vanished.

He drew a deep breath while a tingling current sizzled

and sent his temperature soaring. He had made a tactical mistake, a monumental blunder in his effort to keep everything between them professional and to keep his distance.

That polite, remote relationship of boss and nanny morphed into hot and steamy desire that blasted him. He tried to get his breath as he looked at her.

His eyes had long ago adjusted to the semidarkness. He could see her wide-eyed stare and the knowledge that she felt the heat between them made his temperature soar higher.

"Erin," he whispered.

"Oh, no…" she whispered with her voice trailing away.

"I've tried. For this whole damn week I've tried to leave you alone, to ignore what I feel, to ignore what you obviously react to. We've both tried. What is so wrong about a simple kiss? I'm not going to steal your heart with a couple of kisses.

"I think your brother has lost all sense of perspective," Cade continued, drawing Erin closer. "I don't want to hurt you, but it seems maybe we've forgotten that kisses can be meaningless fun," he whispered, slipping an arm around her waist while he could feel her pounding pulse in the wrist he still held.

"Erin," he whispered. She turned her face up while both her hands now rested on his forearms.

He leaned down to cover her soft lips. His gentle kiss changed to a demanding, passionate kiss that went deep as his arm tightened around her and he held her close against him.

Instantly, arousal rocked him. Powerful. Undeniable. Too late he realized he had been wrong about her kisses being meaningless fun. She set him on fire and he wanted to kiss her all the rest of the night and through tomorrow.

He wanted to make love to her, to seduce her, to never let her go.

As she kissed him back, her mouth was soft, tempting, her tongue an erotic invitation. Her kisses almost buckled his knees and made him hot with desire. He ran his fingers through her soft hair that fell over her nape while he continued to hold her close and kiss her.

"Erin," he whispered, trailing kisses along her throat, down the open V of her sundress, feeling her softness that made him shake with desire. He tried to control it, to hold back, but every move from her only fanned the fire enveloping him.

She pressed against him, her arm holding him tightly. Her other hand stroked his nape, her fingers winding in his hair as she returned his kiss as passionately as he kissed her.

His roaring pulse drowned out all other sounds. Her hips shifted against him and he groaned, wanting her more than he could ever recall wanting any other woman. How could she do this to him? How could her kisses be so spectacular and make him have to struggle to keep from carrying her off to the nearest bedroom?

He should stop, but that was impossible. He knew her kiss wasn't harmless or meaningless, but it also was only a kiss and they couldn't go beyond it. He could continue to kiss for a few more minutes and then he'd have to put an end to the pleasure. He'd have to put the pieces back together afterward because they would have to resume that impersonal nanny and boss relationship.

Right now, though, all he wanted was a beautiful, stunning woman's bone-melting, passionate kisses that were turning his world upside down.

He couldn't keep from running his hand so lightly down her back, feeling her tiny waist and then letting his hand drift lower over the sexy curve of her trim behind, down the back of her thigh that had only the sundress between his fingers and her warm leg.

Her hand closed over his wrist, holding him tightly against her waist until she broke free and stepped back. She released his wrist as she gulped air, trying to get her breath.

"I think we made a mistake, Cade," she whispered. "But it was just once." She gasped for breath as she stared at him without moving. "We can get over that and our kisses won't matter. Kisses that will be forgotten. That's the way it has to be for me to stay here. I'm not risking my heart and you're not interested in anything serious so we both know what has to happen. No more kisses and no flirting. I know you understand."

"It was only kisses, Erin," Cade said. Even as he said the words, he knew their kisses were far from trivial. He'd never had the reaction to kissing a woman that he had with her. Not another woman in his life and he had known some beautiful, sexy women, including one supermodel and one starlet. Both of them should have melted him just from their looks and they had been sexy and exciting, but he couldn't remember their kisses. He knew tonight had been different, far more intense, far more unforgettable. It was the unforgettable part that shook him.

Everything about Erin shook him from the instant she'd opened the door to his office and stepped inside. He should have thanked Luke and hired one of the women from an agency.

He was in deep trouble now. It was taking major willpower to keep from reaching for her to get her back into his arms. With his whole being he wanted to kiss her again.

He couldn't tell how much reaction she was having.

She seemed shaken, but she also had just been through a lot of emotional upheaval.

"Erin—" he said, starting to step toward her. She held up her hand.

"Wait a minute, Cade. I want to tell you good-night and go to my suite. You stay right here. We're not walking through the house together. For a few minutes neither one of us used common sense. We're getting back to that. I'll see you in the morning."

She hurried into the house and as he watched her go, he wondered if she'd be able to stick to that vow. He knew there would absolutely never be any getting back to the way they were before their kisses.

Not for him.

Five

Erin rushed to her room, first stopping to check on Amelia and then going to her suite, closing each door as if she could barricade herself from what she felt.

Cade's kisses had shattered what little peace she had gained. She had never responded to any man the way she just had to Cade, which shook her almost as much as the end of her engagement.

Disturbing her even more, she had almost married Adam, who had never made her feel the way Cade just had. She had only worked a week on this job. She was going to be with him for months to come.

She ran her hands through her hair. Why hadn't she listened to her brother and done exactly what he'd said? He had warned her about Cade—warned her that Cade drew women effortlessly.

It wouldn't be a simple matter of avoiding kissing him again. Every inch of her tingled and desire was a raging

fire inside. She wanted his kisses, his caresses, his lovemaking—something she wouldn't have dreamed possible
when she took the job. She had known she ran a risk to her
heart, but she never thought about this hunger for passion.
And she couldn't let go and make love without her heart
being involved. There was no way sex could ever be casual to her. Her emotions were always tied up in close relationships and intimacy was the strongest emotional tie.

If she didn't guard against more kisses, she would
have a giant heartbreak, something she didn't want to go
through. Not again. Why hadn't she been more careful?

She shook her head and crossed the room to get ready
for bed, but she knew there wouldn't be any sleep for
hours.

Every inch of her tingled for Cade's touch, for his hard
body pressed against her. She tried to stop thinking about
him, placing her fingers against her forehead as if to force
out the thoughts.

"Luke, you were right. Oh, you were right. I should
have listened," she whispered in the empty room.

Stunned that she had such an intense reaction to Cade,
she realized it was probably a reaction to all she had been
through. She realized she must be vulnerable to wanting
to be loved, to make love, to lose herself in passion that
temporarily could drive every vestige of heartache away.

At least she hoped that's all it was. It had been over a
year since she had been with Adam, even kissed a man,
and there had been no one since him until tonight.

Her reasoning calmed her nerves for about one minute, until she remembered Cade's kisses. Who was she
kidding? Her reaction to him wasn't just because of her
breakup. It was a physical reaction to the man himself.
No other man could simply look at her and make her heart

skip a beat. No other man could enter a room and make her pulse jump. No other man could have that effect on her.

It was totally physical, a mutual attraction that she was certain Cade didn't want any more than she did. He was a party guy, never serious, against marriage, unnerved by becoming a guardian. His situation and his attitudes made him the kind of man she planned never to get involved with. Yet she had this intense, heart-pounding reaction to Cade that stopped all her logical thought processes and drove her to do what she knew she would regret.

In his own quiet way Cade was great company. Her brother had always liked him and considered Cade his best friend. Luke trusted Cade and respected him. He also realized how he was about women and long-term relationships.

So why hadn't she heeded Luke's advice?

It wasn't too late. She could get over a kiss. She needed to keep things in perspective and simply avoid becoming more than his employee.

Could she do that for the next few months with him?

Could she do that with Amelia, as well? Or was she going to get hurt again by people she loved? Little Amelia didn't intend to hurt anyone, but after a few months of caring for her, Erin wondered how much it would hurt to tell Amelia goodbye.

If she wasn't careful Erin knew she was going to lose her heart to Amelia and Cade. Sighing in the darkened bedroom, she decided she was making a mountain out of maybe just an anthill. Not even a molehill.

Hereafter she just had to resist him no matter how difficult it might be. When she put Amelia to bed, she would stay away from Cade the rest of the evening. It was that simple.

She stepped out of bed and pulled a chair to the window. Was Cade sleeping peacefully? For a moment she wished he was in as much turmoil as she was, but then she hoped he slept quietly and had forgotten their kiss and was thinking about who he could ask out next Friday night instead of staying home with his little niece and her nanny. If only he would do that, she might be able to sleep again.

Cade woke and heard Amelia's chatter. He cautiously opened the door to her bedroom. She sat up in her crib and spotted him the minute he cracked open the door. She smiled and held out her arms, babbling incoherent sounds.

He had to laugh as he crossed the room to get her, picking her up. "Aren't you the shameless charmer, using all your wiles to get me to rescue you from that prison of a morning bed? Holding out your arms and looking adorable, babbling cute little sounds that make me want to hug you, smiling at me as if you're not up to something and trying to bribe me with a hug. You look adorable, warm and cuddly. That's shameless, Little Miss Heartbreaker. Of course you got what you wanted—a big strong man to rescue you. A chump who will cater to your every whim and try to find exactly what you would like. You flash that cute smile and gaze at me with those big blue eyes and blow bubbles and get exactly what you want without being able to say one word to me. You don't even know how to point to what you want me to get for you, but somehow you manage to get everyone to give you what you want and do what you want and entertain you, sing to you, read to you, even swim with you."

She laughed as if he had said something very funny to her, making him laugh in turn.

"I think you know you're the cutest little child ever, don't you? I suppose I need to get you changed and dressed. Either that or go wake your nanny, which I would enjoy doing, but not with you in my arms and probably a little on the damp side. You just hang on and be patient and let me find you something comfy to slip into—and I do mean slip into."

Smiling, she made smacking sounds with her lips and he had to laugh.

"You're adorable, Amelia," he said, hugging her and setting her back in the crib. "Let me get you changed here and then later your nanny can fix what I've done."

Twenty minutes later Cade placed Amelia in her high chair and leaned down to look at her as she smiled at him. Yeah, he'd do most anything to make her happy.

Soon he sat facing her, placing her sippy cup with milk on her tray. "I don't know what to feed you. Did you know I made your nanny unhappy last night? You don't know or you wouldn't be nearly this happy with me because you like your nanny. I don't blame you. I like her, too. And she is just flat-out beautiful. And so are you, Little Miss Charmer. Now I'll give you some yummy juice and try to find something you like for breakfast. Okay? And if I don't do so well, your nanny will be out of bed soon and come to your rescue. Or maybe she'll come to my rescue." He laughed at himself. "She's had a long night's sleep…unless she couldn't go to sleep at all. I couldn't and it was all because of your beautiful nanny. What do you think of that?"

He didn't expect the reply he got.

"I think I shouldn't have overheard your very personal conversation."

Cade turned and saw Erin standing in the doorway and his heart skipped. She was in cutoffs and a T-shirt and her hair was up in a ponytail. She looked younger and sexier than ever, and he couldn't keep from letting his gaze drift over a pair of million-dollar legs.

"Lady, you should be a model. Those legs could grace any ad."

"Thank you very much. That improved my morning," she replied, "as well as your one-sided conversation with Amelia."

He grinned and shrugged. "That's what you get for eavesdropping."

"It was far too much fun to stop you. Whew! I'm very flattered."

"You should be, although I could have done better talking to you in person."

"I think we're doing what we each vowed not to do," she said. "Maybe I should go out and come in again and we can both forget everything before that."

"Not on your life, darlin'," he drawled while he fed Amelia a bite.

Relief filled him. Last night when they had parted, Erin was upset and he had been swamped with guilt. This morning he was glad to find her smiling and flirting with him, no longer upset with him.

He glanced over his shoulder to see her moving around the kitchen and he assumed she was getting her breakfast. With her back turned, he took another long look at her legs and inhaled deeply because the air in the room had suddenly become blazing hot. In a moment Erin walked closer as she looked at Amelia.

"You're doing a fine job and she's happy, but I'll relieve you if you'd like."

He glanced at the plate in her hand with a piece of toast and a bowl of fresh berries. "Is that your breakfast?"

"Yes, it is, and I can eat as she eats."

"You go ahead and I'll continue what I'm doing as long as she's happy."

"Don't say I didn't give you a chance. You do pay me to take care of her, you know."

"That's right, but I need to learn how to so when you're not around, I'll know what to do."

"It's pretty simple and it looks as if you're getting the hang of it. Let me know if you want me to take over."

"Thank you. We are doing just fine," he said, giving Amelia some more cereal and smiling as she smacked her lips. "She is a noisy eater."

"She'll grow out of that."

"I hope so before she's a teenager."

"Since when did you get so scared of teenagers? You were one back there in your past, you know."

"I think you're laughing at me again. If you suddenly found yourself the guardian of a teenage boy, wouldn't that shake you?" He glanced at her and shook his head. "Ignore that question. You deal with kids, so it probably wouldn't give you a moment's concern."

"Stop worrying about how you'll be with her more than twelve years from now. That's ridiculous, Cade."

When he looked at it like that, he guessed she had a point. Twelve years was a long time to learn. In the meantime, he'd enjoy raising Amelia, with his nanny's help, of course. Speaking of her nanny…

"Let's get Maisie to stay with Amelia tonight and go out to dinner," he suggested. "You deserve a break."

She laughed. "Thank you, but I think we need to keep everything very professional between the guardian and the nanny."

"And stay here just the two adults in this house after she goes to sleep, intimate and cozy at home where temptation is enormous? That's fine with me," he said.

"We can stay here, two adults in the house who, after putting Amelia to bed, will say good-night to each other early and go our separate ways and remain very professional, very remote and very safely in different parts of your very big ranch house." She took a bite of her toast. "Or better yet, you get a date and go out partying."

"That's what I'm trying to do," he said, gazing at her intently enough to make her blush. Her blush changed the moment for him. He had been joking, lightly flirting with her and having fun with her, but her blush reminded him of their reaction to each other, a physical reaction that he had never experienced with any other woman and one he didn't want to share with her. Worse, he knew she didn't want it, either.

That simple fact made for volatile moments and they came without warning. Like now. He drew a deep breath that didn't calm his racing pulse or stop memories of their kiss last night.

Their gazes had locked and he looked into wide green eyes that conveyed desire no matter how much she fought it.

He tried to conjure up thoughts of her brother. Thinking of Luke had become his cold shower. Instead, memories of holding Erin and kissing her were too vivid and he was becoming aroused, wanting her more with each passing second.

He stood. "I think it's time I take you up on your offer to feed Amelia and get the hell out of the kitchen," he said, his voice thick and deep. He turned and walked away without looking back to see if that was agreeable with her or not. He went down the hall and shut himself into his office, closing the door and letting out his breath. His eyes lit on a small snapshot across the room, one taken years earlier and beginning to fade. He picked it up. In the picture he stood with his arm around Luke's shoulders. Both of them were dusty, their hair tangled. They were dressed in jeans and T-shirts and had been playing ball after school in the neighborhood. Luke wore a grin and they looked like great friends who were having a lot of fun together.

"Buddy, I'm trying," he whispered. "I'll try to avoid her the rest of the weekend, but I wish you were here to keep me on track. You probably don't realize what a gorgeous woman your little sister is. You don't, but I sure do and she's about to wreck my life." He replaced the picture, then walked out. He needed to go to work, to do something physical and get his mind off Erin. He should think of someone to party with tonight. Monday, when Maisie would be back in the house, couldn't come fast enough.

The next weekend Cade made arrangements to stay in Dallas and left Erin at the ranch, paying her extra to stay the weekend. During the week, they went their separate ways after she left to put Amelia to bed. She could see that he was doing all he could to keep away from her, to leave her alone, to learn how to take care of Amelia during the day while Maisie was around. In spite of avoiding being alone as often with Erin, she was more aware of him than ever. The awareness they both felt seemed more intense and she knew he still experienced the same volatile reactions she did.

As two more weeks rolled past, Cade wasn't flirting, and he even tried to avoid staying in the same room with her, and arriving in time to eat with her. But that didn't work, either. She was still aware of him anytime he was near her and missed him when he was not.

On the second Friday in September, rain moved in during midafternoon. Erin got Amelia bathed and changed for dinner, wondering if it would just be the two of them after Maisie left.

Cade had gone out last Saturday night and hadn't returned until late Sunday. She wondered who he had been with and if he would be going out again during the coming weekend.

Even though they saw very little of each other, she couldn't get him out of her thoughts. The brief times they were together, her awareness of him had seemed to increase. Even the slightest brush of fingers caused a disturbing current to run through her. Sometimes she caught him looking intently at her, his blue eyes dark and stormy. When that happened, she wanted to leave the room, but the most she could do was look away.

She tried to avoid thinking about his kisses, remembering, speculating, and she made good on her promise to herself to stay away from him by keeping to her room each night after putting Amelia to bed.

Now, Friday afternoon, as thunder rattled the windowpanes and wind whipped around the house, she wondered where he was and what his plans were for the night. She had told Maisie to go home early so she wouldn't get caught in the rain.

Amelia played with her toys while Erin stood at the window and wondered how much danger Cade was in from lightning or flash flooding.

She watched big drops of rain fall on the patio and into the pool. Then more came and the drops came faster until a sheet of gray rain swept over the house. Lightning flashed and she hoped Cade was safe and dry.

As she stood and watched, her heart skipped a beat when a pickup went past the house and made the turn to pull into the portico on the west side. In seconds, she heard him come in. She fought the inclination to go meet him and ask him about the storm, and then he appeared in the door. His hat was gone, his jeans wet from the knees down.

"I'm glad to see you're back safe," she said.

"Thanks. It's a mess out there." He glanced out the window at the unrelenting storm.

"Are you going out tonight?"

He shook his head. "No, I'm not. We'll manage," he said, giving her a direct look. "I'm going to clean up and then I'll come down. It smells wonderful in here."

"Maisie left a big pot of soup made from a tender roast and she made your favorite—strawberry cake."

"Ahh, an evening at home out of the storm with a great dinner, one of my favorites—a pot of soup and strawberry cake. Can we feed any to Amelia? She'll love it."

"She's too little to crunch down strawberries. Just be patient."

"Too bad. I'll be back shortly and I'll be dry. I think I just made it in the nick of time," he remarked as hail began hitting the house and patio and pool, small white balls of ice bouncing in the yard and tearing leaves from the trees.

As he left, she let out her breath. They would be together until she took Amelia to bed. Till then she'd just have to exercise every ounce of self-control. And self-preservation, she added. Dinner went well, and afterward she sat curled in an easy chair, watching Cade play with Amelia on the floor. He talked to the baby, making faces and noises that made her laugh, picking up a hand puppet to entertain her and she laughed with glee, clapping her hands and reaching for the puppet.

He let her have it and sat watching her play with it. He put it on her hand and showed her how to make it look as if it were talking. She laughed and pulled it off her hand to turn it over and look at it.

He propped Amelia into his lap and leaned back against a chair to stretch his long legs in front of him. After a few minutes, she dropped the puppet and leaned back against Cade, closing her eyes.

"She's getting sleepy. I'll put her to bed," Erin said. "She's had a fun evening with you. You're a good dad, Cade."

"I'm trying. She makes it easy to be a good dad. I already love her with all my heart and want to try to do the best I can." He kissed the top of her head. "I'll take her to bed. I'm learning and getting better at this."

"Yes, you are," Erin answered, amused by his insecurity in this one area of his life when he was so confident in things so much more difficult.

"Sit back and enjoy yourself. Watch the rain," he said, turning a lamp off so the lighting was softer. "Our creeks will be up, but I hope that's the only result of this storm. It isn't a real problem. The creeks rise and sometimes flood and cover the bridges, but we aren't usually cut off." A wave of heavy rain hit the house again. "I'm glad to be home tonight." He stood, holding Amelia with great care.

"I should take her and go on to my suite."

"It's a stormy night and we could lose power. Why don't you stay and we can talk or play a game if you prefer. I'll stay on my side of the room like always. That should be safe."

"Nothing is safe," she said quietly and then waved her hand. "See, I shouldn't have said that."

"I'm glad you did. Relax, we're adults. Our kissing was not life-threatening or life-changing and we don't ever have to kiss again," he said, looking down at Amelia in his arms. "You stay. I'll be back and when I return, I don't want to have to sit down here in the rain all alone.

Now I'll take her to bed and if I need help, I'll call you on the monitor."

She smiled at him. "Yes, sir," she replied. He grinned, glanced again at Amelia, who was breathing deeply as she slept. Erin quietly watched him carry Amelia out of the room.

When he returned, he sat in the easy chair across the room from her, as promised. He looked relaxed, sexy and way too appealing. She should have gone with Amelia, but it was fun to sit with Cade instead of spending a lonely evening in her room. Sometimes she didn't mind, but some nights she wanted to be with him and tonight was one. She'd give herself an hour with him and then she'd retire.

"Cade, you're so good with Amelia," she said, thinking about him with the little girl and his feelings about marriage. "Why in the world are you so opposed to marriage?" Erin asked and then blinked. "I'm sorry—that's a personal question you don't have to answer. It's just that I've heard Luke talk about how opposed you are to marriage."

"I figured you knew because your brother does," he said, stretching out his long legs again to cross them at the ankles. He still had his boots kicked off and he wiggled his toes.

"It's because of my dad's rotten marriages," he explained. "I've seen firsthand how unhappy marriage can be and I've seen little firsthand how happy and good it can be. I saw that when I stayed at your house because your folks have a good, happy marriage from what I know. It seems the luck of the draw to end up happily married and I never want to come out on the losing side and get caught in what my folks had."

"That's sad," she said, frowning as she heard from him

a little more about his feelings on marriage and his reasons behind his determination to stay a lifelong bachelor. "You're such a good daddy for Amelia."

"Thanks. That's reassuring because I still feel very unsure of myself with her, but it's a little less worrisome."

Erin's gaze drifted down the long length of him and she felt a tingle. She remembered being in his arms. "You know that's a foolish reason to reject marriage. What your dad did doesn't have a thing to do with the way you'll be," she said. "You're a different man."

"I'm his son. We have the same blood in our veins. I'm scared I'll turn out the way he was. He was in love with all three women before he married them. Even if I don't turn out like my dad, marriage doesn't look like a happy, positive arrangement. I know it is in your family, but I don't want to take that chance. I'll admit, my dad was exceptionally lousy at being a husband and dad—not speaking to his firstborn is a classic example and I would never do anything like that. But marriage seems a huge chance to take, like an amateur trying to cross Niagara Falls on a tightrope. It might work out great and one would have all sorts of attention and laurels. Or you might just fall in and drown."

"That's a gloomy outlook. Can't you see that you're not the kind of father your dad was? It's not something that is inherited or contagious."

"I grew up around him. I hated the fights my parents had. I hated the way he might come home for holidays or he might not. We never knew. He really didn't care about us. He was around some and we got some of his attention, whereas Blake was totally ignored, but all I remember were fights between my parents. I don't know how many nights as a kid I was in bed and would hold my hands over my ears to keep from listening to them and I would vow that I'd never get married."

"That's the view of a child. You probably won't be one little bit like him and you're cutting yourself out of a wonderful life filled with love and joy. I can't imagine life without children in it. Remember her sitting on your lap. She was happy and she likes you and goes to you and holds her arms out for you to take her. Would your dad have done that?"

"Hell, no. I don't know what he did when I was her age, but I never saw him do that with Gabe."

"Don't you want your own kids?"

"One is probably all I can cope with. And as long as we're on this subject and getting personal, I'm sorry for your breakup. I wish you didn't have to go through that, and I wish you the best and lots of luck in the future."

"Thank you," she said quietly. "I still want marriage and a family. Not now, of course, but someday. Adam broke our engagement because I couldn't guarantee I would give him biological children."

"Maybe you're better off without Adam."

"I'm beginning to think I am. I'm sure Luke told you I had a miscarriage and I might not be able to carry a baby to full term. That's very important to some people. It isn't to me. I'll probably adopt my family and that's fine with me." She paused when she got a bit emotional, then added, "That breakup wasn't long ago and I'm still trying to get beyond it."

"As long as we're giving each other marital advice, I've got something to say," he remarked drily and she had to smile, knowing she had started this, so she had to listen to whatever he was going to tell her she should do. "If a guy really loves you, he'll still want to marry you even if you can't give him biological children. As you said, you can adopt."

"Thank you, Mr. Marriage Counselor," she said, smiling at him and trying to avoid thinking about what he just said. "I agree and I brought that bit of advice on myself."

"Yes, you did. I'm as qualified as you are to give marital advice."

"No, you're not," she teased. "You've never been engaged, so I've come closer to actually marrying."

He got up and crossed the room to her, to place his hands on both sides of her chair. "That gives you a little experience, but I've got a lot because I spent fifteen years growing up in a bad marriage until my folks divorced," he said, leaning closer as he talked. "That makes my advice more valid."

"You were going to stay on your side of the room tonight," she warned him.

"See—this is why I shouldn't marry. I don't do what I say I will." His eyes darkened. "Scared of me?"

"Not in the least. I have no intention of marrying you," she said, knowing he was joking. "Now go back to your side of the room and think about my brother."

Cade took her hand to pull her to her feet. "I want to know something else. Give me a straight answer," he said, and her pulse jumped. "I've had time to catch up on the sleep I missed the night after our first kiss. Did you miss any sleep?"

"Cade, we weren't going to do this," she said, suddenly solemn, knowing they had moved beyond teasing and joking about their backgrounds. His probing blue eyes held desire.

"I think you just answered my question," he said in a husky voice as his gaze lowered to her mouth and she tingled in expectation.

For fleeting seconds she knew she should move. Now was the moment to step away from him, but she couldn't. The past year her life had been tough and filled with hurt and loneliness and a lot of hard work. For a few minutes, how disastrous would it be to enjoy some pleasure and excitement? How much could a few more kisses and another sleepless night hurt?

Six

Common sense reared its ugly head. It whispered in her ear—*No*, it screamed, *walk away!* She tried her best to ignore it, instead gazing into his blue eyes that held such desire, she trembled. Still, that voice of reason echoed in her ears.

"Cade," she whispered. "I—I need to go," she said, trying to stay safe, but filled with wanting him.

"I'm not holding you," he whispered in return, kissing her throat and then her ear, light kisses that made her want to wrap her arms around him and pull him close.

Just walk away.

When his tongue caressed her neck, she sighed. If she wasn't careful, his mouth would have her melting right here at his feet. She leaned into his kiss and again the question nagged at her. Would a few little kisses really compound her hurt? She ached to be in his arms, to kiss and be kissed. Could she do that and still keep her heart intact?

She knew better than to fall in love with him, but could she guard her heart against that and still kiss him? Torn between desire and caution, she stood up from the chair while an inner debate raged. He stood mere inches from her, but she already felt his loss. Her head told her to turn and leave him. But she stood rooted to the spot.

Beneath his cheer and friendliness and care of his little niece, beyond his sexy appeal, Cade was cynical and had closed his heart to love. She wanted a long-term relationship—total commitment at some point. She wanted a family like her own. Cade had grown up wanting to avoid the lifestyle she longed for.

He wrapped his arms around her and tilted her chin up so that her eyes met his. She saw the heat in their dark blue depths. "Stop battling yourself," he whispered, his mouth a hairbreadth away from hers. "You know you want to kiss me. You know you liked when we kissed. Just give in to it." He brushed her lips with his and it was like spark to tinder. Her heart pounding, she wrapped her arms around his neck and wound her fingers in his thick short hair at the back of his head.

In spite of all her arguments, in spite of their first kisses and the misery later, she couldn't walk away. She wanted him too much.

His strong arms pulled her flush against him and he took her mouth hard, his tongue going deep.

So inflamed with desire, she could only hold him tightly and kiss him back. She had crossed an invisible line and at the moment she didn't care. She didn't want to go back. Saying goodbye to caution and logic, she thrust her hips against him, finding him hard, aroused, ready to love her.

"Cade," she whispered before his mouth covered hers again and his tongue stroked hers as he held her tightly, his arm a steel band around her waist while his other hand trailed lightly over her curves, moving over her back and down over her bottom, stirring her desire. Her heart pounded and she kissed him eagerly.

He caressed her so lightly in scalding strokes that made her want more. Now that she had let go, she wanted no barriers between them. She wanted to run her hands over his naked skin, wanted to touch and kiss him everywhere. He must have felt the same, because before she knew it, his fingers were at her buttons and then he pushed the top of her dress off her shoulders and it fell around her waist.

She gasped with pleasure as he cupped her naked breasts in his large hands, caressing her, sending streaks of fire to the part of her that ached for him.

As he kissed her, she pulled his shirt free. Her fingers trembled, and he stilled them, yanking his knit shirt over his head in one smooth motion and tossing it aside. He leaned forward to kiss her again, needing her lips on his.

Wanting to explore his marvelous body, she ran her hands over his chest, feeling the curly chest hair beneath her fingers. Her fingers traced solid muscles, lean sinew, then the smooth skin of his upper arms. Finally she wrenched her mouth from his and let it follow the path her fingers had taken. She dragged her lips across his throat and chest.

Groaning, he gripped her head in his hands and pulled her back for another dizzying kiss. She was so overwhelmed with desire that she could only cling to him, close her eyes and be swept along. Until Cade, she hadn't been kissed in so long. If she could ever call what she'd experienced before a kiss. Not after this man.

Running her hands across his strong shoulders, she

moaned with pleasure as he caressed her, his callused hands moving lightly to heighten desire. He swung her into his arms, never breaking contact, and carried her to the sofa where he sat with her on his lap as he continued to run his hand over her and caress her. When she raised her head and looked into his blue eyes, there was no mistaking that he wanted her.

He slipped his hands beneath the full cotton skirt of her sundress. His hands were warm as they trailed up her thighs in light, tingling caresses that made her open her legs and sit astride him.

He cupped her breasts again, his tanned hands dark against her pale, soft skin while he leisurely kissed first one breast and then the other, causing streaks of pleasure that rocked her. Closing her eyes, she clung to his muscled arms.

"You're beautiful," he whispered, "so beautiful." He kissed her mouth and then leaned down to run his tongue around her nipple.

She knew in a few more minutes they would never want to stop. A few more minutes, a few more kisses and tender touches, and she'd surrender to total seduction. Could she? She slipped off his lap, turning away and gasping for breath.

"Cade, I'm not ready for this," she whispered.

He didn't answer and she wondered whether or not he heard her. His hands folded lightly on her shoulders as he kissed her ear and then lifted her hair away to brush kisses on her nape.

She twisted to face him and he held her lightly with his hands on her waist. "We'll stop. I don't want to push you where you don't want to go," he whispered as he continued showering light kisses on her throat, her ear. All the time he kissed her, his hand caressed her breast, first one and then the other.

She wanted him with all her being, and trembled, debating if she could cope with the consequences if they made love tonight. "I want you," she whispered, "but I don't want more hurt."

"I understand," he said, between kisses. He turned her to face him and bent down to lave her breast, his tongue drawing lazy circles around the tip while his hand pulled up her skirt and nestled between her thighs.

"I don't want to hurt you in any way," he whispered. "Stop when you want. You're beautiful, darlin'. I want to kiss you and touch you all night long, but only, only if you want me to."

She thought about her life. She had been alone since her breakup over a year ago. Until Cade, it had been over a year since she had been kissed or held and loved or had any emotional ties to a man. Not that she would have any deep, long-lasting ties with this committed bachelor. But she wanted him nonetheless. Wanted the passion that he inspired, the pleasure that only he could give her.

There was no denying that he was desirable. That he stirred her more than any other man ever had, including the one she had been engaged to marry. Could she deny herself one night with him?

She framed Cade's face with her hands and gazed into his blue eyes that held blatant desire. "I want you," she whispered.

He held her tighter and she swore she saw flames ignite in his eyes.

"I want to make love, Cade, but I don't have any protection."

"I have protection." He cupped her face in his strong hands. "I want to make love to you all night long if that's what you want," he said, slipping his arm around her waist to draw her against him as he leaned down to kiss her, another intense, passionate kiss that made her feel as if he loved her more than anyone or anything on the earth. "Erin, I don't want to hurt you."

She nodded. "I know you don't. I also know we don't want the same things." She responded to Cade as she had never responded to any other man, and right now nothing could stop her from making love with him. But she knew theirs could only be a brief affair before she said goodbye and she'd have to forget him. Was she rushing into another situation where she would be heartbroken?

For this night, this moment, she didn't care. She wanted to make love, to yield to seduction, to grasp joy and life and loving here where it was incredible with him. The moment could be lost and never come again and she chose consequences over regrets.

"Cade, make love to me," she whispered.

It was all the invitation he needed.

He showered kisses on her while his hands drifted up her thighs, caressing her between her legs, stroking her so lightly that she opened to give him access.

He picked her up to carry her to his bedroom, knelt to place her on the mattress. He slipped her sundress over her legs, and then, starting at her ankle, he trailed kisses lightly over every inch of her skin. His breath was warm, his tongue wet, exciting, sensual on her as he moved slowly up, till he met the flimsy fabric of her panties. He slid them down, torturously slow, stopping to caress her here and there, then tossed them aside. He knelt before her and placed her legs over his broad shoulders so he could stroke and love her with his lips and tongue. He took his time, until she was writhing beneath him, her hands fluttering over him.

She cried out, writhing, wanting to kiss him in turn the way he did her. His tongue stroked her relentlessly, making her cry out with need, nearly taking her to the point of no return.

But she didn't want to come like this. Not before she had her taste of him.

With a gasp, she pushed him back. "Let me kiss you the way you kiss me," she said. She slid down his body, her naked breasts rubbing against him, her tongue trailing over his flat, male nipples, until she caressed his manhood.

Then she knelt over him to torment him the way he had her. Her mouth took him in and he groaned. She ran her tongue over him, loving him, and loving each sigh and moan that he emitted. When she felt his body tighten beneath her, he stopped her. Taking her into his arms, he rolled her over, so he was above her. His hands combed into her hair and he gazed down at her, looking into her eyes with a need that made her shake. No man had ever looked at her as if he wanted to devour her and could never get enough of her.

"Cade," she gasped, trying to draw him down to her, to pull him closer so she could hold him against her heart. His dark blue eyes held a need that made her tremble and feel she was the only woman on earth for him.

"Ahh, darlin', you're beautiful," he whispered, a hoarse remark she could barely hear between kisses. "We'll take our time. I want to love you for hours." He ran his hands through her hair.

She couldn't get enough of this man. As if a dam had burst inside, she poured out every drop of passion and the physical expression of her feelings, knowing that Cade was special and this night was unique and then she would have to let it all go. For tonight, he was here in her arms and she could kiss and touch him and try to give him the pleasure he was giving her.

"Kiss me," she whispered.

And he did. A kiss that was hard and passionate. A kiss that told her she had made another monumental mistake with him. Because making love with Cade could never just be once. For her, it was more than a brief fling. He made her feel as if he had offered his body and his heart. She knew better, but that was what she felt and she was in deeper than she dreamed she would be. There was no undoing or turning back now.

She watched him as he opened a drawer in a bedside chest and withdrew a condom. Relishing every moment with him, she watched him put it on and move between her legs. He looked virile, ready to love and incredibly sexy.

She started to sit up, to throw her arms around his neck. Instead, he pushed her to the bed and came down to kiss her, another hot, passionate kiss that made her want him more than ever. "Cade," she whispered. "I want you. Now."

When he lowered his weight, slowly filling her, she gasped with pleasure.

"Put your legs around me," he murmured, and she did as he asked, running her hands down his muscled back and over his hard bottom, tugging him closer to her.

He filled her, hot and hard, moving deliberately as she arched beneath him. She started to cry out, but his mouth covered hers and her cry was muffled. He partially withdrew, driving her need higher, only to thrust into her again and carry her to new heights. Over and over. She held him tightly, giving herself completely to him, giving him complete access to her as she clasped her ankles around his waist. Need pounded in her, until with one final, deep thrust she climaxed. And he followed her. They rocked together as ecstasy overwhelmed her.

But Cade was not done. Minutes later he moved inside her again, slowly at first, then faster, harder, deeper. She thought she was spent, but of their own volition her hips rose to meet his and she was struck with a second shuddering release. Only then did his control finally shatter.

Clinging to him she kept with him, her head thrashing while she held him tightly with her long legs locked around his narrow waist.

"Cade," she whispered. Her fingers dug into his shoulders, and then she ran her hand down his back and over his bottom. Crying out, she was enveloped in rapture.

He shuddered with his release and they pumped together until spent. Euphoria became an invisible cloud wrapping them in a momentary closeness that made them one.

"So wonderful," he whispered, kissing her temple lightly, and she turned her head to kiss him, a long, slow kiss that was satisfaction and union.

Gasping for breath, she hugged him as he held her with his arms wrapped around her and their legs entwined. Gradually their breathing returned to normal. He rolled over, taking her with him and holding her close while he combed her hair gently from her face. "Ahh, darlin', so good, so good," he whispered.

"For a moment I want to hold you. You're strong and solid and sure, all good things that are missing in my life right now."

"No, they're not," he said quietly. "Erin, you're strong and you've been through a lot and you got through it and are moving on. That's strong. You're solid because you know what you want and you're pursuing it and you've picked up the pieces. You're sure because you have confidence in yourself and in your future. They're not missing at all." He kissed the tip of her nose. "But I'm more than happy for you to hold me for the rest of the night if you want. You are a fantastic woman and I'm glad I know you."

"I'm glad, too," she said.

The moment had become more serious and brought reality back. She ran her hands over his shoulder and chest, drawing her fingers lightly through the smattering of chest hair, refusing to think about consequences, choices or even tomorrow morning or the decision she had made tonight.

She was in Cade's arms after the most fantastic sex possible. Lovemaking that had been wild and passionate and fulfilling. She still floated in a euphoria that shut away all the problems in her life. Before she knew it, the bubble would burst and real life would come crashing down to envelope her soon enough, but for a bit more time she was in Cade's arms, still tingling from his caresses and hot, passionate loving.

As she snuggled against him, he brushed another light kiss on her forehead. "This is good, just to hold you close," he said. Beneath her fingers on his chest, she could feel the faint vibrations when he talked.

"I don't want to move."

"I don't want you to move. And I don't want to move, either. This is the perfect place to be." After a few minutes, he shifted on his side, holding her close while she faced him. She combed unruly waves of thick black hair from his forehead. "I'll bet you were a cute little boy." She had no idea where that thought came from. The body before her was all man.

"I was adorable," he said, his blue eyes twinkling.

She laughed. "And probably spoiled rotten as the oldest child."

"Me? Spoiled? Never," he drawled, and they smiled at each other. He trailed light kisses on her temple and rubbed her back lightly as he held her. They were quiet and she felt enveloped in bliss.

"For a while, you made all the problems go away," she whispered. "I know they'll come back because they're real and part of my life, but for the past hour they ceased to exist."

"That's what's meant to be. Sex is magic. It's the icing on life's cake," he said quietly between light kisses.

"So I'm dessert," she remarked drily.

"Definitely," he said, kissing away her laugh. He leaned back after a moment and with his fingers, moved strands of her long hair away from her face. She was still on her side in his arms and she gazed up at him as she ran her hands lightly over his chest and along his muscled arm.

"Cade, this is an intimate moment, a brief time I feel closer to you than I ever have. I'm not pushing for myself because I know I'm going out of your life soon, but I—I wish you'd rethink your views on marriage. You're going to be a wonderful dad for Amelia. You're not like your father."

"Thank heaven for that one," he remarked. "I'm glad for your great faith in me. I'm not as scared to be with her, but right now, I think it's because I know you're here to save me."

She gazed up at him, at the faint shadow of stubble on his jaw. The point was not lost on her that he didn't address her comment. She decided not to push. Not right now.

They became quiet. Wrapped in his arms she refused to think further about the future, or the past. For the next few hours, only tonight existed and she intended to enjoy every moment of it.

"Cade, I didn't know sex could be so good," she whispered.

He smiled. "I'm glad you said that because that's what I was thinking," he said.

She smiled at him, but didn't believe he had been thinking any such thing.

He tightened his arm around her to draw her close and brush light kisses on her forehead. "Ahh, darlin'. This is so good. Stay right here in my arms and let me hold you all night," he said.

She nodded, agreeable to do exactly that. She made her choice tonight and it was done. She stopped thinking and let him pull her close against him.

"So very sexy," he whispered.

She held him tightly as if she had caught happiness for a moment and could hang on to it. But she knew better than to think her happiness was tied up in Cade.

"Will you go out with me next Friday night? We could prevail on Maisie to watch Amelia."

"Shh. Let's not talk about next week or tomorrow or anything beyond the next few hours. And no, we're not going out together."

"Okay, only now and the next few hours. Come closer. You're way too far away," he said, nuzzling her and she giggled.

"I don't think you could get a sheet of paper between us. I'm as close as I can get."

"Are you really? Let me see," he teased, running his hands lightly between them, his fingers drifting over her, squeezing lightly.

"Satisfied?"

"Mmm, ever so, but a repeat performance might be in

the wings," he said. "How about we get in my hot tub and soak and talk and see what happens?"

"You know exactly what will happen and I can't wait," she drawled, and he grinned as he stood and picked her up. Holding her in his arms he kissed her. "I could get used to this really fast," he said.

"Well, don't get too used to it. This is tonight only. I told you, let's just think of now and a few hours from now."

"Of course," he said, carrying her into his bathroom and taking the iPad so they could monitor the nursery.

In minutes they were seated in a hot tub of water as they talked about general topics, the ranch, subjects that were harmless and didn't involve families and the future.

She leaned back against Cade, feeling his muscles flex when he moved. He was warm, hard, wet, all sensations that were sexy and made her think of making love again.

It was almost an hour before he stepped out of the tub and handed her a thick towel. He began to gently dry her and in minutes she was in his arms while they kissed and he carried her back to his big bed.

When she stirred in the first pale light as dawn spilled into the room, Cade drew her into his arms to kiss her and she was lost again to lovemaking. She knew it would end, but night had not completely gone and she felt still captured in the magic of their lovemaking.

It was a sunny morning when she slipped away on her own to shower and dress in jeans and a blue cotton shirt. She braided her hair and by the time she finished Amelia was awake.

They would have the weekend to themselves, just the three of them, and Erin suspected tonight would be a repeat of Friday night which was all right with her. She had given herself over to making love this weekend, even though she knew living with Cade created an emotional risk that would be a real threat to her heart.

She paused in changing Amelia and stood there staring into space as she thought about the past hours in Cade's arms.

She hoped she wasn't already falling in love with him. When she was in the house with him, having made love all night, it was difficult to think about hurting or missing him. Right now, she hoped she could walk away in mid-December with her heart intact. One weekend should not be impossible to get over.

Beyond one weekend, it would be a giant risk. She hoped she hadn't miscalculated and put her heart in jeopardy already. Her response to Cade was different from any other man she had known. That was a warning to take care or she would lose her heart to him and hurt more than she had with the broken engagement.

Amelia stirred, kicking out her feet and calling Erin's attention. She focused on her little charge.

"Hey, little sweetie," she said to Amelia who smiled. "Are you ready for a fun day?" She finished changing her diaper and snapped her pajamas. "Let me brush your hair," she said, working the soft baby brush through her black curls.

"You're a sweet baby. Are you going to make me love you? Am I going to love you and fall in love with your uncle? I can't do that, sweetie, so don't be too adorable. Don't make me miss you every day after I leave here. I want to be able to tell you and your uncle goodbye and not feel as if my heart is being ripped out and locked away here on this Texas ranch." Amelia was paying no attention to her, looking instead at her own toes, seemingly mesmerized by them.

"You'll get a bath after breakfast. In the meantime, let's go to the kitchen. Okay?"

Amelia babbled in reply. She seemed to be enjoying the morning and happy to listen to Erin talk to her. When she carried Amelia to the kitchen, Cade was cooking and had breakfast almost ready.

He turned to put down a spatula, wash and dry his hands and cross the room to Amelia. "How's my baby girl?" he asked as she held out her arms and he took her. "Don't you look pretty this morning? Your nanny has your pretty hair combed and you look adorable." He put her in her chair, glancing back at Erin. "She doesn't cry as often since you joined us. Congratulations on that one. I'm glad because when she cries, I panic and wonder what's disturbing her."

Erin had to bite back a smile at the thought of Cade getting panicky over Amelia crying. "Cade, babies do cry and the world isn't coming to an end, and sometimes when they cry it's just because of nothing more than they're hungry, wet, tired or teething."

"Yeah, common sense tells me that, but I can't bear for her to cry because she can't tell me why. That's what's so scary and—" He stopped, then walked up close to her to look intently at her, as if seeing her for the first time. "She's not the only one looking pretty this morning. You're gorgeous, Erin," he said, trailing his finger along her cheek.

"Thank you." She ignored the thrill that sent goose bumps down her arms. "Are you going to work today?" she asked.

"I am because we have a tree that fell on a fence and a bridge over a creek to repair. First I'll feed Amelia and then I'll help you clean this kitchen. In the meantime, you can eat your breakfast undisturbed."

"Sure. You're free to go at any time and I'll take over Amelia and the kitchen chores."

He turned to Amelia, so Erin got her breakfast and sat eating it while he talked to Amelia and fed her. Later, he shooed Erin out of the kitchen while he cleaned and she bathed and changed Amelia, playing with her in the sitting room. She was winding up a musical jack-in-the-box for Amelia when she heard Cade's boots and looked up to see him standing in the doorway. Her pulse jumped and she wanted to walk into his arms.

He had on a jeans jacket and his broad-brimmed black hat was pushed to the back of his head, framing his face. He looked like a handsome, sexy rancher and she hoped he told her goodbye and left because she wouldn't be able to resist him if he wanted to kiss before he left.

"I'm gone. It's raining again. I have my phone. If you need anything, Harold is nearby and his number is posted by the phone. Just call and he'll be here right away."

"I'll be fine and so will Amelia. You take care. You'll be out in the elements."

"I'll come home to a hot dinner and a warm house and dare I hope, maybe hugs and kisses. Think about that one today."

"Cade, we've been very careful and I don't want to get too involved."

"Let's rethink that one," he said in a deeper, quieter voice, shrugging away from the doorjamb and crossing the kitchen to her, making her pulse quicken again. He placed his hands on her shoulders and she couldn't get her breath. How could he make her melt with a look?

He glanced beyond her at Amelia happily playing with a rag doll. "Stop being afraid of life, Erin," he murmured. "Let go and live a little so you can get what you want out of life," he added, and her heart thudded as she looked into his blue eyes.

"Watch out," she whispered. "I might take your advice."

"Be good if you did," he answered, but desire filled his expression and she didn't think he knew what he replied. He wrapped his arm around her waist, pulled her close and covered her mouth with his.

Her heart slammed against her ribs and the protest she was beginning to think about died instantly. His words echoed in her mind. *"Let go and live a little so you can get what you want..."*

Closing her eyes, she wrapped her arms around his neck and returned his kiss.

Kissing her hard and passionately, he leaned over her, making her heart pound and her pulse drum in her ears. He released her abruptly and she opened her eyes to find him watching her.

"That's better, darlin'," he said and pushed his hat squarely on his head as he turned and left the kitchen. In seconds she heard the back door close, and in a few more minutes his pickup motor started and then faded as he drove away.

Her heart pounded and she tingled all over, wanting to be in his arms, wanting his kisses more than ever, remembering every minute of the night. Were they going to have another long night of lovemaking tonight? Could she resist him? Did she want to resist him? Was he right in telling her to let go and live a little so she could get what she wanted? Maybe she should take his advice.

Cade left to work on a fence that was down from the storm that swept through the area during the night. The wind had been high and broken tree limbs had fallen on fences. He knew his men were scattered on the ranch, moving cattle to other grazing areas and cutting up limbs, hauling them away to clear the area and repairing the bridge, repairing another string of fences and setting up new posts. Working automatically as he cut limbs and then loaded debris into his truck when necessary, he was lost in thoughts about the night.

Making love to Erin had been the best ever—a shocking and unexpected discovery. Along with the most fantastic sex, however, had come a truckload of guilt.

He had promised Luke to look out for his baby sister and then turned around and seduced her. She was vulnerable, hurting still from losses, and he hadn't kept his word, something he couldn't recall ever doing in his life. He definitely had never done it to Luke. He hadn't been true to Luke and he hated that part of what he had done.

Taking off his hat, he wiped his brow with his sleeve. "Dammit," he said quietly. He had always been able to maintain control. What had happened to his self-control?

It had gone flying away the moment he kissed Erin. The one time in his life when self-control was needed badly. He groaned and wanted to gnash his teeth. Erin, of all the women he had known, the little sister of his best friend. He hadn't paid a lick of attention to her when she was a little kid. How he wished he had continued to see her in the same way now that she was grown.

He thought about kissing her, momentarily losing himself in memories that made him hot and temporarily took away his regrets. He would lose Luke's friendship if or when Luke discovered what Cade had done, because he'd broken a trust with his lifelong buddy. It wouldn't matter that the lady was ready and willing, too. It wouldn't matter one tiny bit. Luke meant what he said and he always stuck by what he said. Cade had solid proof of that in the past. And he couldn't blame Luke for being angry when he found out.

Cade propped his foot on a thick oak branch that had fallen and thought about Erin. The worst part of all of this wasn't his guilt or the end of a friendship. What was even worse—he still wanted to go to bed with her. He wanted to make love to her even more than he had last night. The damage was already done to Luke's friendship, that was over and there was no way he would ever get it back.

Maybe if he and Erin were wildly in love everything would be all right with Luke, but they weren't in love. Erin was still all bottled up emotionally and he wasn't a man to fall in love.

She would be gone all too soon in mid-December and once she left, he doubted he would ever see her again.

He hoped with all his heart that Erin had no lasting effects from their lovemaking except good ones. He was certain that during the hours they loved and had been together, she had briefly lost that perpetual hurt that she carried. Time would heal her wounds—at least the broken engagement. Erin was too involved with children and liked them too much to ever completely heal over the loss of her baby. That was in the category of his losing Nate and Lydia. Although he'd had years with Nate, it still was a heartbreaking and permanent loss.

At least he was beginning to catch on how to care for Amelia and eventually, they would start the search for a new nanny.

Again guilt stabbed him. "Sorry, buddy," he said aloud, thinking about Luke and knowing he had broken a trust. If Erin really hurt over their parting, Luke would be able to guess why.

"Dammit," Cade said, unable to fully concentrate on something as mundane as clearing the broken tree limbs and stringing more barbed wire, plus driving in some fence posts. He should have kept a few guys to work with him instead of sending them to different places on the ranch, because clearing limbs and driving posts were a lot easier with four hands than with two.

He leaned on a posthole digger and stared into space and saw only Erin's green eyes, her long hair spilling over her bare shoulders. When they had the evening to themselves later, he wanted her in his arms. Forgetting where he was, Cade thought about her kisses. When he realized he was lost in fantasies about Erin, he turned back to the wire he would string. But in seconds she commandeered his thoughts once again. He shook his head. What kind of spell had she woven with him? When had there been a woman in his life who interfered with what he needed to get done, who captured his thoughts and imagination? Of all the women he had known—the one it shouldn't be was Erin. He groaned and started digging, throwing himself into the job and working as hard and fast as possible, trying to dig her out of his thoughts as he did the earth. How important was she becoming to him? He dismissed that question as ridiculous. She would soon say goodbye and they wouldn't see each other again unless Luke fell in love and married and they crossed paths at the wedding. And that was not likely to happen, at least in the foreseeable future, because Luke was in love with his work.

Cade pulled out his phone, made a call and put his phone back into his pocket. Soon a pickup appeared with three cowboys who came to help.

It was twenty minutes of working alongside his hands before he realized he had paused and was lost in thought about Erin. Startled, he returned to digging furiously. Why couldn't he get her out of his thoughts? A far more persistent question—would she let him make love to her again tonight?

Seven

That night Erin rocked Amelia, finally tucking the sleeping baby into her bed and tiptoeing to her room, closing the door between them because the monitor was on. She turned and faced Cade. He stood in the open door to the hall and she walked into the sitting room to see why. Her heartbeat raced and she wanted to walk into his arms and kiss him.

Cade straightened and approached her. Day by day he was becoming more important, more exciting. When she had to tell him goodbye, she didn't want to look back with regrets.

"I was afraid you'd stay up here without coming back. Let's sit and talk," he said.

Wanting to be with him, she nodded. "Sure," she said and saw the flare of satisfaction in his blue eyes.

He closed the last bit of space between them. "Before we go back to the sitting room…" He slipped his arm around her waist. "This has been a long day and I feel as if we've been apart for a long time," he said. The moment his arm went around her, her heart thudded.

"Cade," she whispered before his mouth covered hers. She held him tightly and kissed him passionately while he picked her up.

He carried her to his suite and sat on his sofa, cradling her against his shoulder, holding her tightly with one arm around her while he caressed her.

She moaned with pleasure, running her hands over him and wanting him more than ever, and with a sense of urgency that she could only assume from his touches he also felt. All the longings she had experienced all day poured out and she kissed him hungrily.

Clothes were flung aside and her hands shook in her haste. She wanted him and was ready to make love to him again. He returned her kisses while his hands moved all over her, pausing only to slip on protection. Then he lifted her over him. As he lowered her onto his thick rod and they moved together in a pounding rhythm, she locked her long legs around him. Crying out, she held him tightly while release shook her and he reached a shuddering climax.

Showering kisses on her face and shoulders and throat, he carried her to his bed, yanked back covers and placed her on the bed to stretch beside her and pull her into his embrace.

"I've wanted you with all my being," he whispered, stroking her damp hair away from her forehead. "All day long you've been in my thoughts and I couldn't wait to be alone with you tonight."

She showered light kisses on his throat and shoulder, stroking him with her long fingers. "Soon I'll be gone and what we have together will be over as it should be, and as both of us want it to be. You're not into permanence and I am—it's that simple."

"That's true, but I want you in my bed and in my arms until you go. Will you move in here until you leave?"

She thought about his question. "No. If Luke would learn that I have, you'd lose a friend no matter what I said. No, I won't move in. I don't want to leave here with a broken heart, either, and if I'm with you that much, I'll fall in love and a broken heart is what will happen. I can't take an affair lightly. You can't take one seriously." She framed his face with her hands to look directly into his dark blue eyes.

"Someday you'll meet someone and fall in love and you'll want marriage—at least I hope you do for your sake and Amelia's. When that happens, you'll be a good husband and a good dad because you're a good man. From what you've told me, you're not like your father. You've told me not to be afraid to live—you shouldn't, either," she said and brushed a light kiss on his cheek.

"Thanks for the vote of confidence," he said, his voice hoarse as it usually became when he was aroused.

"I'll stay as long as I agreed, until mid-December, but I want you to hire another nanny soon and let me help her get settled in. I think the transition would be better for Amelia. She has a lot of new people in her life and she's adjusted well, but hiring a nanny sooner while I'm here will help them get to know each other," she said.

Cade frowned as she finger-combed his black hair back off his forehead. Her hand trailed down over his muscled shoulder, moving lower across his hard chest. "You think that's best?"

"I think it's best for all concerned. I think Amelia will adjust more easily and I think I will be less likely to leave my heart behind when I go. I can start letting the other nanny spend time with Amelia and we'll have her with us in the evening and that will help also."

"I don't see how in sweet hell that will help anything except the new nanny's income. You don't want to be here with me? You don't want to be here in my arms? That isn't what you've indicated in the past hour."

"I don't want to go home with another heartache."

He stared at her, a muscle working in his jaw, and she had no idea what ran through his thoughts. Finally, he nodded. "Very well, I'll move up hiring a new nanny. But right now, you're in my arms, in my bed, and I want you. I want you to stay. I want to kiss you all night," he said, trailing light kisses over her shoulder and scooting down.

Her heart drummed a frantic beat and she knew she couldn't deny him. She wanted to be with him.

He rolled over, holding his weight so he wasn't too heavy. She looked into his eyes and tingled. Desire blazed as if they hadn't just made love.

When his gaze lowered to her mouth, her heart pounded, and when he kissed her she moaned. *Don't fall in love with him. Don't play with fire.* The warnings echoed in her head, but they were too late.

She held him tightly, as if her arms were enough to keep her from having to face tomorrow and to soon say goodbye to him. But she knew that could never be. So instead, she simply let herself live the moment. She gave herself to him and opened up to him.

Later, when she finally started to get out of bed and move to her room, he pulled her back. "Amelia is asleep and no one else is coming in today. Stay with me and let me hold you."

This time there was no hesitation. "I can't say no to that request."

* * *

She would not move in with him, but she was with him every evening. They were becoming a family with little Amelia, and Erin was falling more in love with Cade each day. It wouldn't last, but she had made a choice and taken his advice about letting go and living. She wouldn't think about when she had to tell Cade and Amelia goodbye. That would come all too soon.

One night near the end of September when she was in Cade's arms after making love, she shifted and raised up to gaze into his eyes. "You said you would start interviewing for the new nanny in October. I think we should stick to that schedule. It's only a month earlier and it will make the adjustment for Amelia easier."

Cade wound long locks of her hair around his fingers as he met her gaze. "You're sure that's what you want? This is paradise, Erin."

"I think so, too, but I don't want to leave my heart behind, Cade. I've had enough heartbreak."

A muscle worked in his jaw as he stared at her in silence. "I don't want to hurt you," he said gruffly. "This has been the best, darlin'." Desire flared in the depths of his eyes and his arm slipped around her shoulders as he pulled her to him to kiss her. She wound her arms around him and kissed him in return, refusing to think about parting with him. It was too late to avoid being hurt, but she wasn't going to tell him.

He rolled her over, shifting over her as he plunged into her, and drove thoughts of tomorrow away.

In early October the new nanny interviews started as Cade had said they would. He interviewed each woman and narrowed down the pack to those he thought would be likely candidates as Amelia's new nanny. The next step was to let Erin interview them.

He had four women for her to interview and he listed them in order of his preference. At breakfast when he started to give her the rundown, she shook her head. "You keep your preferences to yourself, and after I interview them I'll make my own list and then we'll compare them. I don't want to be influenced by your choices."

"Fine. We'll do it however you want."

"It's nice you have all this faith in my selection. I'll be long gone."

"You love Amelia and you'll select the best one for her. I know that."

Erin stared at him and his dark brows arched in question. "What? Food on my face? Something I said? What's wrong?"

"It's something you said," she answered. "You said I love Amelia."

"But you do."

She nodded. "I do." She tried not to, but it had been a losing battle.

His blue eyes narrowed and he stared at her. "You knew when you took the job this might be a problem, but you'll get past it. That's just part of letting go and we have to— you know that."

"I thought maybe I could do this without it being so difficult to tell her goodbye," she said, knowing it was going to hurt a lot to say goodbye to Amelia and Cade.

"You definitely can stay and be her nanny until she's grown," he said, smiling at her.

"Thank you for that wonderful offer," she said, shaking her head and laughing with him even though she didn't feel like laughing. She had some tough times ahead when she had to leave them for good. It was going to hurt badly, but he was right. She had known it from the start.

He stood up and crossed the room to her to place his hands on her shoulders. "We're going to be right here on the ranch. Come back anytime you want to see her and stay as long as you want. I hope you and I don't have to say goodbye, either. I have a plane and I can fly to Austin to pick you up at school and fly you back here. We're not saying goodbye forever. I've been seeing you since you were six years old or younger. That won't end when you walk out the door."

Smiling, she nodded, thinking what it would be like if all that he said was the way it turned out to be. She knew when she walked out the door, it would be the end. Cade would go on with his life and someone else would be his latest interest and Amelia would have a new nanny to love, a more permanent nanny hopefully, and both Amelia and Cade would disappear from her life.

She would hear about them from her brother, but that would be seldom and probably even less now that he was out of the country.

The first few months after leaving Cade and Amelia were going to be the ones that would hurt the most. She'd just have to find a way to get through them and forget about the man and baby she'd fallen in love with. And she was in love with them. Both of them. She couldn't be intimate with Cade even for the short term without her heart being totally involved. But she hadn't told him, knowing they had no future.

She loved him, she just didn't know the depth of her feelings for him and she hoped when she got away from him she would begin to get over him and he would become a memory. A memory so hot he had seared a permanent image in her brain.

Just as Adam had faded away and Cade had wiped out that hurt, she wondered if there would be someone to make her forget Cade.

But as her lips met his for a kiss, she already knew the answer to that question.

While Maisie watched Amelia, Erin interviewed the four women Cade had selected, and when the interviews were done, she knocked on the open door and walked into Cade's office.

Leaning back in his chair, he sat with his booted feet propped on the desk. His long jeans-clad legs were crossed and his blue denim shirt sleeves were rolled back. He finished his phone call, swung his feet to the floor and stood.

"Have a seat," he said, his gaze sweeping over her hair that was twisted and pinned behind her head. Looking professional, she wore a tailored brown suit with a tan silk blouse that had a V-shaped neckline and matching tan high-heeled pumps.

"I'm finished with the interviews," she said, handing him her list of candidates in the order in which she liked them.

His eyes scanned the names and he nodded. "We agree on the number one and number two choices, I see."

"Good. I'm glad we agreed on that. I thought our first choice was the perfect candidate. She was very nice and has experience and a sweet manner. And she's a grandmother. They all live in Fort Worth or near there, so that would be a plus."

"Don't sound so eager."

She smiled at him, a bittersweet one. "The time will come when I move on."

He sat back, and she couldn't read the expression that overtook his face. "I've been making plans. I've already talked to Maisie and I've hired her to stay on the weekends for the first two months after you've gone and have Monday and Tuesday off instead. She'll cover the weekends and I'll be here during the week. If I have to travel, Maisie said she would work it out to stay and get someone to temporarily cook for her. How's that sound?"

"As if you've covered all the bases." So why did she feel as if someone had stuck a knife in her chest? The pain only got worse when she realized something. "I won't be here for Amelia's first birthday in January," she said. "I know it's a lot to dare hope you'll send me pictures."

"You could come home for it."

She shook her head. "When I'm gone, Cade. I won't be back," she said. The pain intensified and because she refused to show it to him, she had to get away. "Speaking of Maisie, I should get Amelia from her now, although I think I'll change clothes to something more casual before I take charge of Amelia." When she stood, he came to his feet to circle his desk and walk to her.

"You look gorgeous," he said. His voice had lowered and had a husky note, and she tingled from the desire in his expression. Reaching out, he wrapped his arms around her waist, leaned close and kissed her.

Surprised, she stood for just an instant and then wrapped her arms around his neck to kiss him in return. When he finally released her, she looked up at him. "What was that about?"

"It was because I know I'm going to have to tell you goodbye soon." He dropped another kiss to her lips. "Stay and talk to me after dinner tonight."

"I will, but that isn't really what you're asking me to do," she said, and he smiled at her as he draped his hand on her shoulder and caressed her nape with light strokes that sent tingles dancing down her spine.

"Cade," she whispered, looking up at him. He tightened his arm around her waist, hauling her against him, and leaned down to kiss her, a long, hungry kiss that made her think of lovemaking and long nights together. Finally she stepped back.

"I really need to get Amelia and give Maisie some relief."

"I'll get Amelia. But promise me that you'll sit with me tonight and not go flying off and shut yourself in your suite."

"You have a way of persuading me to do what you want," she said, smiling at him.

"Just sometimes and only when you want to."

"I'll see you at dinner."

"And I'll bring Amelia," he said, watching her walk away. She glanced back over her shoulder at him to see him still standing there, his gaze sweeping every inch of her.

Lara Prentiss started the first of November. Cade had his men help her move and she temporarily took the suite across the hall from Amelia's. When Erin moved out, Lara would move into her suite.

Erin introduced the older woman to Amelia, watching Lara take Amelia and sit in the rocker to talk to her. Short, with graying hair and big blue eyes, Lara looked like Amelia's grandmother and Amelia seemed to like her from the first.

Erin hurt inside. She was losing another little baby in her life. Amelia wasn't her baby, but she loved her deeply and it was going to hurt to tell her goodbye. She had known this day would come and she had no misgivings for taking the job and she would never be sorry about her time with Amelia. She wondered whether she would ever regret being with Cade. Right now, she couldn't regret that, either.

During the day, there were more moments when Lara took Amelia and Erin had to step back and watch and let the older woman hold Amelia and talk to her and dress her.

In those moments she worked on finalizing her arrangements for school and preparing to move. Though she still managed to spend parts of the days and evenings with Amelia, she no longer saw as much of Cade and there were few evenings alone with him or nights with him until her last weekend in December.

Saturday night she was in Cade's arms in his big bed, after they'd made love, and he held her close against him. "What weekend would be good for me to fly to Austin to see you?"

Apparently what she'd told him hadn't sunk in, or he was still resisting. She looked up at him. "Cade, it's like I told you. When we tell each other goodbye here, that might as well be it."

He shifted slightly. "There's no need to cut off seeing each other."

"There's a big need," she said, running her hand over his muscled arm. "Neither of us is serious. Do you want to get married?"

He looked startled. "No. You know I'm not going to marry," he answered, frowning slightly. "That hasn't changed, Erin. I'm just not a marrying man and you know why."

"But I want marriage and children, and if I'm with you, I'll fall in love and want marriage eventually and you won't, so I think to avoid more heartache than I already have, we're breaking it off when I leave here. It's in my best interest. I hope to avoid getting hurt badly again. It's going to be hard enough to leave you and Amelia. I don't want to increase the pain and the longing."

"Well, hell, I don't want to do that, either. I didn't exactly have hurting you in mind. I want to kiss and hold you."

"Ultimately, if we do that, I'll have to know that I can count on those kisses and that love forever and you're not going to promise that or ever want it."

He shook his head. "I'm sorry, Erin, but you've known that from the first," he said, his dark eyes stormy as his thoughts raged. Then, finally, they settled. "All right. I don't want your brother to come home and find you crying over leaving here."

"I promise you he won't. As amazing as it is, I think I may be able to forget you," she teased while deep down, she knew she never would forget him.

He didn't smile, startling her. "Your brother will figure things out no matter what you do. He's always had a knack for coming to the right conclusion."

"Don't worry about Luke. He's at the South Pole and he won't be home until this is history."

"I'm going to miss you," Cade said solemnly. "Come back for Christmas with us. It'll be hell knowing Amelia doesn't have Nate and Lydia. Add to that going through the holidays without you. Come for a few days."

She shook her head. "Sorry, Cade. I'll be wound up in my family and I can't keep going through goodbyes." She wanted to say yes, wanted to be with them, but she couldn't take that emotional upheaval of another big goodbye. "Amelia will have a fun Christmas and she is too little to know what she's lost."

But Erin wasn't. She'd know every moment she'd lost with Cade and his baby.

* * *

When her last day arrived, Erin took Amelia to her suite to tell her goodbye. How would she ever get through saying goodbye and driving away without crying? She sat rocking and talking to Amelia who gazed at her with big blue eyes. Amelia had a new teddy bear from Erin and she was pulling on its eyes and ears.

"You're so sweet. I'll miss you every day and I know you're going to grow so fast that I won't recognize you when I see your pictures. I love you, Amelia. You be a sweet girl and good to your uncle Cade who will be a great daddy for you."

"Da-da," she said, looking at Erin.

"That's right. He's going to be a second daddy and you just call him da-da. He's going to take good care of you and love you to pieces. I'll come back to see you." She pulled Amelia close in her arms, letting tears spill down her cheeks. She stayed that way until Amelia pulled away slightly and settled against her. Erin brushed away her tears, trying to stop thinking about leaving, about missing Amelia and missing Cade. When she had her emotions under control, she stood.

"I think you're ready to go to sleep. I'm going to put you down. When you wake up, Lara will get you."

The door opened and she put her finger over her lips when Cade thrust his head into the room. She carried Amelia to her crib and placed her in it, then turned to tiptoe out.

Cade took her hand and went through the adjoining door into his suite. In his bedroom he turned to wrap his arms around Erin. He leaned forward to kiss her and paused, looking intently at her. He ran his thumb across her cheek.

"I'm going to miss her," she said, feeling tears threaten again. She closed her eyes and he drew her close against him.

"You can come see her anytime you want."

She held him tightly, unable to speak past the lump in her throat.

Finally he walked out with her. Lara told her goodbye inside the house with Maisie and Harold, and Cade was the only one who walked her out to the car.

"If you'll go out with me, I'll fly to Austin next Saturday night."

"Thanks, but no. I'll just be getting settled in my new apartment. No telling what I'll be busy doing." She opened the car door, then turned back around. "Send me a picture of Amelia occasionally."

He smiled. "I'll do that and I'll plan for a visit in the near future."

"Call first. Otherwise, I might be buried in my studies."

"Sure," he said, gazing intently at her. "You're not going to let me come see you, are you?"

"I don't see that as being good for either one of us. I'll think it over."

He put his hand behind her head, held here there for a long, passionate kiss. When he released her and stepped back, she was breathing hard.

"On that note, I better go," she said. "Goodbye, Cade. Thanks for hiring me as your nanny."

"See you, Erin," he said, staring intently at her.

She got in the car and drove away and to her relief, tears didn't start until she was around the first curve that hid his house from view. After a few minutes the tears flowed so freely she had to pull over. She didn't know whether she was crying more over telling Amelia goodbye or telling Cade. She loved the little girl and had many recent pictures of her on her phone, but they would get old. Amelia would grow and this time would be a memory.

And what about Cade? She could see him, and she'd end up sleeping with him, but that would only lead to more hurt. At some point he would tire of seeing her and break it off, or he'd get involved with another woman, one who was available to him. And the pain would just get worse. No, she was doing the right thing. Now had to be the time to end any relationship.

If she'd learned anything in the past few years, it was this. Love hurt. She pulled the car back onto the road and headed to Austin, determined to not get entangled in any relationship. Her heart was still broken from this one.

Erin moved through her tiny Austin apartment getting it ready for when she started school the first week of January. Missing Amelia and Cade more than ever, she constantly took out her phone, started to send a text to Cade and then put away her phone, knowing she had to sever the ties.

When she first moved to Austin, Cade had called a few times and they had talked for over an hour each time as he'd filled her in about Amelia, but now she usually let his calls go unanswered. It was for the best, she told herself.

Tears spilled down Erin's cheeks and she wiped them away. She missed them both more than she had thought she would. When she saw little girls in strollers or dads carrying their little girls, she had to fight back tears.

Even the holidays had been difficult. She had returned home but of course Luke hadn't been there. Though she and her family had talked to him on Christmas, it hadn't been the same as having her brother beside her. And she couldn't stop thinking of the other people she was missing. Cade and Amelia celebrating the day without her.

One of the days at home her mother came into the utility room while Erin was sorting her laundry to pack. "Are you all right, Erin? You don't look like you are."

"I'm fine, Mom."

Her mother stepped close to put her arm around her. "You miss that little girl, don't you?"

Tears filled Erin's eyes and she wiped them away. "I miss her more than I thought I would," she said. "But when I get in school, I'll get over missing her and life will get busy and go on and I'll be okay. Don't you worry. School should take my mind off her."

"Erin, is it just Amelia? It isn't Cade, too, is it?"

She turned to look at her mother and she couldn't tell her anything except the truth. "I miss him, but we didn't have any future together. He's a bachelor. You should know because he and Luke were so close."

"Luke was a little worried when he talked to Cade about hiring you. I really thought you'd be all right."

"I am. I promise. Don't worry about me."

"Well, I know you'll get busy with school, but I hate to see you hurt and I know you're hurting over leaving them."

"I couldn't stay. Cade and I are not good for each other and I can't hang around because of Amelia."

"If you miss Amelia and Cade, go see them."

"I'll think about that, Mom."

Her mother hugged her. "I better check on dinner. Take care of yourself."

"Thanks. I will," she said, thinking the best way to take care of herself was to avoid seeing Cade or Amelia because she would have to go through another goodbye. And her heart couldn't take that.

After New Year's Day, she drove back to Austin. The first week of January her classes started and it was a relief to be so busy, she didn't have time for her mind to wander to life on Cade's ranch.

Who was she kidding? Her mind was never far from there. Amelia would adjust because children did, but did Cade miss her? Was he already seeing someone else? How deep had his feelings run?

Eight

Cade rocked Amelia, who was sprawled against him, one small arm over her head as she slept quietly. He could put her in her crib, but he continued rocking her. He remembered seeing Erin rocking her, a low lamp shining soft light over her.

He missed her more than he thought possible. He knew he would miss her at first, but he expected that to pass, so this constant thinking about Erin, wanting to be with her, wanting to talk to her, surprised him. Missing her not only hadn't diminished, it had gotten worse. He thought he missed her more now than when she'd left in December.

He'd had relationships that had meant something to him and when they had broken up, he had been able to move on. He'd expected that to happen this time, too, because he'd never had anything lasting with Erin. It was brief and then she was gone. And aside from a few phone calls they hadn't kept in touch, which was Erin's doing. She didn't seem to want to keep up with each other or even see each other again. He could fly to Austin, but she hadn't indicated that she wanted him to do so.

It was difficult to concentrate on the ranch and at times during the day he would find his thoughts wandering back to her and he'd forget what he was doing.

He looked down at Amelia who snuggled against him. He still hurt over the loss of Nathan and Lydia and he hurt for Amelia, but he was determined to be the best possible substitute dad for her. He wanted to shield her from hurt.

His thoughts jumped back to Erin. Had she started dating? She wanted marriage and she was gorgeous, so probably she had been asked out. The thought of her kissing another guy, let alone getting married, bothered him. One more shocking turn in his life. He had never felt that way about a woman before. In the past when he'd had an affair, once they had parted, he had never cared what the woman did. Actually, he usually remained friends with them and wished them well.

That was not the case when he thought about Erin.

Amelia stirred and he carefully patted her and sung softly. It was the weekend and Lara had gone to Dallas until Sunday night. He no longer worried about caring for Amelia. He was comfortable with her, sure of himself, and he had fun taking care of her. Too many times he wished Erin was with him to laugh at Amelia's antics or to share a moment.

He sat in the rocker singing softly to her and patting her back lightly. He brushed curls away from her face and realized he loved her as much as he would have if she had been his baby.

"Good night, sweet girl. I'll hear you if you need me," he said, finally placing her in her crib and going to his bedroom, leaving the door open between them.

He took out his cell phone and called Erin. "Answer, Erin," he whispered, wishing she would pick up her phone and wondering where she was and what she was doing. He missed her, and the house was big and empty and Amelia was asleep. He felt restless, dissatisfied, wishing he could talk to Erin. Had she seen that he called and deliberately wasn't taking his call or was she just busy doing something else? Was she out with someone?

That question was torment and he tried to think about other things. But his mind was traveling a single track. He missed Erin and he wanted to see her. He couldn't even get her to answer her phone when he called, so he was certain if he flew to Austin, she wouldn't go out to dinner with him. She wouldn't go out with him when she had been here and he had asked her.

He swore under his breath and stared at his phone, finally sending her a text. There was no answer, so he put away his phone. He couldn't be in love because that wasn't even on his horizon. It was no part of his life. He'd never had a broken heart and he wasn't suffering one now. He just missed her being with him.

A week later he stood on his porch as Blake drove up in his pickup and climbed out, crossing the backyard to the porch. "This is nice of you to let us have Amelia's baby things that she no longer uses, the little basket and the carrier, all the baby blankets. Sierra is due any day now, so she told me to get everything so we can have it ready."

"When are you going back to your house in Dallas?"

"Tonight. Her doctor is in Dallas instead of Downly and that's a bigger hospital. Sierra is there now and we'll stay in Dallas until our baby is born. It's so exciting. I love that we're having a girl because she and Amelia should be close."

"Come on and I'll help you carry everything to your truck. It's all in the storage room."

"What do you hear from Erin Dorsey?" Blake asked as he followed his brother.

"Not much. We don't talk."

Blake stared at him. "Did you part on good terms?"

"Sure. She's just busy with school and we've gone our separate ways."

"How does her brother like the South Pole?"

"That's Luke's deal—he loves it. He'll be at a research center for a year. Glad it's him and not me." Cade opened the door off the utility room to a large storage space with windows on two sides and shelves lining all the walls. "Here's the bassinet and a little tub. All these things go. There's two umbrella strollers because we had three of them. These are extras that we had that were presents." He picked up a toy and held it in his hands, remembering Erin using it to play with Amelia when she first came and making Amelia laugh.

"Cade?"

Startled, he looked around, momentarily dazed, forgetting he had been helping Blake get baby things. "Sorry, I was thinking about when I first got Amelia," he said.

"Sure," Blake said, staring at him and then lifting a box. "Does this go? It has 'Blake' written on it."

Cade looked at it and opened the lid. "Erin marked this for you and Sierra because it's baby things that Amelia has outgrown."

"How's the new nanny working out?"

"Fine. Lara's good and Amelia seems happy with her."

"At least Erin was here to get her started. I wish we had a chance to hire Erin for the first year, but I don't expect she'll be interested in another nanny job."

"She wasn't interested in this one. I paid her extra to get

her to take it," Cade said, looking into another box. As he raised the lid a piece of paper fluttered out. Cade picked it up and looked at a selfie he had taken. Him with Amelia and Erin. He was holding Amelia and had the arm holding the camera around Erin and they were leaning close together. He stared at it now, looking at Erin and missing her, wishing she were here.

"Hey, Cade." Blake's interruption made him look up. "What about this?" He was standing there, holding another box.

Cade shook his head and his brother looked amused as he stepped closer to look at the picture he was obviously so engrossed in. "Good selfie."

Cade smiled. "Sorry. I was thinking about when we took this picture."

"Sure you haven't talked to her recently?"

"No, I haven't. She worked for me and she's gone."

"Maybe you ought to give her a call." He looked down at the stack of baby items they'd amassed. "I'll take all this stuff now and come back and get the rest later," Blake said. But he paused before he bent down to pick up the boxes. "I suppose she knows how opposed you are to marriage."

"Oh, sure. I'll get the rest of this." Cade picked up another carrier and an infant car seat.

They worked in silence to load the pickup and finally Cade jumped down as Blake came around the front of the pickup. "We sure thank you for all this."

"I don't need it now. You wouldn't think one little baby would have so much that a pickup can't hold it all," he said, glancing at the overstuffed truck. "But Erin knew what she had outgrown." As he mentioned her name, he couldn't help thinking of her again.

Blake pushed his hat to the back of his head and wiped

his brow. "You know, since you were old enough to think about it, you swore you would never get married. You may not even know it when you fall in love."

Cade turned to stare at Blake. "Run that by me again."

"You heard me. It's sort of like I was about our father. I was so busy being angry all the years I was growing up that when I started in business, I still thought of him as a big, powerful man. I wanted to compete with him and beat him because when I became an adult, I thought I could. I never factored in that he would get old and weak. I actually felt sorry for him when we finally got together."

"That's hard to figure. You have lots of reasons to dislike him."

"Well, I don't feel the way I did anymore. Maybe you're unrealistic in your views that you shouldn't marry. Our dad is not an example of how the whole world is. He's a frail old man now and I didn't get a shred of satisfaction out of ruining his hotel business. I just didn't look at it closely enough and maybe you aren't, either. Maybe you can't even recognize if you're in love because you've got that warped view of marriage."

"Thank you, Doctor. I'll think about your advice."

"I still say, maybe you ought to try again to get in touch with Erin. You're not quite yourself."

Cade stared at him. "And you're loco. I just think back when I was a kid and how lousy home life was sometimes. I don't want to be tied down and find myself in that kind of situation."

"Maybe you need to see a doctor, then. You're not yourself."

"You wait until your baby arrives and then I can tell you that you're not yourself. Just wait until you're taking care of a little one and see if you don't change. They get you up in the middle of the night and they can't tell you why they're crying. You don't know what they want, or if they hurt—that's new in my life."

Blake shook his head. "Maybe that's it. Time will tell. Thanks again for the baby things."

"Sure. Glad you have them now. Let us know when this little girl arrives."

"You'll know," Blake said. He turned to get into the pickup, then stopped and turned back. "Cade, I hope to hell you and I are both better dads than the one we had."

"I was afraid of that, but now that I'm a dad to Amelia I'm not going to be like our dad. And neither are you. I can't wait to come home to Amelia after I've been out working all day. I think she's awesome. I'll always tell her about Nate, but I feel like her dad, too."

"You *are* her dad, too. And I know you're a good one. And I know you're right that we'll never be like our dad," he said. "Thank goodness." He got into the truck, and then looked out the rolled-down window at Cade. "Better go try to call Erin again," he said, looking amused. "You might be getting back what you've been giving out."

As Blake drove down the road to the highway, Cade walked back to the house, thinking about what his brother had said. Was he in love with Erin and didn't even know it because he had never been in love before?

That night Cade sat in his office, papers shoved aside as he held Erin's picture and wondered about her feelings and about his own.

She had urged him to marry, telling him that he wouldn't be like his father. For the first time in his life, he realized she was right. He'd told Blake as much that afternoon. His parents had fought so much, yet before they married they were in love and that was what had always scared him—people who were in love reaching a point where they were so estranged they were angry with each other anytime they were together.

Maybe it didn't have to get that way.

Erin's parents weren't that way. They had been happily married for over twenty-five years. Maybe his views of himself and marriage were misguided. He had once told Erin to let go and live—maybe he was the one who should rethink long-held beliefs that held him back.

The thought startled him because all his life, as far back as he could recall, he had determined that he would never marry. Could he change that thinking?

A far more important question—was he in love with Erin?

He didn't know anything about falling in love. All he knew was that he wanted her with him. He wanted to hold her, kiss her and love her. He missed her, and he missed her all through the day, not only at night. He missed her laughter, her way with Amelia, her outlook, her jokes. He missed the way he felt when he was with her. Was that love?

Would he want to be married, to live with her for the rest of his life? Would he want her in his bed every night? That question set him on fire and the answer was a no-brainer. Maybe Blake had been right—maybe he was in love with her. So what now? Did he want to propose? Would she be leery about his turnaround and find it difficult to believe that he really was in love and wanted to marry her?

He could easily imagine Erin doubting that he knew what he was doing when it came to proposing marriage. Could he convince her that he meant it with all his heart? That he wasn't like her ex-fiancé and he wanted her for life?

The thought stopped him cold. It was all true. He loved

Erin and he wanted to marry her. He had to make her believe him.

He tried to call her again and got no answer. Cade jammed his hands into his pockets and paced the room. If she wouldn't take his calls, how could he tell her he loved her?

Erin's cell phone buzzed and she looked up from her notebook to grab her phone to see if she had a text from her family. Startled, she saw it was from Luke.

Quickly scanning his brief text she saw he would be in Dallas for meetings later in the week. While he was in the US, he planned to fly to Austin and take her to dinner.

She hurried to a mirror to look at her image. She didn't want Luke to know that she was in love with Cade. Luke would be furious with Cade if he thought Cade had caused her the least bit of hurt. And her brother would blame Cade completely. He would think Cade seduced her and planned on seduction from the first and that she hadn't been able to defend herself from his charm because she was so vulnerable over her broken engagement. He would be so angry with Cade, he would end the friendship and if he saw Cade, he would probably punch him.

She couldn't tell Luke not to come. First of all, she wanted to see him. Second, if she told him not to come, he would know there was a reason and he would come see her. She wrote back that she would be happy to have dinner with him and she couldn't wait to see him. She would just wear something that made her look good and try to be so cheerful that he wouldn't guess that she had been unhappy at all.

Friday night she opened the door to face her brother, who gave her a big hug and then smiled. "It's good to see you. How's the student?"

"Isn't this wonderful? I love it here. You look great. I like your haircut," she said, looking at his thick, short, blond hair that still curled over his head. "I'm so glad you're home and you flew here to see me. While I get my things, come look at my apartment."

Luke stepped inside, but he was clearly more interested in talking than touring her place. "Austin is beautiful," he said. "After the frozen ice cap, I'm in paradise."

"It's still winter, Luke. Come back in the spring and it'll be gorgeous. The bluebonnets will be in bloom and Texas really will be paradise."

"How was the job with Cade?"

"Great and Amelia is the sweetest little baby you ever saw."

"Nate was a great guy. He was younger so I didn't know him like I did Cade. I know little brother Gabe well enough to know he asked you out."

She smiled again. "Yes, he did and no, I didn't go out with him, but he was cheerful and friendly and Amelia liked him."

"Sure. Everyone likes Gabe. He's always got a grin and he loves the pretty ladies, but I figured you'd brush him off. He isn't any more serious about women than Cade, though. Their father really messed up those boys."

"I hope not permanently."

"I think Blake made peace with the old man. You hear from Cade?"

The question was casual, but she knew Luke was paying attention. "No," was all she said, and she hoped that was all Luke would want to know or say about Cade.

"Enough about the Callahans. Mom and Dad said to give you a hug for them. Everything is about the same at home and it was good to be there and eat Mom's beef stew again."

"Don't even talk about it," she joked as she touched her belly and rolled her eyes. "I miss it already. But I do have a good restaurant picked out for tonight. You said not to worry about expense."

"I meant it. I know what it's like to be in college. Always hungry and always broke."

She laughed. "I think that fits the male population more than the female."

They went to an elegant steak house and Luke insisted she order a steak. She couldn't imagine how she would get through even a quarter of the steak, but it would give her leftovers for a few nights.

As they ate, she listened as he described aspects of his environmental engineering job and a new million-dollar wastewater treatment plant and the success in dealing with gray water. She could tell he loved his work and loved the Antarctic.

"Erin, I wish you could see Antarctica. The ice and snow are beautiful. The air isn't polluted and you can see tiny details so much farther away than you can here. It's amazing."

While he talked about a conference in São Paulo and his traveling to Torres del Paine when he had some time off, Erin tried to be filled with cheer. After all, they were on to safe topics now. Or so she thought, until Luke's next question.

"Who did you date while you worked for Cade? I know Cade and I know he won't ever leave things at the status quo. I'm sure he tried to introduce you to someone."

She swallowed her steak. "Actually, no, he didn't. Maybe he's changed. With the responsibility for Amelia, he stuck very close to home."

"Who's he dating?"

She shrugged. "He wasn't. I think he was so worried

about Amelia, he gave up other activities. He was scared to pieces to take care of her."

"That doesn't sound like the Cade I know except for being scared to pieces over his charge," Luke remarked drily. "You didn't go out with anyone and he didn't go out with anyone?"

"That's right. Luke, it's a ranch out in the boonies. We had a baby to take care of, so we concentrated on her. Cade's grandmother was worn-out and couldn't cope when I arrived. Then he hired the next nanny earlier than he had planned originally. That was good because it gave her more time while I was there to get used to Amelia and vice versa."

"Ah, he hired the new nanny early," he repeated, sounding pleased. Luke talked some more about the station where he was, the storms they'd had, the incredible temperatures and the weather. He looked robust, fit and filled with energy.

"Erin, you're not eating anything."

Since he'd brought up Cade and dating, she'd put her fork down. "I had a big lunch today and I'm just not hungry."

He stared at her. "You look really thin."

"It's all the walking I'm doing," she said, getting worried because her brother knew her well.

"How many miles do you walk a day?"

"Luke, stop quizzing me."

"Do you have pictures of Amelia?"

"Yes," she said, relieved to show him the pictures. "I have some here on my phone and I have some more really cute ones on my iPad at home. When we go back, I'll show them to you." As she scrolled through the pictures of Amelia smiling into the camera, she felt the familiar pangs in her heart.

"She's a cute little kid and I can imagine that Cade was worried about taking care of her because he doesn't know one thing about little kids."

"She's really easy to care for," Erin said, knowing Amelia would be in bed asleep now. What would Cade be doing?

"I'm not sure I did you any favors by recommending you to Cade," Luke said quietly, and she looked up at him.

"You really love her, don't you?" he asked.

"Maybe I do, but that's all right. I can go see her whenever I want to and Maisie can keep me posted about her."

"Maisie—I hadn't thought about her. Was she around much?"

"She was there all the time. She would stay on weekends if Cade asked her and she would fill in if needed, although I didn't go anywhere. Maisie helped constantly."

"Did Cade take you out?"

She smiled. "No, Cade did not take me out," she said, thankful again she had turned down his invitation.

"That kind of surprises me."

"I told you, we were busy with Amelia. You try taking care of a baby and see how much spare time you have. I'm a good nanny."

"I know that."

After that, his questions stopped and he signaled the waiter for the check. When he'd paid, he said, "Let's go back so I can get a good look at your apartment."

After she'd given him the tour they sat in her small front room and Luke sipped a cold beer while she drank ice water.

"Where are the pictures of Amelia you said you'd show me? I got you into that job and I'd like to know that it worked out well and you were happy."

"Didn't I look happy in the pictures that were on my phone?"

"Yes, you looked very happy. Happier than you do now."

"You're imagining things," she said. "Maybe I should quiz you and see if you're really happy in the frozen south because that sounds miserably cold."

"It is miserably cold, but I like the work. It's what I wanted to do and I'm learning a lot, using my education some. I like what I do."

"Well, good. I'll get you another beer."

"I'll get it," he said, getting up. "Stay where you are. Want anything?"

"No, thanks. I'm fine." He left the room and she sipped her water. A few minutes later he returned with pictures in his hands.

"I saw these in the kitchen. You printed them out."

"Yes. Sit on the sofa and I'll look at them with you," she said, wishing she had taken out the one of Cade with her. She guessed Luke would make an issue of it.

She sat close beside him as he looked through them. When he took a draft of his beer she said, "That's your last beer because you're driving."

"Sure, Mom. I'll drink a big glass of water before I leave. That'll help."

"Yes, it will. I'll go get you one."

"You stay where you are. I'm not going to drink water with my beer. I'll get it soon." He flipped to the next photo. "Ahh, she's a cute little girl. That wreck of Nate's really tore Cade up and I can understand. It seemed so senseless and tragic."

The next picture was the one of her and Cade. She stood beside him and he had his arm around her shoulders, his face close to hers and they were both laughing.

Luke stared at it and then looked at her. She saw the realization and accusation in his eyes before he spoke. "This is why you're so thin and you look like you're going to burst into tears."

"I miss them and I miss Amelia and I'm going to burst into tears if you don't stop."

"Dammit. I debated telling him about you and urging him to hire you, but there were so many reasons I thought he'd leave you alone."

"Will you listen?" she said. "You're going to upset me and that I don't need. Cade and I don't communicate and don't intend to in the future. I told him and Amelia goodbye. They're out of my life."

"Yet you have these pictures you went to the trouble to print. Especially this one." He held up the photo of her and Cade. "Dammit, I told him all you had gone through."

"Stop getting angrier at him. He didn't do anything and we've parted forever. I'm in school and I made a lot of money working for him. I loved being a nanny and I loved little Amelia. Now promise me you'll leave him alone."

"Hell, no, I'm not leaving him alone." Luke caught her chin in his hand. "You're in love with him, aren't you?" he said, his blue eyes boring into her. "You are."

"You're being a bossy big brother. I'll get over Cade and you forget this," she snapped, jerking her chin out of his hand and taking her pictures from him. She crossed the room to sit and glare at him.

"Now, you're not going to do anything foolish, are you?" she asked.

"No, I'm not. I don't have time for Cade and I hope you meet some nice guy getting his PhD, date him and marry him."

She had to laugh. "Stop trying to marry me off. You've been in the frozen south too long. You need to get back with your penguins." Luke grinned and she wondered if he really had lost his anger. "You leave Cade alone. I'm fine and I don't want him around. Okay?"

"Okay. You know what you want, but if he tries to hire you back or anything else, then he'll hear from me when I get back in the USA."

"Luke, promise me you won't do anything rash. I'm fine. I won't take his calls because I see no point in it."

Luke turned his head. "You don't take his calls?"

"No. Didn't you just hear what I said? I don't take Cade's calls. We're through. I'm enrolled in school. I'm halfway across Texas from him. He's out of my life for good. What more could you want? Now if you go punch him, then I'll have to go see about him. Is that what you want?"

"Hell, no," he said. "Okay, you made your point and I'll forget Cade, but he didn't do what I asked and I'm sorry if I sent you somewhere that caused you more trouble."

"Forget it. I got the job, got paid way more than it was worth. I did get to take care of little Amelia who is a sweetheart. I miss her, but that's natural. Cade is out of my life forever," she said, feeling something squeeze inside. "What more could you want?"

"I guess not anything. That's good." Luke stood. "Sis, I better head back. I don't want the plane to go to Dallas without me."

"Thanks for coming out to see me. Bossy as you are, I wish you could stay just one night."

"I'd like to, but I haven't spent enough time with our folks. I'll go home and do that and then be on my way back to the Polar Regions."

She hugged him. "You're a good brother, Luke."

"I'm a super brother," he corrected her and then chuckled, and she punched his upper arm playfully as they walked to the door. He hugged her lightly. "Take care of yourself and stay away from Cade. He won't ever get serious."

"I know," she said, "and I want marriage and a family."

"That's because our family is a good one and we all love each other." He kissed her cheek.

"Be careful, Luke," she said. She worried about him going back to the Antarctic. They argued, but he was her brother and she loved him and looked up to him and wanted him to be safe.

"I'll be careful and I'll be in Texas for a few more days."

She watched him drive away and then she rushed to phone Cade. She paused with her hand on her phone. "Just call him and tell him about Luke and get off the phone," she whispered to herself. "Don't talk to him for an hour," she added, knowing she would be tempted.

But could she do it? She stood there arguing with herself about calling him. Several times she put down her phone and walked away and then stopped and rethought what she should do. Finally, taking a deep breath, she pressed his number.

The moment she heard his deep voice, tingles raced over her nerves and her pulse beat faster. Silently, she reminded herself to avoid letting him know how much she missed him.

"Cade, this is Erin. Listen to me," she blurted out. "My brother is home for a week and he flew here to have dinner with me. He's on his way back home to Downly. I think he's really angry. Promise me you won't see him." She said it all in one breath and then she waited for his answer.

Nine

"Did you hear me?"

"I heard you and I'm not home and I won't see him," Cade said, and she let out her breath with relief.

"I'm sorry. He saw some pictures, those selfies you took and he got angry and started quizzing me."

"I'm far more interested in talking to you than hearing about Luke. I'm glad you called me. I've missed you."

Her heart thudded and she gripped the phone tightly. "I've missed you and Amelia so much," she admitted, tears coming because she just wanted to walk into Cade's strong arms and kiss him.

"Well, we can remedy some of that real soon."

She wiped her eyes. "How's that?" she asked, hoping he couldn't tell she was crying.

"Open your front door."

Shocked, she turned to stare at her door. She dropped her phone and ran to the door to open it. Cade stood on her porch and she felt as if she were in a dream. He had his black Stetson squarely on his head. He wore a leather Western jacket and jeans and boots and he looked more wonderful than he ever had before. She flung herself into his arms as he stepped into her house. He kissed her, walking her backward into the apartment and kicking the door closed behind him.

"Why are you here?" she whispered.

"Because I missed you and I love you," he answered, his blue eyes darker than ever. "And you wouldn't answer my calls, so I had to come in person."

"Cade," she gasped. "I've missed you so much."

"Then why in the hell didn't you take my calls? I've called and called," he said between light kisses.

"Because we don't have any future together," she said, tears welling again. He kissed her passionately, and she forgot about the future as she clung to him, kissing him, pouring all her longing into her kiss and pressing tightly against him. Her heart pounded with joy. For right now, he was here in her arms. She would worry about saying goodbye later.

Picking her up, he glanced around. "Bedroom?"

She pulled his head down to kiss him as she pointed over her shoulder. She held him tightly with one arm around his neck while her other hand roamed over him as if to make sure he was really there.

Cade carried her to her bed and set her on her feet while still kissing her. As her hands fluttered over him and she tugged off his shirt, unfastened and opened his belt, he pulled her sweater over her head and unfastened her jeans to push them away. He paused a moment to look at her, framing her face with his warm hands. "I've missed you like hell."

"I'm glad," she whispered, standing on tiptoe to kiss

him. Her hands shook with eagerness and she continued kissing him. She couldn't believe he was here and she could kiss and hold him.

He picked her up, gazing into her eyes. "I love you, Erin," he said, and her heart thudded.

"I love you," she whispered in return, meaning it with all her heart. "More than anyone ever," she added and then kissed him.

Over an hour later she lay in Cade's arms, stroking his back while euphoria enveloped her. She wanted the night to last forever, to stay in his arms, to have his kisses, to be able to hold and love him.

"I love you so much," she whispered.

He shifted, placing her on the bed and rising up to look down at her. "I love you, Erin. And I mean this with all my heart and all my being—will you marry me?"

Erin's heart slammed against her ribs and she couldn't get her breath. Her arms tightened around his neck as she pulled him down to kiss him. Finally, she raised her head to look at him. "I love you, Cade. I love you and I'll always love you, but you've spent your life determined you would never marry. This isn't like you. Do you know what you're doing?"

"I'm more certain than I've ever been in my life. It was easy to say I didn't want to marry and never would want to, because I wasn't in love. Now I'm in love with you and I want to spend my life with you."

She framed his face with her hands. "I love you. You're a wonderful daddy for Amelia. You'll be a wonderful dad for all your children, Cade, but you have to be really sure. You may just want me in your bed and you're not accustomed to hearing no. Marriage is a giant change in your life."

He smiled at her and caressed her nape, making her tingle. "I'm really sure. It is a giant change I'm ready to make. Amelia was a revelation in my life—I can be a dad to her. That was a miracle to me. You've helped me see that I'm a good dad to her. You're right, Erin. I'm not like my father. I don't have to avoid marriage if I really love someone and now I do. I love you with all my heart."

Her heart pounded as she gazed at him and he looked at her, waiting without talking. "You mean that, don't you?" she asked. "And you're not scared I might not be able to have your biological children? We might have to adopt."

"Erin, I'm adopting Amelia. Why would I object to adopting another child?"

"Or children," she said, smiling at him. "I want a big family."

"And I want you. I'm not worried about your ability to have children. I think you can." He stopped her with a kiss when she started to deny his words. "I know—I'm an optimist. That's true, but love can do a lot in our lives. Whatever happens, we'll be together. Any kids we have, any way we have them, we'll love them. Darlin', I need you in my life. I've learned that during the past month. I love you," he whispered and kissed her hard and long.

She wanted him, loved him and wanted to yield to him, to toss cares and worries and common sense aside and tell him yes, she would marry him because she loved him and she loved Amelia and they would be a family. But she never got the chance. He rambled on, like a man who had a lot to say and he wasn't letting anything or anyone get in his way.

"I'm not scared to take a chance on being a husband or a dad. I've been miserable without you. I've thought about your career—you can still get your degree and you can work with children or human services or whatever you want. There will be needy families and children in Dallas, Fort Worth, Downly—you won't have any difficulty going on with your career if you want—part-time or full-time."

The more he spoke, the more her surprise grew. "You've thought about this a lot," she said, a small smile teasing her lips.

"I have thought about it and I put off Amelia's first birthday party because she's too little to know the difference. I wanted you there for it, so I waited."

Delighted, Erin hugged him as she kissed him again. "Thank you! I'm so glad. That will be fun. I love Amelia." She gazed up at him, looking into those dark blue eyes that she loved so much. "I love you with all my heart, but I'm stunned. How long have you thought about marriage?"

"Not a long time because I didn't realize I'd fallen in love. I've never really been in love before. Not the real thing—the forever kind of love." He kissed her and she held him tightly, kissing him in return while her heart pounded with joy.

She heard a car door slam, but paid little attention until she heard pounding on her door.

"What the hell?" Cade snapped, frowning.

She slipped out of bed and began yanking on clothes. "I just know that's Luke. He left, but somehow he must have found out you're here," she said. "I'll take care of him."

"You leave him to me," Cade said, passing her. He already had his jeans on and his feet jammed into his boots. He yanked on his shirt as he left the room. She buttoned her blouse and tucked it in, hurrying as fast as possible because she wanted to get the door and keep Luke and Cade apart.

"Cade, wait," she cried, running toward the front door to try to reach it before he did. But she didn't make it.

Cade yanked open the door and Luke stepped forward. "Dammit, Cade. I told you not to hurt her," he snapped as he swung his fist and hit Cade, knocking him off his feet.

As Cade slammed against a chair and went down, Erin screamed and went to him.

"Cade," she said, cradling his cheeks in her hands and turning his head toward her, afraid Luke had knocked him unconscious. Blood streamed from a cut on his cheekbone but he was alert. She looked into his eyes and all her anger with her brother evaporated. All she saw was the love and the desire she felt mirrored in Cade's gaze.

"Get up, dammit," Luke snapped.

She wrapped her arms around Cade's neck and hugged him. As long as she was over him, holding him, he wouldn't get up and her brother couldn't hit him. She gazed into his dark eyes.

"You never answered me," Cade said.

For a moment she thought he wasn't thinking straight, that her brother's punch had done more damage.

"This wasn't the way I imagined proposing to you," he went on to say, "but I can't wait. I love you. Will you marry me?"

"Get up, Cade," Luke ground out between clenched teeth. "Stop hiding behind Erin."

Cade ignored his friend's words. His eyes never wavered from hers. "Darlin', I love you."

"What the hell is going on?" Luke asked. "Get out of the way, Erin."

"Darlin', you still haven't answered my question. Will you marry me?" Cade asked.

"Yes," she gasped, giving up and wanting him and hoping she wasn't doing something that she would regret, but she couldn't say no. She loved him.

She kissed him, and then raised her head. "Cade, you're hurt—"

"I feel no pain." He grinned. "Because you'll marry me."

This time when Luke barked his command, Erin turned, scrambled up and faced her brother with her fists clenched.

"Don't you dare hit him again," she snapped. "I'm going to marry him. You hit him, Luke, and I don't know if I'll ever forgive you. You hit the man I'm going to marry. He's going to be your brother-in-law," she repeated louder as Cade came to his feet, wrapped his arm around her waist and lifted her out of his way while he faced Luke.

Luke's mouth dropped open as he stared from his sister to Cade.

"What the hell is going on? You're marrying my sister?"

"Yes, I am, as soon as I can."

"You owe him an apology and me an apology, Luke Dorsey," she said, getting between them again.

"Well, I'll be damned," Luke said, shaking his head. "Cade, I'm sorry."

Wiping his cheek with his handkerchief, Cade drew Erin into his arms to kiss her again. He held her tightly and finally raised his head to look into her eyes. "You'll really marry me?"

"Yes, I'll really marry you," she said, her heart pounding with joy as she clung to him to pull his head down to kiss him again. While they kissed, Cade reached behind him and closed the door.

"Where's Luke?" she asked, looking around.

"I don't know. I think he had the good sense to go." Cade reached into his jeans pocket and pulled out a small box that he handed to her. "This is for you. I got this in case I could talk you into saying yes."

Her lips smiling and her hands shaking, she opened the box. She gasped when she saw a large diamond surrounded by dazzling emeralds.

"Cade, this is beautiful."

"So's my love," he said, drawing her to him to kiss her again. He picked her up and carried her to the bedroom to set her on her feet right beside the bed. She still held the ring and he took it from her to slip it onto her finger. "I need to ask your dad for your hand in marriage."

She laughed. "That's old-fashioned and I love it and he will probably be impressed because he asked my granddad. Some old customs still hang around in our family."

"How about kissing the bride-to-be and taking her to bed for a night of love?"

"I think that's perfect," she said, holding him tightly as if she might lose him again. "I might even drop out of school for you."

"Don't decide that tonight because I think you'll want to finish and get that degree," he said and kissed away her answer. "There are a lot of things you can do to help little kids when you have it."

She kissed Cade, joy chasing away all doubts and fears as she held him tightly and thought about Amelia. Erin's joy grew because she would get to be a real second mother for Amelia. She would be Cade's wife. She held him tightly, not wanting to ever let him go again.

Epilogue

On a sunny March morning Erin stood in the back room of the church while her mother smoothed the skirt of her white silk wedding dress that had narrow straps over her shoulders, a tiny waist and straight skirt. She wore the emerald and diamond necklace Cade had given her that matched her engagement ring and her hair was in spiral curls framing her face.

Erin held Amelia in her arms. Amelia had a pink hair bow in her dark curls and she wore a pink organdy dress.

"Mama," she said, playing with Erin's necklace.

"She calls me that and Cade dada," she told her own mother, unable to hide the pleasure in her voice. "When she's a little older, we'll tell her about her real mother and daddy. She already recognizes their pictures." They had two big paintings of them in their ranch house, among some family pictures, and a wonderful photo taken with Amelia the week before the crash that they'd framed and hung on the wall, too.

"That's good, honey," her mother said, smiling at Amelia. She took her from Erin and set her on her feet, holding her hand. "She's a strong little girl."

"She's a joy every day to me. Mom, I'm so happy."

Her mother moved close to hug her lightly and step back. "I'm glad. Cade loves you and he's a good person." She nodded toward the door and the full church beyond. "He has a lot of relatives here. His father is here and his mother, but I don't think they've spoken. Dirkson has another wife here, I see."

"That's Blake's mother." Blake's wife, Sierra, was her matron of honor and Sierra's mother was there, too, holding their new baby. Emily Callahan would be just two months old next week. "When Blake's daughter gets a little older, I think she'll be able to play with Amelia."

"She will." Her mother nodded. "His wife looks lovely. All the attendants do, but none more lovely than the bride. She is gorgeous."

Erin smiled again. "Thanks, Mom. The bride is the happiest person here. I can't stop smiling."

"No one wants you to. I'm sure that Cade doesn't. I don't think he can stop smiling, either."

The wedding planner poked her head in then, motioning to Erin. Her mother picked up Amelia and walked on ahead into the church. With one more glance at herself, Erin stepped out to meet her dad, who waited in the vestibule. She wrapped her arm around his and brushed a kiss on his cheek. "I love you, Daddy," she whispered, and he smiled, patting her hand.

"I love you, too. I hope you and Cade are always this happy."

"Thanks, Dad. I hope so, too." She turned from her father and looked up the aisle at Cade. The sight of him had her tingling with happiness. Her tall rancher fiancé was breathtakingly handsome in his black tux. Beside him stood Blake, the best man, and her brother and Gabe Callahan who were the groomsmen along with three of Cade's friends.

As organ music filled the church and trumpets played, the guests stood and she walked with her father until they reached the altar where her hand was placed in Cade's. She gazed into his dark blue eyes and saw the love and joy she felt reflected there.

They said their vows and Erin knew they were more than words. They were promises that she and Cade would hold forever. Then they were presented to the guests as Mr. and Mrs. Cade Callahan and as everyone applauded, they rushed back to the back of the church. After pictures, when they were in the limo on the way to the country club, Cade kissed her.

"This marriage will be good, Mrs. Callahan."

"It'll be very good," she answered, smiling at him. "Cade, I'm the happiest person on earth right now."

He shook his head. "Absolutely not. That would be me. It's going to be great, darlin'. I promise I'm going to do everything in my power to be the best husband and daddy possible for you and all our kids."

She smiled at him, taking his optimistic outlook and knowing they would have kids, biological or adopted. Either way, they would have a family and they would be loved. She kissed him again, then leaned back to look at him.

"Do you have a handkerchief? Wipe your mouth where I kissed you before we get to the reception."

He grinned at her wickedly. "I'd like to just keep going and start our honeymoon now."

"Not yet. Everyone came to party and celebrate with us."

"It is a celebration, Erin," he said, suddenly looking serious. "A celebration that I feel can go on for the next sixty or seventy years. We're going to have a good marriage."

She smiled up at him. "Yes, we are," she answered, feeling they could deal with the problems that would come up because their love was strong.

An hour later, Cade took her hand to walk to the dance floor at the country club for the first dance as husband and wife. "I'm glad this first one's just for me," he told her. "From here on out you'll have to dance with my brothers and with yours and with assorted relatives."

"My next dance is reserved for my dad."

"Well, you won't have to dance with mine. He doesn't dance." Cade searched the crowd for his father and found him sitting at his table. "Look at him. I don't think he's paid any attention to either of his little granddaughters, but frankly, I'm not surprised. I don't think he knows how to deal with kids, much less little girls."

Erin turned his face to her and changed the subject. "So now your brother Gabe is the only single guy in the Callahan clan. I have three friends out there who are drooling over him."

"Well, he'll like that. It won't take him long to find them if he hasn't already. Gabe likes the ladies and always has."

"I think that runs in your family," she remarked, and he grinned.

"Erin, you look so beautiful today. I will never forget watching you come down the aisle," he said.

"Thank you," she answered. Her heart beat with love for him. "I'll be glad when we're alone and I'm in your arms. We've had a lot of parties and public moments lately but now I'm ready for some private ones. And you, my very handsome husband, make my heart race to look at you. I love you, Cade Callahan. I'll spend my life showing you."

"I hope so," he said as they danced. She lost all awareness of everyone else, gazing into Cade's eyes. "Cade, I'm willing to try soon for our baby if you are."

"Darlin', I want whatever you want," he answered. "You have no idea how much I love you, but I intend to show you."

His arm tightened slightly around her waist and he drew her closer as he swept her into the dance. She couldn't imagine she could ever be happier than at that moment in his arms.

The next dance was with her father and Cade danced with his mother.

To her surprise, Dirkson Callahan asked her for the next dance. She politely danced with Cade's father. "Welcome to the Callahan clan," he said. "You're a beautiful young woman and Cade is a lucky fellow. I hear you aim to finish your education and get that PhD, which I think is commendable. I'm proud of my sons and now all of them except Gabe have married beautiful and smart women."

"Thank you. Come visit anytime. We'll be happy to have you. You can get to know your granddaughter."

"I'm not very good with children."

"She's sweet and doesn't require you to do much except smile at her. I'll show you sometime," Erin said. "Your son is a good dad."

"I'm glad to hear that because he can make up for my shortcomings." He shook his head. "But enough of family problems." He smiled at her. "Have a grand honeymoon. I told Cade I left your wedding present on his desk at his house and I have a plane to catch before too long."

"Thank you. I'm glad you were here for the wedding," she said, wondering whether he had danced with Sierra or talked much to Blake. She knew they had talked last night at the rehearsal dinner. She had seen Dirkson and all his sons standing in a circle once, talking and laughing, which surprised her after all she had heard about Blake and his feelings for his father.

Their dance ended and she turned to see Luke waiting to dance with her.

"You look beautiful, Erin," he said. "I'm glad you're happy."

"Thank you. You look quite nice yourself."

"I'm glad I told him to hire you. I've told you that before, but I'll say it again today—one last time. He'll be good for you and good to you. Cade is a good guy."

She grinned at him. "You are, too, except you're a little bossy as a big brother."

"Don't start in with me about slugging him. I've apologized sufficiently for that. How was I to know that he asked you to marry him?"

"You might have asked before you started swinging. Anyway, that's past." She patted his shoulder and looked around the room. "Isn't Amelia the prettiest little toddler?"

Luke turned to look at the child. "That she is. But I'm going to laugh when she's a teen and Cade has to deal with her."

"Cade will manage."

"Yeah, he probably will. I'm happy for both of you. I think I see his little brother lining up and focused on us. Gabe probably intends to ask you to dance next." He let out a laugh. "Besides the bride, he will dance with every beautiful single woman here. You can bet on that one and he's as opposed to marriage as Cade seemed to be, but for a different reason. Gabe just isn't ready to settle down. Cade wasn't, either, until he met you."

"I think Amelia gets the most credit for Cade wanting to settle down."

"Well, however it worked out, it's all for the best. Happy marriage, Erin," Luke said, planting a kiss on her cheek. "If you ever need me, you know you can call."

"Thanks, Luke," she said. "Thanks for coming from the South Pole for our wedding."

The music changed tempo and for the next dance most of the guests spilled out onto the floor, waving their arms and stepping in time to a lively beat while Gabe danced facing her with a big smile. When the music stopped, he placed his hand on her shoulder. "Welcome to the Callahan clan. We need you in this family, Erin. You're great for Cade and Amelia."

"Thank you. I'm happy to join the Callahan clan. And now you're related to the Dorseys, too."

"I didn't think the sun would rise on a day when I'd be related to Luke, but that's good. Luke will come back to Texas with all sorts of knowledge of penguins and icebergs and other useful stuff."

She laughed as Cade stepped to her side. "I'm claiming my bride, bro. I'm sure you can find some gorgeous single guest to flirt with."

"That's a good idea and I'm going to try my best," Gabe said, laughing and walking away.

"I'll bet I'll have white hair when he falls in love."

"You didn't think you ever would and look at you now," she said, looking at his thick black hair and wanting to run her fingers through it.

"That's because I met you," he said, gazing at her with desire in his eyes. "By the way, Dad left us a wedding present." He placed an envelope in her hand. She saw it had been opened and she saw a check inside. She looked up at Cade. He took it from her and tucked it into his pocket. "It'll go into the trust we'll set up. It's one million dollars."

"Oh, my heavens."

"That's my dad. He's all about money. Sometimes just to have him come home for Christmas would have been a bigger deal."

"I think you're already a great dad for Amelia."

He smiled at her. "Thanks. I'm trying. Let's go."

Though she was tempted to leave now with her handsome husband, she put a hand on his arm. "Soon. Just be patient and keep mingling."

They were swarmed with well-wishers and it was midafternoon when she was alone again with Cade.

"Hi. Remember me?" he asked when he sidled up to her.

She laughed. "Can we go now? I feel as if I've talked to everyone who lives in Texas."

"There are still a lot of guests here partying. Enough that I don't think we'll be missed. There's a big white limo parked and waiting in the front, and they all expect us to leave in that." He wagged his brows. "But I have a small sports car out there behind the bushes and it's ready to go. What do you say?

"I say yes to that sports car." Her parents had taken Amelia home to the ranch for a nap, and they would be babysitting her while she and Cade were on their honeymoon.

Cade didn't hesitate. "C'mon, Mrs. Callahan."

In minutes Cade drove sedately away from the church, reached the highway and sped up. Laughing, she took off her veil. "This is so much better. Now what's this surprise you have in store for me for our honeymoon?"

"Patience, love. I'll show you soon," he replied, and she laughed, her dimple showing.

Six hours later Erin stood in a sprawling one-story house of glass and stone, overlooking the blue Pacific Ocean near Monterey, California. "Cade, this is the most beautiful house and place on earth. Sure you want to stay a rancher? We can bring Amelia out here to live forever."

"I'm glad you like it. It's leased for the next six months so we can come back anytime we want. I've also leased a house in Colorado for the summer when it gets really hot at home. If you like Colorado, we can build out there and go every summer."

She threw her arms around his neck and leaned against him. For the flight she had changed to a red linen dress that ended at her knees and matching high-heeled pumps with a short matching red linen jacket. She had tossed aside the jacket.

"We'll come here or go to Colorado whenever you want—within reason," he added. "I'm adding that because I'm not leaving Texas for long periods of time."

"Oh, you're not?" she purred, rubbing her hips against him.

He shook his head. "I have plans for us there." He wrapped his arm tightly around her and kissed her passionately. She melted against him, holding him and kissing him in return, enveloped in happiness and joy. She thought of Amelia waiting at home in Texas for them and the family they had made and would add to. They'd already decided to try to have a baby as soon as possible.

Erin couldn't be happier. She was thrilled and so totally in love with her handsome Texas rancher—the man who would always make her feel loved and be a wonderful husband and a wonderful daddy for all their children.

* * * * *

MILLS & BOON®

Desire™

PASSIONATE AND DRAMATIC LOVE STORIES

A sneak peek at next month's titles...

In stores from 12th January 2017:

The Heir's Unexpected Baby – Jules Bennett *and*
From Enemies to Expecting – Kat Cantrell

Two-Week Texas Seduction – Cat Schield *and*
One Night with the Texan – Lauren Canan

The Pregnancy Affair – Elizabeth Bevarly *and*
Reining in the Billionaire – Dani Wade

Just can't wait?
Buy our books online a month before they hit the shops!
www.millsandboon.co.uk

Also available as eBooks.

MILLS & BOON®

Why shop at millsandboon.co.uk?

Each year, thousands of romance readers find their perfect read at millsandboon.co.uk. That's because we're passionate about bringing you the very best romantic fiction. Here are some of the advantages of shopping at www.millsandboon.co.uk:

* **Get new books first**—you'll be able to buy your favourite books one month before they hit the shops

* **Get exclusive discounts**—you'll also be able to buy our specially created monthly collections, with up to 50% off the RRP

* **Find your favourite authors**—latest news, interviews and new releases for all your favourite authors and series on our website, plus ideas for what to try next

* **Join in**—once you've bought your favourite books, don't forget to register with us to rate, review and join in the discussions

Visit **www.millsandboon.co.uk**
for all this and more today!